PRAISE FOR
NO ONE KNOWS

"Enthralling! Ellison's twisty-turny thriller is my kind of novel: interesting characters, complex plotting, and an ending you'll never see coming. Suspense at its finest!"

—Lisa Gardner, #1 *New York Times* bestselling author of *Find Her*

"J.T. Ellison has created one hell of a brain bender. *No One Knows* is a masterfully written shell game in which a grief-stricken woman is forced to reckon with her past until everything she believes about love, hope, and trust is tested. Ellison's storytelling powers are on sharp display in this literary thriller, proving that no one is who they claim to be and everyone has secrets worth protecting. Compelling, perceptive, unsettling, and with an ending so on point I wish I could read it again for the first time. I inhaled this novel."

—Ariel Lawhon, *New York Times* bestselling author of *Flight of Dreams*

"The unreliable female narrator is all the rage, and Aubrey Hamilton is up there with the slipperiest of them all."

—*Kirkus Reviews*

"A dark domestic thriller that is sure to leave you guessing until the final page."

—SheReads.org

P9-EMO-586

"*No One Knows* will have readers guessing who can be believed and what their ulterior motives are. Ellison messes with the characters' heads as well as the reader's with her many twists and turns."

—*Military Press*

"Ellison clearly belongs in the top echelon of thriller writers. . . ."

—*Booklist* (starred review)

"*No One Knows* stands out most perhaps for characters who are so realistically crafted, so sufficiently complex that it's difficult to conclude who is most, or least, sympathetic. No one in this novel is without serious lapses in judgment and fatal flaws. It's an absorbing thriller with hairpin twists and turns that readers can't possibly see coming."

—*Chapter 16*

MORE BOOKS BY J.T. ELLISON

Standalone Novels

Lie to Me
Tear Me Apart

A Brit in the FBI Series
with Catherine Coulter

The Final Cut
The Lost Key
The End Game
The Devil's Triangle
The Sixth Day
The Last Second

Lieutenant Taylor Jackson Series

Field of Graves
All the Pretty Girls
14
Judas Kiss
The Cold Room
The Immortals
So Close the Hand of Death
Where All the Dead Lie

Dr. Samantha Owens Series

A Deeper Darkness
Edge of Black
When Shadows Fall
What Lies Behind

NO ONE KNOWS

J.T. ELLISON

POCKET BOOKS

New York   London   Toronto   Sydney   New Delhi

Pocket Books
An Imprint of Simon & Schuster, Inc.
1230 Avenue of the Americas
New York, NY 10020

This book is a work of fiction. Any references to historical events, real people, or real places are used fictitiously. Other names, characters, places, and events are products of the author's imagination, and any resemblance to actual events or places or persons, living or dead, is entirely coincidental.

First Pocket Books paperback edition October 2019

POCKET and colophon are registered trademarks of Simon & Schuster, Inc.

For information about special discounts for bulk purchases, please contact Simon & Schuster Special Sales at 1-866-506-1949 or business@simonandschuster.com.

The Simon & Schuster Speakers Bureau can bring authors to your live event. For more information or to book an event, contact the Simon & Schuster Speakers Bureau at 1-866-248-3049 or visit our website at www.simonspeakers.com.

Manufactured in the United States of America

10 9 8 7 6 5 4 3 2 1

ISBN 978-1-9821-2881-4
ISBN 978-1-5011-1849-4 (ebook)

For Scott, Linda, Laura, Blake, Harlan, and,
as always, Randy

PART ONE

As contraries are known by contraries,
so is the delight of presence
best known by the torments of absence.
                              —Alcibiades

CHAPTER 1

Aubrey
Nashville
Today

One thousand eight hundred and seventy-five days after Joshua Hamilton went missing, the State of Tennessee declared him legally dead.

Aubrey, his wife—or former wife, or ex-wife, or widow, she had no idea how to refer to herself anymore—received the certified letter on a Friday. It came to the Montessori school where she taught, the very one she and Josh had attended as children. Came to her door in the middle of reading time, borne on the hands of Linda Pierce, the school's long-standing principal, who looked as if someone had died.

Which, in a way, they had.

He had.

Or so the State of Tennessee had officially declared.

Aubrey had been against the declaration-of-death petition from the beginning. She didn't want Josh's estate settled. Didn't want a date engraved on that stupid family stone obelisk that loomed over the graves of his ancestors at Mount Olivet Cemetery. Didn't want to say good-bye forever.

But Josh's mother had insisted. She wanted

closure. She wanted to move on with her life. She wanted Aubrey to move on with hers, too. She'd petitioned the court for the early ruling, and clearly the courts agreed.

Everyone was ready to move on. Everyone but Aubrey.

She'd felt poorly this morning when she woke, almost a portent of the day to come, but today was the last day of school before spring break, so she had to show, and be cheery, and help the kids with their party, and give them their extra-credit reading assignments.

From the second they arrived, her students buzzed around her. It didn't take long for Aubrey to catch the children's enthusiasm and drop her previous malaise. It was a beautiful day: the sun glowed in the sky, dropping beams through the windows, creating slats of light on the multihued carpet. The kids spun through the light, whirling dervishes against a yellow backdrop. She didn't even try to contain them; watching them, she felt exactly the same way. Breaks signaled many things to her, freedom most of all. Freedom to go her own way for a bit, to explore, to read, to gather herself.

But when her classroom door opened unexpectedly, and Principal Pierce came into the room, the nausea returned with a vengeance, and her head started to pound. Aubrey watched her coming closer and closer. Her old friend's face was strained, the furrows carved into her upper lip collapsed in on each other,

her yellowed forefinger tapping against the pristine white-and-blue envelope. She needed to file her nails.

What was it about moments, the ones that start with a capital *M*, that made you notice each and every detail?

Aubrey reminded herself of her situation. The children were watching. Trying to ignore the stares of the more precocious ones scattered about the classroom, gifted youngsters whose sensitivity to the emotions of others was finely honed, Aubrey took the letter from Linda, handed off the class into the woman's very capable nicotine-stained hands, and went to the ladies' room in the staff lounge to read the contents.

The letter was from her mother-in-law. Aubrey knew exactly what it contained.

She tried to pretend her hands weren't shaking.

She flipped the lid down on the toilet, locked the door, then sat and ripped open the envelope. Inside was a piece of paper folded into thirds, topped with a handwritten note on a cheery yellow daisy-covered Post-it. Aubrey felt that added just the right touch. Her mother-in-law always had been wildly incapable of any form of tact.

There was no denying it now; her hands trembled violently as she unfolded the page. She looked to the handwritten note first. The words were carefully formed, a schoolgirl's roundness to the old-fashioned cursive.

Aubrey,

For your records.

Daisy Hamilton

Scribbled in print beneath the painstakingly properly written note were the words:

Joshua's Mother

Well, no kidding, Daisy. Like I could forget.

The sticky note was attached to a printout of an email. It was from Daisy's lawyer, the one who'd helped put this vehicle in motion last year, when Daisy decided to petition the courts to have Josh declared legally dead.

Aubrey fingered the scar on her lip as she read.

Dear Daisy,

Per our earlier conversation, attached please find a copy of the Order entered from the civil court today by Judge Robinson. As I explained to you on the phone, this Order directs the Department of Vital Statistics to issue a death certificate for your son, Joshua David Hamilton, as of April 19 of this year.

Now that this Order has been officially entered, we should take another look at the estate plan. Josh's life insurance policy will be fulfilled as soon as the declaration is received, and I'd like you to be fully prepared if you plan

to contest the contents. I will be forwarding you
a final bill for my services on this matter in the
next couple of days.

> *Best personal regards,*
> *Rick Saeger*

And now it was official.

In the eyes of the law, Joshua David Hamilton was no longer of this earth. No longer Aubrey's husband. No longer Daisy's son.

No longer.

Aubrey was suddenly unable to breathe. Even though she'd been expecting it, seeing the words in black-and-white, adorned by Daisy's snippy little missive, killed her. Tears slid down her face, and she crumpled the letter against her thigh.

Daisy was a bitch, always had been, and Aubrey got the message loud and clear.

Get over it. Get on with your life. And watch out, kid, because I'm coming for that life insurance money.

But just how do you move on when you can't bury your husband? Five years later, there were still no good answers to the puzzle of Josh's evaporation. One minute there, the next gone. Poof. Disappeared. Missing. Kidnapped, hit over the head, and suffering from severe amnesia, or—worse than the idea of his heart no longer beating—he'd chosen to leave her. Dead, but not dead. Without a body, how could they know for sure?

Damn you, Josh.

He *was* dead. Even Aubrey had to admit that

to herself. It had taken a year to formulate that conclusion, a year of the worst possible days imaginable. As much as she hated to believe he was really gone, she knew he was.

Because if he wasn't, he would have let her know. He was the other half of her. The better half. The responsible half. The serious half.

For him to be taken, or to have run away—no. He would never leave her of his own volition.

Which meant he *must* be dead.

The circle that was her life, a snake forever eating its tail.

Aubrey didn't know the answers to the riddle. Only knew that one thousand eight hundred and seventy-five days ago, Josh had been nagging at her to hurry up and get in the car because they were late for one of his closest friend's joint bachelor/bachelorette party. That they'd had a serious fender bender on the way to the party, which resulted in the small white scar that intersected Aubrey's top lip in a way that didn't detract from her heart-shaped face. That they'd arrived at the hotel over an hour late, and Aubrey had offered to get them checked in while Josh went to find the groom and join the party. That he'd kissed her deeply before he went, making the cut on her lip throb in time with her heart. That he'd glanced back over his shoulder and given her that devastating half smile that had been melting her insides since she was seven and he was nine and he'd pushed her down on the hard playground asphalt and made her cry.

That she'd repeated the words of this story so

many times it had become a mantra. To the police. To the lawyers. To the media. To Daisy. To herself.

Her world was broken into thirds.

Seven and seventeen and five.

Seven years before he came into her life.

Seventeen in-between years when she'd seen Josh almost every day. Seventeen years of joy and fury and love and sex and marriage and heartache and happiness. Of prepubescent mating rituals, teenage angst, young-adult dawning realization, the inescapable knowledge that they couldn't live without each other, culminating in a small wedding and three years of marital bliss.

Five years of After. Five years of wondering.

She thought they were happy. Late at night, in the After time, Aubrey would lie in their bed, still on her side, wearing one of his white oxford shirts she pretended held the lingering bits of his scent, and wonder: *Weren't we? Weren't we happy?*

What was happiness? Where did it come from? How did you measure it? She'd always looked at the little things he did—from a sweet note in whatever book she was reading, to bringing her freshly cut apples when she was vacuuming, or having a travel mug of hot Earl Grey tea waiting for her in the morning as she rushed out the door—as signs that he loved her. That he was happy, too.

But then he was gone, and she had to pick up the pieces of their once life, shattered like the reflective glass of a broken mirror on the floor.

Seven, and seventeen, and then five. Five years of emptiness, solitude, loneliness.

The State of Tennessee didn't care about any of that.

All the state cared about were the cold hard facts: one thousand eight hundred and seventy-five days ago, Joshua David Hamilton disappeared from the face of the earth, and now enough time had passed that a stranger had declared him legally dead.

CHAPTER 2

Aubrey heard the door to the teachers' lounge open. Glanced at her watch—she'd been sitting in the bathroom for nearly an hour, and school was in dismissal. She wiped her eyes, smoothed her unruly hair, straightened her pencil skirt, and emerged to find Linda waiting for her with a look of genuine compassion on her face. Wonderful Linda, who had never believed the nonsense the district attorney spouted and gave Aubrey her teaching job back the moment she got out of jail, even though they lost students over her rehiring.

Aubrey accepted a hug from the older woman.

"You okay?" Linda asked.

"I suppose," Aubrey answered. She handed Linda the letter. Stared at her own left hand while Linda read. She still wore the wedding band and engagement ring Josh had placed on her finger. The small half-carat diamond solitaire, all he could afford at the time, was still a very high-quality stone. It flashed in the overhead fluorescent light, sparkling, and Aubrey remembered an old wives' adage: *When your ring smiles, your man is thinking of you.*

Her man. Her man was gone. How was he

thinking of her? Looking down upon her from heaven? She used to believe in things like heaven, and God, and faith, and saviors. Hope.

No more. She'd been living in purgatory too long to believe in anything but hell for sinners anymore.

Linda folded the paper and slowly put it back into the envelope. Her brown eyes were soft and compassionate. "I see your mother-in-law hasn't changed a lick."

"Daisy is as Daisy does. At least there's one constant in my life."

"I doubt she'll ever change. She's always been this way. Even when you were children, she was . . . difficult."

Sometimes Aubrey forgot that Linda had known Daisy longer than Aubrey had. Linda had been a part of the school for more than twenty years now, rising up the ranks. She'd been friends with Aubrey's mother, but not Josh's. Very few women were friends with Daisy.

Linda slid to the window and glanced out. The lounge faced the playground on the back of the school, empty now that the children were headed home. It was the perfect sanctuary when the teachers needed a smoke. Linda's ancient Zippo lighter flared, and a quick breeze came through the slitted glass. Aubrey smelled the fragrant oil, nearly drifted back in time again, but the snap of the metal brought her back.

Linda blew a long stream of blue smoke out the window, smiled at her young friend.

"More than one constant, Aubrey. Are you working tonight?"

Aubrey made ends meet working two jobs now—teaching at the Montessori school and working part-time at Frothy Joe's, a coffee shop near her house.

She shook her head. She had the evening off.

"Why don't you join me then? It's open mike night at Frothy Joe's. We can have a little dinner afterward."

"That's kind of you, Linda, but I think I'll pass. I need . . . time."

Time. *Stupid excuse, Aubrey.* She'd had five years already—what were another few hours going to gain her?

Linda set the burning cigarette on the window ledge and took both of Aubrey's hands in hers. "Aubrey. Listen to me. You are entering dangerous territory here. You have to keep moving forward. You can't shut down again. We nearly lost you last time. If you're not up for dinner out tonight, why don't I come over and make you something instead?"

Alone, alone, alone. I want to be alone.

Aubrey shook her head. Her voice was still unsteady, but she drew a deep breath and forced a smile. "I'll be okay, Linda. Promise. I'm going to draw a bath, pour a glass of wine, and relax. Nothing about tonight is different from the past five years' worth of nights. Josh is still gone. This is just a piece of paper for his mother so she can get the *closure* she so wants. It doesn't mean anything more."

"She's going to contest the life insurance policy."

"Let her. I don't want Josh's money anyway."

Linda looked doubtful but, good friend that she was, simply hugged Aubrey to her chest, silently released her. The cloud of cigarette smoke settled on Aubrey's blouse, and she nearly choked.

Back to her classroom, down the now quiet hallways. The mantra ringing in her ears.

Alone, alone, alone.

Aubrey gathered her purse and keys and walked to the parking lot. The thirdhand Audi Quattro she and Josh had wrecked the afternoon of his disappearance sat forlornly in the parking lot. She needed to get a new car, it had started leaking oil last month and she didn't have the money to get it properly fixed, but she was loath to part with this one. Josh was so proud the day they bought it, so happy that he'd managed to get such a great deal. She'd gotten the damage to the front bumper and hood fixed, made sure it got regular oil changes, and rotated the tires. Other than the small leak, it ran well enough, reliably turning over day after day.

But it was a constant reminder.

She sat in the driver's seat, stared at the odometer.

Death is an inevitability. Aubrey knew that. People will die, and the essence that was their soul will go wherever they believe it will go, and a new life will join the world in their place. Wax and wane. Yin and yang. Even her car would die one day, and she'd have to remove yet another link to her previous life.

Perhaps this was what she'd been waiting for. Perhaps the fact that Josh had been declared dead would help her find the internal fortitude to finally move on. If the state agreed, then she could mourn and grieve properly, and wake to a new day, a new life.

As if there were any way to move past this.

Home was ten minutes from school. She managed to get there without forgetting a single stop sign.

The house on West Linden Avenue was looking a bit shabby around the edges, not that it had ever looked smart and polished. Aubrey did the best she could, relied on the kindness of the people around her to help with the projects she couldn't manage on her own, but the harsh winter had stripped away the last vestiges of paint around the eaves and bleached the shutters, making the whole outside look shaggy and worn. She'd have to paint before summer was over.

She'd been forced to give up their gorgeous house in leafy, tony Green Hills to pay her legal bills. The house on Woodmont was one they'd dreamed of and saved for, scrimping even more than usual. A no-interest loan made it reachable, if not affordable, on their meager salaries. A house to grow into, Josh said, hinting at a future filled with love and laughter and the pitter-patter of tiny feet.

The day they'd closed had been triumphant.

They'd moved in with hardly any furniture, just enough to make it look like someone was squatting in the house. That first night, they'd had pizza and a bottle of Korbel champagne, the best they could afford—the only they could afford—and built a fire in the fireplace even though it was still warm outside. They made love in front of the fire, and fell asleep in the midst of their own party.

Content.

Their house belonged to someone else now, and Aubrey lived in the shabby little house on West Linden, on the other side of the highway, because the life insurance policy underwritten on Josh was tied up since there was no body, and Aubrey had been forced to sell their dream to make ends meet.

Moving away from their house tore her heart apart. Even though she knew he was dead, a little voice in the back of her head whispered, *When he comes home, he won't know where you are.*

Angels are supposed to follow you everywhere, though. Watching, guarding, caring.

Someone would show him. Tell him.

Or not.

Looking forward wasn't the hardest element of the path she was on; the overlying specter of making a mistake, of doing something that would sever the connection with her previous life, had drowned out all her other worries and concerns.

And yet today, coming home felt different. Was it acceptance? Sorrow? Freedom?

She couldn't put it into words, didn't even try,

defying the therapist's orders that she accept each emotion as it came to her, examine it minutely, then let it go so she wouldn't get dragged into the undertow of sadness. A handy tool if one was truly able to disconnect from the moment-by-moment, all-consuming emotions that came with losing your husband.

She pulled into the concrete drive, turned off the car and let it settle, then headed into the kitchen, dropping her bag on the counter as she went.

She heard the scrabble of nails, the joyous woof. Winston, their—her—Weimaraner, came wiggling into the kitchen. He pushed his wet nose into her hand and turned his sleek blue-gray body sideways into her legs, a warm, weighty comfort. Without Winston, she didn't know if she would have made it through. More than a companion, he'd become the man in her life, a platonic four-legged husband.

She dropped to her knees and gathered him close.

"How's my baby?" she crooned, rubbing her fingers into his silken ears. He arched his neck in pleasure, rewarded her attentions with a gentle lick on the nose, then went to the door and sat expectantly, blue eyes smiling.

He'd always been a happy dog.

They'd found him in a box on the side of the road, one Sunday when they'd gone on a drive in the country, down Highway 96 into Williamson County. Green grass, and cows, and a puppy.

Aubrey had spied the small gray tail sticking out of the cardboard. Josh had pulled the car to the shoulder to investigate. The puppy, thin, tired, looked up at them with such trust, there'd been no question about keeping him. They'd bundled him home, fed and watered him, trained him to a pad, and been worshipped in return. They named him for Churchill, Josh's childhood fascination.

Winston missed Josh. Sometimes Aubrey called and he didn't come, and she knew where she'd find him: in the laundry room, curled on a ratty old ragbag sweater of Josh's, inconsolable.

She didn't blame him. If she had the choice, she'd have gone to sleep on Josh's sweater, too, and never woken up.

She let Winston out into the backyard, climbed the short staircase to her bedroom, changed, and tied on her sneakers. A run might help clear her head.

She went back downstairs and opened the sliding door. "Winston, wanna run?"

Sometimes Winston came along, sometimes he didn't. She always left it up to him.

The dog was having a tussle fight with one of his chew toys. He glanced up at her, and she could swear she saw him shrug. Today he chose to stay in the backyard.

She unlatched the doggie door so he could get back inside, locked the front door behind her, and tied her key to her shoelace. Always-careful Aubrey. She set a brisk pace, let the soothing motion of her feet carry her toward oblivion.

For the first couple of years after Josh was gone, after the investigation was finished, after she was exonerated, she'd come home to the shabby little house, let Winston out, and open a bottle of wine. When she started opening a second bottle before she went to bed, when she'd withdrawn so far that she started missing work because she was still passed out from the night before, and had her little accident, she was forced into a moment of clarity and stood back to examine her life.

The consensus? She was trying to dull the pain.

It was a big pain, one that needed to be dulled. But nothing was working. The therapy, the drinking, work, her friends, the dog, the occasional suicidal ideation, none of that was taking enough of the edge off so she could sleep at night. So she could function. So she could stop missing him so very badly.

An escape was a necessity. She had to have something to do. Drowning in her sorrows, literally, wasn't going to work. It wasn't helping, and Josh would be embarrassed by it. In all things, his approval mattered the most to her. Even dead, she sought his admiration.

So she turned to running.

The first mile was behind her now, and she hit her stride. She never planned her route beforehand, changed it up depending on her energy level that day and her level of paranoia. After her brief stints in jail, the horror stories she'd heard, she knew enough to vary her routines.

Today, breath was her friend, her salvation. It gave her purpose, renewed her spirit. Cleansed her worries. She let the air flow into her lungs as she pushed harder, up the rolling hills of her neighborhood, legs pumping, sweat drying in the cool air, skimming past the school, the new construction, monstrous houses replacing the small cottages, onto the grounds of Vanderbilt University. She circled the campus. Five miles in now, and the sky was purpling with the impending sunset. She needed to turn back but pushed for another ten minutes, then swerved across Blakemore and dashed into Dragon Park, until she hit the tree.

Their tree.

She pulled up short, caught by surprise. She hadn't intended to come here. She was trying to escape, and instead, she'd run headlong into her past.

The tree was a century-old oak, a witness to most love affairs in town. The gnarled bark had been stripped clean, replaced with a full-sleeve tattoo of carvings. There wasn't a square inch untouched from the ground six feet up the tree's height.

Aubrey turned to go. She didn't need to see it. Didn't want to see it. But a gossamer thread of desire pulled her back, to the north-facing side of the tree.

There, carved in the hard oak flesh, intertwined inside a crooked heart, were the letters $JDH + AMT = TLA$.

Josh David Hamilton plus Aubrey Marie Trenton equals True Love Always.

He'd carved it for the first time when they were thirteen and eleven, respectively. Each year, on their anniversary, they came back and he carved it again, deeper and deeper into the tree. For some reason, other lovers seemed to respect their mark and didn't try to carve over it.

She ran her fingers over the letters and allowed herself a moment. A capital-*M* moment. No one needed to know. She didn't have to report in to her therapist. She could have this for herself, this last wallow in her past, ignore the knife stroke against her heart.

There were no tears. She couldn't allow that. But she could allow herself to think back to that night, the longest night of her life, the night Josh disappeared.

CHAPTER 3

Aubrey
Five Years Ago

The accident.

On the way to the party, in his rush, Josh rear-ended a black sedan driven by an older man. Aubrey would never forget the look on the man's face when he came roaring out of the car to scream at Josh. His rage made her shrink back against the seat, but just as quickly, concern over the car, and worry for Josh, drove her out to face him.

The man's car was barely dented; the bumper of their precious Audi was caved in, sagging to the left as if exhausted by its ordeal. Josh was physically fine, just bruised, and Aubrey was as well, except for the small piece of flying glass from the broken passenger-side window that hit her mouth and sliced her upper lip. She was ministered to by her husband at the scene; two stitches' worth of thread and a butterfly bandage from the kit Josh always carried closed the tiny gash. She should have listened to him and gone to a plastic surgeon to have it repaired properly, but she would hear nothing of it: Josh was in his third year of medical school, with plans to become a family practitioner, or maybe a surgeon, he hadn't decided.

But stitches, that was med school 101. It seemed wrong, somehow hypocritical, not to take his care for herself.

When things were wrapped at the accident scene, they texted their friends that they were okay and hurrying, then called a cab to take them to the Opryland Hotel. Late and anxious, Josh kissed her at the concierge stand and hurried away to the bachelor party. Aubrey snuck into the girls' extravaganza, took a seat in a low chair in the back of the room, and discreetly rubbed her neck. Her mood was dampened by the accident, yes, but she already despised the forced hilarity of the traditional bachelorette event: the shrieking girls ogling an oiled-up beefcake in a ridiculously tiny thong shaking his package in their faces while they played some random game of touch and shoot— the stripper touches you, you have to do a shot.

She was embarrassed by the looks they were getting from the people around them, half pitying, half jealous. Aubrey knew these girls, knew every single one of them was internally rolling her eyes and wishing she could just be somewhere else. But for some reason they were all in the back room of the restaurant, drunk, surrounding a half-naked man like a pack of starving wolves and throwing dollar bills at him, pretending they were having the time of their lives.

The stripper moved closer to Aubrey, and she instinctively pulled back, then halfheartedly tossed a dollar at him—there was no way on God's green earth she was going to let his sweaty hip touch her. When the attention focused on the next woman, she edged away from the group and slipped out to the ladies' room. Splashed a little water on her face. Glanced at her wide brown eyes and the unruly mess of Medusa-like curls that crowned her head. The straightening shampoo her hairdresser had talked her into was a joke. Even with an hour of excessive flat ironing, there was no way to tame her tresses into any semblance of smooth, silky waterfall hair. She'd wasted that fifteen bucks. Looking back, she kicked herself. They were going to need every dime to pay for the repairs on the car.

Her lip was swollen, the little stitches slightly bloody beneath their butterfly bandage, like a sepia train track. People paid good cash money to get their lips this puffy. Little did they know a simple car accident could save them thousands in surgical procedures.

She started back to the group. High-pitched squealing made her stop short. Janie, the bride, was being molested by the stripper now, twirling and dancing in his arms. God, she must really be hammered. All this crew was concerned with was getting as loaded as possible as quickly as possible, and it looked like the drinks had done the trick. They were up to their ears in the party's signature cocktail, pink piña coladas. Aubrey was allergic to coconut, so every time the waitstaff moved through with the concoctions on their trays, Aubrey passed.

But she did want something. No one would

notice if she disappeared for a longer stretch. This party wasn't about her. No one would miss her.

She walked down the hallway to the first quiet bar she found. The Opryland resort was gigantic. It housed multiple restaurants and bars, all situated along a garden-like atrium on the lowest level of the hotel, each with a different theme, a commercial identity crisis like no other. You can't be all things to all people, but Opryland was trying.

And truth be told, she wanted to check on Josh. He wouldn't mind; she knew he wouldn't. He was probably worrying about her this very second, just as she was worried about him. They had a connection like that. She could think of him, and he'd call, almost as if she'd summoned him.

The silence of the bar was welcome. She settled herself on a stool and sent him a text.

> Utterly bored. Come meet me for a drink? I'm in the Jack Daniel's Lounge.

Five minutes passed with no word. She figured he was distracted and hadn't looked at his phone, and wondered what, exactly, the groom, Kevin Sulman, and his friends had devised for the male cohort's entertainment that had her husband so transfixed. Strippers, probably, though Sulman had claimed to his bride-to-be that he was skipping the tradition. Janie had assured him she would follow suit. So much for that.

And if there were strippers, Josh was a healthy

young man, and would certainly be looking. Aubrey tamped down the spurt of anger. He would look, but he wouldn't touch. He'd promised. And she trusted him.

She gathered her purse and phone to leave when a waiter came through from the back of the bar with a tray balanced on his hand. Centered perfectly was a single highball of clear liquid, garnished with a slice of lime. He caught her eye, made a beeline to her seat, set the drink on the bar in front of her with a smile, then turned with a flourish and disappeared back the way he'd come. She hadn't even had time to grab her wallet from her bag.

She sniffed the drink, and a wide smile broke over her face—Tanqueray and tonic, her favorite. Josh was such a silly romantic. She loved that about him the most. He was surprising, and fun, and smart and sexy and wonderful, but under all of that ran a streak of romanticism that would make Eros proud.

Like sending a gin and tonic to her in the middle of a boring party. More than a drink. A promise.

She settled back onto the bar stool to wait for him, expecting him to appear from around the corner with a sly grin on his face, tickled to death that he'd surprised her. Texted him again—*You are the best husband EVAH!*—and waited.

Aubrey sipped the drink and let the cool, piney taste coat the back of her throat, once again considering how incredibly lucky she was. Having money would be nice, but it couldn't buy her the love of a good man, or friendship, or the kind of happy, settled contentment she'd always felt when she thought of her husband—the things she valued most in this world.

She thought back to their own wedding three years earlier, a quiet, subdued affair but, in her mind, much more fun. They'd both been excited, a little nervous. Josh's hands had shaken when he put the ring on her finger, but his voice never wavered as he said his vows. She didn't remember all the details, but would never forget looking into his denim-blue eyes as he said the words that would bind them together forever. She'd gotten goose bumps, so strong was his intensity, and she knew he meant every word down to his bones.

She glanced at her watch. She'd sent the first text at 9:45 p.m. It was now almost 10:15. Her drink was three-quarters gone. She toyed with the lime on the edge of the glass. Where was he?

She had a nice little debate with herself. She was tired. Sore and bruised from the accident. The drink had made her sleepy, and they had a beautiful king-size bed waiting upstairs. Share a hot bath, maybe get crazy and raid the minibar, definitely break in the bed—these things sounded like heaven. So if he wasn't going to come to her, the least she could do was go to him.

She finished the drink, wound her way through the acreage of the hotel to the concierge desk, and asked where the Sulman party was taking place. The concierge didn't hesitate, told her the room number immediately, which gave Aubrey pause. Did he think she was part of the entertainment? Her dress wasn't that revealing, was it?

She turned her back and started toward the bachelor party. To be fair—she was always fair with him—she texted Josh, *THX for the drink. I'm coming to get you, we have things to do upstairs*, ended with a smiley face.

She got lost immediately. The hotel was so big that she didn't know how the people who worked there found their way around. Fifteen minutes passed, twenty. She was hopelessly lost. Finally, a man dressed in the pink-and-gold livery of the hotel appeared around a corner. She flagged him down, and he showed her to one of the little golf carts that buzzed around the site. "I'll take you. Hop in. It's on the other side of the property. A two-minute ride."

She got into the cart, wondered if this qualified as getting in the car with a stranger. It was chilly; the sun had long since disappeared, and the early spring evening fought with the last vestiges of winter for control.

"Where're you from?"

Aubrey started. "Oh. I'm local. We're here for a wedding. My husband and I, that is."

He smiled. "No worries. We see lots of people like you here."

Aubrey's back stiffened. The damn dress. She *did* look like a stripper. Or a swinger, or something else equally unsavory.

The man didn't say anything more, just pulled up to a pink-and-gold building with *Lounge* written on the doors.

"Here you go, ma'am."

He waited, and she opened her purse and

fished out a dollar. He took the money with a smile and buzzed off, leaving her standing alone in the dark.

The door to the lounge sprang open, and one of Josh's best friends, Arlo Tonturian, stumbled out. His eyes were nearly crossed, but he recognized Aubrey.

"Hey, hey, sexy lady. You must excuse me for a moment." He weaved over to the bushes and proceeded to vomit. Yes, she'd definitely arrived in the right place.

She didn't want to wait. She wanted to go inside, grab Josh, go to bed, but Arlo was in pretty bad shape, so she went to him and put a hand on his back.

"Can I help?"

He retched again, stood up, spit a few times. He looked slightly more normal, but still pale, and still drunk.

"Jesus, why do I ever agree to Jägerbombs? Shit makes me sick every time. Josh not feeling good either?"

"I don't know. He's been doing Jägerbombs, too?" Great. They didn't make him sick, but they certainly didn't make him amorous. More like passed out cold.

Arlo gave her another slightly cross-eyed look. "He never showed, princess. And trust me, Sulman is mightily pissed."

CHAPTER 4

Aubrey was getting annoyed.

"You're drunk, Arlo. Josh is inside. He took off for the party the minute we arrived." She glanced at her phone; it was nearing midnight. "That was over three hours ago. We were late, we had an accident on the way over. Didn't you hear?"

Arlo rubbed his eyes and gave her that soft grin he used when he wanted to be charming. "I'm drunk all right. As a fucking skunk. But he ain't inside. We called his cell phone, but he never answered. He's missing the strips, too. They have ta-taaaaas." Arlo's face turned white. "You didn't hear that. Don't tell Janie. She's not cool like you."

So Sulman *had* fallen prey to the strippers.

"I won't say anything." Aubrey reached for the door, but Arlo stumbled over and slammed it shut.

"No way, sexy lady. You can't go in there. Men only." He looked a little more sober now, and Aubrey shook her head. God knew what Sulman was up to in there—or Josh. Was that why Arlo was blocking her way? Was Josh doing something he shouldn't have been? She had a flash of anger and jealousy so intense that she felt like if she didn't scream she'd explode.

No. No way. He would never. Not after . . .

She shouldered Arlo out of the way and flung the door open. His slurry voice followed her down the dark hallway.

"Aubrey. Aubrey, really. You don't want to go in there."

She stormed into the corridor and followed the noise. A heavy bass beat thumped in time with her slamming heart. She pulled the double doors open and strode into the bacchanal. Her eyes took a few moments to adjust to the gloom. When they did, her first emotion was relief. What she saw wasn't terribly shocking. Not great, but it could have been worse.

Kevin Sulman, the groom, was being kissed and groped rather forcefully by a random stripper, and looking like he was enjoying her attentions. A few of the boys had their hands and mouths in places that they shouldn't have, but no one was naked but the hired girls.

And there was no Josh.

What the hell?

Arlo was right behind her. He grabbed her by the waist and yanked her from the room.

The doors swung closed, but the music barely faded. Arlo pulled her by the hand down the corridor and into the parking lot. He was humming under his breath. Once they hit the tarmac, he put both hands on her shoulders. His breath was sour on her face.

"Aubs, you can't say anything to Janie. She will roast Sulman on a spit."

"She won't, Arlo, but I don't care about them. Where is Josh?"

"I told you. He didn't show." He stepped back, fumbled in his pocket for a pack of cigarettes. "We thought he either felt bad after the accident or y'all decided to go home."

"In our imaginary car?" Aubrey heard the note in her voice. Heard it, and it scared her. She'd gone up several decibels and an octave, all at once. Arlo heard it, too. He stopped fumbling with his smokes.

"Don't freak, Aubrey. Have you called him?"

"Yes. He's not answering."

Her breath started to come short. What if Josh was dead? An intracranial bleed caused by the accident? A collapsed lung? A pneumothorax? All those terms she'd been helping him study for the past three years tumbled around with the threatening panic inside her head. Maybe he was in the emergency room right now, intubated, unable to talk, unable to call her and let her know.

As she rang Josh's phone again, she asked Arlo, "Do you know the way to the main hotel?"

"Yeah. It's through the back of this place. You came the long way around, I take it?"

"Yes. I want to check the room. Show me the fastest way back."

He tossed his cigarette on the ground and pulled the door open for her. She followed, phone to her ear. Josh's voicemail clicked on. She left him a message. Followed Arlo past the thumping walls of the party, out into a long corridor that attached back to the hotel lobby. Damn concierge had sent her the wrong way, but she didn't care about that now. They found the first elevator up, and she hit the button for the fourth floor.

It took forever. Aubrey thought she'd lose her mind. She had her key in one hand and the phone, steadily redialing, in the other. The doors finally dinged open, and she took off at a run toward their room.

She wrestled with the keycard but got the door open.

The room was empty.

Aubrey knew then something was wrong. Very, very wrong. Like that sixth sense that tells you when something bad is going to happen, and the phone rings with news that someone you love is sick, or has died.

She tried to stay focused. Maybe he'd gone back to the house for something. She rang their home phone, but the machine picked up—with that stupid, goofy message they'd recorded one night when they'd both had too much to drink. Individually: "This is Aubrey." "And this is Josh." Together: "These are the voyages of the Starship *Hamilton*. Our mission: to bodily go where no married couple has gone before. Which means we're really busy right now. You know what to do!"

No one but friends had the home number—all their business was done on their cell phones—but she really needed to change that message.

At the beep, she said, "Josh? Hon, where are

you? I'm at the hotel looking for you. Call me as soon as you get this, okay?"

Arlo was finally catching her concern.

"Maybe he went home?"

Aubrey looked at him sharply. "I just called. He's not answering there, either. Let's check with the hotel staff. Maybe he left a message for me downstairs."

She wrote a note and left it on the bed. They went to the front desk. She fought the urge to run, carefully placing one heeled foot in front of the other. She ignored Arlo's occasional assurances that things would be fine, that they'd find him. With every step she said a little prayer, which quickly became a loop in her head: *Please be okay, please be okay, please be okay.*

When she knew in her heart things were never going to be okay again.

CHAPTER 5

Aubrey
Today

That was the moment. The moment that changed During into After. Where the seven and seventeen ended and the five began.

A beeping car horn pulled Aubrey back from her reverie. She looked up to see the intersection crowded with drivers, all of them heading into their own worlds, their own lives. Stars of their own plays.

What did all those people do? Strangers who passed her each and every day—did they have sorrow and pain and loss like she did? Surely she wasn't the only person in the world who suffered, by whatever means.

Her therapist had once tried to get her involved in a group therapy grief program. It had been a complete disaster. The people in group were just so . . . damaged. There was a dizzying array of loss on parade, from the woman whose young daughter had drowned in the bathtub while she went to answer the phone, to the man who'd run his car into a tree and killed his girlfriend, to the quiet teenager who'd shared some bad Ecstasy with her best friend, resulting in the girl having a heart attack on the dance floor of their favorite club.

Aubrey didn't fit into their construct.

They all had answers. Funerals to attend. Bodies to bury. Self-flagellation to attend to, especially seeing as everyone in the group was somehow responsible for the death of their loved one.

Now, Aubrey. Responsibility and accidents are different beasts entirely. You know that.

Bullshit.

Aubrey had no anchors. She had no body, no closure, and certainly bore no responsibility for Josh's death. For a time, they didn't even know for sure that he was truly gone. For a time.

Two things were certain: Aubrey hadn't killed her husband. And she knew Josh had sent her the gin and tonic that night.

It *had* to be him.

But he never came to her rescue. Through the weeks of investigation, police harassment, the legal proceedings, the trial, the months that turned into years, through the moments when During became After, when Aubrey could finally sleep through the night without thinking about the handcuffs being slapped around her wrists and the hard metal of the county jail pallet they called a bed under her body, when she was set free and came back to their empty home and startled dog and faced his mother's decision to petition the courts to declare Josh dead so she could steal away the insurance money, he never came.

He never came.

She had to reconcile the silly romantic she'd married with the concept of a man so callous, so vengeful, that he would allow the woman he claimed to love to be dragged through the mud, accused of his murder, hounded by the press, the police, without stepping forward to save her.

She couldn't. Josh would never let that happen.

And that's why she knew, without a doubt, that he was dead.

More traffic noise, and she jumped. How much time had she just lost? Her lizard brain reacted. *Run more.* She did, running away from the tree, away from the happy and the sad, up the hill into the darkness.

One foot in front of the other.

Again and again and again.

CHAPTER 6

Daisy
Today

Daisy Hamilton ran her finger along the icy tumbler of vodka, her third in as many minutes. She tossed the freezing alcohol against the back of her throat, filled the glass to the brim one more time, shoved the bottle back into the freezer, and took the shot onto her back deck. She sat hard in the Adirondack chair that faced the gardens and lit a Virginia Slim. The letter from Rick Saeger sat on the table next to her, mocking. The promise of the money, mocking. The promise of closure, mocking.

When the phone call came this morning, rapidly followed by the letter, Daisy went into overdrive. She needed someone to share in her sadness, her horror, her fear. Aubrey was the first person who came to mind. The first one who always came to mind. The loss of Josh wasn't enough punishment for that girl. Daisy wanted to tear her open and watch her bleed on the pavement.

Dropping the envelope at that little bitch's school had consumed her. She needed the girl to hurt, just like Daisy hurt, though she didn't know why she bothered; Aubrey was as walled off as they came. Daisy had always thought Aubrey was one of those people who had no emotions, no conscience. A sociopath. But if that were the case, would Josh have married her in the first place?

She'd never be able to ask him.

When she pulled out of the Montessori parking lot, her pointless arrow slung, Daisy had driven aimlessly around town, looking at all the places Josh played as a little boy. She ignored the transparent ghost of the girl, stuck to him like glue, sapping all of his energy, pulling his attention away from the only woman who truly loved him.

She'd stopped for a drink. Just one. Fortified, she'd driven through town to the Mount Olivet Cemetery office and given them the second date for the gravestone.

An expiration date.

She sipped the vodka. Thought back, the way she always did. Wondered if she would ever have peace.

It started on a Tuesday. A Tuesday that should have been like every other Tuesday before, not like every Tuesday to come.

Daisy had been making cookies, and the hour spent standing and stirring and bending before the oven made the crick in her back flare up, the one that started several years earlier after she'd fallen down the stairs. She knew she should stop and take some ibuprofen, but she wanted to get this last batch in the oven. Then she could rest. Then she could give in to the nagging pain that was her life.

But the door to the garage slammed, and in came her son, calling like a frightened jaybird.

"Mama! Mama! Mama!"

Her heart had sped up for a moment, then calmed. She recognized the alarm in his voice, she who was so attuned to every nuance of her child: every cry, every smile, every tear, every tooth; the way the skin on the inside of his arms was silky smooth and the scent of his hair told her he needed a bath, and the after, when he bundled into the towel, wet and clean and sleepy in her arms. His voice was filled with distress, but he was not hurt or in physical pain. His concern was for another.

Probably a squirrel hit by a car, or a bird flown into the window. Nothing to worry about. Nothing that couldn't be soothed with a kiss and a cookie.

How wrong she was.

Josh had skidded into the kitchen, his rumpled hair sticking up in the back, the cowlick that refused to be tamed no matter what she did to it.

"Mama!"

She turned to him, wiping her hands on a dish towel. "Josh, stop yelling. I'm right here."

"Mama! Something *awful's* happened."

Awful. To a ten-year-old, that could be anything from dropping his toothbrush in the toilet to remembering the toad he'd left in the pocket of the jeans she had just put in the wash. Awful was running out of milk to go with his cookies. Awful was relative.

"What happened, Josh?"

Her voice was weary. She hadn't meant it to be. She didn't know exactly when it started, the lassitude. The first time Ed had hit her, maybe? When she asked for the restraining order? When she'd filed the divorce papers and he'd come screaming at the door, the police having to cart him away? When she'd remarried—Tom, good, steady, boring Tom, who didn't drink, didn't hit, and loved Josh like his own child? She was a good mother. She'd done all the right things for her son. Her happiness was irrelevant in the face of his love and joy. So what if she felt trapped?

"Mama, Mrs. Pierce told us Aubrey's parents went to heaven."

She'd set the wooden spoon she was using to mix the cookie dough on the sideboard and wiped her hands on the dish towel. Josh had stopped five feet from her, his eyes wild, tears threatening to spill over. He thought he was too old to cry, and was fighting his emotions so hard. She took him by the hand and went to the table, sat down, and pulled him between her knees.

The accident had happened three days before. One of those things, her mind told her; one of those things that happened to other families. The Trentons, good people, town favorites, hired a babysitter for their young daughter, Aubrey, had themselves a night out on the town, and managed to get sideswiped by a tractor-trailer on their way home. The story had made the late local news. Daisy had been drinking a glass of wine and stopped short when she saw the accident scene, the crushed car, the yellow drape. She hardly noticed spilling a bit of wine down the front of her shirt. Her mixed emotions.

Daisy had taken an instant dislike to Marie Trenton, who always managed to make her feel like an incompetent harpy. Marie was a fixture on the Montessori's PTA, perpetually in charge. Always put together. Always gentle in her rebukes.

She was sorry for their deaths; of course she was. But something in her couldn't help but feel like Marie Trenton had gotten exactly what she deserved. But she couldn't say *that* to Josh.

"They had an accident. I know you must be scared, sweetie. But nothing is going to happen to your daddy or me. I promise."

"I know that. But why didn't anyone *tell* me?"

Josh was going through an adult stage where he felt everything needed to be shared with him. He was right this time, though. She should have told him. He liked playing with the little Trenton girl, and the school was so small. Surely they were all talking about it today.

She'd had a flash of anger toward Linda Pierce, Josh's teacher. She should have called to warn Daisy she was going to share this momentous news with Daisy's son.

But how do you explain a sudden death to a child?

Why hadn't Daisy told him herself? Perhaps because Josh had lived through Ed, though he didn't, couldn't, remember, and she wanted to shelter him from more pain.

"Sweetie, sometimes things that happen to grown-ups aren't good for children to hear."

That answer wasn't going to be good enough; she saw his mind begin to churn. He bit his lip and leaned in to her. She enveloped her son in a hug, and he whispered in her ear.

"But Aubrey has no one. Where will she go?"

This was more than a rhetorical, philosophical question. After the weekend, after fate had dealt this cruel blow, Aubrey indeed had no family. The Trentons, having left a lifetime of longing for their own child behind them, were older when they adopted Aubrey from some crack-addled teen mother who subsequently overdosed. The school had actually used their family as a model to help other young families struggling with infertility make the decision to adopt. But as only children themselves, with parents long dead, the Trentons were alone in the world. There was no one on record to take in small, orphaned Aubrey.

Who would take Josh if I died? Dear God, not Ed. Please not Ed.

She'd made a mental note to thank Tom again for adopting Josh, for his protection of her son and her sanity, forced aside the glum thoughts, gave Josh a quick squeeze.

"Aubrey is going to be just fine. There is a system. They will take care of her, and give her a new family."

"No!" It was somewhere between a proclamation and wail.

"Josh, honey. You're going to have to trust me. This is hard for you to understand, but you're my big man now. Sometimes grown-ups make decisions we don't agree with, but they are the right decisions. Aubrey will go live with a foster family."

"Strangers. They'll kill her."

"Of course they won't kill her."

"It happens. I've seen it."

Seen it on television, some damn cop show she'd caught him watching in the middle of the night about a year back.

"I told you, Josh. That was make-believe."

She could feel him vibrating in her arms, didn't know if it was tears or fury. Josh didn't like being told he was wrong. Even at ten, he got his back up.

"But why can't she come live here? With us? We could be her family."

He pulled back, staring at her, pleading with his eyes.

"Oh, Josh. That wouldn't be . . . I mean, we couldn't . . . We're not equipped."

For the briefest moment, panic filled her. *Me, raise Marie Trenton's daughter? Like hell I will.* And then . . . *He didn't know. He couldn't know.*

"But, Mama . . ."

She stood, quicker than she'd intended, signaling the end of the conversation. She ignored the pain in her back—getting Josh off the subject of the Trenton girl was more important. She needed to finish the cookies and start dinner before Tom came home, exhausted from his long day at the university, ready to eat and watch some television and maybe wrestle with the bills in his office or tinker in his basement before going to sleep.

There was no question of helping. They didn't have the money to take on another mouth. And damn that kid for making her feel like less of a mother, a person. She should want to reach out to the little orphan girl, reach out and bring her to her bosom. But the idea of managing two kids made her queasy. Add to that she'd spend the rest of her life hearing Marie Trenton's voice every time Aubrey spoke . . . Well, that just wouldn't do. The girl would survive. She'd always struck Daisy as a survivor.

Josh stood by the table, still uncertain, like a dog that's been kicked but wants to come back and try to be petted again. He knew that she'd made up her mind, but he was going to press the issue. She could tell.

But he didn't, not in the way she expected. Instead he slung a sentence at her that would resonate for years, the first thing he'd ever said to be purposely hurtful. She didn't know where, or who, he learned it from, but his intent to upset her succeeded.

"I thought mommies were supposed to love everyone."

Daisy's hands had warmed the vodka. The glass was half empty, but she couldn't bear the taste anymore. She tossed the drink in the bed of the cypress tree and lit another cigarette.

Idiot. She'd been such an idiot. She'd pushed

him right into Aubrey Trenton's skinny little arms without even meaning to.

Josh had made his choice that day. He'd chosen an eight-year-old stranger over the woman who gave birth to him, nurtured him, loved him. Given his heart to a parentless waif, an orphan twice over, a child he'd spend the next sixteen years catering to.

An eight-year-old stranger who'd grown into his wife.

A choice that had gotten him killed.

CHAPTER 7

Aubrey
Today

Dusk shrouded the sky in an inky gray-and-pink blanket. Aubrey's calves screamed. She was gulping air and pumping her arms to try to keep up with the punishing pace her demons set forth. She needed to slow down or she'd be too sore to walk.

She shortened her stride to a manageable jog, finished the last hundred yards around Dragon Park, and walked for a bit with her hands on her hips as her breath finally steadied.

She'd done her daily penance. It was over. Time for her to make her way back to the house, shower, maybe heat up a frozen dinner or, better yet, scoop some ice cream into a bowl and crash on the couch with Winston.

She wasn't that far from home, but the idea of getting there under her own steam was suddenly overwhelming. The darkness didn't bother her; she'd been known to run when she couldn't sleep. Midnight, two in the morning, four, they were all her friends. But she was exhausted, and smart enough to recognize it. She'd done more than sixteen miles, at a seven-minute-mile pace, and hadn't been prepared with water, a snack, protein pack, nothing.

Ignoring the giant mosaic dragon rising out of the playground, the screams of the happy children scaling its spiny back, she walked to the water fountain at the entrance to the park. Sucked down a gallon of warm city water, slowly walked to 21st Avenue, stuck her hand out in the universal gesture of "I need a cab."

It only took a minute, remarkable, really. Nashville wasn't terribly large, and cabs weren't a given occurrence like they were in many cities. This end of town, where Vanderbilt met Dragon Park, wasn't a big spot for tourists; outside of the Pancake Pantry, all the exciting bits were on the other side of campus, near Centennial Park and the Parthenon. She could always call for an Uber car, but she didn't trust them; she'd had a bad experience once and had no desire to repeat it.

A yellow sedan edged to the curb, and Aubrey saw the outline of a man in the backseat. He reached over and handed the driver some money, opening the door almost before the car had come to a stop. He stepped out, head turned from hers, and pulled a briefcase from the backseat. He began to walk away.

Her heart began to beat, loud and crazy and insistent.

She knew that walk.

Josh.

She took off after the man, rushing before he disappeared into the crowd, her heart soaring.

He'd come back. He was here!

"Josh!" she called. The man didn't turn.

She reached him in just a few seconds, put her arm on his shoulder, and whirled him to face her. Older, midthirties, blond hair, lightening a bit at the temples where he'd gray in a few years, brown eyes, straight nose—her mind screaming, *No no no no no no*.

It wasn't him.

"Hi there. Can I help you?" the stranger asked, his eyes confused.

Aubrey shook her head. Dejected, she turned and walked away.

How many men had she chased down in the street, thinking they were her husband? How many times had she been fooled? The perfect word, *fooled*.

Aubrey, you are a stupid little fool. A stupid, desperate fool chasing something you know doesn't exist anymore.

She had to wait ten minutes for another cab. She stretched across the backseat, rubbing her sore muscles, her head resting against the window.

He's dead and gone, Aubrey. Dead and gone and rotting in the ground somewhere, and just because you don't know where doesn't change the fact that he is no longer.

And he's never coming back.

Dear Josh,

I thought of you today. Of course I did, that's a stupid way of saying it. I think of you every day, all of the time. I just wish I knew where you were.

I thought of you today when I was walking on the beach. Kevin and Janie have forced me on an out-of-town weekend, to the house in Nags Head. Remember the time we went there, that ridiculously long drive, and the place was boarded up and we had to sleep in the car?

They claim they want to get me away from town, away from the memories, away from the press clamoring after me, but the truth is, they are embarrassed by all the attention. Our friends are embarrassed by me.

I hate it here. It's wrong to sleep in our room without you. All I can do is walk, escape, get away from the insincere, solicitous smiles. The air is thick and wet, but down by the water there is a touch of a breeze, a whisper, really, and that's where I go.

There were rocks on the beach. Not shells, nothing crushed underfoot, but a wide expanse of sand dotted with stones. I collected them, one by one, eight in all. One for every month you've been gone.

I know you're out there. Everyone tells me you're dead. But I know you're there. I can feel you, as strongly as if you were walking beside me, scattering the stones in my path for me to chase. But when I look back, there is only one set of footprints.

All I can do is hope that one day, you will come back to me.

Always,
Aubrey

CHAPTER 8

Aubrey
Today

The house was dead quiet when she returned, emptier than usual. Winston was asleep in the living room, snoring lightly, paws up in the air. He didn't even budge when she put his food down. She stood in the kitchen in her bare feet and drank two large glasses of water. She wasn't hungry, but she forced herself into a frozen dinner all the same, knowing that her run had depleted so many calories that she'd be weak in the morning if she didn't refuel.

The light on the answering machine was blinking.

She went to the phone and pressed the Message button. Linda's cheerful voice sprang from the machine.

"Aubrey, honey, if you change your mind about wanting company, I'll be at Frothy Joe's at eight. I'd love to see you come out tonight."

Aubrey deleted the message and glanced at the clock. It was 7:45 p.m. already. She didn't want to talk about poetry tonight, see Linda's solicitous smiles. She was dripping wet and so tired she couldn't think straight.

And yet something drove her to set her fork

down, mount the stairs, take a shower, whip a comb through her wickedly curly hair, slip on a cotton dress, and gather her car keys.

The house was just so empty tonight.

She couldn't face it alone.

Frothy Joe's was a quaint little coffee shop on 21st Avenue, hugely popular with the Vandy students. The original owner, now deceased, was from Colorado, and had a thing for bears, which took over every corner of the coffee shop. Between the scent of freshly ground coffee beans and the decor—mountain chic, so unlike anything else in Nashville—Aubrey found she could almost imagine she was somewhere else. Anywhere else.

The store was currently owned by Meghan Lassiter, Aubrey's best friend and confidante, who had happily given Aubrey the part-time gig when she'd applied. Meghan was independently wealthy, and always seemed to have room for a few extra employees.

Meghan's exact background was a mystery. She'd told so many stories about from whence she came, all with a sly wink and an engaging smile, that no one knew what was real and what was fabricated. Which was exactly what Meghan wanted. She felt it imperative that her life's story be full of mystery and excitement.

There was one truth to Meghan that Aubrey knew: she kept a well-loved, tattered copy of Daniel Wallace's *Big Fish* in her purse. Aubrey wondered which of the crazy characters from Meghan's life would come parading out at her funeral.

It didn't matter where Meghan had come from. All that mattered was she was here now and, despite the boss-employee relationship, functioned as the combo-platter sister, aunt, and fairy godmother Aubrey didn't have.

Aubrey opened the door to the shop slowly and carefully so the chimes wouldn't ring and interrupt the students studying. She needn't have worried. She'd forgotten it was open mike night. There was a buzz in the air. The crowd was quite large, standing room only. Aubrey could see folks packed in cheek by jowl, all facing away from the door. Good. All the more opportunity for her to get lost in the shadows. Singers and slam poets spoke in the back corner of the shop, behind an incongruous wall divider stacked with coffee-stained, dog-eared books. A lending library of sorts. Meghan had put up the wall to separate the two areas of the store, dropped a few paperbacks on the shelves, and the students had done the rest. There was an honor system: if you took a book, you needed to replace it with another.

She heard a deep voice droning on behind the shelving—some poet or another reading from his work.

Meghan was standing against the far wall, arms crossed and one leg propped up behind her like a stork, one eye on the poet, another on the counter. She was somewhere in her midthirties, a few years older than Aubrey, her black hair in a pixie cut, the sprinkling of freckles across her nose echoing Aubrey's own. She smiled widely when she saw Aubrey, green eyes sparkling against her peaches-and-cream skin. She launched off the wall and went straight to Aubrey like a bullet, enveloped her in a rib-cracking hug. She motioned with her head toward the front of the store, where they could chat without disturbing the event.

"You're not scheduled tonight. And after the day you've had, I didn't think you'd be out and about. You look like hell."

"Linda told you about the letter?"

"Yes. Are you okay?"

Aubrey shrugged. "I went for a run. I accidentally did sixteen miles."

Meghan shook her head. "Who accidentally runs sixteen miles?"

"Me. I just lost track of time."

"Sure. Did you eat? I have fresh muffins. And those spinach pinwheels you like."

"That's all right. I'm really not hungry. Who's the poet?"

Meghan eyed her again but backed off. "Some guy. His stuff's a little much for me, but what do I know? I just make the coffee."

"And he turned out this big a crowd? Good for him."

"Slam poetry junkies. Always looking for something to snap their fingers about. Besides, he is rather hot."

She winked slowly, the black fringe of lashes surrounding her green eyes succeeding in making it look suggestive. Meghan, for all her attempts at androgyny, was a singularly sexual creature. And equal opportunity with her playmates, Aubrey knew. Not from firsthand experience, of course. Meghan liked to brag.

"So now your looks predicate how big your crowd is?"

"You know that's not true. Just look at—" Before Meghan could finish, applause started. "Oh, I gotta go. Help yourself to something, sugar. You need to eat. You're getting downright anorexic."

Then she was gone. Aubrey watched her scoot to the back, her calf-high Doc Martens silent on the wooden floor. Meghan had a tiny tattoo centered on the nape of her neck, in an Asian language, but wouldn't tell anyone what it meant. Rather, she had a new story for how and why she got the tattoo, and what it stood for, each and every day, but none of them were remotely factual.

Aubrey often wondered if she would have survived the past five years without Meghan cheering her on. She'd held her, commanded her, forced her, loved her, and simply carried her when she wasn't able to carry herself. Aubrey had never had a friend like her, and something told her she would never find that combination of friend, confessor, and partner in anyone again, barring a husband.

Great. Now Meghan was the husband she'd never have.

At least she'd moved up to bipeds.

To appease her friend, Aubrey moved to the food table and selected a couple of savories. She choked down a spinach pinwheel. Despite the fact that they were incredibly tasty, Aubrey just wasn't hungry. People began filtering from the back, and Aubrey saw an opportunity for distraction. She went to the register, logged in under her employee ID, and began to sling refills.

Forty-five minutes later, Meghan came to the front of the store with the evening's star in tow. Aubrey was counting the till but could hear them coming, his deep voice contrasting nicely with Meghan's contralto. There was a coquettishness to the conversation, and Aubrey realized Meghan was going to go home with the poet tonight. It was a foregone conclusion. What Meghan wanted, Meghan got. She was a stalking lioness when someone turned her crank. People fell under her hypnotic spell whether they wanted to or not.

Aubrey normally envied her that. Though honestly, tonight, she just didn't want to watch the carnage.

"Excuse me. Can I get a refill?"

Aubrey turned toward the voice and felt a shock, the trilling of her blood rising to the surface. It was the man from the cab, the one she'd chased down earlier. She was transfixed. She couldn't move. The man's eyes stayed on hers, and she felt like he was staring deeply into her soul.

It could have been two heartbeats or two years later when he finally spoke. "It's you."

Aubrey felt herself leaning forward, drowning in his eyes, dark like the deepest coffee.

"Um, Aubs, are you going to fill the man's cup, or do I need to do it?"

The spell was broken. Aubrey tore her eyes away. She glanced at Meghan, who was looking at her with undisguised curiosity. Flustered, she grabbed the man's cup. Their fingers touched, and she pulled her hand back as if she'd been burned. The man didn't look away; he continued to stare at Aubrey with something akin to wonderment.

Meghan's eyes narrowed.

"Do you know each other?"

"We don't," Aubrey said, as the man chimed in, "Yes, we do."

Meghan cleared her throat. "Well then. I need to get things cleaned up. Why don't you two catch up?" She turned tail and scooted away, seizing upon Linda, making her way toward Aubrey and the stranger like a crocheted guided missile, and steered her off course to the back of the store, but not before Linda caught Aubrey's eye and gave her a small thumbs-up.

Aubrey was filled with guilt, and shame, and embarrassment. What must that have looked like? Had she just panted after a strange man like a dog in heat, in front of two of her dearest friends? This was not acceptable. Yes, he was handsome, and had a nice voice, and beautiful eyes. But her husband was dead, officially, as of today. She wasn't an idiot. She knew where the asserted attachment was coming from. She was tired of being lonely. But now was not the right time.

"I must be going as well," she managed, untying her smock.

The man was still watching her closely. "You can't just leave."

"Sure I can."

"I've been thinking about you since I ran into you at the park."

"How nice." She started to move around the counter toward the door.

"My name is Chase. And you are?"

He stuck out his hand to shake, and without thinking, she took it. "Aubrey, and I have an early day tomorrow."

"Tomorrow is Saturday. How early can you get started on a weekend? Let me buy you a drink."

"Is this how you end all your days? Asking strange women out for drinks?" And she smiled.

What the hell was that? It had been so long since she flirted with anyone that she didn't recognize the warmth when he responded in kind, took a step closer to her, and leaned on the counter.

"We aren't strangers. You're Aubrey, and I'm Chase. We bumped into each other earlier today. Obviously, we are destined to have a drink. Come on. Just one. You can tell me who Josh is. You seemed like you were surprised I wasn't him."

Aubrey felt like she'd been slapped. She shook

her head. *No. No way.* He wasn't allowed to use the name so carelessly, so easily. She couldn't tell a complete stranger the story, much less a man with espresso eyes.

Meghan popped up. Figured she was lurking nearby, eavesdropping.

"Oh, go on, Aubrey. Sam's is still open. Linda and I will meet you over there in a bit."

Aubrey heard the unspoken promise: *We won't leave you alone with a stranger, honey. Go on, have a drink. We'll be right behind you to make sure you're okay.*

"Yes, please join us," Chase said, and Aubrey could hear the slightest tinge of annoyance in his tone. For some reason, that made her feel good. He wanted to be alone with her.

Aubrey Marie Trenton Hamilton, you are a first-class idiot.

But there was something about this man that she simply couldn't understand, some draw that she hadn't felt in many, many years.

Josh's face floated into her mind, his blue eyes smiling, nodding, almost as if to say, *Yes, Aubrey. Go.* She wanted to hold on to that image so badly, of him smiling at her, but the moment her mind reached out to grab it, it dissipated like smoke.

Five years. Five years later, she was bumping into her future at last.

The truth was, Chase reminded her of Josh, and tonight, she wanted to find a way to be close to him.

She watched him watching her, nodded.

"All right. But just one drink."

CHAPTER 9

Sam's: dark wood, gleaming brass fixtures, a long bar punctuated by comfortable stools, and wooden tables spread higgledy-piggledy throughout. It was easy to pull up a chair, gather the tables into groups for larger parties, or slip one off by its own for a twosome. Students rubbed elbows with songwriters and country music stars and Titans players and off-duty doctors and soccer moms. Just one of those Nashville things. Everyone came to this town with a dream, and ended up kaleidoscoped together into a single shifting, pulsing entity.

As usual, the bar was packed. Aubrey didn't particularly want to run into anyone she knew; this used to be their hangout, hers and Josh's, and many of their friends still popped in on occasion. Of course, all of them were busy with their own lives now, raising families, and didn't get out unless there was money for a babysitter. Date night, they called it. For a woman who'd only ever operated under the auspices of every night being date night, Aubrey worried for them. Having to schedule time with your husband to be married seemed counterproductive.

She was a bit confused as to why Meghan suggested Sam's, of all places, actually. But she didn't want to worry about it too much. She was feeling reckless and slightly daring. She hadn't so much as glanced at a man in a friendly way for the past five years, and yet here she was, about to have a drink with a stranger, one whose walk reminded her of Josh.

The extended, unprepped run had clearly deprived her brain of necessary oxygen.

She knew the din lessened a bit in the back. Two birds with one stone. It was quieter, and away from most of the prying eyes. She gestured for him to follow her, found a table for four in the far corner. He pulled her chair out for her. Once she was settled, he looked around.

"Nice place. Should I go to the bar and get our drinks?" Chase asked.

"That's all right. Someone will be here in a minute."

"Okay."

He sat opposite her, one hand on the table, palm open, relaxed.

What did that mean? When Josh had done that, it was an invitation for her to take his hand, where he would rub the underside of her wrist and make tingles shoot between her legs.

They lapsed into silence. He was watching her, gauging, and she truly had no idea where to start. Or why she was here.

She was saved by Vincenzo, one of the regular waiters. He came out of the back and saw her sitting in the corner, immediately joined them with a big grin on his perpetually tanned moon face. He pulled her to her feet and hugged her.

"Aubrey! It's been too long. How are you? You're too skinny, let me get you some food."

"Everyone keeps trying to feed me. Really, I'm fine."

Vincenzo shook his head and poured on the accent. "In Italia, we like our women to have some meat on their bones." He traced an hourglass in the air, waggling his considerable eyebrows.

"You're from Franklin, Vinny. Nice try."

He laughed and gestured inquisitively toward Chase.

"Who's this?"

She was surprised at the welcoming tone— Vinny and Josh had been good friends. Apparently, everyone wanted to feed her, and see her get laid. Everyone had moved on but her.

"Chase—um . . ."

"Boden," he supplied helpfully.

God, how embarrassing. But Vinnie seemed unfazed.

Chase put out a hand. "I'm from Chicago, actually, just here in town to see the sights. Aubrey and I have bumped into each other twice today, I figured it was a sign."

"He was at Frothy Joe's. We're just waiting for Meghan and Linda. Having a quick drink."

"Nice ta meetcha." Vinny shook Chase's hand, then moved his mother hen act back to Aubrey. "You work too much, you never come see me anymore. I see you run by sometimes."

"I'll do better, I promise."

Chase was smiling at her. "What would you like to drink?" he asked.

"I'll have what you're having."

Chase looked up at Vinny. "Tanqueray and tonic, with a slice of lime. Tall, if you don't mind." He looked back at her. "Is that okay?"

Aubrey felt that crazy zing again. "Yes, that's fine. My favorite, actually."

"That's funny. Mine, too."

With his words came an easy smile. She got it now. He was playing her. Anger bubbled to the surface.

She stood. "Chase, I'm sorry. I need to go."

He stood, too. "Why?" He looked genuinely confused.

"I think there's been some sort of misunderstanding. I wasn't even supposed to work tonight. It was a lark on my part. I've had a very long, very bad day. It's been a long five years, as a matter of fact. And I don't know what Meghan told you about me, but I'm not into that. This. You. I can't go there. So you'll excuse me. Thanks for . . . Well, see ya."

She was three feet away, congratulating herself on getting out while the getting was good, when she felt his hand on her arm.

His hand.

Her breath left her in a whoosh.

He turned her slowly. After a second's resistance, she allowed herself to be maneuvered to face him.

Those dark chocolate eyes bored into her.

"Aubrey, I don't know what you're talking about. I don't know anything about you outside of the fact that you chased me down earlier, called me Josh, then showed up at the coffee shop behind the counter when I needed a refill. For all I know, you're stalking me."

He smiled, and it was crooked, the left edge of his lip quirking up—just like Josh's—and she shut her eyes and pretended that the hand on her arm belonged to the ghost of a man she missed dreadfully. After a few moments, she opened her eyes, nodded, and let Chase lead her back in the chair.

"Want to tell me what's going on?" he asked.

Vinny arrived with the drinks. She was silent until he left, took a huge long pull on the straw, felt the familiar, bitter pull of the gin. Liquid courage.

She met Chase's eyes again.

"My husband . . ."

He actually sat back in his chair. She really knew how to grab someone's attention.

"I didn't know you were married."

How could he miss that? She glanced down at her finger. Her ring wasn't on.

She panicked for a moment, then remembered. She'd slipped it off before the shower like she always did after a long run, because getting soap in the grooves chafed the swollen flesh.

And she'd forgotten to put it back on.

Holy shit.

She took a deep breath. Her therapist had always told her things happen for a reason.

But her wedding ring?

On the day he was declared dead?

And here she was, sitting across from another man. She was a terrible person.

"Chase, I don't know what's wrong with me. I never leave my house without it. I know, I am a walking contradiction. Yes. I'm married. Was married. Am. He, Josh, went missing five years ago."

"What happened?"

This should fix things.

"The police think I murdered him."

He didn't miss a beat. "Did you?"

"No. But it didn't stop them from putting me through hell."

"Jesus. That sounds like a mystery novel."

She laughed humorlessly. "He disappeared the night of his best friend's bachelor party. The courts have just declared him legally dead. Today, I mean."

He sat back in his chair, looking stunned. "You must be terribly upset."

"Yeah. I am. So you see, now isn't really a good time for me to . . ."

She realized she'd finished the drink. It felt good. Good to have a little buzz. Good to talk to someone. Good to get it off her chest for once, instead of holding herself together.

Her mind said, *Careful, Aubrey.*

The rest of her said, *Fuck off. For once, just leave me alone.*

Too bad she couldn't listen to her own good advice.

"Chase, you seem like a nice guy. I don't think you want to get rolled up in my drama. I should probably go."

He actually looked hurt. "When are you going to stop trying to run away from me?"

"I can't help it. You remind me of him."

"Do we look similar?"

"Not at all. You are the exact opposite of him in many ways. But you walk alike."

And when you put your skin to mine, I feel like an electrical storm is surging through my body. Just like I did with him. And you're only ever supposed to feel that with one person. That's all it's supposed to be. You get one chance at this in life. One. No one really gets two bites at the apple, do they?

Chase had another half smile on his face.

"So I walk like your dead husband. Josh."

"Stop using his name," she snapped.

"Sorry. I thought . . ."

God, Aubrey. Extricate yourself already.

She wanted to leave. She wanted to walk out the door. But something was holding her there. Something . . .

"No, it's okay. This is my problem, not yours. I'm not ready to get involved with someone."

He was quiet for a moment, then said, "I see."

Vinny brought another drink. She took a large sip. Another. Another. Her head was feeling swimmy. She felt the edges slip away, that familiar rush.

She wasn't an alcoholic, far from it. Just a girl who got very drunk, very quickly, off any manner of alcohol. And didn't know when to stop.

The second drink was gone now. She signaled Vinny for another.

"You couldn't possibly understand," she said. "It doesn't even make sense to me."

"Couldn't I, Aubrey? There's no way for me to possibly understand?"

He took her hand. His thumb slid across the inside of her wrist. She was frozen.

"You know he's dead, but there's no body. So somewhere, deep inside you, in a place you don't ever acknowledge, there's a tiny quivering bead of hope."

Whisper-soft swipes against her skin. His touch was hypnotic.

"Yes."

"And you've been faithful to him, all these years."

"Yes."

"You were humiliated and embarrassed by the police and the press. Lost the respect of your peers, your friends, your family."

"Yes," she whispered.

He dropped his voice, and she heard something in there, something so familiar.

"I understand, Aubrey. I understand more than you could possibly know. You are a diamond, shining in the dark. It would be impossible for someone to leave you of their own volition."

His gaze was pulling her under. She felt herself slipping into the abyss. It would be so easy to get lost in those brown depths, to drown in them. She leaned forward, toward him, not sure what she intended. His face was shaped like Josh's, but his chin was different. His eyes were, too. Honestly, he looked nothing like her husband. But there was something about him . . .

"Hey, you two. What's up?"

Meghan's cheer yanked Aubrey back into her chair, and she pulled her hand from Chase's grip.

"Hi, Meghan. Nothing major. We're just chatting." She heard the slur in her voice. Damn. She needed some water. Her head. It was so thick, so full.

Meghan sat next to Aubrey, giving her shoulder a squeeze. "You might want to slow down there, sugar pop. Linda went home. I'm glad you're still here. I was afraid you might have slipped off into the night."

"Not yet," Chase said lightly. "We were just getting to know each other."

Meghan looked at the two of them closely and raised an eyebrow. "Am I interrupting?"

Aubrey laughed. It was a high-pitched whinny, bordering on hysteria. Drunk laugh. Drunk girl. The thought made her giggle again. "Of course not. We were just talking about . . . Chase, start again. What were you saying?"

He didn't miss a beat, and Aubrey liked him for it. Almost as if he knew she was getting too toasted and wanted to protect her secret.

"Like I was saying, Chicago's had the worst

winter in decades. We've all been freezing. The idea of some warmer weather seemed like a good one when I booked the ticket."

Yada yada yada. Aubrey watched his mouth move. It was a good mouth, full lipped but not overly so, just the right amount of cushion. She didn't like kissing lipless men.

Good God. She really was drunk.

Meghan had a beer, dark and thick, Guinness, from the looks of it. She took a sip, and the foam gathered on her upper lip. "So you've just been sitting here, talking about the weather. Uh-huh. Chase, what do you do?"

Aubrey could have sworn a cloud passed across his face. "I write freelance. Articles. Boring stuff, computers mostly. It pays the bills." He launched into a funny story about a jail-broken iPhone found on the L, and the tension passed.

They talked, and talked, and talked, Chase regaling them with stories, Meghan countering with some of her tall tales. Aubrey pretended she was an ordinary woman, out for an ordinary evening, with ordinary friends. She went along for the ride, enjoyed it even, until she looked at the clock and realized it was almost one in the morning. She was more than tipsy, and exhausted, and ready to go home. After Meghan's arrival, things had gone back to normal for her and Chase, just two people who found some common ground having a drink. Ships passing in the night.

She stood carefully. "Guys, this has been fun,

but I really have to head out. That sixteen miles is catching up with me."

Meghan gave her a hug. "I'm staying. I don't need to open the store until noon tomorrow. Chase? Another?"

"Actually, Meghan, I have to go, too. I'm supposed to fly back to Chicago in the morning. Aubrey, why don't I walk you out?"

He met Aubrey's eyes. She stared back, willing herself not to get lost.

It all flashed before her, how the night was going to go.

They wouldn't speak. It was almost as if words would break the spell, and they both knew it. They'd just walk out of the bar and around the corner to the parking lot behind the coffee shop, not touching but very aware of each other. The drive would take less than five minutes. He would follow her into the kitchen, and when the door was closed and the alarm set, he would pull her into his arms.

And when his lips touched hers, she would know.

Josh.

The tenuous hold she had on her emotions would be broken. She'd accept his caresses and return them ravenously. They wouldn't even make it out of the kitchen.

Without breaking the kiss, he would simply lift her onto the counter, push her dress up and out of the way, slide off her panties, and sheath himself in one stroke. She would moan, deep in her throat, and he would answer her cry. It would be over too quickly.

They would move to the bedroom and do it all over again. And again.

She didn't know how much time had passed, whether a minute or an hour. Years would have gone by too quickly. She had missed him, so much. And now he had come home.

CHAPTER 10

Daisy
Today

It was dark out, and Daisy was still on the back deck when Tom came home from work.

He took one look at her and sat in the matching Adirondack chair. He reached a hand out and touched her knee.

"What's wrong?"

Tom had a way of asking questions that Daisy didn't know how to answer: *How are you? Are you all right? Do you still love me?*

"The letter," she said, shrugged at the paper.

He picked it up and read, lips moving slightly as he sounded out the words. It was a tic that drove her mad sometimes.

He finished and set the paper in his lap. He didn't say anything, just looked out over the gardens. She waited. Tom would have some sort of platitude. Words meant to be comforting that she would hear as an indictment.

She looked away from his face and lit a cigarette. The pack was nearly empty. Did she have more in the refrigerator? Or was this the last one?

Five minutes passed. She felt rather than saw movement, risked a glance. Tom was crying, silently, tears rolling down his worn, lined face.

She didn't know what to do. She didn't know how to react. Josh wasn't Tom's son, not really, yet Tom had adopted him soon after their marriage began, had always loved him like his own, even when Josh was at his worst. She didn't like having to share her grief with her husband. It was hers, hers alone, a tight ball of perpetually sustained energy that kept her body animated, jerking along like a zombie from day to night to day again. An internal supernova that happened one thousand eight hundred and seventy-four days earlier. One thousand eight hundred and seventy-four, not one thousand eight hundred and seventy-five, because Aubrey hadn't told her right away.

Sometimes Daisy was happy about that. That she'd spent one last day in ignorant bliss, not knowing that her son was most likely dead.

And other days, days like today, she wanted to rip the little bitch's head off for not calling immediately. What in the hell had she been thinking? No, that wasn't the right question. What had Aubrey been *doing*?

Daisy knew exactly what. Killing her son.

Five Years Ago

Daisy was in her car, taking a first drive in her much-coveted Mercedes CLK, the one Tom had surprised her with the night before. The day was sunny, blue skies, puffy white clouds. Flowers bloomed, and the heavy scent of honeysuckle gathered in her nose.

She was happy.

She'd been truly astonished last night when the car rolled into the driveway. She caught a glimpse of something in the front yard and glanced out the kitchen window. She knew immediately what was happening, rushed out the door. The car purred on the cracked concrete, dark and sleek, a midnight blue so deep it was nearly black, the halogen headlights ringed in . . .

"What's this? Tom, what have you done? It has eyelashes? My car has eyelashes?"

Tom laughed, and she could see he was thrilled at her overwhelming joy. Daisy was a hard woman to please—she knew this. Tom knew it as well, and spent much of his time thinking about ways he could make Daisy smile. Delivering the vehicle she'd dropped so many hints about loving was only one gesture in a long line of gestures.

But this one was worth something to her.

She rewarded him with some bedroom acrobatics that she wasn't sure she still had in her, but was happy to find she did. The car symbolized a new beginning. A fresh start for them.

But as she drove, imagining the simmering jealousy behind the admiring glances of her friends at the club, and enjoying every minute of being able to finally, finally, throw her bounty in their smug faces, her cell phone rang. The navigation display popped up with the number for her daughter-in-law. Tom had set up the Bluetooth in

the car so all Daisy had to do was click a button
on the steering wheel to answer.

Daisy's good mood slid away. To say she wasn't
fond of the woman who shared her son's bed was
an understatement. She'd never warmed up to
the girl, thought she was trouble from day one.
Like mother, like daughter. That day, so long ago,
when Josh had taken her side, always rankled.
Josh had always liked Aubrey, yes, but Daisy never
imagined he'd marry the little brat.

What did they say—*A daughter is a daughter
for all of your life, a son was a son 'til he took him
a wife*? Even knowing her son would grow up
and leave her eventually, that he'd chosen to do
so with Aubrey Trenton was enough to send her
blood pressure through the roof. Daisy relegated
to second place by Marie Trenton's little girl, of
all people?

It wasn't right—Daisy and Josh had been
pals, best friends. She'd sacrificed everything for
him. Created a new life with a man she didn't
necessarily love in order to give her son stability, a
good, solid, loving world to grow up in. And little
orphan Aubrey stepped in and ruined everything.

She took a deep breath and answered.

"Yes?"

"Daisy?"

There were tears in Aubrey's voice, beneath
the steel, which was surprising. The hard, sharp
edge of the girl was all Daisy ever saw. Daisy
supposed she couldn't blame her for needing to
protect herself, after the hullabaloo, but when

speaking to her family, she should adopt a more pleasant tone.

"What is it?"

"Daisy, you need to come over. Josh is missing."

Today

The cigarette pack was empty.

Tom had stopped crying.

"Are you really going to contest?" he asked.

"The insurance payout? Of course. Josh and I had a deal: I cosign on the house, he makes me the beneficiary."

"We don't need the money."

"Well, that little sociopath doesn't deserve it."

His lips thinned in the way that made her cringe. "Daisy. Aubrey is not a sociopath, and damn it, Josh loved her. He wanted her to be taken care of. That's why he had the life insurance policy in the first place."

"And what about me, Tom? I was his mother. I raised him, and loved him, and tried to keep him safe. Safe from his real father. Safe from her."

The comment struck a nerve. He quietly stood, took the overspilling ashtray and the empty tumbler, and said, "You should probably eat something, dear."

Daisy tried not to glare at Tom. She really did. How was she supposed to eat? Her son was dead, and the woman who killed him lived.

She'd lost nearly forty pounds in the past

five years, twenty of which she'd needed to lose, another twenty that made her look like a washed-up model still trying to cut it on the runway. Some of it was muscle—she tried to keep up her tennis game—but she was mostly just skin and bones and sinew. A walking bag of seething loss.

Tom was right. Vodka and cigarettes and regret were only enough to sustain her temporarily.

She stood mechanically and went to the kitchen. Tom followed. She sensed he wanted to talk more, to be touched. To have her apologize for throwing Ed in his face. To something. But she kept her eyes and hands averted, started a pan of leftover soup to warm, put a small baguette in the oven, placed napkins and spoons on the table.

They ate in silence. That is to say, Tom ate. Daisy just swirled her spoon around in the thick gold broth. When the scrape of metal against china signaled that Tom's bowl was empty, she stood. Tom stood as well. He started to open his mouth, closed it again, sighed, and shuffled to the basement door, disappearing down into the gloom.

Daisy grabbed both bowls, dumped her meal down the disposal, tidied the kitchen.

She took the vodka from the freezer and poured one last shot. There was a bottle of pills in the cabinet, ones designed to help her sleep. Help her forget. She reached for the orange plastic, dumped two in her palm. Dropped them on her tongue and used the vodka to chase them down her throat.

Day one thousand eight hundred and seventy-four was over.

CHAPTER 11

Aubrey
Today

When Aubrey woke, she was acutely aware of three things. One, the sun was well up in the sky, which meant it was late morning. Two, her head was splitting, caught in a vise grip of throbbing pain. Three—and despite the pain, she was at once relieved and disappointed—her bed was devoid of the man she'd met last night. The man who'd so passionately made love to her. The man whose touch, whose kiss, reminded her of what she'd lost.

What a dream. What a delicious dream.

Eyes closed, she stretched, and felt the soreness in her legs, and between them. She wanted the fantasy to continue. To pretend that the world she knew was something different.

Josh.

Josh always had risen before her. Was he in the kitchen, making breakfast? She didn't smell anything. No coffee. No bacon and eggs and toast. Only the stale breath of a hangover, and a sudden brimstone whiff of regret for what she'd done.

She opened her eyes, worried, glanced at the pillow. No one there.

Her drowsy mind caught up to the situation. Not Josh. *Chase.*

Jesus. She'd actually brought a stranger home and slept with him. How could she have let that happen?

What did you expect, Aubrey? You had enough alcohol to drown a horse. This is why you don't drink anymore. You black out. You lose time. You do stupid, reckless things.

She got up and walked downstairs.

The house was very empty.

The alarm was set.

She was alone.

Winston was asleep in a pool of sunshine by the kitchen door. She must have let him out when she got home last night, so he'd slept through his morning constitutional. She roused him, took him out into the yard, played for a few moments, left him to his business. Went back inside to make herself some coffee.

Maybe take a few aspirin.

Should she try to eat? Her stomach flipped, and she decided no, not yet. Let the coffee get in first. Then she could self-flagellate.

She saw the edge of a piece of paper under the phone. It had been ripped from a notebook.

Her heart skipped a beat. She picked up the paper. Read with incredulity.

Aubrey,

Last night was . . . Well, I'm speechless. I can't wait to see you again. I apologize for slipping out this morning. I had an early flight and

didn't want to wake you. I'll call you later.
I hope that's okay. I'd love to come back and
spend some time. Maybe next weekend? Or
maybe even before that. If you'd like, that is.
Anyway, thank you. It was a lovely night.

He'd signed it simply, a one-word scrawl:
Chase.

She leaned back against the kitchen counter,
running the paper across her lips. Her grazed lips
swollen from his kisses, the tender skin abraded by
his beard. At least he hadn't disappeared without a
word. That would have been too much to bear.

What have you done?

She slid down onto the floor. She felt dirty.
Tainted. When he'd touched her, when he'd
kissed her—she'd felt Josh.

The Josh.

All of him. And so she'd allowed him to be.

There are things you don't forget. The way a
man makes you feel, the way he moves his mouth,
his hands, his body. The way he walks. None of
those things could be changed. Could they?

Aubrey, listen to yourself. Be rational. Think, for a
moment, about what you're saying.

She did. She thought it through, from the first
moment, at the edge of the park—their park—
when he got out of the cab. His gait, the shoulders squared, the cock of his head.

She'd been so sure. And when he kissed her
last night, she'd known, without a doubt, Chase
was Josh.

Impossible.

Wishful thinking?

Wish fulfillment. Bolstered by bits of lunacy brought about by the horrid news about Josh being declared dead, delivered in such a hurtful way by his beast of a mother, coupled with a very long run with no prep and a major overindulgence in adult beverages.

That was all.

Winston came in through the open door and cuddled against her. She stroked his ears.

One of the things she'd learned in therapy: the mind is a very powerful entity. It can play tricks. It can be manipulated. Hers in particular had been strained to the point of breaking by Josh's disappearance, and the harassment, the trial, and the alcohol abuse. By her past. She was an easy mark, should someone want to take advantage of her fragility.

Had Chase Boden taken advantage of that? Maybe he'd been lying all along, maybe he knew all about Josh and her background. Maybe she was just another notch on his belt. Maybe she fucked a new girl in every town and slipped out in the morning, leaving behind a note.

God. She'd been played. No, it was worse than that. She'd allowed herself to be played.

You stupid, stupid girl.

She screamed, the harsh sound echoing in the house. Winston leaped away, flinching, then scooted next to her, tongue lolling, worried. She buried her face in his flank and cried.

Her thoughts chased themselves, piling up

like snowflakes in a winter storm, melting under her memory's withering heat. She indulged her demons. Dreamed of a world in which Josh was alive, that he'd come back for her. It was a warm and happy feeling, one that she wanted to stay wrapped up in like a blanket, heated from within with happy memories.

Now, Aubrey. No need for that. Go easy on yourself. You suffered a trauma yesterday, whether you want to admit it or not. And you reacted in a completely healthy way. Probably the healthiest way you could have. Josh is not coming back. You must move on. Your rational mind accepts this, even if your subconscious occasionally betrays you. Why else would you have acted so out of character yesterday—drinks with a stranger only the top of the heap?

She had no idea how long she sat on the cold kitchen floor, the hard tile making her buttocks ache. She couldn't shake the thought that somehow, some way, Chase was Josh.

Her therapist wanted her to reach out when she felt herself drowning in uncertainties. But she didn't want to hear that emotionless, clinical voice right now.

What do you think, Aubrey? How does that make you feel?

If I knew, would I be coming to you for the answers? No, you stupid shrink. I'd decide for myself.

There was only one thing left to do. She called Meghan, who answered on the first ring.

"Yo! What up, buttercup? How are you feeling this morning?"

"Hi, Meghan. I'm . . . okay."

The languorous tone was gone. "Aubrey, what's wrong?"

"It's . . . I need to talk about Chase Boden."

Meghan chuckled. The all-knowingness of it set Aubrey's teeth on edge. She rarely got angry with Meghan—that was counterproductive. Meghan was a fairy, an ethereal spirit, uncontrolled, uncouth, un-everything. She didn't respond to anger, or any emotion save actual pain.

"Stop laughing."

"Ah. I see. He did seem rather intent on getting you home safely."

"Meghan, I don't know anything about him."

"Did you sleep with him?"

"Meghan!"

"You did! Oh, my God, Aubrey, I am so proud of you! You've needed to do this for a long time. Shake off the cobwebs. You know your cherry was growing back. Bad things happen to women who don't have sex. How was he? The way that man moves, his hips sway. When I watched the two of you heading out the door, all I could think about was—"

"Could you back off for just one second, please? I'm not kidding around here. I need to know who this guy is."

"What's the matter, sweetie? Did he eat and run?"

Meghan's tone was unmistakable. Aubrey could practically see her eyebrows waggling lasciviously.

"Don't be gauche, Meghan. I'm serious. I need to know everything I can about him."

"He said he was a writer. Google him. He probably has a website. Listen, I have to go. The store beckons. Call me later. I'm really proud of you."

"Meghan, I need to talk to you now."

A muttered curse. "Sorry, shut the door on my hand. All right. The store can wait a minute. Shoot."

"In person. There's more. I can't do this over the phone. Please come over. Please?"

Meghan sighed deeply, then said, "I'll be there in five. But I don't have long, sugar. No offense, but there's a lot to be done today."

Aubrey hung up and waited, unmoving, at the table. The thick wooden round had been in Josh's family for years. He'd done his homework at it—they'd done their homework at it—and Aubrey knew on the underside of the table Josh had written in big black marker, *I love Aubrey*. His mother had never found out. God, Daisy would have shot him dead for defiling the furniture, especially with a declaration of love for Aubrey, of all people.

Daisy had thrown roadblock after roadblock in the way of the burgeoning romance the minute she saw it might be something more than puppy love. Aubrey never understood what it was about her that Daisy hated so. Josh told her it wasn't true, that Daisy just needed time to wrap her head around their relationship, but it never happened.

Aubrey tried so hard, too, to be friendly, and kind, and loving, but the witch would never let her in. After a few years of Daisy's open hostility, Aubrey came to detest Daisy as well.

Some people are just meant to rub each other wrong.

Whatever thread, however thin, that held them together after Josh's disappearance was severed permanently during Aubrey's trial. Daisy's gaunt, bony face swiveling to see who was watching her enter the courtroom, the stylish black suit, even the pillbox hat complete with veil— come on, how precious could you be?—seemed tailor-made for the prosecution. Aubrey would never forget the look on Daisy's face as she sat on the witness stand, the manic glee in her eyes. "I have no doubt she played a role in my son's disappearance. She's always been off, that girl. From the moment I met her, I knew she'd be the death of Josh."

Thanks a lot, Daisy.

Five minutes later, Winston rose to his feet and stared at the door. There was a knock, shave and a haircut. She answered it, and before Meghan even got inside Aubrey said, "It's Josh."

Her friend's face, usually inscrutable, softened. "Sugar, no one blames you. It's been five years. He's dead. He won't care."

"That's not what I meant."

Meghan leaned back and crossed her arms, assuming her usual stance. The move killed all her soft edges, made her look tough, uncompromising. She could be a biker assassin just as easily as a coffee shop owner.

"Speak to me."

Aubrey took a deep breath.

"This may sound crazy. But hear me out. Chase reminds me so much of Josh. It's almost like . . . almost like he knows him. Or knew him." *Or is him, but of course that isn't true, it couldn't be. It just couldn't. A girl knows these things.*

To her credit, Meghan held back the laughter, though Aubrey could see her mouth twitching. She shook her head. "Sweetie. You need a nice cup of tea. Maybe with a little whisky in it. Hair of the dog. You really did tie one on last night."

"I'm serious."

"Come on now, Aubrey. Josh is dead. He's been gone for years. If he were alive, he would have come back. You know that. And if Boden knew your husband, he would have said something."

"He did things, things only Josh knew I liked." She sounded ridiculous, she knew, but she needed to push forward on this.

Meghan sighed. "Aubrey, honey. When's the last time you saw your doctor? Have you been taking your meds?"

"Damn it, Meghan. I'm not hallucinating, or imagining things. Not this time. There's a connection between them. I swear it."

Meghan sighed deeply and ran her hand through her cropped hair. There were a few strands of gray mixed into the black. When had they started to age? Aubrey didn't feel any older than she had when Josh was here, though she must have gotten older, if her heart was still beating. She had to think for a moment when her birthday was—she hadn't allowed a celebration in five years. May. In just a few weeks, she was going to be thirty.

"You know, we've been through this before," she said, and Aubrey heard the recriminations in her tone. The solicitude of dealing with the madwoman in the attic.

"Not like this. This time it's different. I swear. I slept with the man, for God's sake. Does that not mean anything? Do you think I would do that with just anyone?"

Meghan stared deep into Aubrey's eyes, assessing. Aubrey imagined she was looking for the madness within, hoping to touch it, capture it, stamp it out.

"No, sugar, I don't think you slept with him carelessly. I think you've been repressing so many emotions over the past five years that it finally all came to the surface." She leaned forward. "Listen to me. This isn't rocket science. You fucked a guy, Aubrey. The first one since your husband disappeared. It's frightening and unnerving, but it is *not* a sin. You are still a good person."

"Jesus, Meghan. Are you not listening to anything I've been saying?"

"Yes, I have. I ask again, have you been taking your medicine?"

"Meghan. I'm not joking around here. Something—"

"Aubrey, honey." Meghan ran her hands along Aubrey's arms. The gesture was meant to be reassuring, but only served to distress Aubrey more. She hated to be touched when she was upset. She shuddered and yanked away and walked to the other side of the table, out of reach.

Meghan eyed her coolly. She knew better than to try to touch Aubrey again. "Okay. Let me run this down for you. Chase doesn't look anything like Josh. He has a completely different build. His hair and eyes are different. His face shape is different. He has a history. A family. A life. Do you agree with all of that?"

"Yes."

"Verifiable information."

"Probably."

"Definitely. Then you understand where I'm coming from. He is not your missing husband."

"I don't think he *is* Josh, I just think . . . Dear God, Meghan, you of all people should know how easy it is to fake a background. You've been doing it successfully for years."

The dart found its mark. Meghan flinched, her mouth narrowing into a fine line.

"Point taken. But, Aubrey, it's one thing to fudge a few things about your past so people don't go looking and making assumptions. It's a completely different thing to morph into another person entirely. Now. You had a lot to drink last night. You had a one-night stand with a relative stranger. And it's a good thing. You look more alive today than you have in years. Don't regret it. Just let it go."

"Meghan—" Aubrey began, but the woman held up a hand.

"No more. I have to get going. Relax. Take your pills. You're just having a little bit of buyer's remorse."

Buyer's remorse. How dare she. How *dare* she?

"You can see yourself out," she snapped.

"Come on, sugar—"

"Out. Now."

Meghan shrugged and wandered out the door. Aubrey slammed it behind her.

She went into her office and opened her laptop. It took her less than a minute to find the right Chase Boden. She should have done this first, before she talked to Meghan. She clicked on his website and scanned until she found the bio page. With the picture. And his background. He had been modest; he was clearly a respected journalist, with multitudes of articles to his name.

As she burrowed into his website, her head began to swim.

The large, glossy professional portrait definitely showed the man from last night. Square jaw, little cleft, floppy blond hair, deep brown eyes. God, he was handsome.

Stop that, Aubrey. Focus.

She scanned the bio. It was a bit short, but had all the relevant details: After graduating from Dartmouth, he'd joined his family business, a now-defunct jewelry store just outside Philadelphia, in an area called Upper Darby. An image search brought up more pictures, Chase with people she assumed must be his family—his father, stooped a bit, with graying hair, but a smile that mimicked Chase's own; his mother, a stern-looking woman with light dancing behind her eyes.

Of course Chase wasn't Josh. But maybe he'd met him, or knew him . . .

She closed the browser and sat back in her chair.

You're grasping at straws, Aubrey. You're so desperate to have Josh back you're trying to turn a stranger into him.

What a fool she was. Meghan was right; Aubrey *had* gone off her meds, and maybe that wasn't a good thing. She saw no point in taking them when she was feeling fine, but if she *was* starting to imagine things again, maybe she should, even if only for a little while. At the very least, she could have some of the blessed numbness back. The pills wiped her clean, let her skate lightly through her daily life, not connecting fully with anyone or anything.

Winston began to bark, loud and insistent, the kind of frantic baying that signaled a stranger was near the house. Probably Meghan coming back to apologize. Aubrey rose and glanced out the window down to the front steps. There was no way to see to the front door from the dormers, but she could see onto the street. A dark blue beat-to-hell Camry was sitting in front of the mailbox, half on and half off the curb.

Oh, *shit*. Shit, shit, shit.

The doorbell rang, and Winston's bark reached a fever pitch.

She could pretend she wasn't home. But he started yelling.

"I saw you look out the window, little sis. Come on down."

CHAPTER 12

Aubrey
Twenty-one Years Ago

Aubrey is allowed one toy. She has no idea which to choose—how to choose. They are all dear to her. And they will all be gone, just like the rest of her world. The teddy bear will be the best; he works as an extra pillow. She sleeps with him at night, her head resting on his, her curly hair mimicking his own curly fur. Yes, the bear is the right choice. Especially if there is no bed, no pillows, wherever she is going.

She looks to the dark-haired woman sent from the bad place, who is tapping her foot in impatience. She wants to ask if she may have permission to take two, but she is afraid. She reaches for Bear, careful not to meet the inquisitive button eyes of the rest of her brood. She knows they feel she is abandoning them. She understands their concern completely.

"All set?"

Aubrey looks at the walls of her room, painted a rosy pink. There is a picture of her parents next to her bed. She is too frightened to ask if she may take it with her, stow it inside her bag, her tiny little bag with three changes of clothes and one worn bear. When the woman glances away, she shoves the frame under Bear, trusting him to protect her secret.

"Aubrey? You hear me?"

"Yes."

"Are you all set?"

She nods. What other choice does she have?

"Good girl."

The dark-haired woman stops at McDonald's, buys Aubrey a Happy Meal. The car smells of fake evergreen and grease and cigarettes, and Aubrey can barely choke down the sandwich and fries. She leaves the small movie cowboy in the paper box. The woman said only one toy.

With rush hour traffic and lights, the drive takes twenty minutes, give or take. Aubrey forgot to look at the clock as they left the house, but as they leave McDonald's, she locks eyes on the little digital display and watches the minutes tick away.

Twenty minutes by car.

If you are traveling in a car that is going forty miles an hour, and you travel for twenty minutes, how many miles have you traveled?

The dark-haired woman whistles.

Aubrey clings to Bear.

The car slows just after dark. The dark-haired woman mutters under her breath, grabs a piece of paper from her purse. She does a U-turn in the street and takes the first left, then stops in front of a small yellow house. Aubrey's eyes slide across the yard, which has two tricycles, a boy's bike, and various other items that tell her children live here.

She is at once relieved and frightened.

"Come on," the dark-haired woman says.

"Where are we?" Aubrey asks.

"This is your new home. For a while, at least. It's a foster home."

Aubrey does not know what *foster* means. She does, though, understand the concept of home, and knows, without a doubt, this is not hers.

She climbs from the backseat, clinging to Bear. One of the porch lights is out, and she can see a large cobweb littered with dead insects strung around the other. Not the fun, fake kind her parents used to put up for Halloween, but a real one. A spider, as big as a cherry, sits patiently in the middle, ready to drain an unwary being into a dried-out husk.

Aubrey begins to shiver. It is not cold—no, she hasn't felt a bodily sensation like hot or cold anytime since her parents failed to come home and the policeman knocked on the door and the babysitter screamed. This is the kind of shiver that comes from inside, one that can only be comforted by loving arms and gentle kisses. The arms and kisses and kind, loving faces of people she will never see again.

The door opens, and a smallish woman with her mousy brown hair in a frowsy bun on top of her head looks down at her.

Her face creases into a smile, and Aubrey sees that the woman is missing the same front tooth that Aubrey is. She takes this as a good sign.

"Come in, come in. I was just sitting everyone down to dinner."

The dark-haired woman pushes Aubrey lightly on the back.

"This is Sandra," she says. "She's going to take good care of you. I'll come see you in a few days and see how you like it. Okay?"

Aubrey is suddenly exhausted. She didn't know it was possible to be this tired. Beyond tired. She closes her eyes and feels the colors of the day swirl behind her lids.

"Okay, Aubrey?"

She nods, not knowing what else to do.

The woman named Sandra takes Aubrey by the hand and gently pulls her into the house. The door shuts behind them with a slam. Aubrey feels the air around her draw close, and her vision begins to swim.

"No, no, sweetie, don't cry. You'll be happy here, I promise."

When the woman speaks, there is a long hiss on the *s*'s. Aubrey knows that is called a lisp, and it is a bad thing. She changes her mind about the missing tooth.

"Come meet your new brother and sisters. There's a good girl."

There are four children strategically placed around a kitchen table, each in various stages of age and dress and cleanliness. Three, the girls, ignore her, but one, the oldest, a boy who looks to be at least twelve, though she'll find out later he is only ten, stops eating and stares at her. He has olive skin and dark blue eyes, one of which squints a bit.

"Your parents are dead," he says, not a question, just a flat, empty statement of fact.

Aubrey nods.

"Mine are, too," he says. "Sit here. My name is Tyler."

CHAPTER 13

Aubrey
Today

Aubrey walked down the stairs slowly, carefully. Winston was pawing at the front door, mouth moving so frantically that spittle flew from the corners. His gray tail stood straight out behind him like a pointer.

"Winston. Stop!"

She didn't mean for her voice to be so sharp, but she couldn't help it. Winston looked at her in surprise but quit barking. He sat down hard, still staring at the door.

Knock, knock, KNOCK!

He wasn't being polite anymore. The hits reverberated through, making the wood shimmer. Aubrey took a deep breath and turned the knob.

She was greeted with the smile of a handsome dark-haired man. His visage was both completely foreign to her and utterly familiar. One bulkily muscled arm leaned against the doorjamb. His dirty hair was shaggy, unkempt, long over his collar, and he sported a Titans football jersey in pale blue. It had the number 9 and *MCNAIR* on the back. She recognized this not because she was a football fan, but because she mailed the shirt to him at the penitentiary as a Christmas present the year McNair was murdered.

That he'd shown up wearing her shirt was meant to be a message:

I come in peace.

No. Never peace. Not from her past.

"Tyler," she said, cautiously. Not a greeting, a welcome, or an invitation, just a statement. She knew better than to leave any room for interpretation.

"How ya doin', little sis?"

"Don't call me that."

"Why? You're my sister, just as good as if you were born that way."

Aubrey didn't respond.

"Aren't you gonna invite me in?"

"No."

Tyler flashed his grin again. Tyler had impeccably white teeth that were remarkably straight for one who'd never benefited from orthodontia. She wondered how it was possible that he had maintained them, after all these years, all his problems. Stayed off the crack, stuck with the needle. Smart of him. When he smiled, it took her back, and she didn't want to go there.

Since that day, when she was such a young girl, so scared, so lost, Tyler had stepped up and she'd thought him a leader. But she soon learned he was the follower, desperate to be liked, respected, feared. Once he found that the weightier the gun in his hand, the more respect he earned, he was lost to her forever. When he started using the product he was selling, it was over for him.

"When did you get out?" Aubrey asked.

"Invite me in, sister." It was not a request. Aubrey moved away from the door and allowed him entry. She couldn't stop him if he wanted in anyway—he was twice her size—though it was nice to pretend he'd have some respect for her wishes. Then again, he never had, so why start now?

She shut the door behind him and wedged her back up against it. Winston, seeing Tyler, sniffed the air a few times and steadily backed away, disappearing into the kitchen.

"When did you get out?" Aubrey asked again.

Tyler's eyes slid to the side. She looked at what he looked at, wondering. Together, they took in the small living room: the brown leatherette couch that had a large rip in the middle cushion, the tan carpet that needed vacuuming, Aubrey's running shoes stacked against the back door, the vertical blinds, half open, half-mast, dusty. A mess, but it could be worse. At least there were no signs of Boden.

She hoped the flush she felt when she thought of him didn't show on her cheeks.

What did Tyler want? What was he looking for?

Now, Aubrey, why do you immediately assume he's after something? Why can't you let him come say hello after a long absence? Why do you have to turn it into something else?

Because you know him, better than anyone.

"I got out a few days ago," Tyler finally replied. He was hedging.

The hangover came back, biting at her stomach and head with vicious snaps. She didn't have the energy for this.

"I'm making a cup of tea. Would you like one?" She broke Tyler's gaze and left him standing in the foyer. Walked toward the kitchen. He followed.

"Tea? What kind of pussy do you take me for?"

She tossed a smile over her shoulder, and at the same time, they both said, "A biiiiiig fuckin' pussy."

She relaxed. Tyler was just here as a brother, wanting to mooch some money, food, and alcohol, and he'd be on his way.

"Got any eggs?" he asked hopefully, following her into the kitchen.

"No. Tea is it. Unless you want a frozen dinner?"

"Nope. And if that's all you have, you need to go to Publix. You look like you're starving to death."

The ice was broken now. They could pretend they were friends, if not forever connected through their pasts, through the system. Both systems. He'd never believed she'd killed Josh. He knew her. In his own weird way, he loved her.

She could have had a terribly difficult time while awaiting her bond hearing. Instead, Tyler's influence had managed to keep her from the worst the county jail had to offer a pretty young white thing.

"So. You seeing anyone?" he asked.

Aubrey froze, disguised the movement by gracefully reaching for the teapot. She didn't turn.

He couldn't know. There was no way he could know. Unless he was staking out the house, waiting.

She arranged the cups, dropped in the tea bags.

"Tyler, what do you want?"

"I can't just drop in on my little sister because I want to say hello?"

"Not a week out of jail, jonesing for a fix and reeking of alcohol. No."

She turned to face him. Tyler was unpredictable at the best of times—he could be here to intimidate or woo, depending on his mood and where he was in the cycle. Tyler was forever getting clean, forever relapsing. The people around him bore the brunt of his failures.

His face contorted for a brief second, the attack coming. Instead, he breathed in deeply and his lazy smile returned. Yes, he wanted something. He was willing to swallow his explosive temper to get it as well.

"I hear Josh was declared dead at last."

"Yes." Her chin inched a bit higher. "What about it?"

"There's some serious coin coming your way, I expect."

"No, actually."

His eyes widened for the briefest of seconds, then narrowed, mean as a snake.

"Don't bullshit me, little sister. The world knows all about his 'estate.' And the life insurance policy. Why do you think they thought you killed him in the first place? That's an awful lot of money for a kid to take out on his own life. So"—he leaned against the counter—"I was hoping you would share a bit of your good fortune with your big brother."

She met his gaze, the dark blue depths muddy, the bloodshot whites tinged with the tiniest hint of yellow. Jaundice. Too many needles. Tyler played the role of crippled junkie too well. It had saved him from being killed more than once; his bosses didn't like the runners sampling the wares, but he managed to keep them satisfied enough to spare his life. They understood, with the high-grade heroin they were selling, some of their foot soldiers were bound to fall prey to the goods.

Aubrey liked to run away from everything, too, find that blessed oblivion. The only difference between them: her drugs were legal. Honestly, she understood Tyler getting hooked on drugs more than she understood the strange power he felt when carrying a gun. He claimed it was for protection. All the dealers carried. But she wondered if, deep down, he was just a walking time bomb, and the gun his easy way out.

"There's nothing to share. I'm not going to get any money from the 'estate.' Daisy is going to contest and get everything."

"Daisy. That bitch don't deserve a penny of Josh's money."

"Tyler, quit talking like you're some gangsta.

You have every bit the command of the language as I do."

Now she was needling him, and it felt good. He flushed, eyes squinting even farther.

"Don't fuck with me, *teacher*."

He made it sound dirty, and small.

"Oh, come off it. Do I need to remind you of that time—"

"Shut up." This was said flatly, no more affection, just a warning from a brother that she'd gone too far. She'd made her point. The teakettle whistled. They stared at each other for a few more moments. She poured the hot water into the cups, careful not to splash.

"You know I'm telling you the truth. Daisy already let me know she'd be fighting the payout. In her mind, the insurance company screwed up and the money belongs to her. It was her bargain with Josh when we were trying to buy the house. We couldn't afford the payments, and he asked her to cosign. She agreed on one condition: that she be sole beneficiary of his life insurance policy, the one she and his stepfather had taken out on him years before, and she'd have control of the property in case we defaulted. He agreed, thinking once we had a few years under our belts he could go in and change everything back to me. But you know all this already."

"Then why did Josh add so much money to the policy right before he disappeared?"

"For the thousandth time, I don't know."

"But when he did add to the policy, the insurance company put your name down as a default, since you were his wife."

"And he died before he could sign off on the change to move it back to Daisy." She smiled meanly. "Daisy was beside herself."

"That woman never has liked you."

She shook herself a little, remembering. "None of this matters. It's blood money. I don't want it. I'm not going to fight her. She can have it all."

Tyler sidled up behind her. She felt the cold, hard steel of the weapon in the small of her back. She didn't flinch. Tyler responded poorly to shows of weakness.

"Have we all been wrong, Aubrey?" he whispered in her ear. "*Did* you kill him?" The gun traced small circles on her spine. "You can tell me. It's official now, he's dead and gone in the eyes of the courts, and you were acquitted. The cops won't be knocking on your door."

Aubrey turned around slowly, felt the muzzle trace around her ribs until it was pointing straight into her abdomen.

"You of all people know I didn't kill him, Tyler. And he has to be dead because Josh would never, ever put me through this hell."

Tyler used the gun to tease the bottom of her shirt up, revealing the hard flesh of her stomach. She met his eyes. Dared him.

"I loved him more than my own life. Part of me died with him. Killing him would have been like killing myself. Now put that stupid gun away before you accidentally blow off your cock."

He coughed out a laugh, gave her a soft kiss on the cheek, tucked the gun into the waistband of his jeans, grabbed the cup of tea, and sat down at the table. He picked up the saltshaker, unscrewed the top, and poured the contents on the wood. Pictures emerged from the tip of his finger, outlines: an engorged penis, a heart, a big question mark.

Aubrey brought her tea to the table and sat opposite her foster brother.

"I have a little bit of cash. It's not much. But if it will help get you on your feet, it's yours. I'm sorry I didn't know you got out. I would have been there."

The words were insincere but had the placating effect she was going for.

"I'm clean, though I'm sure you don't believe me. They had a program, in jail."

"You've been through programs before."

"It's different this time." He went quiet. "Maybe a hundred or so. Just until I can find some work. I'll pay you back."

She knew *work* to Tyler meant something illegal. What was she going to do, tell him to get a straight job? Tyler had lived in the recesses of society his whole life. She didn't blame him for being who he was: an addict, struggling along like the rest of the world.

She blamed his mother, a whore with a crack habit; his father, a businessman who'd slipped down to Donelson Pike one afternoon and made a deposit, then disappeared forever; and the dealer-slash-pimp who kept his mother's legs spread and mouth occupied to line his coffers. Tyler had spent the first three years of his life in malnourished squalor until a local cop found him next to his mother's lifeless body.

His freedom was traded for a series of well-meaning foster parents.

Just like hers.

She rose from the table and went for her purse. Enabler she would be if it meant getting him the hell out of the house. She got it out of her wallet and handed it to him silently. He took the money without meeting her eye, used the edges to turn the salt into pretend lines of coke. She noticed Tyler's hands shaking and knew without a doubt he was too newly clean. The money would go straight into his arm. Sadness overwhelmed her.

Tyler never had a chance. At least Josh had pulled her from the ashes before she went down the same road.

Why wasn't he leaving?

"It's all I've got, Tyler."

"Thank you."

"You're welcome."

He didn't move, so she stood, arms crossed, and waited. God, she just wanted to lie down. Her head had started pounding again; her stomach was roiling.

"You've always been good to me, Aubrey."

"Good grief, Tyler. Did you find God in prison or something? Get. Scat. Leave. I have stuff to do."

He smiled at her, a flash of childhood, their adventures, their fears, their moments of innocence. His gold necklace caught the light from the kitchen window. He'd had it as long as she'd known him. It would be easy to pawn, to get some money to put in his arm, but he held on to it like a lifeline.

"I didn't find God, Aubrey. But I am straight." He squared his shoulders. "I've always been honest with you. I told you from the beginning Hamilton was no good."

Here we go.

"Tyler, he's gone. Doing the 'I told you so' dance won't change things."

"I'm not kidding around, Aubrey. I heard some shit while I was in."

Aubrey burst out laughing. "About Josh? *My* Josh? He was training to be a doctor, Tyler, not a criminal. We left that element up to your side of the family."

Tyler pushed back from the table so hard the chair tipped over onto the floor and Winston jumped.

"It never ends with you, does it?"

"Josh wouldn't know the first thing about doing anything illegal. You knew him. He wouldn't even bet on a football game. Good God, listen to yourself."

"You honestly think—Jesus, Aubrey! When will you see he wasn't the man you thought he was?"

"Fuck you, Tyler. He was twice the man you'll ever be."

He flinched away from her. Her words had always been sharp.

"Tyler—"

His voice was deadly quiet. "You're from the gutter, Aubrey, just like me, and don't you ever forget it."

He stormed from the room. She heard him fling open the front door. Moments later, the engine of the Camry came to life with a roar.

She went to the front door and closed it softly. Leaned back against it.

"Damn."

Tyler had always been a mess. He'd gotten himself involved in drugs, and ran with a gang of boys whose sole purpose in life was to get into trouble. That same gang of boys grew up and turned into a tight-knit group of serious troublemakers who ran drugs for a branch of the Dixie Mafia.

She didn't want to know the things Tyler had done. Thirty-one—the same age Josh would be if he'd lived—and he'd been in and out of jail, in and out of rehab, so many times that she couldn't keep track.

She knew this wasn't the life he wanted. He'd fallen into it and hadn't had the energy, or desire, to extricate himself. Or the love. If someone would just love him properly, he might find his way again.

That's your fault, Aubrey. You know it is. You created him.

She shook off the thought and tried to focus on what he'd told her before he stormed out instead.

He'd always hated Josh, and she'd never fully understood why. Oh, she got it; Tyler had a thing about people he perceived as "better" than him, and he liked to play the role of the protective older brother. *Hurt her and I'll hurt you*, those sorts of empty threats.

Except for when the threats weren't empty.

She'd been attracted to Josh because he was Tyler's opposite, in every way. Where Tyler was brash and hurtful, Josh was kind and generous. Tyler had little use for morality; Josh spent years trying to teach Aubrey the right way to do things. Tyler was horribly jealous of Josh's goodness, seeing something inside Josh he would never possess.

Josh was a good man. Decent through and through. Even as a child he'd been gallant and honest and implacable, a source of strength, of honor. He'd grown into a man who wanted nothing more than to help people, which was why he was training to be a doctor.

She was well aware of her tendency to make Josh out to be perfect, a hero even. Her therapist had chided her when Aubrey started to immortalize him and his selflessness.

No one is perfect, Aubrey. One day, you'll start to remember Josh's faults, too.

Yes, Josh had a fault.

He'd died.

Dear Josh,

Did I ever tell you that I see my death? It's nothing concrete, more of an overwhelming moment of imagination, like a dream, but I'm awake. Sometimes it's a plane spiraling down to earth. Other times it's a wave crashing over my head. The riptide pulls me out to sea, tumbling me against the sand until I open my mouth and scream water into my lungs. Sometimes it's a tree on the side of the road, and my car flies into it and my head cracks against the windshield and everything goes black. Sometimes, it's the handful of pills I want to take.

Oh, Josh, I can't go on like this. I miss you too much. We were supposed to be in this together. I know you're dead, but my mind can't believe that you're really gone. If I could just know for sure, I'd be able to make a decision about what to do next. But we're caught in this limbo, between the worlds, where you've disappeared and, frankly, so have I.

Always,
Aubrey

CHAPTER 14

Aubrey
Today

After Tyler's Camry backfired its way away from the curb, Aubrey felt her hands begin to shake, the anger coming in waves. Damn that man. He was forever forcing himself into her life, through coercion or intimidation or manipulation, whatever it took. Why wouldn't he just go away? He reminded her of the worst parts of her world, the parts she spent so much time locking away, screwing them down into the furthest bit of her soul so she wouldn't ever have to think about them.

Tyler must have been desperate to rush over when he got out of jail and claim he'd overheard Josh had been wrapped up in something bad. Trying to hurt her, to punish her for gaining her freedom when his was wrenched from him, or leverage the information for something. He was trying to drag her into his unhappiness again. Tyler's morass was all-encompassing.

Aubrey felt the rabbit hole closing in on her, so she did the only thing she knew to do. She took an Ativan and put on her running shoes.

One foot in front of the other. Again and again and again and again.

Pace became breath became her body, all of her

parts working together to find some meditative calm. The hangover began to recede. She let the memories wash over her.

She tested her emotions. Thought about the previous night. *Chase.* She tried to ignore the warm flush of excitement that coursed through her, followed by anger and regret. It was wrong, wrong to think of him and Josh at the same time. She would have to find a way to separate the two in her thoughts.

Where was Chase now?

She didn't know anything about his life in Chicago. Did he have a woman? A house? Did he spend his Saturday afternoons mowing the yard so he could watch the game on Sunday in peace? No, he was probably combing the bars, looking for another strange woman to screw.

She pushed the pace, upped her flow.

Come on, Aubrey. You're making pretty big assumptions. Maybe he was telling the truth. Maybe he did enjoy your company. Face it, nothing about the last twenty-four hours was normal, by any stretch of the imagination. You're under stress, and stress does wonky things to your mind.

Running relieved that stress and allowed her to think rationally. After a while, she was able to see there were two plausible scenarios for what happened last night.

Either she'd been used by a player on the road who had no intention of ever calling her again, or he'd actually liked her and his note stating he wanted to see her again was sincere. That was all. There were no machinations, no clandestine insights to be gained. They were just a man and a woman who'd had sex. All the weirdness in her life aside, it boiled down to that. She'd gotten paranoid. She read into everything, looked for ulterior motives, unspoken statements, danger.

And her mind had finally played the biggest trick of all on her. She'd wanted to believe he was Josh so badly, she'd almost convinced herself last night it was his arms she slept in.

Her feet pounded the pavement, and she felt more settled. The grass of Dragon Park ended, and she veered off onto Blakemore. She'd run through the Vanderbilt campus, look at all the happy kids, and pretend she was one of them. She put Tyler and Chase and Josh and Meghan and Daisy out of her mind, and let her legs take her into oblivion.

She didn't see the dark blue sedan following her around the edges of the park.

CHAPTER 15

Aubrey was done in, her legs shaking from the exertion. She needed to go home, but she veered away from her turn. She didn't know what possessed her to take one more lap around Dragon Park and return to the tree.

That was a lie. She knew exactly what drove her there. And though she didn't want to indulge the demon, she did it anyway.

It had been years since they'd played the game. It was a childhood fancy, something silly. As teens it had become the most singularly romantic thing that Aubrey could ever imagine. But once they were together—dating, engaged, married—there was no reason to continue. They had instant access to each other anytime they liked. They didn't need to arrange illicit assignations.

But after Josh went missing, the lovers' oak called to her. It seemed fitting, since they were separated, that she resurrect their old method of communicating. When they were kids, the tree's hidden hole had probably once been the home of a squirrel, or some birds, but when the city started spraying for mosquitoes, the tree had been vacated.

She wrote him a letter and stashed it in the

oak's trunk, in the little indentation that seemed made for their missives.

For the first year, after the media shit storm died down, after she went back to work, when she was trying to return to an even keel, she'd run to the tree every night, put her hand in the small hole, and feel for a new piece of paper. Hoping. Praying.

There never was one. The crevice was always void of anything but the pages she'd laid there.

Aubrey coped the only way she knew how. She wrote more letters. And more. But now she did it on the computer and clicked the Send button when she was finished. She'd left Josh's email account open, hoping against hope that one day he'd see her notes and write back.

Insanity is filled with wishful thoughts.

Of course, she knew that was impossible. The blood at the house confirmed it. He'd been gravely injured the night he went missing. Injured enough that the DA tried his best to hang a murder charge on Aubrey's slender shoulders based on the blood pool alone.

The letters were her one link to the world in those first maddeningly scary months. Especially the time she was incarcerated, before the trial, when she'd lost her temper and punched the investigating cop and they'd tossed her in county overnight. She'd mouthed off to the judge and he'd given her three more days to cool her heels while they decided whether to make things official. She couldn't sleep, not a wink. The jail's doctor had finally given her Ambien because they were afraid she was going to get psychotic without proper rest. She slept. The sleep of the dead. Every night for two months, they gave her the pills.

When she got out, she couldn't sleep without them. She liked the deep oblivion they gave her. They kept her sane. Every night, she'd write until the pills washed her brain clean of thoughts and sleep dragged her under.

The letters didn't take a cohesive form. Some were long, rambling accounts of her moments, some short snippets. Some were angry, some full of longing. Some pleaded, some accused.

But none were ever answered.

As the days stretched into months stretched into years, she continued the habit. Her therapist had suggested it as a way for her to cope, and Aubrey found the idea appealing. It made her feel and look weak, so she didn't tell anyone what she was doing. After a while, she realized she was using the letters to hold on to her sanity. Even during that time, the time she didn't like to remember, when she'd slipped, she kept writing. The letters became her lifeline, a way she could talk to Josh again.

They added up. Pages and pages and pages. She printed them out and kept them all in boxes, coded by year, one through five. There were hundreds. Details of her life without him, of what he was missing. Of what she missed about him.

She knew the words to all the communiqués.

One of her favorite pastimes was opening the boxes and reading through them. Sometimes it was a good exercise, a measurable gauge that she was moving on, getting by. Other readings would devastate her for days. She could conjure them in her mind as if she had the photocopies sitting in front of her, and often ran them through her head while she jogged. There was a section of letters she didn't like to revisit, from the time before she found the physical outlet, but the rest she had memorized. It was obsessive, yes, but it helped her cope.

She stroked the carved initials on the tree. She could almost fit her pinkie finger into the edges of the heart.

The sad segments of her life: Before, During, After—seven, seventeen, and five. Happiness, bliss even, replaced by shock and isolation and fear. Aubrey knew the exact moment when Before turned into During. And when During became After. When the blur began to focus, and she woke, half a woman.

She fingered the scar on her lip and pulled her cell phone from inside her running shirt's zipper pocket. It was an outdated iPhone, no longer manufactured, but she didn't want to get a new one because it had the text messages she'd sent Josh the night he'd disappeared. The police had given it back to her when the trial ended; they had no use for it.

The last text was at 11:59 p.m. the day of Sulman's party. That's how she knew the exact moment her life changed forever. A little gray screen with a green bubble that read *You are the best husband EVAH!* with a string of *x*'s and *o*'s, four of each, followed by quieter, more desperate messages as the night progressed, culminating with *Josh, we can't find you. We're going to the house. Arlo wants to call the police. Please, please call me.*

She didn't have the heart to delete the texts.

He was dead. She knew he was dead. It was wishful thinking that he could be alive somewhere. Hurt, forgotten, unable to return . . . that was fantasyland, a fantasy Aubrey discarded when the police slapped the cuffs on her and threw her in jail, and she stood before the judge, all alone.

But she could still dream.

Unhealthy as it was, she could conjure Josh at will: the smooth skin of his forearm, the feel of his hands across her neck. The way he smiled at her, without reservation, always happy, always willing. The way he teased, and the way he loved. She'd been with him for so many years that she didn't really remember the time before, when she had a mother and a father to tuck her in at night.

A college kid in a black-and-gold Vanderbilt ball cap ran by, stared at her crying by the tree. She could see the hitch in his step as he decided whether to stop and see if she was okay. She gave him a little shake of her head, and he jogged on toward campus, clearly relieved.

You're getting maudlin, Aubrey. Best get going.

As she ran back toward the house, with Josh's face and the words that tied her to him fresh in her mind, she realized she hadn't written him last night. It was the first time in years she'd skipped the ritual.

She kicked up the pace a notch. Something was wrong with her. First she'd forgotten to put on her ring. Then she'd met a man, brought him home, and slept with him. Now she'd forsaken the one ritual that had given her a lifeline back to the real world.

Maybe she'd just been waiting, in suspended animation, for the official ruling of death. Maybe her subconscious was doing its level best to protect her, to keep her from harm, and it somehow knew there had finally been a last line written in the book of Josh and Aubrey.

She struggled against the rising tide of fear and relief that coursed through her brain. For five years the thought of Josh had been an open wound, one that Aubrey touched nearly every day, ripping off the meager scab so she could feel the pain fresh and anew. Yet somehow, some way, when Daisy gave her the letter, things had suddenly felt different.

It's you who is different, Aubrey. You've finally come to terms with his loss.

The realization hit her hard. She didn't know whether to laugh or cry. All she knew was she needed to say good-bye properly. It was time. It was finally time.

The sun was just beginning to slide toward the horizon. She propelled herself back to the house, to her haven, her refuge. She'd sweated out all the booze and bad feelings, was left with the euphoria she always felt when she finished a run. It was a high—no different than the one she got from the consumption of alcohol or the ingestion of drugs, just comprised of natural endorphins instead of chemical ones—and her mood was suitably lightened.

She put Winston out in the backyard, then mounted the stairs to her office. That was a rather grand term for the room; it was a large closet she'd converted, just big enough for a small desk, a chair, and a computer. No storage, no shelves. Very minimalist. But it served its purpose: it was a sanctuary for her thoughts to run free.

With a deep breath, she pulled up her email and hit Compose.

The blank square popped up. She stared at the empty subject line. Normally she didn't bother with a subject—these were pro forma emails—but she felt compelled to type a single word into this one:

Good-bye.

Dear Josh,

It is official. The letter has come from the state, and the judge on your case has declared you dead. Your mother took it well, as you can imagine. She will now fight to get the money from your estate, and honestly, I am fine with that. She needs that sense of control, of possession, and if it makes her feel better, so be it. You know money has never been important to me.

But something has happened to me as well. As if that letter unshackled me, and I didn't know I'd been chained to the floor with metal and locks.

Do you remember the first time I went away? The morning after we'd lost our virginity? Your mother came home and caught us naked in the living room and called the police? They came to Sandy's house to arrest me for breaking and entering, trespassing, the works. When they put the cuffs on my wrists, I felt like an animal in a cage, one whose sole purpose was entertainment. They laughed at me when I freaked out. I will never forget that—the sun rising in the background, being in the back of the car, Tyler banging on the window to have them let me out, Sandy standing on the porch, so disappointed, with the ring in her hand to give to them, and I got claustrophobic in the hot backseat and started to hyperventilate. I thought my heart was going to break out of my chest. A full-blown panic attack. And they just laughed, pulled away from the curb, and told me to shut up. And they ended up shipping me to that place . . .

Josh, that's how I've felt every day since you disappeared. I've been in a cage, panicked, desperate to find you, to figure out what happened. And suddenly, when the letter came, a peace filled me. The responsibility was taken from me. Someone else had made the decision for me.

You will always be my first and best love. I wouldn't have survived my childhood if you hadn't reached out to me, loved me, made me yours. But now it is time for me to say good-bye. To move forward with my life. To try and have the life you wanted for me. Without you by my side, it will not mean as much. But I'm going to try, Josh. I'm going to try.

I love you, darling. I always will.
Aubrey

She was sobbing as she typed in her name and hit Send. Before she could change her mind, she hit Print, exported the Send folder, and wiped the email account clean. She went to Gmail, created a new account, and sent out a message from her old Yahoo account with her new email address. She closed the Yahoo account, sent them a follow-up email requesting that the account be disabled, and repeated the process with Josh's address.

She logged out of the computer, deleted the bookmark, and breathed out a huge sigh. The tears stopped. She wiped her eyes and sat back in her chair.

She should have closed his email much sooner than this. That last tangible link to him, to his world, had been keeping her from seeing her future. She had finally, finally done the right thing. It was time to move on.

Aubrey suddenly found she was hungry. She decided to call Meghan and ask her to meet at

Sam's. They could have some food, some drinks, a laugh or two. They could talk about Chase, and what he might hold in store for her. They would talk about everything, everything but Aubrey's dead husband.

CHAPTER 16

Meghan didn't answer her phone, so Aubrey satisfied her burning desire to start over with a cup of chamomile tea, hopeful that she'd done the right thing. She was already starting to feel the small edges of regret, those lingering emotions that derailed her so often.

Don't fret, Aubrey. You're making strides, literally.

She finished her tea and was just heading up the stairs to take a shower when the phone rang.

She didn't recognize the number, so she let it go to the answering machine. A moment later, a man's voice spilled into the kitchen.

"Hi, uh, Aubrey? This is Chase."

She didn't allow herself to think, instead about-faced and picked up the receiver.

"Hi."

"Oh, you're home." He sounded very much relieved, and she smiled. She'd forgotten what this kind of awkwardness was like. She'd only experienced it once before, when Josh suddenly realized he was in love with his best friend and became a shy, stammering, blushing fool for exactly one week before he finally got up his nerve to ask Aubrey out on a date. Their first official date.

She swallowed the lump in her throat and told Josh, firmly, to go away.

"You're still there, right?" Chase asked.

"Yes, I am. Sorry. How are you? How was your trip home? I hope everything is good in Chicago. Is the weather nice?"

Aubrey, you sound like a schoolmarm.

"Chicago is rather lonely, actually." His voiced dropped, became warm and conspiratorial. "It would have been much better if I'd stuck around."

She felt an answering pull in her gut and realized that she was smiling. "I'm afraid I was a little drunk last night."

"I know. It was charming."

"Gracious of you. I hardly imagine that's true, but there it is. Thank you for . . ."

For what? For getting her shit-faced and taking advantage of her? For helping her move on, something she'd never have had the courage to do on her own? For leaving her alone to grapple with her emotions?

It hit her, that's exactly what he'd done. He hadn't abandoned her this morning. He'd given her some space to come to terms with what happened.

Oh.

"Just . . . thank you."

"You're welcome. Thank you for taking my call. I don't normally— Well, none of this is normal for me. I'd really like to see you again, Aubrey. Last night, yesterday, today . . . I can't stop thinking about you."

Her heart beat a rapid tattoo inside her chest, a sudden rush of adrenaline that signaled something abnormal, something unique, something different. It flooded her body, and she felt tingly all over. It was almost as if, with Chase's words, the band of invisible metal around her heart had sprung loose, and she could suddenly see, hear, and feel again. She took a breath for courage.

"I'd like to see you again, too," she whispered.

"I'm so happy to hear that." She could practically see the edges of his brown eyes crinkling, like they had last night, when she memorized the movement. "I can come back to Nashville tomorrow. Catch the first flight out of O'Hare so we can spend Sunday together. Are you busy? Maybe we could go to the movies? If you like that sort of thing."

"I do. I can't remember the last time I went to one, though."

"Then we need to rectify that. You pick. I'm game for anything."

Josh had never been game for anything. He had distinct ideas of what he wanted to see. Action, thrillers, and war movies, mostly. He hated chick flicks, or romantic comedies, or anything that involved period costumes. She'd always gone along with his decisions because, honestly, she didn't really care. She could watch her movies when he was at school, the long hours away she'd need to fill with something. But it was nice to have a choice.

Stop it, Aubrey. You can't move forward if you measure each piece of the man against a ghost.

She glanced at the clock. It was nearly six. Twelve hours suddenly seemed too long to wait. What was she going to do with herself?

"Do you want me to pick you up?" she asked. Oh, God, now he was going to think she was desperate.

He laughed instead. "It's okay. I can get a car. I'll come straight over, all right? We can make a day of it."

"All right. See you tomorrow." Unsure of what to do next, she hung up. The air in her kitchen seemed full and happy, pregnant with possibility. He wanted to see her again. He hadn't just used her for sex and disappeared.

She mounted the stairs with a spring in her step. The shower felt good, all her earlier aches and grumbles gone. She had a date with a man she couldn't stop thinking about.

It was disloyal, certainly. But it had been five years. She'd been in her widow's weeds the entire time. Surely Josh would understand. Surely he would want her to be happy. She hadn't planned this at all, hadn't even thought to start dating again. But there was something about Chase that made her want to throw caution to the wind.

Hair combed out and sweats on, she went outside to join Winston for a play date in the backyard, frolicking in the grass. He caught her mood and capered like a puppy, all legs and barks and rolling silliness. They were both in high spirits when they came back in the house.

She fixed a quick Lean Cuisine for dinner, and as the microwave irradiated her meal, she remembered Tyler's warning and finally allowed herself to think about what her foster brother had said.

Josh, not the man she'd thought he was. Involved with bad people.

Rivers of goose bumps slithered their way across her body. Damn Tyler. Couldn't he just leave well enough alone? Did he have to come and throw this in her face again?

She didn't want to relive any of it, especially the days when she was so scared every noise made her jump, and she couldn't sleep for fear that whoever had harmed Josh was coming for her, too.

The familiar panic began, racing through her chest.

She needed a distraction.

She stalked from the kitchen to the living room. Ran her fingers along the bookshelf, touching the spines of her favorite novels. No, reading would take too much energy. TV, then. She sat on the couch and flipped through the stations, but nothing caught her eye.

She poured a glass of wine.

And another.

Could Tyler know what really happened?

She picked up her phone and dialed his number, hoping it was still in service. Hoping he'd be coherent. It was a risk, at this hour, especially if he'd used the money she gave him.

He answered on the first ring, voice clear and lucid.

"Hey, sis. I thought you were pissed at me?"

"I am. Were you just mouthing off, or did you really hear something about Josh?"

CHAPTER 17

Chase

Chase clicked off his cell phone and felt vaguely uneasy. He was good at fabrication. He was a writer. Embellishment was his forte. But he was doing more than adding in a few flourishes to make the ends come together neatly.

He was staying at the Sheraton on Union, only a couple of blocks off the main strip. The room was anonymously nice: fourteenth floor, a corner king with large glass windows overlooking the small downtown area called Lower Broadway, and the well-lit bridges over the Cumberland River that led to East Nashville.

He had *omitted* that little detail when he talked to Aubrey. She was under the impression he'd gone home to Chicago and was coming back, and he'd done nothing to dispel that assumption. There was no way for her to check on him; all he had to do was show up at her house at the right time in a new set of clothes, and she'd believe. She'd told him she didn't go downtown much; he felt confident he wouldn't run into her by accident.

She'd been pretty bombed, anyway, the first time. They'd gotten back to her house and were going at it hot and heavy when he stopped, worried she might be one of those who have next-day second thoughts, but she'd urged him on, and he asked if it was okay to go all the way, and she said yes, that's what she wanted. She was wasted, but still together enough that he didn't feel she wasn't serious, and it had been rather amazing, screwing in her kitchen. She wanted to fuck, and she wanted to talk. About her dead husband, about the trial. And she wanted to fuck again, so he took her to her bedroom and laid her down on the soft sheets, but she didn't want it gentle, and the dog watched mournfully from the corner as she rode him.

He got turned on again just thinking about it. She was an athlete, had the grace and unconscious security that came with being in good shape, and the liquor had killed whatever other lingering inhibitions she might normally carry around. If he were honest, it was the best sex he'd ever had.

He wanted to go back and do it again. He wanted to feel her lips on him, that hair tickling his thighs, driving him mad, those strong legs urging him on. Wanted to run his hands all over her body. Wanted.

Now that he was in, so to speak, in the most personal way possible, he didn't want to mess it up.

He found a table at the hotel bar and ordered a beer. His mind kept drifting back to Aubrey. She was prettier than he'd imagined. The mug shots and court photos didn't do her justice. She'd looked scared and lost and hopeless. Now she was strong and resilient, her skin glowed, and he couldn't help remembering running his hand along her strong, taut leg. She'd given herself to him unreservedly last night, sparking a passion in him he'd never felt before with any woman.

There was an intoxicating darkness within her, swimming behind her eyes. He'd felt it the first time they touched, when she took his mug at the coffee shop, her eyes landing on his briefly as the spark shot between them. Electric and dark and unfathomably deep. Something secret. Something she was hiding from the rest of the world.

Remember, Chase. Remember your purpose.

He was getting nowhere. He finished his beer, tossed a five on the table. The lights of Nashville beckoned him. He decided to go for a stroll.

Music blared from speakers on every street corner. There were lines around the block to several bars: Legends Corner, Tootsies. Drunk girls weaved on too-high platforms and too-short skirts, arms around one another. Bridal parties crowded the sidewalks, none of them looking at all happy. He didn't understand that. Wasn't a wedding supposed to be a dream? Or had women these days gotten so entitled, so ferociously into themselves, that even the fun parts of the process were misery? Were they simply marrying because it was expected?

Was that what happened with Aubrey and Josh?

She'd told him they'd been childhood sweethearts. That she worked two jobs so Josh could go to medical school. He couldn't help but think Hamilton was a total idiot. Clearly he'd gotten greedy somewhere along the way. He'd been up to no good.

"Watch out, asshole!"

Two drunk girls had weaved into his path, bumping his arm, spitting their vitriol his way instead of apologizing. He almost retorted, but the face of the one on the left was green, and he figured he would be safer just stepping away rather than getting puked on. He liked his Italian leather loafers, thank you very much.

The heaving mass of humanity on the Saturday night streets was endlessly fascinating. He parked himself on the rooftop of Rippy's, ordered a barbecue sandwich and a beer, and watched.

And thought about innocence, and curly blond hair spilling carelessly across a white pillow, and his next moves.

CHAPTER 18

Aubrey
Five Years Ago

"9-1-1, what is your emergency?"

Stay cool, Aubrey. Don't get hysterical.

"My husband has gone missing."

Aubrey felt rather than heard the sigh on the other end of the line.

"How long has he been gone, ma'am?"

"It's been a little over four hours since anyone has seen him."

"I'm sorry, ma'am, but we can't take a report until he's been gone for twenty-four hours."

"No, you have to listen to me. We were in a car accident this afternoon. He seemed fine, but he could have some sort of medical issue that we weren't aware of. He's a doctor. Please. Something is wrong. I can feel it."

"Ma'am, our policy—"

"Fuck your policy. This is my husband we're talking about."

Aubrey heard the woman's sharp "Ma'am!" before Arlo wrenched the phone from her ear.

"My name is Arlo Tonturian. I am a friend of the missing man, and I'm also a lawyer here in town. Josh Hamilton is supposed to be the best man at his best friend's wedding tomorrow. He never showed up to the bachelor party, despite arriving on the premises of the hotel where the party was located four hours ago. We fear there has been foul play. We would appreciate being able to speak to a detective immediately."

Arlo gave Aubrey the thumbs-up, his brown eyes soft but insistent. Aubrey mouthed a thank-you, sat on the floor with her arms wrapped around her legs, listening with half an ear.

She and Arlo had looked everywhere in the hotel for Josh. He'd vanished into thin air. No one seemed to remember seeing him. Without some sort of warrant, the hotel security people weren't willing to look at their videotapes. Everyone—the hotel staff, their security—seemed to think Josh had just left her. Walked away after giving her a kiss, off into the sunset. They were all acting like this was nothing, that he'd probably snuck off to meet someone, a lover, perhaps, not expecting people to be looking for him. She didn't even know how to combat that sort of idiocy. All she could do was tell them, over and over, Josh wouldn't do that. She knew it, deep down. He was loyal to the core.

Especially since that day when she'd seen him at Starbucks, talking to a fellow med student, a pretty girl with shiny blond hair, straight as a whip, who laughed with her head thrown back and touched Josh's hand, making him smile widely, and lost her ever-loving mind at him when he got home. In the face of her rage, he'd assured her they were just friends, he hadn't been doing anything, he'd never loved anyone but her.

He never had. She knew that was true.

Arlo bent down to her, squeezed her shoulder gently. "I think they're going to help. They want to know what he was wearing. Do you remember?"

She thought back to the moment she walked down the stairs at the house, Josh's wide smile floating into her mind. She fought back tears.

"White button-down, khakis, Topsiders, dark brown with a white sole."

"His exact height?"

"Six foot one. He weighs one seventy-five now."

"Okay." Arlo relayed the information, along with brown hair, blue eyes. He listened for a moment, looked at Aubrey. "Any scars? I know he doesn't have any tattoos."

She glanced at Arlo, coloring. "He has that scar in the shape of a U on the inside of his right leg. By his groin."

"Right." He relayed the information. "She put me on hold. These are good details."

"For when he's found dead."

Arlo looked at her in horror. She couldn't believe she'd said it aloud. But it was true. She watched all the cop shows. They needed identifying features to match his body to the one lying in a cold steel drawer under a crisp white sheet. She knew there were no sheets, not really, but the image stuck in her brain—Josh cold and silent, unmoving, gaping wide incisions across his chest from the autopsy, his organs dumped in a plastic bag and shoved inside his stomach cavity. He'd done a rotation in forensic pathology; he'd shown her what it all looked like. She didn't want that, didn't want them to cut him open, mar that perfect expanse of sun-dappled skin that stretched across his strong chest. It was profane.

No, no, he was okay; she knew he was.

"I don't want an autopsy. Tell them, Arlo. Tell them."

Arlo hung up the cell phone.

"You didn't tell them," she said dully.

"Aubs, let's cross that bridge when—if—we need to, okay? They said to call back tomorrow if he doesn't show. They can't file an official missing person's report for twenty-four hours. We're just going to have to keep looking ourselves." He helped her to her feet. "We can go to the station, see if a personal plea will work. I can throw my boss's name around, too."

Arlo smelled like vomit. What if the police arrested him for being drunk in public? It would be her fault. All her fault.

"Arlo, you might want to change, maybe brush your teeth."

He started, looking guilty. "Yeah, I'm probably pretty rank. I'll take some gum if you have it."

She didn't have gum, but managed to dig out an old roll of spearmint Life Savers she'd left in her fancy bag the last time she'd carried it. She gave it to him.

"You're a good friend, Arlo."

She saw him shaking his head. He popped a

Life Saver in his mouth and started to crunch it to pieces.

"Josh's been my best friend for years. I'm as worried as you are."

"I want to go home," Aubrey said. It wasn't so much a statement as a whimper. She cleared her throat and spoke again, stronger this time. "Let's go to the house first, Arlo. Maybe he did leave me behind, maybe he did go home. We need to check there, too."

Arlo hit himself in the forehead. "Yeah. Sorry, I'm not thinking clearly. We should do that before we go to the police. Maybe he just got tired and decided to go home, and he's passed out."

Neither one of them believed that, but doing something was better than sitting around doing nothing.

CHAPTER 19

Aubrey
Today

Aubrey had the phone to her ear, listened carefully to Tyler's story.

"All I heard was bits and pieces, braggings. Word was some med student at Vanderbilt had gotten himself mixed up with some folks who were really bad. He had access to drugs through the hospital. Oxy. Hillbilly heroin. They'd talked him into doing some work for them. Dude sounded mobbed up. That's all I know."

"Why do you think he was talking about Josh? It could have been anyone in the program with access to the pharmacy, right?"

"Maybe. But the timing fits. And someone did kill Josh. These men, they aren't nice, Aubrey. It wouldn't be the first time they killed someone who got in their way."

"Jesus. When did you hear this?"

"Last week. I was in the temporary holding cells down at County, waiting for my parole hearing. We got stuck there overnight—remember that awful storm we had? With the tornado warnings? The guy was telling some wild stories, but this one sounded . . . plausible. Oxy is hard to get nowadays. Someone with access to the pharmacy would be invaluable."

"Why didn't you come to me immediately?"

"Do I look like a carrier pigeon?"

"Tyler, stop it. I'm serious. If you heard something that might explain what happened to Josh, you should have come to me right away. Or called."

"And say what? 'Hey, sis, I overheard some guy in the jail cell next to me claiming he heard there was a Vandy doc running drugs'? You would have thrown me out the door even faster than you did. Besides, I came, didn't I? I told you. Not that it matters. It's too late now. Even if he was involved, dude's dead."

She bit back her retort, took a deep breath. "That *dude* was my husband. Give me names, Tyler. Please. Who told you this? I need to know." *So I can track them down and talk to them myself. Wring their fucking necks.*

His tone changed, as if one of his so-called friends had shown up and he started showing off. "No idea, beyotch." He hung up on her.

She tossed the phone onto the table next to her and sat back onto the couch. She felt sick.

All Josh had ever wanted to do was save lives. He had a savior complex. He'd gotten a taste of what it was like to help someone with Aubrey and her awkward childhood situations, and that feeling of accomplishment had stuck.

Josh as a criminal mastermind was laughable. But someone had killed him. That was irrefutable.

And good people didn't murder innocent doctors.

She felt her heart speed up a bit. What if this was it, at last? What if the bragging Tyler had overheard was the key?

Aubrey had spent the past five years breathing, running, drinking, getting up in the morning and going to work, sleeping when she could, showering when she remembered. Finding out what truly happened to Josh would be heaven on earth.

A good man gone bad—a young doctor, no less—murdered when he tried to do the right thing? Was this the story she would ultimately share with the world?

She'd thought she was ready to move on, to put Josh's disappearance behind her, but felt the familiar threads of obsession beginning to pull at her. She'd searched for answers before. She'd never had any luck.

Heard Meghan's voice in her head: *This way lies madness, Aubrey. You know that.*

I know. I know. This will be the last time, I promise.

She had to find out who killed her husband.

And then she'd kill them herself.

CHAPTER 20

Aubrey went upstairs, took a familiar path: down the hall to the small, dark closet that housed a rickety ladder leading directly to the tiny storage space in the eaves above her bedroom. The boxes were in the eaves. The boxes were full of the case files: trial transcripts, newspaper articles, DVD recordings of the local news, photographs, her own arrest and trial records, everything she'd collected that had to do with Josh's disappearance.

Aubrey had been forced to part with most of Josh's things when she sold the house and moved to the small space off West Linden. She couldn't afford a storage unit, so she'd compromised by packing nearly everything into plastic boxes and allowing Daisy to haul them off in her stupid Mercedes with those ridiculous eyelashes on the lights. Daisy had no idea how senseless she looked, but Aubrey wasn't about to be the one to spring it on her. Especially since, despite the grumbling and bitching, Daisy taking the boxes, trip after trip after trip, saved Aubrey from throwing all of Josh's things away.

Three hard-sided cardboard boxes waited at the top of the ladder. She hauled them down to her bedroom one by one.

She'd just gotten the lid off the first box when

she heard Winston rouse from his slumber and start to whine.

She stopped, listened. It was a quiet night. No wind, no rain, no leaves and branches brushing up against the house. The moon had set, and the sky was very dark. She realized she hadn't drawn the blinds; though no one could really see in through the dormer, she still liked the security of having that window dark to the outside.

She heard nothing. The light at her back meant she couldn't see out the window to the street, either.

Winston whimpered again, and a shiver began to curl around her tailbone.

She wasn't usually afraid to be in her own home at night. She didn't have a gun, but she did have a large aerosol bottle of wasp spray that she kept near the bed. She figured she had a better chance of hitting an intruder with the spray than she would with a bullet. It was a trick she'd learned of in jail.

A bump now, right outside the front door. She scrambled to the other side of the bed and grabbed the spray, took the lid off, and slid to the corner of the bedroom nearest the door. No one would be able to get in without passing by her.

She adjusted the bottle, got her finger on the trigger.

Winston began barking, and each yelp reverberated in her spine. She heard him running up the stairs toward her.

Great. Even the dog was scared.

Which meant she would have to check and see what was happening herself.

She hoped for Tyler. Maybe he'd been irritated enough at her to come back and have words. No. Tyler would slam his fists against the door in anger. The only way he knew to deal with the rage that ate away at him from the inside was brute physicality.

Winston arrived in the hallway and cuddled up next to her, his tongue out, panting loudly. She set the spray down and used both hands to close his mouth so she could listen. He didn't like that, fought back, his head wiggling out of her grasp. He woofed again, and she shushed him.

A discreet knocking started.

Quiet, soft. She swallowed hard, tightened her hold on the can of wasp spray, and decided.

She crept down the stairs. The knocking started again, then stopped.

Who the hell was knocking on her door at four in the morning?

The door was silent.

She got to the bottom of the stairs and fumbled for the phone. Dialed 9-1-1 but didn't hit the Send key.

"Who's there?" Her voice sounded stronger, surer than she felt. "I have a gun. Don't even think about breaking in here."

"Aubrey? Don't shoot. It's me."

She recognized his voice immediately. Her heart gave a little bump in her chest, and she allowed herself a deep breath.

"Hold on." She unlocked the door, opened it partially. "Chase? What are you doing here?"

The night seemed to disappear when he smiled, his brown eyes crinkling. "I couldn't wait to see you. So I drove down."

"From Chicago? That's a long drive."

"I know. Trust me, I know. I was going to wait until morning, but I saw the light on and heard the dog . . . Can I come in?"

She was touched, and surprised, and a little bit nervous. But most of all, she was glad to see him. So very glad.

"Of course. Please."

She stepped back and he came into the little foyer. Winston barked once in hello and trotted back to his nest in the kitchen.

The moment she shut the front door behind Chase, he had her in his arms. The phone dropped to the floor, forgotten.

"I couldn't wait," he whispered. "I couldn't wait."

He kissed her, and she forgot she was supposed to be thinking of Josh, instead melted into him. Kissing Chase was like riding a wave, back and forth, up and down. He had a hand in her panties, and she only struggled for a moment getting his belt unbuckled.

She didn't allow herself to think, just feel.

And it felt so, so good.

They gathered themselves off the living room floor. Aubrey pulled on Chase's shirt, loving the feeling of the cool cotton on her bare skin, and went to the kitchen. She made tea and returned to the living room with their cups, suddenly shy. Shy and sore and dying to take him upstairs and do it all again.

She handed him the hot mug, liking how her fingers prickled when he brushed against them. She was sad to see he was wearing his jeans again, though he'd left the top button undone.

"I can't believe you drove all night."

He scooted over on the couch, made room for her to sit. She did, leaning back just a bit so she could see his eyes. They were the deepest brown she'd ever seen.

"I told you, I couldn't wait to see you. There's something about you that's intoxicating."

"Intoxicated, you mean."

He shook his head. "Don't do that. Don't deflect. I'm giving you a compliment."

She smoothed down her hair and took a sip of the tea. She needed to be honest with him. It was only fair.

"I don't know how to do this," she said.

He smiled widely. "Don't know how to do what? You seem to be quite on top of things, if you know what I mean." He ran his hand up her leg and leaned in to kiss her. She shut her eyes and focused on the softness of his lips. She wanted him. So much. He finally stopped and pulled back, one eyebrow raised.

"See?"

"It's not that. I'm a mess, Chase. I have to give

you fair warning. You may want to run away as fast as you can."

He smiled. "I'm willing to do whatever I have to, Aubrey. You are one in a million. I can see that already. I'm just looking forward to getting to know what's in here"—he tapped her right temple—"as well as what's in here." His other hand moved all the way up her leg this time, and he cupped her, moving inside.

She felt the impact through her whole body. Her back arched a bit, allowing him to settle deeper. He didn't move to kiss her again, just stared deep in her eyes as he moved his finger slowly. Her breath came short, and before she could stop herself, stop the feelings, she began to shake. Only then did he kiss her, and drive himself inside her. She rode him, wave after wave after wave, and felt all the parts of her shatter.

PART TWO

Days of absence, sad and dreary,
Clothed in sorrow's dark array,
Days of absence, I am weary;
She I love is far away.

—Jean-Jacques Rousseau

CHAPTER 21

Josh
Eighteen Years Ago

Josh closed his pocketknife, put it back in its small leather pouch, and returned it to his front pocket, smiling at Aubrey the entire time. Small curlings of bark and pale tree flesh clung to his forearm.

"For you," he said, flushing his hand toward the lovers' oak, bursting with a nearly indefinable combination of lust, love, and pride.

The small furrow appeared between her sun-bleached blond eyebrows.

"'JDH plus AMT equals TLA.' Josh, what does that mean?"

Aubrey and Josh were at the huge old oak tree in Dragon Park, their tree, the place they met when Josh could get out from under Daisy's ever-watchful eye. It was easier when school was out—Josh could talk Daisy into letting him do things alone, go to the library, go for a walk. Anything to get out of the house, away from his bitchy, disapproving mother, and closer to Aubrey.

But when school was in, he had to cut class, and if his mom knew he'd skipped out to go meet Aubrey, she'd kill him. But a man had to do what a man had to do. That was Tom's favorite quote. Tom, his stepfather, the man who'd adopted Josh, who loved him, who didn't mind if Josh wanted to go meet up with the little Trenton girl. Tom, who, when Josh was twelve and Aubrey ten, sat him down and explained things—the "facts of life," he called them.

Tom was a good man. Josh liked him a lot. He knew he wasn't his real father, though Daisy tried to pass that off. Josh remembered more than his mother would have liked about his biological father. Daisy didn't like to talk about Ed Hardsten. She'd divorced him when Josh was four. He remembered that night clearly. She'd practically set the house on fire burning all the pictures. A neighbor smelled smoke and called 9-1-1, and the fire department came and put out the small bonfire she'd set in the backyard, and a fireman took Daisy in the house. After what seemed like forever, she came back outside, calmer, controlled, and gathered Josh in her arms.

"Mommy, what's wrong? Where's Daddy?"

"Daddy's gone, Josh. Daddy's gone away and won't ever come back. He's gone to . . . to heaven."

He was only four; he couldn't know his mother was lying to him. Ed Hardsten didn't go to heaven. He went to jail. He was corrupt. He worked with bad men, men who didn't care about sad mommies or scared little boys. He stole from people, and cheated, and lied. There were rumors that he'd killed two men, never proven, and bedded a floozy. Josh learned the term later, *floozy*. It reminded him of voluminous curtains blowing in the wind, and forever more in his mind he pictured his father standing with an ethereal lace angel dressed in striped white-on-white linen by his side.

"Josh?"

He came back down to earth.

"Sorry, Aubs. It means 'Joshua David Hamilton plus Aubrey Marie Trenton equals True Love Always.' See?" He traced the lines he'd just cut into the tree's bark with his finger. "It means you and I are tied together, forever."

"Oh." Aubrey stared at the letters, eyes wide, and looked back to Josh. "Forever? Even if you go away?"

"I'm not going anywhere, Aubrey." He wanted to hug her, to reassure her. Only mothers and fathers went away. Kids didn't. But that was a concept that might be lost on her. In a burst of bravado, he spilled out a whopper. "You know, Tom's not my real dad. Mine . . . died when I was four."

He'd figured out his mother lied to him a couple of years earlier when he caught sight of a letter in her top drawer, signed by a man named Ed Hardsten. A letter that demanded Daisy allow him to see his son. Dead men can't write letters.

You're dead . . . to me.

"Really?" Aubrey asked.

He could see the intrigue in her eyes. It took a lot to impress her, and he was pleased with himself, and embellished a bit.

"Really. My mom doesn't let me talk about it. I think he broke her heart." He said this with gravitas, a knowing statement, and Aubrey nodded. Heartbreak was something she understood completely.

"Thank you for telling me." Serious Aubrey, with her curls sticking out from the undersides of a too-big raggedy baseball cap, was starting to look older than her years. That made Josh sad, though he couldn't really explain it. The day had gotten entirely too serious, as a matter of fact. They needed to break this mood. He didn't get to spend enough time with her as it was; he didn't want to waste it being unhappy. Time to move along.

"What do you want to do today?" he asked, smiling, cheerful.

"How much time do we have?"

"All day. I might get grounded tonight, but I don't care. It's worth it." He said it with reckless abandon. He'd fashioned notes excusing both of them from school for doctor's appointments. If the office called and checked, he would be in huge trouble. If they didn't, well, what was the harm? Besides, a day out of school in the park with his best friend was worth whatever punishment he'd get.

"I don't know. Movies?" They started walking again, along the path, and Josh caught Aubrey glance back at the tree with a small, satisfied smile on her face.

His heart swelled with pride. He'd entertained her and made her smile. She was such a serious girl, so silent and quiet. That's what attracted him to her in the first place: she was so quiet. Like a mountain, or a tree, something that needs to be watched over, sat by, explored without touching.

"Movies would be good. We could go see the new Tarantino."

"That's rated R. We can't get in without an adult. What about the one with the bugs who talk? That looked funny."

"That's a kids' movie."

Her face fell. He forgot sometimes that he was her elder, and some of the things that might appeal to her seemed childish to him. "Maybe we could just walk around and talk. I have some money, we could go to McDonald's. Or the Soda Shop on Elliston Place."

Her eyes lit up. "Oh, can we? I'd love a float. I haven't had ice cream in forever. Sandy doesn't have money for extras like that."

He couldn't imagine a world without money for ice cream, but he bit his tongue. It was decided. He'd buy her a treat.

"Sure. Stick with me, kid. I'll show you the world." He stuck out his arm, and Aubrey hesitated for a moment, then put hers tentatively through his. Wow, it worked. He'd seen the move in a movie once. He was going to have to try some more things like that.

The Soda Shop was quiet. They got a booth in the back, ordered root beer floats. The waitress eyed them suspiciously. It was clear they were cutting school, two kids in their khakis-and-white-polo-shirt school uniforms at a soda shop at 11:30 in the morning—Josh's a real-life Polo from Ralph Lauren that Daisy bought at Hecht's in Green Hills Mall, Aubrey's a knock-off on sale from Kmart—but when Josh put the money on the table she shrugged and went ahead with their order. They slurped down the floats. Josh ordered some cheese fries, too.

Aubrey ate and drank with gusto, like the starving little feral creature she was.

Josh had fed a wild cat once. It would never let him get close, just watched from the bushes, eyes glowing, soft grumbling meows coming from its little chest. It wouldn't come out and eat until Josh went inside and the cat felt safe. Then it scrambled from the brush and gobbled down the food and retreated into the bushes to await the next encounter. Josh fed it for weeks. One day, it didn't show, and he was sad. He'd named it Lucky, and felt like the cat belonged to him.

Aubrey reminded him of Lucky. She had that same look in her eye, like she'd bolt at the first loud noise or approaching footfall. That's why he was always so careful to be gentle around her, not to startle her.

"You kids want to play a game?" A man was standing by their table, watching them with interest.

Aubrey jumped, and Josh put his hand across the table onto her arm to calm her. His mom did that to him sometimes, and it worked.

"No," he told the man. He knew they weren't supposed to talk to strangers—that was a rule he didn't want to break today. He knew all about Stranger Danger. He'd been through all sorts of lectures, especially when he went on his first overnight camping trip with the Scouts. Tom had explained, in no uncertain way, what could happen should Josh allow a stranger, especially a strange man, near him. Strangers snatched kids and did bad things to them. A waitress in their local soda shop was one thing, but a strange man who approached them? No way, José.

The man wasn't deterred. "Really. Just a quick game. If I can guess your names, you come for a ride with me."

Josh stared at Aubrey, whose eyes were as big as saucers. She stepped on his foot under the table, her lips thin and tight. She shook her head. Josh agreed: this guy was creepy. Shit. They should have gone to see the movie about the talking bugs after all.

"We aren't going anywhere with you." Josh's voice was full of bravado he wasn't feeling. His voice cracked, too—he'd just started to inhabit a lower register, beginning his path to manhood, and here he was sounding like a little boy again, not a strapping lad of thirteen.

"Oh, come on, Josh. Don't you want to take a ride with your pops? You and little Aubrey? I can give you a lift home. I bet your mom would be PO'd to find out you're not in school."

He knew their names. This was really, really bad. And his was Pops? What did that . . . Oh, Pops. Pop. Like Dad. He had one friend at school who called his dad Pop. It seemed weird, like soda pop. Who calls their dad soda pop?

"You know Josh's mom?" Aubrey asked. Aubrey was fascinated by Daisy. She knew the woman didn't like her, and just assumed it was because Aubrey was a lost child, without parents, without a real home. Dirty. People were supposed to be sympathetic to lost children. Not Daisy.

The man grinned. "Do I know Josh's mom? Of course. Scootch." He used his arm to push Aubrey deeper into the booth and sat with them. Josh's heart was beating out of his chest, and it only got worse when the man spoke again.

"I'm Ed Hardsten, Josh. I'm your dad. Don't you recognize me, son?"

Aubrey looked confusedly between Josh and Hardsten. "You said your dad was dead."

Josh found his voice at last. "My dad is dead. You aren't my dad." His shoulders squared. "And I'm going to tell the waitress if you don't leave right now."

Hardsten just laughed. "Oh, son. Daisy told you I died? That bitch. Don't believe me? Here."

He tossed a photograph down on the table. Josh crooked his head to look at it. He picked it up, mouth open. It was a picture of Ed Hardsten and his mom. His mom held a boy in her arms. Josh recognized a young picture of himself.

This wasn't good. Not only had he been caught in a lie, this man scared him. Maybe his plan was to kidnap them. Kidnap them, cross state lines, then kill them and bury their bodies in a shallow grave.

He kicked Aubrey under the table to get her

attention. Tried to send her a message with his eyes.

When I say go, run!

"You bothering these kids?" The waitress— her plastic name tag read *Cherry*—stood at the end of their table with one hand on her hip. She had a coffeepot in the other and looked about ready to clock the stranger.

"I'm not bothering them. He's my son."

"Oh. That so?"

Josh met the waitress's eyes. His must have been filled with shock and fear because her brows came together and she stepped a little closer to him.

"You supposed to be seeing this one like this? His mama know you're here with him? You got unsupervised visitation?"

Hardsten sat back, relaxed his arm on the top of the booth. "Now, no need for that. You know how custody goes. I just haven't seen my boy in a while. I'll shove off here in a minute. Okay?"

"I've got my eye on you, mister. You try to leave with either of these kids, I'm calling the cops."

"No need, ma'am. No need. Just wanted to say hi."

He stood and took the picture back from Josh's grasp, ruffled the boy's hair. "I'll be on my way. Josh, I'm sorry your mom told you lies about me. But now that I'm out, I hope you and I can talk again."

With that, the man winked at the waitress and sauntered away.

CHAPTER 22

Aubrey
Eighteen Years Ago

Aubrey was confused. First Josh said his father was dead, and she'd felt a kinship with him, something that they could share. Then this man showed up, trouble on a stick, as Sandy would say, all muscles and rolled sleeves and bits of tattooed ink running up his arm, and Josh freaked. Totally, completely freaked.

The minute the man left, Josh grabbed Aubrey by the hand and hauled her from the booth. "We gotta go."

"Where?"

"To my house." They were out of the Soda Shop now, into the beautiful day, Josh dragging her so fast that they were jogging up the street toward Dragon Park. The sun seemed sinister now, not cheery, and Aubrey hated the bad feeling that flooded her chest.

She dug in her heels and made him stop.

"Aubrey, let go. We need to go home."

"Josh, I can't go to your house. Your mother, she doesn't like me."

He swallowed hard, and Aubrey saw tears in his eyes. "I can't do this alone, Aubrey. Please, please come with me."

"Shouldn't we wait until later? When school's out? She's going to be furious with you for cutting. Especially once you tell her what happened."

She didn't need to say the rest: *Especially because you were with me.*

That drew him up short. "You may have a point."

"It's noon now." Aubrey made a show of looking at her watch, a digital piece of crap Sandy had picked up at Sears. At least it worked, unlike many of the things Sandy brought home. "School's out in two hours. Do you think you can wait?"

He sat down hard in the grass. She sat next to him, wanting to reach over and touch him but not knowing if that was allowed. It was amazing to her that this boy liked her. He liked to spend time with her. He talked to her like she was his equal. He never called her bitch, like Tyler did. He called her by her real name, Aubrey, and once, last month, honey, which had made her chest expand and tears come to her eyes.

"What about the library? Aren't you allowed to use it because of your dad? I mean, Tom."

"Why do you want to go to the library?"

"We could go look him up. Find out where he's been."

"Ed Hardsten? My . . ." He paused, brows knitting, as if he couldn't find a way to put the proper name together with the one that should symbolize love and caring and acceptance and security. He finally managed it, a whisper so soft she barely heard him because he was staring at the ground between his legs and couldn't meet her eye. "My father."

"Yes."

"What do you mean, look him up and see where he's been?"

Aubrey explained the lingo she'd heard from Hardsten. "He said 'now that I'm out.' In our house, that means he just got out of jail."

"Jail." Josh's voice was flat. She understood. It was someplace he'd never go, or even know that much about. Jail was for bad people who did bad things. Josh was shining-light good. For the first time in their relationship, Aubrey was the one with the experience, with the knowledge, with the ability to help. It made her proud, and her chest puffed out a bit.

"The library will have answers. And it will take some time." She braved it then, reached for his hand. "If he's really your dad, then he's alive. And that's a good thing, right?"

"I don't know. Maybe."

"So the library?"

"Okay."

They got up and crossed Blakemore, walked onto the Vanderbilt campus. Tom was a professor at Vandy, biology, so Josh had access to Vanderbilt's library anytime he wanted, but they'd have to be discreet.

Josh was quiet, vibrating with emotion. Who could blame him? He'd just had the worst and best news of his life dropped on him without warning. He was embarrassed, too. He shouldn't have lied. And he really didn't want to get reported for cutting.

"You were four when he died . . . went away?" Aubrey asked.

Josh nodded.

"Okay. Let me talk."

That wasn't hard. He was still caved in on himself, speechless. He followed her through the doors and to the resource desk. The reference librarian behind the counter barely looked their way when Aubrey asked for *The Tennessean* archives from nine years ago. She was impressively businesslike. They were just a couple of kids doing an assignment.

A minute later, the librarian handed over the box and pointed them to the microfiche machine. Aubrey fed the film into the machine like she'd done it a hundred times.

Josh whispered, "What are we looking for?"

"The name Ed Hardsten connected with a crime."

"That will take years."

"No, it won't. What month did this all happen?"

"April."

"Easy. Trust me."

The first story they found wasn't front-page news, but it was the lead on the local section. The headline read *Local Man Indicted on Fraud and Conspiracy to Murder: Ed Hardsten to Serve Ten Years.*

Aubrey read the story to Josh, stumbling a little over some of the Latin terms, but they got the gist of it. As her foster brother, Tyler, would say, Ed Hardsten was a bad dude.

Aubrey could understand why Daisy had said he was dead. She was rather fascinated, actually. Perfect Daisy, who looked down her nose at Aubrey, had been married to a tattooed, clearly naughty almost-murderer.

Aubrey expertly printed out the story, then searched some more. She found one more reference to Hardsten, in another murder investigation a few years later, but couldn't find anything else. It was enough, though. Josh was satisfied.

They returned the microfiche to the librarian. Aubrey folded the page into a small square and put it in the back pocket of her jeans. She could tell Josh didn't want it. That would be too much to ask.

"It's two o'clock. We can go home now."

Josh nodded, and they headed toward his house. His neighborhood bordered the back edge of Dragon Park, Craftsman-style houses in dark wood with short driveways and green lawns, sheltered by tall leafy trees. An upstanding area. Near where Aubrey used to live. Before death and Sandy and Tyler—her uncomfortable new life. She hated coming here. Hated remembering.

The huge mosaic-covered cement dragon cast shadows on them as they walked by. Community art, it was called, this massive plaything that gave the park its name. Every once in a while, Metro would sponsor a picnic, and the neighbors would come to glue fresh tiles to the dragon's side.

Aubrey briefly touched the small square tips of cracked tiles that made up her favorite mosaic, the girl in red, as they passed by. A delighted scream sounded near her head. She watched a small girl slide off the dragon's nose and fly into a heap at her laughing mother's feet. Bitterness swelled inside her.

That should be me. I should have a red dress like that, and live on the edge of the park, and spend the afternoon playing with my mother.

She picked up a rock. Took a step toward the girl. Josh slowed, looked at her queerly.

Aubrey swallowed, pocketed the rock, stowed her anger. It was Josh's turn to be upset now. Josh, who had all the things Aubrey wanted but threw them away at every turn. For her.

They timed it so they'd arrive at 2:30 p.m. on the dot. School was normally dismissed at 2:25 and the walk was short, only five minutes. He couldn't wait anymore, practically pulled her along in his haste to get home.

When they arrived, legs sore from the walk, Aubrey hung back outside the house.

"I should probably go."

"No, Aubrey, please. Please stay with me." His face was still crumpled, and he was pale. Even so, he was the most handsome boy she'd ever seen. How could she abandon him now, when he needed her the most?

Against her better judgment, she agreed. He gave her a brief, hard hug, and they went into the house.

Daisy was in the kitchen, making cookies. There were always fresh cookies at Josh's house. Aubrey's stomach rumbled. She'd really like to live in a world where she could come home to fresh cookies instead of the unwashed, snaggle-toothed glory that was Sandy.

But then she'd have to have someone like Daisy to tell her what to do.

Aubrey was sure her mother was never like Daisy. She was sure of it. The memories she had of her mother and father were beginning to fade a bit. She couldn't remember the exact color of her mother's eyes, or her father's voice. But she remembered real warmth, real love. Daisy's smiles and cookies and hugs, they just didn't feel genuine.

"Hey, Joshie. Home early today. How was school?" Smile, smile, toothy crocodile smile, until she saw Aubrey lingering by the garage door, and the corners of her mouth turned down. "Oh. You brought *her* along."

Josh lost his composure the minute the tone of his mother's voice changed.

"You said he was dead."

"Said who was dead, Josh?"

"My father!"

Aubrey was reminded of a rabbit she'd once seen caught in a trap. Daisy's eyes went wild and wide; her mouth opened in shock. After a moment, she recovered and whispered in a harsh, nasty voice, "What did you just say?"

"Ed Hardsten. That's my dad's name, right?"

"Josh—"

"He's not dead. He was in jail. For being hired to murder someone. But you knew that. You've been lying to me for years." He gestured to Aubrey, who realized at once that handing over the incriminating paper was going to make it look like she was the culprit here. She cursed herself for not thinking of that sooner.

"Aubrey, give it."

She took a deep breath and pulled the paper from her back pocket. Josh ripped it from her hand and unfolded it, practically threw it at Daisy. She glanced at the headline, then looked up, assuming the worst, as she always did.

"You little bitch. How dare you egg my son into looking for his father? Leave, now. You are not welcome in this house," Daisy said to Aubrey.

"She had nothing to do with it, and she's staying," Josh proclaimed.

Daisy's stare was malevolent; Aubrey started backing away.

"He just got *out*," Josh said, poison in his voice.

Daisy broke the hateful gaze, looked at her son. "What?"

"You heard me. He isn't dead. He's been alive this whole time, and you've been keeping it from me. When were you planning to tell me the truth, *Mother*?"

It was too overwhelming. Aubrey felt tears well up in her eyes. She'd never heard hatred in Josh's voice before. He and his mother were in some sort of glaring standoff, and she wasn't exactly sure what was happening.

Daisy crumpled the paper into a little ball. "He's dead to me," she said. "He should be dead to you. After what he did. All the people he hurt. He was supposed to stay away from you, from us. It's part of the agreement. How did you find out?"

"I've known this whole time that he was alive. He came to see me today."

Daisy sucked in her breath. She and Josh circled each other like rabid dogs, staring, neither one saying anything. Aubrey hated this. She hated to see Josh in pain, and she hated Daisy for putting him through this. A little voice registered what he'd said. *He'd known all along his father was alive.*

He'd lied to her, and that stung. But the lie suddenly felt bigger, meaner, and she looked at Josh with new respect. This was important to him. Important enough to create a fiction for her sake. She should be angry, but instead, she was flooded with love.

Daisy finally stopped moving and turned to Aubrey, her voice ringing with authority. She pointed toward the door, enunciated every word.

"This is a family matter. You are not a part of this family. Leave now."

This time, Josh didn't argue with his mother, so Aubrey did the only thing she knew to do. She ran.

She didn't see Josh again for a week, and when she did, he was reserved. Still sweet and loving, but there was a new shadow hiding behind his eyes. She hated to see it. He was supposed to be pure and clean; she was the one with the secrets and shadows.

Knowing his dad was the worst kind of criminal changed Josh. He vowed to never be that kind of person. He was so adamant about it that Aubrey felt kind of bad because Tyler was "that kind of person." Tyler, who stole sweets from the Walgreens for her, who brought her water when she had nightmares. Who, at thirteen, had already spent a night in jail. Who was teaching Aubrey all his little tricks, how to palm a pack of gum, slide a magazine down the back of her pants, how to inhale on a cigarette.

Josh would be furious with her if he knew. She'd accepted that she'd have to deal with Josh's straight-arrow ways, that it was part of loving him. The price of doing business. A price she was more than willing to pay. Josh didn't need to know everything.

CHAPTER 23

Aubrey
Today

The sun broke through the windows, spilling onto their shoulders. They'd never made it off the couch, and Aubrey's eyes opened to the happy pale blues of Winston standing nearby, tail wagging, ready to go out.

She tried to wriggle out from underneath Chase's still sleeping form, but he had her pinned. No help for it, she'd have to wake him.

She shifted her arm, realized it was wedged between them, resting against his cock. Without opening his eyes, Chase gave a small groan and smiled. "Do that again." She giggled, she downright giggled, and moved her hand gently.

"Mmm. I like waking up like this."

"Well, if you don't stop liking it so much, Winston will pee on the rug. Give me a minute, all right?"

Reluctantly, she rolled away, whipped a shirt over her head, opened the back door, and let Winston run into the yard.

When she turned back, Chase was propped up on one elbow, sunlight glowing on his skin, an eyebrow cocked.

"Nice view," he said.

Her stomach flipped. Amazing how he could

do that with two words. She let her eyes sweep over his body. "Agreed. Want some coffee?"

"Tea. And only if you promise we can drink it in bed."

"That I can do."

She went into the kitchen, acutely aware of the breeze between her legs. This felt so normal, so right. Parading around half naked in front of a man she hardly knew, and it didn't faze her. He made her feel safe. She was glad he'd come.

They had the tea, made love again, took a shower together. Hungry, they went down to make breakfast. It was a nice day, so after they'd eaten, she suggested they sit outside and get some vitamin D.

They settled on her tiny front porch. Chase threw a stick for Winston, who went mad with the game, making them both laugh.

Chase held her hand. "The other night, you were telling me about the trial. Were you ever afraid you would be found guilty, even though you weren't?"

"That's a serious topic for such a lovely day."

"We don't have to talk about it if you don't want to. I was just curious, what it must have been like. I can't even imagine being falsely accused."

"It was hell," she said, remembering. "They didn't believe me at all, in the beginning."

Five Years Ago

The cop—his name was Parks—spoke with a southern accent, slow and smooth, trying to keep her calm while getting at the truth. He didn't believe her. She could tell he didn't believe her, and the panic welled in her chest once again.

"Mrs. Hamilton, please describe what your husband was wearing to me again."

"White button-down, khakis, Topsiders with a white sole. I've told you this already."

Aubrey's voice shifted into monotone. It had been five hours since Josh's disappearance. Five of the longest hours she'd ever experienced.

"How long has he been gone?"

You know how long. Five motherfucking hours, and you're just sitting here smirking at me instead of helping me find him.

Aubrey tried to say the words aloud and found them stuck in her throat. Instead, she took a sip of the water the cop placed in front of her and tried again.

"There's blood all over my house. We need to be looking for him, not sitting here talking. Please, why won't you listen to me? Why won't you help?"

The cop looked at her with something that could be interpreted as humor, or could just be a tic that he had, a quirk that made his mouth sneak into a smile when he listened to Aubrey talk. Like he didn't believe a word of what Aubrey was saying. Like he knew something he wasn't sharing. Like he thought . . .

"Mrs. Hamilton. Where could he have gone? You say you came to the hotel with him, and he left to join the bachelor party. But no one at the hotel can confirm that you arrived with your husband."

"This is insane. You're acting like I have a clue where Josh might be. I don't. Not at all. I kissed him good-bye at the front desk, in front of the concierge, for God's sake. Surely he remembers that."

"The concierge doesn't remember seeing either one of you."

Aubrey smacked her hand onto the table, the slap against the wood reverberating in the tiny room. The emotions from the past five hours were sneaking up on her. Never good at pretending she was fine when she wasn't, Aubrey felt the tears begin to prick at the corners of her eyes. She fought them, knowing it would be a losing battle.

"I do not know where he is. Please. You have to help me."

Hold it together, Aubrey. Don't cry in front of this man. He won't understand.

She couldn't help it. A tear slipped down her cheek, another. Suddenly she was gushing so hard the cop had the decency to look embarrassed.

"I don't know where he is," she managed between sobs. "He would never just leave. He sent me a drink, at the bar, after I texted him that I was bored. I expected him to show up, but he didn't. That's all I know. Something has happened to him. Please. You have to help me find him."

●　●　●

The tears dried up. She hired a lawyer. Told him the story without inflection, or losing control the way she had with the cop.

About the accident. She'd been in the bar. She'd texted Josh. He sent her a drink. He'd never shown.

After an hour of waiting, she'd gone looking for him, ran across Arlo, one of the groomsmen, getting sick in the bushes. She'd helped him, and he told her how upset Sulman was that Josh hadn't shown for the bachelor party.

She'd panicked. Known instantly something was wrong. It took two hours to convince everyone else.

By then it was too late.

Josh was gone. Without a trace.

The police hadn't believed her story. Oh, they'd been solicitous, but she could feel the eyes on the back of her neck, the sly whispers. When the investigation into Josh's disappearance began in earnest, they'd pull Aubrey in to the CJC to "talk," stop by her house at all hours. Metro homicide interviewed the waitstaff at the hotel, and none would admit to delivering a gin and tonic to a lone woman in the Jack Daniel's Lounge. Aubrey had gone through photos of the staff herself and hadn't seen the waiter either, but she really hadn't been paying attention.

That particular instance became one of great interest to the detective assigned to Josh's case. There was nothing to corroborate her story about the drink. Which meant, in the detective's mind, there were nearly three lost hours in her story, after the accident and before she connected with Arlo Tonturian.

Nothing physical tied Aubrey to the blood-soaked scene at their house, but that didn't matter. They always look at the spouse first, and those three hours of doubt were enough for the police to tear apart her life. Once they unsealed her juvenile record and realized Aubrey wasn't a plain-Jane suburban housewife, they went at her doubly hard. When they found out about the insurance policy, the $5 million Aubrey would get in the event of Josh's death, put into place a week before, the district attorney decided to go forward with the case. There wasn't enough evidence from the start, but that didn't stop him. He bandied around the possibility of a murder for hire, and the grand jury bought it. His performance must have been masterful because she was bound over for trial and arrested for first-degree murder. The DA went on the news that night, a self-satisfied smirk on his face, bragging that they'd gotten murder convictions without bodies before.

The Nashville media joined in and did quite a job on her, turning her into a devious liar with a sordid past. A black widow nestled in their midst. They posited she'd snuck away from the party, murdered her husband, planted herself in the bar for an alibi, and, after the appropriate amount of time had passed, made a show of looking for him. After all, $5 million was a lot of money.

In the middle of all of this, as hours grew to days grew to weeks, Josh was simply gone. During the long, cold, hard days after he disappeared, as Aubrey was buffeted by the hurricane-force winds of the investigation and arrest and trial, she became the queen of vacillation.

Maybe she'd imagined the drink. Maybe the media was right, she had some sort of Jekyll-and-Hyde split personality, one side a mild-mannered Montessori teacher, the other a scheming Mata Hari who, with malice aforethought, murdered her husband and successfully discarded his body where no one could find it.

The reports became more salacious by the day. Her lawyer always brought her the papers when he came to discuss the next day's testimony; the headlines screamed at her.

She could almost believe she was as wicked as they claimed.

Daisy had not helped things. She'd volunteered to be a witness for the prosecution. Aubrey had to sit in the stifling courtroom looking at the face of the woman she'd known for so many years as she spun truth into lies, making Aubrey's entire life look like one long episode of *Law & Order*.

After a week of listening to people cast aspersions on her character, it was her turn. Her attorney did a wonderful job, setting everything perfectly. She told her story without crying, stayed strong, resolute, humble.

And then it was time for the cross-examination. The DA started kind, gentle, even. He ran her through the events of that night. Asked her a million questions. Pointed out she had a history of violence. Postulated that Aubrey had been drunk, so drunk and out of control that in a fit of rage she'd murdered Josh and didn't remember doing so.

She told him wearily she hadn't been drinking, not until the G&T at the bar.

With a smile that said he was about to nail shut the lid of her coffin, he said he had just been informed of two new witnesses, waiters who claimed they'd seen her drinking the bachelorette party's signature pink piña coladas.

Her defense attorney quickly raised a polite objection, pointed out Aubrey had a severe, well-documented allergy to coconut. He calmly explained that a woman in the grips of both a violent drunk and anaphylactic shock could hardly manage to kill her husband and disappear his body off the face of the earth so effectively that no trace had been found outside of the blood in their living room, which was ten miles away. Without a car, without a taxi arriving at the hotel to take her, without a friend who would admit to driving her to her assignation, and without an EpiPen to counteract the effects of the coconut. It was just too preposterous to imagine.

The jury agreed.

If the glove don't fit, you must acquit.

It had always been a long shot, a circumstantial case. They simply didn't have any proof.

The DA, who'd outkicked his coverage with his Hail Mary piña colada accusation, was forced to withdraw the charge of first-degree homicide. He tried to get Aubrey to plead to manslaughter. She refused. A not-guilty verdict was returned in under an hour, the jury thanked for their service, and Aubrey sent blinking into the light of freedom with her reputation sullied but not entirely smeared black.

Today

Aubrey stretched, curled her legs underneath her. "And that's the whole story. Linda gave me my job back, I endured the whispers and stares, and then, people . . . forgot." She played with her now empty teacup. "I never did," she whispered.

Chase leaned over and gave her a supportive kiss. "Troublemaker."

He had a knack for making her feel less pitiful about the whole thing. "I guess I was."

"What did you do when you were a kid, to get into so much trouble?"

But Aubrey heard something, looked up. "What in the name of God?"

CHAPTER 24

Daisy
Today

Daisy stared at the gaunt face in the mirror and wondered when she'd gotten so very old. She had a tennis game this morning, then an appointment with her lawyer to finalize the paperwork for contesting Josh's life insurance policy. It had started as a simple $50,000 underwrite. Something the bank suggested she and Tom do for Josh while he was a child. He could cash it out when he was thirty-five, and it drew a bit of interest each year.

Two weeks before he disappeared—*died, Daisy, died*—Josh had changed it to term life, upped the policy to $5 million. And put Aubrey's name on the beneficiary line.

Five million dollars. And he'd left it to that tramp. Well, she wasn't going to get any of it if Daisy had her way.

Daisy needed the money. It could give her an escape. A divorce. A new life in a different city where no one would recognize her, no one would know that she was the mother of a missing boy. Where no one would talk behind her back and be solicitous to her face to the point of arrogance. Where no one would pity her.

Tom wouldn't fight her. He'd probably be

relieved. They hadn't been happy for a long, long time, and Josh's disappearance—*No, Daisy. His death. Josh's death*—had made things that much worse. Tom didn't approve of the fact that Daisy felt she should keep the money. They'd gone rounds over it, but Daisy would always have the last word.

"Josh would have wanted me to have it," she told him. "After everything I've done for him, he would want me to be happy. He made me the beneficiary, after all. It was a technical mistake by the bank that put that girl's name in my place. We have to correct the mistake, is all."

Oh, screw Tom and his judgment. Josh was her son, hers, not his.

She slipped into the kitchen and grabbed an apple and a bottle of water from the refrigerator. She tried not to think about the vodka bottle in the freezer, just inches away from her hand. But the second her consciousness acknowledged it, her brain remembered the feeling of numbness, the oblivion it could bring, how good the chilled bitter liquor felt sliding down her throat, and she could think of nothing else.

No one needed to know.

She opened the freezer, pulled the bottle from its shelf, and took a belt. The glass was freezing on her hands and lips. She took one more shot for good measure, let the strong taste flood her tongue. She swallowed, then raced back upstairs and brushed her teeth. Wouldn't do to have the women at the club smell vodka on her breath, though God knew how many of them were doing the same thing right now.

Hypocrites. They were all a bunch of flaming hypocrites.

She slammed back down the stairs, grabbed her bag, and threw it in the back of the CLK. The bag tipped sideways, dumping yellow balls and her locker key on the floor. She'd worry about it when she got there.

She whipped the car out of the garage and headed toward Richland Country Club. Spring was beautiful in this part of town, with the wide, hilly lawns, the centuries-old trees leafing out, languorously shading the huge, multilevel brick homes. Radnor Lake was only a few miles away. She used to take Josh there, to walk around the beautiful nature preserve. He'd hold her hand and pick up rocks for her to admire.

She wasn't going to escape the memories of her son this morning, so she let them in and wiped her eyes carefully when she was finished.

She was nearly to the club when her cell beeped. She hadn't noticed that there was a message—sometimes they got no reception in the house. She played the voicemail: Bobbie, her tennis date, had to cancel. She'd just gotten an emergency call from her daughter, who needed her to go babysit.

Well.

Now Daisy had the morning free. Most everyone else she knew was attending church services—that's what people who still had something to believe in did in this city on Sunday mornings—so there wouldn't be a pickup game to be had at the club, not yet. Tom would still be on the course, playing his weekly round with his buddies. She had no one. No one to be with. No one to count on.

She could go to the lake, take a walk around.

But even as she thought it, she aimed the car downtown. Ten minutes later, almost without thinking, she ended up on West End, across from Centennial Park, in front of one of her favorite restaurants, Tin Angel. Almost without thinking, because one small part of her knew that they had a lavish Sunday brunch with pitchers of delicious mimosas.

The valet greeted her like she was an old friend, even though she'd never seen him before in her life. There was a line—there was always a line; Tin Angel didn't take reservations—but she bypassed the waiting horde and went to the hostess stand.

"I'm just going to the bar," she said.

The girl, long brown hair with a deep purple streak, and innocent, so innocent, smiled winningly and waved her through.

The first glass of chilled champagne and fresh squeezed orange juice went down smoothly. The second followed on its heels like it was afraid to be parted from its friend.

When had this become her life?

She was getting light-headed, but she poured a third glass.

"Can I get you something to eat, ma'am?" The bartender must have noticed she was weaving in her seat a bit; he had his arms crossed disapprovingly.

The idea of food made her want to vomit, but she played along. "Just some fruit and toast, please."

"What's your name?"

"Why?"

"Just being friendly. No eggs? We have a great omelet on special today. Goat cheese and arugula."

Arugula. Arugularugularugala.

Pull yourself together, Daisy.

"No, thank you. Just the fruit."

When he turned away to put the order in, she hurriedly drank the rest of the mimosa, tossed a twenty on the bar, and left.

The valet had put her car in the slot closest to the door, well aware that if something happened to an expensive vehicle on his watch he'd be paying for it out of his own pocket. She took the keys from him in exchange for a five, got in the car, and locked the doors.

She hadn't liked the way the bartender was looking at her.

As if he'd known.

The day was fine, the traffic somewhat light. She had another hour to kill before meeting her lawyer—he being one of those tethered to the confines of the pulpit on any given Sunday. She put the car in gear and pulled away, headed down West End toward Lower Broad, toward the river.

The Sunday morning streets teemed with visiting tourists, almost all families. It hurt her, stabbed her insides to see them walking along with their children in tow, so happy, so carefree. She wanted to scream at them: *Don't you know they could die? Don't you know they can be stolen from you? How dare you not be worrying about keeping them safe?*

It wasn't supposed to be like this. You're supposed to precede your children into death.

She consoled herself with the thought that sometime soon she'd have a hefty check in her hand. She'd fill a bag, gas up the car, and head onto the open road, without a word to anyone. She wasn't sure where she wanted to go, only knew she wanted away. Away from Nashville, from her memories, her very life.

Daisy fumed and plotted and dreamed and wound around the downtown streets—Broadway, Church, State, Union, Broadway again, left on First—then turned left again and headed back out toward the capitol, careful to drive slowly and responsibly.

She somehow ended up behind Vanderbilt Children's Hospital. She'd driven in a big circle, and realized she was only a few streets away from Aubrey's house.

This was all Aubrey's fault.

Daisy turned off Blakemore onto 25th Street. She had no intention of stopping. But what would it hurt to drive past? Little bitch probably wasn't home anyway. She was probably at brunch with her own group of friends. Daisy had seen her last week, with that woman who owned the coffee shop, their heads together, laughing over a private joke. Aubrey had moved on.

Aubrey's house was at the end of West Linden, where it met the plain dead-end street. It should have been a cul-de-sac, but the builders had gotten lazy and there was no half-moon to delineate it, so the street ended abruptly in a dirty guardrail. Daisy turned down the road and could see the shabby little bungalow. Its dormer windows stared at her accusingly.

Aubrey was sitting on the front porch, the dog—Josh's dog—frolicking off his lead in the dormant, nubby grass. There was a man sitting next to her.

Daisy drove closer. Her heart sped up. The way the man sat, his hands loose between his legs, his shoulders cocked forward, his head titled to one side . . .

Josh!

Daisy floored the accelerator. The Mercedes, unhappily goosed, leaped forward, and Daisy struggled to keep it in check. She went for the brake but missed somehow. The car continued to accelerate. Daisy held on tight to the steering wheel, her mind not moving fast enough to force her hands to turn it, just so overwhelmingly happy he'd come back at last, before she slammed across the curb, over the sidewalk, and directly into the corner of Aubrey's house.

CHAPTER 25

Aubrey

Aubrey saw the car coming, recognized the lashes on the headlights, realized who was driving, all in the fragment of a moment before the car jumped the curb and barreled directly into her living room. There was no slow motion, no dawning realization that the accident was going to occur. The car appeared one second and smashed into the side of the house the next.

Winston began to bark, howling and frantic, and something mechanical in Aubrey kicked in. "Call 9-1-1," she shouted at Chase, then ran around to the driver's side of the car. The air bag had deployed. Aubrey could see Daisy leaned back into the seat, eyes closed, mouth agape, blood streaming from her nose. She was not wearing a seat belt.

Her hands were deathly still in her lap, and Aubrey was filled with foreboding. She tugged at the door, but it was locked. She ran to the passenger side—it, too, was secure.

Chase was talking into his phone, looking over at her wildly. She ran the ten feet back to him.

"Tell them we need an ambulance. She's hurt really bad. The doors are locked, I can't get in to help her."

The car was still running, the purr of the engine altered, sounding more like a spitting, snarling beast. Daisy's foot was jammed on the gas; the tires tried to gain purchase, grating the grass beneath them into a muddy mess.

"Hammer?" he shouted at her.

"In the garage."

Chase tossed the phone to her. "Stay on the line, they want to hear more details."

He ran back in the house. Aubrey put the phone to her ear.

"Please hurry," she said. "I think Daisy's badly hurt."

"Do you know the woman in the car, ma'am?"

"Yes. Her name is Daisy Hamilton. She used to be my mother-in-law." Aubrey heard the thin wail of sirens bleeding into the air. "They're coming, I can hear them."

"They're only a minute away, ma'am."

Nashville. An ambulance was always only moments away.

Chase dashed out of the house and down the stairs toward the car. He had a hammer in his hand.

"Wait, Chase."

He glanced back up at her, and she pointed over his shoulder. The heavy grinding of the fire truck's engine preceded the vehicle, and a moment later the wail of the siren grew to a fever pitch, and they pulled onto the street.

Neighbors were popping out of houses like groundhogs, eager to see what was happening.

Aubrey heard murmurs and shouts and barely noticed that Chase had ignored her and plunged the hammer through the passenger window. The glass shattered, showering Daisy with small shards. She looked like she was covered in diamonds. Chase reached in and pressed the button that controlled the engine. The engine cut off, the growling stopped, and just as quickly, a fireman pulled him away from the car.

An ambulance rolled into the street, along with a white-and-blue patrol car.

Aubrey took Winston by the collar and dragged the panicky dog into the house.

"It's okay, baby," she crooned. "It's all okay."

She caught a glimpse of the living room. The car hadn't torn a complete hole but had wrecked the wall. The lamp had fallen on the floor, and the sofa was five feet into the center of the small room.

"Stay, Winston."

She went back out onto the steps. Chase returned to Aubrey's side and put his arm around her shoulders. She couldn't help it; she moved in closer. It felt so good to have someone hold on to her again.

They watched the melee. Daisy was fitted with a hard neck brace, brought gently from the car on a backboard, set carefully on a stretcher. Her eyes were still shut, the front of her tennis whites covered in thick red blood.

A patrol officer came to the steps and barked, "What happened here?"

Aubrey had to drag her attention away from Daisy—they were putting something down her throat and attaching IVs to her veins—to the officer.

"Is she going to be okay?"

The officer softened a bit. "They're doing all they can. Can you tell me what happened?"

"I don't know what she was doing here. She never comes over here. There was no reason for her to be here anymore."

Chase tightened his hold on Aubrey's shoulder. She was babbling, the shock of the accident taking over. He spoke in her stead.

"The car came flying up the street, directly into the side of the house. She didn't brake, didn't slow down at all. Almost as if she was aiming at it."

The patrol officer frowned. "You sure she wasn't aiming at you and changed her mind at the last minute?"

"That could have been the case," Chase said gravely.

Daisy disappeared into the back of the ambulance. Aubrey tore her gaze from the scene and looked back at the officer.

"No. No, not at all. She was going too fast, the car was flying. She just gunned it and went into the yard. She lost control. She had to be going sixty or so when she hit."

The cop turned to Chase. "Sir, you killed the engine?"

"I did. I was afraid the engine might blow. I could smell gas."

"Wouldn't have happened like that, but good

thinking regardless." Aubrey saw the cop's name-plate and felt small a spike of fear. *B. Parks.* God, was he related to that asshole who'd arrested her? It was a small town—he must be. Her wrists started to itch; just the thought of the cuffs on his waist made her jumpy.

He was talking to her again. "You know the woman driving the vehicle, ma'am? Dispatch said she's your mother-in-law?"

"Ex. My ex-mother-in law. Her name is Daisy Hamilton."

"And your name is . . . ?"

"Aubrey Hamilton."

The officer started to write in his reporter's notebook, then stopped and glanced at her curi-ously. Aubrey recognized that look. She'd been on its receiving end many a time.

She closed her eyes for a brief second and sighed. "Yes. That Aubrey Hamilton. Do we have a problem?"

"Aubrey," Chase said, a note of warning in his voice.

The officer shook his head. "No problem at all. I just need to get a couple of people on the horn."

"Like who?" She heard the edge in her voice. Daisy had run the car into her house, and already people were starting to act like Aubrey had done something to cause it. A ripple of aggravation drove through her system. Something in her expression gave her away because the officer leaned forward with his hand on his weapon.

"Ma'am, relax. I'm just putting word out to my

training officer—he's a few blocks away on another accident scene. It's my first week on the job. I don't want to have anything in question, okay?"

"Babe, it's okay," Chase said. "He's just crossing the t's."

"Ha," Aubrey said. "You have no idea what this is like for me. You have no idea." Her voice ended in a shout, which did nothing to help soothe the fears the new cop was having.

"Ma'am? Ms. Hamilton? Why don't we step inside for a moment?"

The tone of his voice made her nerves go into overdrive. Chase caught her distress and squeezed her arm, but it was Josh's voice she heard in her head. *Aubrey, calm down. If you don't act like a normal person, they might think you had something to do with this and arrest you again.*

Aubrey shut her eyes again and nodded. She let Chase lead her into the house like she was a lost child. Winston jumped to her side, whining, and bared his teeth at the cop. Chase reached for Winston's collar and said, "No, boy." The dog immediately calmed, and Aubrey glanced sharply over at Chase. When she and Josh had been training the puppy, Josh had always grabbed the dog's collar and said, "No, boy," with that exact inflection.

Aubrey was just plain living in a surreal netherworld where strangers seemed like friends and everything had gone topsy-turvy.

Chase sat her down at the kitchen table, then started making tea.

The police officer talked into his shoulder for a few minutes, giving and getting instructions. She watched him warily, wondered who he was calling.

He keyed his mike once more, said, "10-4," then turned to her. He took the seat opposite her at the table, blocking her view out the window into the street, where the ambulance was pulling away.

"Okay, Ms. Hamilton. Let's go over everything that happened leading up to the accident."

"Your father is Officer Bob Parks, isn't he?"

The officer looked surprised. "How'd you know that?"

"He worked my husband's case, when he went missing. You look just like him."

"Yes, ma'am. I'm his son, Brent. He's Sergeant Parks now."

Of course he is. Life moves on, Aubrey. Everyone's life has moved forward except for yours. Until yesterday. And look where that got you.

Chase brought three cups and a freshly brewed pot of tea. He sat and offered the mugs around, then poured out, like the perfect host. The cop accepted the steaming liquid, took a polite sip, then set the cup down and opened his notebook.

"Thank you, sir. Could you state your name for the record?"

"Of course. Chase Boden. I'm a friend of Ms. Hamilton."

Had he lingered suggestively on the word *friend*, or had she just imagined it?

Whatever he said seemed to appease the cop for the moment because he started back in on Aubrey.

She relayed the story again, and a third time, before the doorbell rang.

"I'll get it," Chase said. She watched as he crossed to the front door and opened it. An older, grayer version of the young officer sitting at her kitchen table stood in the doorway, along with two more police officers.

Great. He'd called his dad. This should be interesting.

Chase let them all in, then resumed his spot at the table. He placed a comforting arm on Aubrey's leg, very much the man of the house.

Surreal. Surreal, surreal, surreal.

The officers spoke among themselves for a moment, then the older one, the asshole she knew as Bob Parks, addressed her.

"Nice to see you again, Mrs. Hamilton." There was a slight tone of amusement in his voice; apparently he didn't hold a grudge. Five years ago when Parks tried to cuff her, she'd fought, hard, and blackened his eye. She sent him a look.

Please don't mention I hit you, not in front of Chase. Please.

"And you. I hear you've made sergeant. Congratulations."

"Thank you. Ma'am, your mother-in-law has been transported to Midtown. Have you called her husband yet to let him know about the accident?"

"Oh, God, Tom. I should do that. Is she okay? What should I tell him?"

"I don't have that information. I would like to hear what happened, though."

Chase stood. "Come now. Aubrey has already repeated the story several times. We were sitting on the front step, playing with the dog, and this woman came flying up the street and rammed into the house. There's nothing more for us to add at this point."

Us.

Nothing more for *us* to add.

Aubrey felt her shoulders square. The last time, she hadn't had anyone there to stop them from questioning her again and again and again. She took strength in the fact that Chase was so much in charge and relayed her own requests.

"I'd like to call Daisy's husband now. And then I'd like to go to the hospital and see how she's doing."

Both Parkses weighed her words, then nodded in time, almost as if they were twins, not father and son.

The sergeant spoke first. "That's fine, Mrs. Hamilton. Thank you for being so cooperative." He started to hand her his card, thought better of it, handed it to Chase instead. "We'll be in touch if there's anything else we need from you, and you feel free to call if you remember anything else. You have homeowner's insurance, I presume? A report will be left with you in a few hours for you to give them."

"I do. With the Farm Bureau. Thank you very much."

The officers left through the front door, and Aubrey sagged against the chair.

Chase knelt beside her, brushed her hair back off her forehead. "Are you okay?"

She gazed at him, struck by how loving he was, how sweet, how concerned. She almost didn't know how to react to that. But this wasn't about her right now. She needed it to be about Daisy. As much as she despised the woman, as often as she'd hoped that Daisy would get drunk and drive herself into a tree, leave this world behind, leave her constant disapproval behind, she didn't truly wish her dead. Now that the impossible had happened, Aubrey felt a sudden kinship, a need to take charge. It's what Josh would want.

"I am. I need to call Tom."

Chase reached behind her and retrieved the phone. "Here you go."

"Thank you, Chase. For everything."

He just smiled and ran his palm against her cheek.

"Anything for you, Aubrey."

CHAPTER 26

Aubrey
Nineteen Years Ago

Aubrey is ten. She has just been given a valentine by a boy named Josh Hamilton. She has known Josh for three years. A lifetime. He has beautiful blue eyes, and a smile that makes her happy.

Not much makes her happy now. She lives in the house with Sandy, and Tyler, and Julia and Becka and Latesha, and the men who parade through to give Sandy money in exchange for their pleasure with her foster mother. It is an existence, not a life.

She sleeps in the same bed as Latesha because they are the closest in age. Latesha and Tyler are *doing it*. Aubrey has to pretend she doesn't know this, but they groan and grunt and fight in the bed every night like small animals. Tyler pushes Aubrey off the bed sometimes and makes her sleep on the floor. She doesn't like the floor; Sandy isn't the best housekeeper, and small things skitter around in the corners during the night, but it is better than being part of the fun. She can't sleep with them playing in the bed.

Once, they allowed her to stay, and Latesha held her hand while Tyler ran his palms over

Aubrey's still invisible breasts, but she hadn't liked that, so now when Tyler comes into the room, she grabs her pillow and decamps without making a fuss.

Aubrey is sworn to secrecy, but wonders if Tyler knows he is just one in a long line of boys who are sticking their things in Latesha. She was caught last week at school going down on one of the teacher's aides, and Sandy was furious.

Aubrey knows what sex is, what *going down* means, what *pussy* and *dick* and *cunt* and *whore* mean, and vaguely thinks these are words and actions that no ten-year-old should know so intimately.

But now, Josh Hamilton has handed her a small red heart cut out of construction paper with *B My Valentine* written in crooked letters with blue ink, and she can't help but wonder if that means he wants to put his thing into her, or maybe he just wants her to take the piece of paper and smile and say yes, she'll be his valentine. So that's what she does. She smiles and says yes, and he smiles back, leans in, and kisses her forehead, then darts off.

She is bewildered, and suddenly the center of attention for all the girls in class.

Two approach, and Aubrey is reminded of the lions stalking a wildebeest in a television show on Animal Planet that Sandy made them watch with the volume turned up real loud last night while she entertained a guest. The nature shows are where Tyler and Latesha got the idea to couple in the first place. Sandy thought the kids were getting wholesome entertainment. How could there be anything bad on a channel focused solely on cute zoo animals? But instead of the gentle education Sandy was hoping for, they were exposed to sex and violence and gore and sadness.

Life.

The taller of the two, a girl with a wide forehead named Hilary, smiles disarmingly, then snatches the valentine from Aubrey's hand and reads the inscription.

She turns to the smaller girl, Danielle, and says, "Oooh, looky here. It says 'Josh loves Aubrey.'"

She begins to chant the words aloud, and Danielle joins in, the two becoming a miniature Indian circle, hooting and hollering and pointing, and others arrive from various areas around the room to join in, not knowing why they are dancing around little Aubrey Trenton, or why she has tears in her eyes, or why there are small torn bits of red construction paper near her feet, only that the gang leader has called and the gang leader must be answered.

Their teacher, Linda Pierce, sees the situation unfold and hustles over to stop it. Aubrey is forever being picked on. She is different. She no longer has parents. She lives with strangers. She is on scholarship. She comes to school, hair wild about her solemn and sad face, not speaking, not interacting with anyone but Josh Hamilton, who has set out to save the small, desolate little girl.

The crowd disperses, back to their own activities. They will be sat down for a conflict-resolution session shortly, so there is no chance of misunderstanding that what they've just done isn't acceptable, and will do some role-playing exercises to find a different, healthier approach to acting out. Mrs. Pierce wipes Aubrey's tears, helps her pick up the shredded valentine.

Aubrey wonders if Josh could be talked into making her another. But he is gone, back to his classroom, back to his perfect world, where parents are alive and mothers don't have sex with strangers.

Mrs. Pierce hands her the Scotch tape, and together they piece the red thing back into being.

Aubrey hides in the coatroom and hugs it to her heart, plotting her revenge on the girls who tried to take his love away.

Dear Josh,

I saw Kevin and Janie's boys today. They've moved to Pensacola. (I know, can you imagine the Sulmans out of the Outer Banks?) I never get to see them or the kids anymore. God, they are huge. And precocious, and funny. I can't believe how much you're missing. I can't believe what I'm missing. I thought we'd have babies by now, curly-headed little girls I'd dress in frilly pink outfits and solemn-faced boys who wanted to play with trains and you'd share your music with.

I will admit it, I broke down. I don't do that much anymore. But as I watched them playing in the yard, I lost it. Simply, cleanly, completely. Cried, and hid my tears behind my sunglasses. Parker came up with a beetle to show me and said, "Auntie, your nose is all red," and I blamed it on sunburn.

It's just not fair. Where are you? Why won't you come home to me? Was it something I did? Did I make you unhappy? Was there anything that I could have done differently? I can't help but feel that you ran away from me, that I drove you away. And for what?

I don't know how much longer I can do this, Josh. You were everything to me, and I feel so incomplete. Like I am half a woman.

Come home, darling. I don't want to live without you anymore. I can't.

Always,
Aubrey

CHAPTER 27

Daisy
Today

Daisy heard snippets of language but couldn't decipher them. She felt like she was asleep, underwater, locked inside a room that didn't allow for air. She couldn't breathe. Every part of her body hurt, and though she was afraid to move, afraid it would hurt more, the idea of lying still any longer made her claustrophobic. Eyes. Eyes had to open. Her eyes wouldn't open.

She thrashed. Oh, dear God, she couldn't breathe. She began to choke, to gag.

"Whoa, whoa, whoa, she's waking up."

This she heard clearly, in her right ear. Waking up from what? What was happening?

The warm cotton of heavy sleep began to flow through her. She recognized the feeling, a brief moment of clarity. She'd had anesthesia once before. And as she began to be cognizant of that thought, the darkness overwhelmed her.

Later.

Long, low beeps. Daisy could hear them clearly, getting louder and louder. The hiss of air. Her chest—oh, the pain was unbearable.

She opened her eyes. She couldn't move her head. The feelings of claustrophobia returned; she saw Tom leaning over her.

"Oh, Daisy. Honey. Thank God. Nurse!"

Thank God for what? Tom's face disappeared, replaced by whiteness, intense and harsh, so bright it made her reflexively shut her eyes. She tried to sit up and saw red. The pain was immediate, flaring into her brain. She stopped moving, just clenched her teeth together, prayed for it all to end.

"Daisy?"

She opened her eyes. Tom's face was back, wavering above her.

"Baby, you were in an accident. Do you remember?"

An accident? She didn't remember anything. She tried to shake her head, to say no, but nothing worked.

A brown-skinned sloe-eyed woman appeared. A genie. She looked like a genie. Where was her bottle?

"Daisy, I'm Rasha. I'm your nurse. You have a tube down your throat to help you breathe. You have sustained several injuries, including a broken sternum and some cracked vertebrae in your neck. You're in a halo, to keep your head still. You're going to be very sore, so I want you to tell me, on a scale of one to ten, how badly you hurt. So blink for me, sweetie. Blink for how badly you hurt on a scale of one to ten."

Daisy fluttered her eyes as quickly as she could.

"Wow, okay. Let me get you some relief here."

She couldn't see what was happening, but within moments her body was flooded with liquid gold, warm and soft as cashmere in her bones. She tried to take a deep breath, a reflex reaction to the soothing relief she felt, but couldn't.

It didn't matter anymore. A gentle darkness surrounded her, carried her away.

The sun was coming through the blinds. Daisy could feel the shift, that instant when she knew she was awake. There was a brief, intoxicating moment while she forgot what was happening. Reality crept back in, and the pain began.

It burned and ached and simmered in her chest. Each breath was agony.

But pain was her companion. It told her she was alive.

Tom stood nearby; she could smell his fear and sweat over the antiseptic coldness of the room. The nurse, Rasha, offered more meds, but Daisy blinked once for no. She wanted to know what was going on. Where she was. What had happened.

Using only her eyes, she looked left and right and left and right, trying to communicate something, anything, so they'd know she wanted to hear about why she was here and what the hell was going on.

Tom asked her a few inane questions: "Do you have to pee? Go ahead, you have a catheter. Do you want a drink? You can't have one, I know your mouth must be dry, but they're giving you fluids. Do you hurt? Of course you hurt, that was stupid of me. What do you want, sweetheart?"

She shut her eyes and kept them closed. Amazing, even drugged and broken, she could still get annoyed with the man. He never had understood her.

She opened her eyes again and frowned at him.

"I don't know what she wants," he said, voice needy with helplessness.

A voice that made Daisy's blood pressure tick up several notches answered. "Let me try."

Tom's face was replaced by the curly-haired bitch who'd gotten Josh killed.

Aubrey.

If Daisy could only raise her arms, she'd scratch her eyes out.

"Daisy," Aubrey started in a soothing discoursing-with-the-inmates tone, "you've been in an accident. You drove your car into my house. You're hurt badly, you're in intensive care. They've done surgery to put you back together. Your neck was broken, they fused the vertebrae together, so you have to stay in the halo for a while. It's screwed in, so you won't be able to turn your head. And your sternum had a crack in it. They need to keep you as immobile as possible for the time being while things start to knit back together. Blink twice if you understand."

As much as she didn't want to obey the little

wretch, she was more starved for information, so she blinked slowly, once, twice.

"Good. They're going to keep you sedated until things are calmed down. You've given everyone quite the scare, Daisy. It's going to be a rough few days, but they think they'll be able to take you off the ventilator soon. And then you'll be able to talk."

Something in Aubrey's eyes actually telegraphed concern. Daisy blinked twice.

"We'll stay with you, Daisy, as much as they'll let us. The visiting hours are limited here in Intensive Care. No matter what, you won't be alone. One of us will be nearby twenty-four/seven."

Tom's worried face hovered into Daisy's field of vision. He was nodding at each of Aubrey's well-enunciated statements.

Daisy shut her eyes. Looking at them upside down and sideways above her was making her nauseous. She didn't remember the accident. She'd hit Aubrey's house with her car? She thought back, searching her bruised mind for something, anything to hang on to.

Images floated through her mind—tennis, her house, vodka, Tom.

Nothing. She was blank.

She opened her eyes and another face appeared in her field of vision. A young man, thirty or so, with dark eyes. He looked so familiar. So very familiar. She had no idea who he was, and yet she knew him intimately. Every ache, every pain. Every whisper in the night, the smooth skin on the underside of his arm. She loved him. Even in high school, when he hated her, she loved him.

Her brain worked to make the connections, tried to process and spit out the answer, but it just wouldn't come.

And then he sprang into her consciousness, and she realized it had all been a terrible, awful dream. She'd been dreaming.

Josh. Her Josh. He was right here, standing with her. She didn't even care that the wretch was with him. She was flooded with happiness.

It was so good to have the family back together.

Exhausted, she let her eyes close, and slid into darkness again.

CHAPTER 28

Josh
Seventeen Years Ago

The beginning of Josh's first day in high school was shaping up to be incredibly painful. The Montessori school he'd attended since kindergarten only went up to eighth grade, and then the students moved on to regular, mainstream public schools or pricey private schools. Private school wasn't in Tom's budget, so instead of walking down the street to school, Josh had to get on a bus, with strangers, to go to Hillsboro High School. Josh hated strangers. He liked things safe and sane and comfortable.

At fourteen he wasn't big for his age either, which worried him. He knew he was going to get picked on. New kid, new school, new class—yeah, things were going to be different, that was for sure.

The bus smelled like vomit. Someone more scared than he was, then. He ignored the curious looks, took the first empty seat, and attempted to become invisible, shrinking into the green pleather, face attached to the window. The glass was cool and felt good against his cheek.

He didn't know how he was going to stand being away from Aubrey.

She was so small, so wounded. Who was going

to take care of her? Who was going to defend her? Without him there to give her that invisible layer of armor, she would be vulnerable to attack.

Last night, when they'd talked on the phone, she told him that she missed him. It made his heart swell up, and he'd snuck off to the bathroom for another shower and spent his time under the water's spray imagining all sorts of naughty things that he'd like to try with Aubrey. Things his mother would probably shoot him for.

But Aubrey was only twelve. A mature twelve—she'd seen too much at the foster home where she lived—but twelve nonetheless, and the way Josh looked at it, it wouldn't be right to have the real thing between them for a while. He knew of a girl in his neighborhood who'd gotten pregnant, and the idea of that happening to Aubrey was frightening to him. He'd gone to the library and looked up several books on childbirth, and learned exactly what happened when a man and woman had unprotected sex. No, that wouldn't do.

So he had to be content with pleasuring himself in the shower, which really wasn't all bad, though he would have liked to at least have Aubrey's hand in place of his own. That would be safe. They wouldn't get into trouble that way. She'd do it, too, without complaining. She would do anything for him.

His fantasy about the shower lasted him until the bus pulled up in front of the school, and he realized he had a painful erection. God, how was he going to get off the bus?

He fiddled with his backpack, praying things would calm down. *Dead puppies.* No, that didn't work. *Daisy.* Yes, that did the trick. Just one mental glance at his mother's disapproving glare sent things shrinking back down to normal.

He swallowed and got off the bus, knowing he must be beet red. He looked down at the ground and hurried up the stairs, being jostled by boys and girls much bigger than he.

"Josh?"

He heard his name and looked up. Aubrey was over by the doors. He couldn't help himself; his face broke into a huge grin and he loped toward her, oblivious to the people pushing and shoving around him. God, she was beautiful, that curly hair sticking out at angles from her face, her lips redder and fuller than any girl's he'd ever seen. She was starting to fill out, too, her body on its continental drift toward womanhood, a swell of hips and small breasts. She had long legs though she was only five feet tall, legs tight with muscles from all the walking and running and biking she did. Anything to stay moving. Aubrey was perpetually in motion.

"What are you doing here?" he asked.

"Don't be mad. I wanted to see you off."

"But you're late for school."

"I'll blame it on Sandy. Mrs. Pierce won't know any different. I borrowed a bike and rode over here."

Borrowed. Josh cringed at the word. *Borrowed* was her slang for *stole*, and it was something she did more than Josh liked. Aubrey's versions of right and wrong were colored in shades of gray Josh didn't completely understand.

"Be sure you take it back, Aubrey."

"Yes, Mom," she said, and flashed him a grin. He couldn't stay mad at that face for long. She really had no idea what effect she had on him, on everyone around her.

The bell rang, and Josh jumped. "I better go. I'm glad you came by."

"Me, too." Aubrey looked like she wanted to do something, or say something. He waited, bouncing on the balls of his feet for a moment, then said, "Well, bye."

"Bye," she replied, then bit her lip and, faster than a cobra, leaned into his space and touched her lips briefly to his. Without a word, she turned and jogged back to the bike, hopped on, and rode away. Josh stood there, staring after her.

She'd kissed him. *She* kissed *him*. After all the horrible imaginings, and the pleasurable ones, of trying to figure out how to get her to let *him* kiss *her*, she'd gone and reversed things on him.

He smiled. Oh, God. She really liked him.

"Yo, kid. Was that your girlfriend?"

Josh was pulled back to reality by the voice. He cringed inside, not knowing what to expect, turned with his fists clenched. The boy was taller than him, with dark hair and dark eyes, a beak of a nose. He looked strong, and Josh immediately put his weight on his toes, ready to punch and run.

"Yeah, that's my girlfriend," he said. Casually. Cool. Just the hint of a challenge in his tone.

The older boy's face broke into a knowing smile. "Nice." The boy bumped Josh's shoulder with his knuckles. "I'm Arlo."

"Josh Hamilton."

"You ever been laid?"

Should he push his luck? Maybe not. This guy looked like he could see through most things.

"No."

"Yeah, me neither. But you're certainly on the way. She's a little hottie. We should go in. Are you going to try out for football? I'm varsity this year. You're awful quick—I saw you take off from the bus. You might make a good running back."

Arlo chatted nonstop as they walked into the school. Josh followed him, dumbstruck when Arlo introduced Josh around to his friends, all obviously not ninth graders. They were practically men.

Josh thought back five minutes, to Aubrey's darting eyes just before she leaned in and kissed him. She'd known people were watching. In one fell swoop, Aubrey had given him credibility in his strange new life.

And then he realized she'd done it on purpose, a gift for him. She'd anticipated his fears, his concerns, known that he would have a hard time, so had shown up—on a stolen bike, no less—to help him transition into this more grown-up world.

How did she do that?

He shouldn't ask. She knew too much as it was. Insightful Aubrey.

His heart blossomed with something new and different, a feeling of warmth and excitement and depth that he'd never felt before. He shook hands with his new friends, went off toward his homeroom with strength in his step. High school was going to be just fine.

CHAPTER 29

Aubrey
Today

Three days passed with frustrating slowness. Aubrey and Tom took turns at the hospital, Tom during the day, Aubrey at night. They did twelve-hour shifts, watching, waiting, anticipating. Daisy had good moments and bad, but she'd been on an upswing for the past two days, and the doctors thought they'd be able to remove the ventilator by the end of the week.

Aubrey was completely exhausted. Exhausted and off her schedule and struggling with her emotions because, though she should be feeling nothing but pity and remorse, in all honesty, she enjoyed Daisy's silence. Enjoyed her pain. That made her a bad person, she knew. But the woman had always been so cruel, so horrible, that Aubrey had a hard time mustering up too much sympathy for her.

She'd been anesthetized against compassion. That made her a sociopath, didn't it?

It was a horrifying thought. Surely it wasn't entirely true.

Not entirely. She'd loved Josh desperately. And in her way, she loved Tyler. And she certainly had some sort of feelings for Chase. She would kill anyone who hurt Winston. She could cry when upset.

A psychopath then. Able to feel, but always choosing to follow the wrong path.

Aubrey checked the clock. Nearly two in the morning. Daisy was sleeping and, if the pattern she'd fallen into held, would be out until the overnight nurse came to do her vitals at four. Aubrey yawned and decided to risk a trip down to the cafeteria for a cup of coffee.

She crept out of the room so as not to wake her mother-in-law, and closed the door quietly behind her. The hallway lights were bright; she rubbed her eyes against the sudden glare. A man she didn't recognize walked by, toward the last bank of rooms, and she realized just how unsecure a hospital was. The thought set her heart to beating hard, a tiny rush of adrenaline. Anyone could be here. Anyone could claim familial ties and walk the hallways at all hours. It totally creeped her out.

She alerted the nurse where she was headed in case of emergency, then took the elevator to the first floor. The hospital itself was a labyrinth, one she'd never thought she'd know so well. Too bad they hadn't taken Daisy to Vanderbilt, which Aubrey knew well from Josh's time there.

Instead, the first few days in Midtown, she'd ended up in parking lots and cardiac care units and outpatient surgery centers before she started to get a feel for the veering hallways that led to the appropriate bank of elevators. A person could get lost too easily around here, and it was rare to find people who could direct you to the right place; three-quarters of them were lost as well, and the others were busy rushing to their assigned spots. It could be quite frustrating.

But she finally got the hang of it.

Aubrey exited the elevator, smelled the dim antiseptic air that indicated freshly mopped floors. She was chilly, clutched her arms together for warmth. Yes, a coffee would be good. Maybe even a quick granola bar or some chocolate. Fuel.

The cafeteria was open with modified service, self-service, and prepacked foods only. A sleepy clerk sat on a stool by the register, his head nodding.

Aubrey got a large cup of coffee and a Hershey bar. She paid the attendant and decided to sit and drink for a bit. She had time. Daisy wouldn't wake up. She'd never know.

She took a hard plastic seat by the window, even though there was nothing to see in the dark. The trees had small, dim lights planted in the mulch shining up their thin trunks, but this was an interior courtyard, so there was nothing outside to distract from the quiet.

She sipped the coffee and wondered what was next. Chase had gone back to Chicago. He had to work, an article due. He'd be back Thursday night. She was looking forward to seeing him. To talking with him. To touching him and smelling his scent and feeling his hands caress her body.

But she didn't know where she wanted things

to go yet. It was a silly thing to worry about, but Aubrey had only ever been in love with one man, and was a monogamous creature at heart. She wanted to know what to expect, what to plan for. For the schedule to magically appear: You will date for three months; he'll suggest moving in. Since you have the yard for the dog, he'll want to live in Nashville. And on New Year's Eve, he will propose, and you will be torn as to what to answer. You'll want to say yes, but have you spent enough time getting to know him? And then there's the question of children . . .

God, Aubrey. Cart before the horse much? You don't even know if he's trustworthy.

"Is this seat taken?"

Aubrey jumped. A man was standing at her elbow. Silvery hair, dark eyes. Jeans and a sweater. Oddly familiar. He made her uncomfortable, but she didn't want to seem rude.

"Um, no?"

"Oh, good." He sat down across from her, his own cup of coffee to hand. "It gets so lonely here at night. It's nice to see another civilian. Mom sick?"

"Mother-in-law."

"Ah. The toughest relationship. You've stolen her son away, he's chosen you over her. Oedipal complex aside, it's always fraught with danger."

Aubrey couldn't shake the eerie feeling she was getting from this guy.

"Your . . . wife is ill?" she guessed.

"Ah, no. Just a friend." He smiled and took a sip of his coffee. Aubrey realized he was the strange man from the hallway upstairs—that's where she'd seen him—but now, face-to-face, he seemed even more familiar.

"Have we met?"

"I don't know. Have we?" He cocked his head to the side and smiled. Aubrey stared at him. She totally knew him, and not just from the hospital. But from where?

"May I?"

With a small smile, he broke off a piece of her chocolate bar. The audacity of the move shocked her. She grabbed the chocolate bar, pulled her chair and person back from the table.

"Don't you love chocolate? It makes the day more special." He smiled a little, and chills ran down her spine.

Aubrey stood, picking up her cup and the chocolate. "I need to get back upstairs."

"Oh, don't go just yet. Let's talk some more."

"Thanks, but I'm going to head up."

"How is your husband?"

She didn't answer, just started toward the coffee urns again to top off.

She heard the man approaching from behind.

"Aubrey, right? Aubrey Hamilton? Really, how is your husband? His name is Josh, if I recall."

Aubrey whirled around, out of patience. "Good night." She started away, but he grabbed her arm.

"I asked you a question. How is dear Josh?" His voice was no longer friendly and inquisitive. Now it was filled with menace.

She tried to pull her arm from his grasp, but he had her in a steel grip. "He's dead, you sick bastard. My husband died five years ago."

"Now, now. Doesn't do to lie. I saw you with him earlier in the week. In the elevator. Yes, I'm sure it was you."

"That's just a friend of mine. My husband is dead."

The man stroked his chin. He spoke almost to himself, sotto voce. "Really? After all this time, too. Fascinating."

She jerked on her arm. He let go, and she started away.

"Mrs. Hamilton?"

She turned to glance back at him.

"If you hear from him, do let me know." He handed her a card.

Aubrey was too shocked to do anything but take it. She finally came to her senses and scurried back to the elevator. The man didn't follow her, just stood grinning by the coffee urns.

When the doors closed, she remembered to breathe.

She was shaking, her hands trembling so hard that hot coffee sloshed out of the opening in the lid, spilling on the card and burning her hand.

"Son of a bitch!"

The elevator stopped on the fifth floor while she was cursing. The nurse on duty saw her and jumped up from behind the desk. "Are you okay?"

Aubrey nodded, left the elevator, cradling her hand. "Coffee burn."

"Let me see it," the nurse commanded. Aubrey stopped and held out her hand. The nurse tsked over it for a moment, then said, "Go rinse it in cool water. It's not too bad. Hey, by the way, your mother-in-law is awake."

"Thanks," Aubrey said. Great. Just what she needed. She went to the room and set her coffee and the ruined card on the small shelf above the radiator, then made eye contact with Daisy, who was burning mad. Aubrey could see it in her eyes.

"Are you okay?"

One big blink for no.

"Do you hurt? I can get the nurse to supplement your last shot."

Another single blink.

Aubrey sighed. "I wish I could read your mind, Daisy. Or that you could write. Do you want to try?"

Two blinks. *Yes.*

"Okay." This was something they'd been working on. Daisy wanted to communicate, but she hadn't had enough energy to make the pen move properly. Decoding her chicken scratchings had been difficult. The doctors said with practice she'd get better. But there was one word she had managed to write, several times.

Aubrey got out her Sharpie and notepad and placed the pen in Daisy's grasp. Aubrey held the pad up at an angle so Daisy could see it properly. She wrote shakily, halting, but miraculously, the word finally made it onto the page. Aubrey turned it around and read it.

Josh?

She sighed, heavy and impatient. How many times were they going to go through this?

"Daisy, Josh is dead."

Her tone lacked conviction, and Daisy started a string of blinks indicating emphatic nos.

"The man you saw here isn't Josh. That's Chase. He's my friend, my . . . boyfriend. He's a freelance writer from Chicago. Josh passed away five years ago."

Daisy waved the pen toward the pad again. Aubrey obliged, and the older woman wrote some more. Her hand fell to her side, limp. Aubrey looked at the pad again.

Not dead.

Jesus. What the hell was going on today?

She patted Daisy's arm and nodded. "Okay, Daisy. Time for you to get some sleep."

She started to press Daisy's morphine button, but Daisy had already closed her eyes and was starting to drift.

Aubrey stepped back to her uncomfortable chair and wedged herself on the cushion, legs drawn up underneath her.

What had just happened? Who was the man who'd appeared downstairs, asking about Josh? And why did he seem so familiar?

She picked up the coffee-stained card gingerly, as if it were a bomb that might go off. *DC*

Investigations—Private, Secure, Discreet. There was no address, just a handwritten phone number, the last three digits smeared out of recognition from the coffee spill. Shit. She held it to the light. Maybe that last number was a seven, or a four? She turned the card over and saw a name written on the back.

Derek Allen.

She knew that name. But where from?

Damn it, she shouldn't have taken the pills. They made her foggy, and she suddenly realized she needed to be sharp right now.

She shook her head. This was all crazy. Utterly nuts. She couldn't go through this again. She knew Josh was gone. Knew it in her soul.

So why were two people suddenly claiming he was still alive?

She looked blindly out into the blank night. The answers were there, if she was willing to face them. And Derek Allen was the key.

CHAPTER 30

After several hours of worrying, and shaking off the fear that crowded in to fuel her nightmares, Aubrey finally fell asleep in the hospital chair. She managed to stay under for a full hour. When she woke, the sun slinking through the blinds, she had a sleepy thought: Keep her head in the sand. Dismiss the craziness from last night as exactly that. The guy from the cafeteria was wrong. And Daisy, well, Daisy had suffered a head injury. Insisting Josh was alive . . .

So much for running from the truth.

Aubrey awakened more fully, finally allowing the thoughts she'd been trying to pretend she wasn't having to come to the fore.

There was a clear resemblance between Josh and Chase. She'd seen it from the very beginning; that's what had intrigued her in the first place. It wasn't looks: Josh was fair, with blue eyes and brown hair. Chase had darker skin, not tan, just more olive, with coffee-colored eyes and blond hair. The basics were different. The bone structure was different. But there was something similar in the way they walked, the way they talked, the way they kissed, the way they made love. Something similar, but so very different.

Josh had a scar on the inside of his right thigh, and a constellation of freckles on his back with which Aubrey, for fun, used to play connect the dots. The result was a lopsided Mickey Mouse. Chase didn't have freckles on his back or a scar on his thigh. She'd seen both areas and she knew they weren't there.

The whole idea that Josh was Chase, that Chase was Josh, was ridiculous.

So why was she sitting in her mother-in-law's hospital room wondering if it was possible? And trying desperately to deny the fact that somewhere, deep inside, she wished it were true?

Reality check, Aubrey.

She'd spent years making Faustian bargains with God, offering to do almost anything to get Josh back. And now, now that she'd finally started to sew up the gaping hole in her heart, she had a chance to start over, and she'd be damned if she was going to let it pass her by.

Chase had woken her from a deep sleep. They'd been talking, a lot, about her past and her life, about his dreams for the future. Even about Josh. She was developing real feelings for him, strong, raw, and unrestrained emotions. Emotions she almost didn't recognize as possible to belong to her. Emotions that made her feel alive again.

Continuing to see him, to allow her heart free rein, was a disaster in the making. But the thought of never seeing him again, never being with him, hurt. She had to find a way to continue the affair and protect her fragile heart at the same time.

She'd never been without Josh. Even in death, he'd been as real and tangible to her as if he'd been alive, whispering in her ear. But a part of her had never forgiven him for leaving. For dying. My God, what if she had been found guilty and had gone to jail for murder?

She shuddered. It wasn't the first time she'd played the what-if game. But now, she had a path out. She couldn't—no, she wouldn't—let anyone ruin this for her.

She turned the card over in her hands. The day Josh was declared dead, Chase showed up. And only a few days later, here was another guy appearing out of the blue, giving her a card with the name Derek Allen, offering answers. It was time to take off the blinders. Hiding the truth from herself wasn't going to work anymore. She didn't want to drag herself through it all again, but she'd be damned if she would miss an opportunity to find out exactly what had happened to Josh.

But she was going to need help. She couldn't do this alone.

She needed Tyler.

CHAPTER 31

Josh
Fifteen Years Ago

"Yo, Hamilton. Tonight's the night, huh? You finally gonna bone that girl or what?"

Josh pushed against the lineman, forcing him back into the secondary.

"Fuck you, Kowalski." Josh wrenched the older, bigger boy to the ground. The whistle sounded. The coach shouted, "All right, all right, line up again. Hamilton, quit jawing with Kowalski. Cover Sulman."

Josh gave Kowalski one last hard shake, then turned to Kevin Sulman. Arlo lined up next to him this time.

"Let's tag-team his pansy ass."

"Oh, yeah."

The whistle sounded and they attacked, tossing Sulman to the ground like a sack of air. He was no match for the two of them together.

Josh had put on a solid twenty pounds of muscle since the beginning of the summer training season and, thankfully, started a growth spurt that had him eye-to-eye with Arlo. That wasn't all that was right with his world. Freshman and sophomore years were over, he was moving on to his junior year, he was on the varsity football team, and Aubrey would be starting as a freshman in the fall. Josh's grades were top notch, football was going great, and he was being pushed to consider running for class president. Arlo Tonturian and Kevin Sulman, his two best friends, would be graduating after this year, and he'd most likely be made captain of the team for his senior year. With any luck, he'd get a football scholarship and have a full ride for undergrad before he started the long slog through medical school.

Everything was perfect. Absolutely perfect. And there was one thing that was going to make it even better.

Tonight, he had a date with Aubrey.

The date.

His mom and dad were out of town. He'd sworn up, down, and sideways he wouldn't have anyone—"That means Aubrey, too, Josh, especially her"—over to the house. But fuck that shit. He wasn't about to lose this opportunity. He wanted their first time to be perfect, special, and he'd be damned if he was going to let an empty house go to waste.

He was buzzing with anticipation. Literally felt his skin shivering. Arlo and Kevin knew what was up; they'd been teasing him all afternoon. "Don't you want to wait for prom? Won't that make it the most *perfect night ever*?"

"Fuck off," he'd told them with a grin. He didn't care if they wanted to tease him. He knew they would stand by him, thick or thin. They loved Aubrey as much as he did. She did that to people. You couldn't help yourself from falling in love with her.

Everyone except his mom. Daisy continued to despise Aubrey with a passion. He could never figure out why. He knew the surface reasons: she'd hated Aubrey's real mom, hated that Aubrey was a foster child, that she lived in a bad part of town (Daisy was a complete snob; anything that wasn't considered a feeder neighborhood for the country club was immediately labeled "bad"), that she didn't have money, like that was a fourteen-year-old girl's fault. Money was vital to Daisy, and she always wanted to be richer than she was. Appearances were everything to her. Coveting was her favorite pastime. She took keeping up with the Joneses to previously unknown levels.

But the true reason for her enmity eluded him. Aubrey had never been anything but sweet and respectful with Daisy, a little shy even, but she'd been treated like hell for years.

Not like he was going to ask and open that can of worms. He just did his best not to mention when he was going to be with Aubrey, and he called her instead of her calling him. Daisy wasn't mellowing, but she was calming down a bit. Slightly. She could still go nuclear at a moment's notice if caught at the wrong time.

Daisy didn't seem to realize that Josh was tied to Aubrey in ways even he didn't completely understand. She'd just shake her head when she looked at him getting ready to go out, carefully shaved and combed and tucked, and spit venom at him. "That girl is trouble, Josh. She's no good. She's going to drag you down with her one of these days."

Thinking about the animosity between his mother and Aubrey upset him, and he missed an easy tackle. He forced it from his mind and tried to focus on football.

He didn't think practice was ever going to end, but it did, finally, and he hit the showers and dressed as fast as he could. He needed to pick up a few things for their night together, and he only had an hour before she was supposed to come over.

Arlo had secured him some beer, but he drew the line at buying his friends' personal protection. Josh needed to stop at Walgreens and pick up condoms. Aubrey was on the pill—the school nurse gave them out like they were raspberry Pez—but Arlo had told him that the first time was often hard on a girl and a little extra lube could go a long way toward making things easier.

Arlo had deflowered enough virgins around school that Josh didn't question the advice, but scooted to the back aisle and looked for the words *spermicidal lubricant* on the Trojan box. Only Trojans would do—big ones, he had that clear in his mind, at least.

The pharmacist narrowed his eyes at Josh but didn't say a word, rang up the purchase, and put it in one of those white plastic bags that were so thin they were practically clear. The ones that fairly screamed, *Look, look! I have something private and embarrassing inside me!*

The mortification over, he swung by Publix and grabbed a spray of roses and a frozen pizza. Plus Moose Tracks ice cream—Aubrey's favorite.

When he got home he busied himself with setting things up: flowers in a vase, candles on the table, pizza in the oven, beer in the fridge, ice cream in the freezer, condoms in the drawer next to his bed. He went up and shaved, just to be doubly smooth, and spent ten minutes deciding which T-shirt to wear.

At seven on the dot the doorbell rang, and Josh, clad in jeans and a black Pixies tee, launched himself down the stairs.

Aubrey was on the step, looking demure in a white dress and sandals. He nearly grabbed her and dragged her straight upstairs, but he had a protocol to follow.

They ate and laughed and were shy with each other. Aubrey drank a beer and got giggly. Josh drank one and got anxious. What if he wasn't any good? What if he really did hurt her?

He had another, and some of the fears were assuaged. Tipsy, they ran upstairs, and Josh coaxed Aubrey into trying on some of Daisy's things. Pretty clothes, jewelry. A pearl ring he'd always liked. Things he couldn't give her. Not yet.

She twirled around like a ballerina in his mother's favorite red chiffon dress, looking for all the world like a model. As he admired her, she twirled right into the dresser, knocking a slew of perfume bottles onto the floor. "Whoops!" She giggled, bending over to pick them up. Too big, the dress slid off her shoulders, and he was suddenly face-to-face with Aubrey's smooth white back.

Do it. Do it now.

He took a step toward her, and she looked back over her shoulder at him, stripped off the dress, grabbed her clothes, and ran, laughing, downstairs.

Leaving the disarray to clean up later, he followed.

He found Aubrey in the living room, wearing only a bra and panties. He had planned to start the evening here anyway.

He turned on some music, watching her edge around the room. She suddenly looked nervous, so he offered her another beer. She drank it, eyeing him over the edge of the can.

He sat down on the couch and patted the seat next to him. Aubrey joined him. They kissed for what seemed like years. Aubrey followed his lead with each step, and when his jeans were unbuttoned and her smooth hands were buried in his shorts and wrapped around his cock, he slid a finger inside her. They'd gone this far before, so he waited to see what she would do.

She kissed him again, then looked deep into his eyes.

"Get naked," she whispered.

"Let's go back upstairs," he replied.

"No. I don't want to move."

He understood that sentiment. He kept one finger inside her and used his other hand to shed the rest of her garments. She did the same for him, pulling off his jeans and boxers, and he realized this was happening, it was really happening. He lay down with her, skin to skin, legs to legs, belly to belly.

"Now," she whispered.

"I need a condom."

"I'm on the pill. It's fine. I don't want one."

"But it will hurt."

She shushed him with a kiss and reached between his legs. Her touch burned, and he didn't need any more coaxing. He used his thigh to spread her knees, then on a whim, scooted down and licked her. The taste was foreign, salt and silver and smooth, and he did it again, enjoying the sensation of her moving beneath him. It was the most intimate thing he'd ever done, and he was shocked when she moaned a little, like she was enjoying it. So he did it again, and again, and again, until his head started to swim.

Then he slid up her body and placed the tip of his cock against the spot he'd been licking. Aubrey hesitated for a moment, he felt her shift a bit and the smooth muscle of her thighs contract, but then she sighed and relaxed her legs apart. He started in, and the sensation blew his mind. Silk and soft and the richest warmth he'd ever felt. Dear God, no wonder people were obsessed with this. Aubrey gasped a little and tensed, then pulled him against her, hard, and before he knew it he was inside her all the way.

"Are you okay?" he asked, not moving, totally breathless.

"Go," she replied, so he did, sliding in and out, gritting his teeth as the sensations started to flood him. He couldn't help himself; he couldn't stop. He went faster and faster until everything exploded. It took him a full minute to come back down to earth.

When he could focus again, he saw Aubrey was looking up at him with a huge grin on her face.

"We should do that again." She smoothed a kiss against his lips.

"Are you okay? I didn't hurt you?"

"I love you, Josh. You could never hurt me."

He disentangled himself from her reluctantly. She looked like the Cheshire cat, happy and pleased with herself. He felt like a king. An emperor. This was his woman, and he'd just taken her. They'd been swept up in the moment and didn't even need the condom.

He pulled Aubrey into his arms and kissed her, with every intention of following up his inaugural performance with another, one that might last a bit longer. He was hard again so fast and above her, ready, when the voice froze him in place.

"Joshua David Hamilton! What in the name of God are you doing?"

Move. Move, Josh.

Aubrey's arms fell away from his back, and he jumped up from the couch to see Daisy standing in the door to the living room, her face aghast.

"Oh, shit," Aubrey said, and that did it. Daisy went ballistic. But she didn't curse at Josh, or hit him, or any of the things he expected. Instead, she marched to the phone and dialed. She pointed a finger at Aubrey, who was trying to get into her bra. "I'm done with you, missy."

"Mom, relax. We were just—"

"I know exactly what you were doing with that little slut. I saw my bedroom. Letting her try on my clothes? Having sex with her on my couch? You're disgusting. Yes, police?"

"Mom—"

"Mrs. Hamilton—"

"Shut it, both of you. Yes, ma'am. I've just returned home to find that my house has been broken into. I have the girl who did it here in my living room. I insist you send a patrol car to arrest her immediately. She's underage, and it looks like she brought alcohol in the house as well. Yes. Yes, I have her name. Aubrey Trenton."

Daisy hung up the phone with a manic gleam in her eyes.

"You've got it coming," she spit at Aubrey. "Josh, you are grounded, and I forbid you from seeing this girl ever again."

"Mom, you're overreacting."

Daisy ignored him, went to guard the front door.

Aubrey was crying. Josh was torn. Calm his mother, get her to cancel her threats, call off the police—Jesus, she'd called the cops?—or comfort Aubrey. He chose Aubrey, tried to put his arms around her, but she stood, frozen, a statue in his living room. Heard a little gasp come from his mother, like she'd been cut with a knife, ignored it.

"It's okay. I won't let them in. I promise."

Aubrey didn't respond, just stood there crying, eyes downcast.

He decided to try reasoning with Daisy.

"Wait for me. I'll fix this."

Aubrey didn't acknowledge him, so he caressed the top of her head and left her in the living room. His mother was stationed at the front door, arms crossed on her chest, face drawn. He could feel her fury from across the room; waves of negative energy spilled off her body.

"Mom. You can't do this. You can't call the police on her. I invited her here. This is my fault."

"I just did. Oh, and look. Here they are." She flung open the door and waved to the officer who'd pulled into the drive.

Josh didn't know what to do. *My God, how had the night gotten so off track?*

The policeman conferred with his mother. He put his hand on his gun belt and started into the house. Josh stepped in front of him, decision made. He wouldn't let this happen.

"I'm sorry, sir, but my mother is mistaken. No one broke in here. I invited my girlfriend over for dinner. My *mother*"—he couldn't help himself, the disdain came through loud and clear on the first note of her name—"caught us fooling around and has overreacted. She isn't fond of my girlfriend, you see."

"That's not true. Josh wasn't home when I

arrived. It was just that girl, and she was in my jewelry box, trying to steal things. She has stolen one of my rings, it's missing from the jewelry box, it has a pearl in it, and—"

"Mom!" Josh was shocked. He couldn't believe she'd lie to the police.

"Now, son," the man said, reasonable and kindly. "Move out of the way. I just want to talk to the girl."

"Aubrey Trenton, that's her name. She's a little criminal. Lives with criminals, it's not surprising she's become one herself." Daisy was screeching. Josh gritted his teeth and turned on her.

"You are lying, Mother. Stop this."

She just pointed over his shoulder.

"See? Am I lying? Look. The back door's been broken out."

Josh and the policeman looked where she indicated. The door was broken. The only way to lock and unlock the door was with a key for the deadbolt. Daisy liked it for security; Tom always warned that it was a fire hazard. Josh saw the splintered wood and his stomach dropped. He turned and went to the living room, not surprised to find it empty.

An animal, when cornered, will do most anything to escape.

CHAPTER 32

Aubrey
Today

It was nearly six in the evening, the hospital buzzing with shift changes. In Daisy's room, they were just getting ready to make the pass-off from Tom to Aubrey when the doctor came in, all kinds of jovial.

"Hi, Tom, Aubrey." He turned to the bed. "Evening, Miss Daisy. Want to get that tube out of your throat?"

Daisy blinked rapidly, her sign for absolutely, yes.

Rasha joined the group, and the doctor shooed Aubrey and Tom out into the hall.

It wasn't even a full five minutes before Rasha came and grabbed them. "She did great. But let's not tire her out too quickly, okay?"

Daisy was sitting up in the bed, looking wan and pale, the bits of the halo biting into the skin of her forehead, making the surrounding tissue red and angry. She ignored Tom, focused laser-like on Aubrey.

The first thing she asked was "Where . . . is . . . Josh?"

Aubrey was tempted to smooth the hair back from Daisy's forehead but resisted, knowing the gesture wouldn't be welcome. Instead, she played with her own hair, trying to get the curls secured behind her ear. She glanced at Tom, who gave a half shrug and a nod.

"Daisy, I've told you this before, but you've been under a lot of sedation. I'm not sure how much of your memory has been affected by the accident. But Josh passed away. Five years ago."

Daisy's bruised face wrinkled in thought. Her words came out in a horrifying rasp. Aubrey could only imagine how much it hurt Daisy to speak.

"That's . . . not . . . right. You're . . . wrong. I swear . . . I saw . . . him here."

Here we go again.

"That was Chase. He's my . . . friend."

A friend. That was putting it mildly. Yes, their dating had evolved differently from the normal "boy meets girl, three dates, and then it's okay to have sex" setup. Instead they'd started with the passion, and were only now getting to know each other.

Chase was erudite, and funny, and compassionate. Similar to Josh in many ways, selflessness and generosity just the beginning. He was due back in Nashville tomorrow, and she couldn't wait to see him again.

Daisy snorted, her face pinched at the word *friend*. Her voice was getting stronger now.

"I know I saw Josh. I know it. Why are you keeping him from me, Aubrey? Why won't you let me see my son?"

"Daisy, I promise you. Chase is not Josh. Josh is dead, Daisy. Even the courts say so."

"Tom?" Daisy turned to her husband, imploring. "Tell her she's wrong. Tell her I saw him. He was right here. He was at her house. I saw him."

The beeping monitors ratcheted up a few notches, and Rasha stepped in.

"We need to keep her calm. Why don't we talk about something else? Daisy, you're such a quick healer. If things keep going well, we'll be able to unscrew the halo. And then you'll be able to go—"

"Shut up!" Daisy shrieked, then started to cough. The monitors went crazy, and Rasha hurried them away.

In the overlit hallway, Tom turned to Aubrey. "I think you should go on home now. I'll handle her tonight."

As disloyal as it was—Tom had been on duty for hours and must be exhausted—Aubrey felt nothing but pure relief. It was one thing to watch over Daisy when she couldn't fling her vitriol, but now that she was talking again, Aubrey would become the target, and she really didn't want to be forced into arguing with a woman who'd nearly died, even one as horrible as Daisy. "Are you sure?"

"Yeah. I'll get her on the right page. You can come back tomorrow."

"Okay, Tom. If you think it's best." She gave him a hug and tried not to let the skip in her step show. She'd be able to get a run in, shower, and actually spend the night in her own bed. And Winston would be in heaven—he missed his mommy. Meghan and Linda had been taking turns on the nightly and morning walks.

After her run, Aubrey could continue her long-distance seduction of Chase. And see if Tyler had had any luck tracking down the man named Derek Allen.

CHAPTER 33

Chase

Chase stared out the window of his apartment in Lincoln Park, watching the neighborhood women pushing strollers toward the zoo. It was a perfect Chicago spring day, almost warm, bright and sunny, and it felt like the whole city had emerged to get some fresh air.

Aubrey.

Focus, Chase.

He tapped the keyboard again, pulling his notes together. Cursed his naïveté for thinking he could play fast and loose with his own reality.

Every investigative reporter dreams about the moment he uncovers something no one else has and breaks a story wide open. Chase thought he just might have the lead he needed to blow the Joshua Hamilton story out of the water. And he'd been sitting on it for two hours because he now had a bigger problem on his hands.

He couldn't stop thinking about Aubrey Hamilton.

Chase wasn't a player. Yes, he'd bedded his fair share of women, but he'd never been with one who he wanted to protect. He'd felt downright chivalrous when the police had shown up at Aubrey's door and started hounding her. He wanted to punch the officer in the face, had forced himself to take a breath and speak calmly. It had hurt him to see Aubrey getting upset, to watch her walls go back up. He'd hated to leave the next day, but he had to get back to Chicago to file a piece on the new MacBook and get his assignments for the week. The whole time, all he could think about was getting back to Nashville, holding her in his arms.

He had a whole alternate reality going on. He was supposed to be investigating Aubrey. Instead, he was helping her with her mother-in-law, bolstering the family in their time of need. He'd liked Tom Hamilton, and while he wanted to get as far away from Daisy as possible, he also hated to leave them. And it was tearing him up because he knew that was crazy. He was looking for a story, not a family.

His boss had warned him about this. Getting too close to a subject. Becoming involved. It killed your perspective, made the story into something it wasn't.

How was he going to keep on this path? He couldn't betray Aubrey. She'd been betrayed by too many others.

He heard his boss in his head: *That girl must have a magic cooch to get you off the scent.*

Maybe you need to follow that line of thinking, Chase. Like the papers said, Mata Hari and all that. You know she has something to do with her husband's disappearance. You know it.

Yet he didn't care. All he really wanted was to

run his hands along her body, and bury himself inside her. To smell her scent and make her laugh. To wake up with her beside him, curled in a snug little ball against his stomach.

He went back to the window, feeling terribly low. These were dangerous thoughts. Especially after the things the investigation had shown about her. That there was a coldness in her. That she'd acted off from the beginning. That he needed to look deeply into her background, the life she'd led, the people she'd hung out with. Criminals, all.

He didn't want to see Aubrey get hurt, knew he couldn't trust her. But . . .

The demon on his shoulder laughed uproariously. *You can't be in love, you idiot. You've only seen her twice.*

Love?

The idea shocked him into action. The demon was right. He was simply in lust. Aubrey Hamilton was a pretty, vulnerable woman, but she was a story to him. He'd made a mistake bedding her; that was stupid, the result of desire, too much drink, and a deep-seated need to get to the bottom of her mystery and make a name for himself.

But he wasn't in love. He absolutely wasn't.

But he was completely compromised, and it was time to own up to the truth.

He called his editor, told him what was going on. That he couldn't go forward with the story until the wife knew he was doing the piece on her husband. Because, really, unless Josh Hamilton *was* alive and came back for her, there'd be no story anyway. That he'd find out the truth faster this way, that she'd absolutely play along, and no, of course he wasn't doing anything stupid.

His editor balked, but Chase promised this was the right angle. Get the wife on board, come at it from the inside.

His editor refused. Push through, he said. This is a huge piece. Career-making, for you and for the paper.

Chase said no. And his editor gave him a choice.

Do the piece, or get a new job.

Without hesitating, he agreed to the latter and quit. Hung up on his boss and his career, ignored the phone when it rang back, his boss's voice on the answering machine telling him to take a few days and think it over, and clicked on his notes again.

He was going to have to show this picture to Aubrey at some point. Coming clean meant coming clean all the way.

How would she react? How would she feel? Destroyed all over again, probably.

Well, Chase might be the harbinger of ill tidings, but he also planned to stick around and pick up the pieces.

CHAPTER 34

Aubrey
Today

Aubrey purposefully walked by the cafeteria as she left, just in case the creep was there waiting. She didn't see him, and sagged a bit in relief. Despite her bravado, she didn't know if she was up for another confrontation.

She couldn't get Josh out of her mind, and Daisy's attack had left her drained and upset. All the old doubts were rising to the surface, her concerns and worries. She used to be so strong. So fearless. With Josh at her side, she could conquer the world.

The new Aubrey was prone to anxiety, carried her Ativan with her everywhere. She recognized that a pill was in order, so she went to the parking garage on the second floor where she'd seen a soda machine once when she was lost in the night. She slid a dollar into the slot and got a bottle of water.

Josh wasn't the man you knew, Aubrey. Oh, she knew him. Knew every inch of him.

Pill taken, she headed around the building to the aboveground parking lot. She refused to park in the underground lot at night. It was too dark, too lonely. Unsafe.

Aubrey dialed Tyler's number, put the cell to her ear. Voicemail, again. She left him another message: "Tyler, I need to talk. Please call me when you get this."

Damn it, she needed Tyler to find out what he could about this Derek Allen character, but he'd dropped off the radar. Aubrey knew there was a good chance he was holed up with a bag and a syringe, and would emerge sometime soon needing money, or bail. So she was left to figure out the secrets alone.

She handed the ticket to the valet. He ran off to retrieve her car, and she thought about Daisy, lying in the bed upstairs, convinced Chase was her long-dead son. It was interesting that she'd seen the resemblance between Josh and Chase, too. At least Aubrey knew she wasn't losing her mind entirely. Meghan couldn't see it at all. Meghan was too rational, too fixed. Too focused on helping Aubrey move past her tragedy and start living again.

Meghan.

Perfect.

Aubrey glanced at her watch. Meghan had insisted Aubrey take a few days off from the store to deal with the Daisy situation, so they hadn't talked outside of scheduling walks for Winston. She would still be at work.

The valet returned with the Audi, and she headed toward Frothy Joe's.

Spring had absolutely rioted overnight. Buttery daffodils bloomed across the Vanderbilt campus, and the trees had greened up. The suddenness of the seasons in Nashville sometimes caught Aubrey off guard. One day it would be frigid, and the next the forsythia would scramble out, desperate to be seen by all passersby, the sun would linger in the evening sky, and a hint of warmth would pulsate in the breeze. The bank sign said it was seventy degrees—a certain harbinger of the impending weather shift. They went winter to summer many years, without a discernible spring.

But this year was different. This year, they were having the lost season.

Traffic was light, and she arrived at the coffee shop in less than ten minutes. Meghan was setting up for another poetry slam when Aubrey arrived.

"Heya, kid. How're you doing? How's Daisy?"

Aubrey gave Meghan a quick hug. "They finally took her off the ventilator. She immediately started asking for Josh. She thinks Chase is Josh."

"Looney tunes." Meghan smiled at Aubrey. "Chase is back in town tomorrow?"

"Yes." Aubrey couldn't help but smile back.

"Slut."

"I'm not." But she had to admit, she enjoyed the teasing. Who would have thought?

"Are you going to stick around tonight? We have another event, and I could use the help."

Aubrey considered for a moment. Linda was going to walk Winston at nine—she'd have time to get home before then. "All right. I was hoping to have some quiet time, but mercenary that I am,

I could use the money. And you and I can talk—I have a favor to ask."

"Deal. Now get crackin', sister. This place won't set itself up."

Aubrey stuck out her tongue at her best friend and got to it. She went in the back and started bringing out chairs. The extra help made things go quicker. The whole room was set in five minutes. The event began at seven. When she'd done the author introduction, Meghan signaled to Aubrey and they went to the front of the store. There were a few students, headphones in, heads bobbing to an invisible beat. Private enough.

Meghan grabbed them each a cup of coffee, and they settled themselves on the stools at the counter.

"So . . . ?" she said, watching Aubrey carefully.

"I need your help. But you have to promise to hear me out, okay? Don't interrupt. Let me tell you the whole story, and then you can make a decision."

Meghan gave her that cocked-head "are you off your rocker again?" look.

"Seriously, Meghan. This is important."

"Okay, okay. I will sit and sip my coffee and let you spin me a tale."

"Good. Thank you. A man approached me at the hospital last night. He implied that Josh was alive, and if I wanted answers to call him. He gave me his card, but I spilled coffee on it, so I can't see the number. He seemed really familiar, but I can't place him."

"Let me see the card."

Aubrey handed it over. Meghan glanced at it, and Aubrey could have sworn her face paled. She set it down carefully on the counter.

"Go on."

"All right. You know how when I saw Chase for the first time, I thought he was Josh? So did Daisy. She was so convinced it was him, she drove into my house. She got excited, her foot jammed on the gas. She—"

"Was drunk off her ass. Didn't you say her blood alcohol level was .23?"

"Meghan. Interruption."

"Oh, forgive me. Please, by all means, continueth." She grinned contritely, and Aubrey shook her head.

"As I was saying. She was so convinced he was Josh that she slammed into the house. When she got the tube out, the first thing she said was 'Where is Josh?' I figured she'd just forgotten he was dead, but when we talked, she just didn't believe me. She thinks I'm holding him back.

"And when Tyler showed up, he told me he spent a night in holding with a guy who claimed he was running drugs with a med student out of Vandy."

Meghan sat there for a moment, then said, "Oh, I'm allowed to speak now?"

"Yes. I need to find out if the med student he was talking about was Josh."

Meghan leaned forward. "Your Josh? Running drugs? That's ridiculous."

Aubrey swallowed. "I don't know if it is, Meghan.

I'm going to ask Chase for help. He's a reporter. Maybe he can do some digging or something." She sat back and watched the emotions course over her best friend's face. At least Meghan didn't laugh.

Meghan got up and poured them fresh coffees, then turned back to Aubrey.

"This is insane, you know that."

"I do," Aubrey replied. "You didn't know him, Meghan. He was born to save people. He saved me. And all he wanted to do was help others. He wasn't a criminal, didn't have that kind of mindset. If he got himself into something and got in over his head, and they killed him for it, and people are starting to talk about it . . . I have to know. I have to find out what really happened."

"No one's perfect, sugar. Especially saviors."

Aubrey sighed. "I know. But he was pretty damn close."

"What do you think Chase will say about all of this?"

"No idea. He's been very interested in the story, as you can imagine. He may walk, he may want to help. I won't know unless I ask."

Meghan straightened the napkins on the bar. She shook her head while she thought, the small diamond in her left ear cartilage winking, like a star moving in and out of the clouds. Aubrey sat silently, waiting. Either Meghan would believe her and want to help, or she'd laugh her out of the store, and Aubrey would be forced to try elsewhere.

"Do you honestly think Josh could have been involved in an illegal drug ring?"

"Someone killed him, Meghan. At this point, anything is possible."

"But don't you think the police would have followed that trail back then? Do you remember them saying anything about Josh being involved in something?"

"They weren't exactly talking to me, and it didn't come up in the trial. But Josh was acting strange before he disappeared. I thought it was the stress from school, and his extra job at the ME's office. He wasn't getting a lot of sleep. Burning the candle."

"The ME's office?"

"Yeah. We needed extra money. He had changed his mind about his specialty. It was going to add time to his schooling, so he took the job at the morgue to supplement our income."

Meghan looked at her strangely. "You realize no one has ever mentioned he worked at the medical examiner's office."

Aubrey stilled. "What do you mean?"

"I mean in every article I've ever read about Josh, none ever mentioned he had a second job. Did you tell the police this?"

"Of course. Why were you reading about Josh?"

Meghan laughed shortly. "Aubrey, you're my best friend. Of course I read about your husband's case. Knowing stuff about him helped me help you. When you were having bad times."

"Let's not go there."

"Agreed. Though you start digging into this, you could end up right back in the hospital. You know that, right?"

Aubrey looked into the depths of her coffee. "I am a lot stronger now than I was."

"All right. So maybe he lied to you about working at the ME's office. Let me ask you this. Did you ever find anything odd, something that you didn't know Josh had? Keys, notebooks, parking stubs? Drugs? Anything that might be suspicious?"

"Meghan, no. Not that I know of. I was grieving, though, and they put me through hell, interrogating me, harassing me. I wasn't exactly looking for lost keys or parking stubs, and the drugs I was taking were my own. Then we packed everything up and Daisy took it. I don't even have it anymore."

They both drifted into silence. Meghan pulled out her laptop from under the counter, was clicking the keys. Aubrey didn't know what she was looking up; she just kept shaking her head, muttering "This is crazy" under her breath over and over. Aubrey understood that sentiment. She felt the same way.

"Whoa. Look at this."

"What is it?"

"Derek Allen. If this is the same guy, Aubrey . . . he was held for questioning in the murder of a drug kingpin out of Mexico." She tapped away, then pulled up the Davidson County

Criminal Court website. "I can plug in his name and see his arrest record."

"Are there pictures?"

"Not in this database, no. And a Google search isn't picking anything up."

"What about DC Investigations? That was on the card he gave me."

Meghan's brows furrowed. "Nothing. Aubrey, I think you need to go to the police, and tell them he came to see you."

"You're kidding, right? Me, go to the police?"

"This Derek Allen guy is trouble." She flipped the computer around. "Look at his sheet. His most recent arrest was for aggravated murder. He was sentenced, he's been in jail. He's no one to be playing with."

"No police. No way." Aubrey thought back to the conversation she had with Tyler. "This has to be the guy Tyler was talking about who was being released. But why would he come to me and say these things about Josh?"

Meghan finally closed the browser and looked at Aubrey speculatively.

"Sometimes you can be so charmingly naive."

"I am not. And Josh is dead."

Meghan sipped her coffee. "Listen. I've never told you this, but years ago, I used to be married to a private investigator. If you won't go to the cops, I could ask him to look into this for you."

Aubrey felt her pulse begin to race. "You were married to a PI?"

Meghan shrugged. "He was always off on

stakeouts trying to catch men in awkward positions so their wives could divorce them and get a bundle of cash. It was unseemly, really."

"Still. I'm your best friend. I can't believe you never told me."

Meghan sighed. "It was a lifetime ago, sugar, and it didn't end well. Besides, sharing, it's not my way. Once something is done, it's over, and there's no sense looking back over your shoulder and wishing things could be different. That way lies madness."

As soon as the words were out, Meghan winced.

Aubrey looked at the floor. "Ouch."

"Sorry. My bad. Let's get back to the matter at hand. Daniel and I are friends of a sort, now that we have some distance. And I have to admit, you've got me intrigued. Though I'm shocked that none of this came up during the initial investigation."

"Why would it?" Aubrey asked. "Why would anyone tie an upstanding young doctor-to-be who went missing from his friend's bachelor party to a drug dealer?"

"If the investigators were worth their salt, they would have looked at every angle."

"But it's such an obtuse angle, Meghan. They were looking at me. Maybe they missed it."

"You don't know that."

Aubrey narrowed her eyes. "You don't know that they did."

"We'll have to find out. We have to go at this

from two ends." Meghan stood and started straightening the counter. "It's just crazy enough to make sense, though. That Josh was involved in a drug ring, got himself hurt, but got away, and now that he's been declared dead, he's back from the grave, looking for the insurance money."

Aubrey felt the familiar sense of unease at the idea of the insurance payout. "Wow, Meghan. You should write novels. Josh is dead. We all know that. He can't come back from the grave for the money."

"When does the settlement go through?"

"Friday."

Meghan shrugged. "It's a jumping-off point. And you're still planning to tell Chase what you've found out?"

"Yes. I think he might be able to help."

Meghan fiddled with her cup. "I don't know if you should."

"Why not?"

"Isn't that obvious, Aubrey?"

"No. It isn't."

"Look at this clearly, Aubrey. You have an emotional stake in the outcome. And that's going to cloud your judgment. It looks to me like someone's messing with you. You can't be sure it's not Chase. He could be behind all of this."

"Meghan, that's ridiculous. Chase is not involved in this."

Meghan just nodded, curt, and Aubrey had to bite back a nasty retort. She didn't believe that; she couldn't. Chase was a good guy caught up in a strange situation. Instead, she said, "I can't tell you how much I appreciate your help."

Meghan smiled. "I can't promise anything. But now you have me intrigued." They heard clapping from the back of the store. "I can break this down. Go home, get some sleep. I'll call you tomorrow after I've had a chance to talk to Daniel."

CHAPTER 35

Aubrey left Frothy Joe's feeling oddly optimistic. She was on the path to finding real answers about what happened to Josh.

She couldn't believe Meghan had held out on her like this. She'd been married to a PI? Why hadn't she offered his help with Josh before?

Because Josh was dead. And her responsibility as your friend was to help keep you sane and functioning.

And Meghan had done just that. For five years she'd been by Aubrey's side, wiping away tears, fixing meals, taking away the empty bottles, reminding her to take her medicine.

Five years of friendship, of laughter, of sorrow. Aubrey hadn't ever had a friend like Meghan before. No, that wasn't true. She'd had Josh.

She was home in five minutes. The gaping hole in the brick made the already shabby house look horrible. She'd have to call the insurance company again tomorrow and see when they could get someone out to assess the damage. Shaking her head, she went inside. Winston was overjoyed to see her, licked her on the face, then went to his lead. He wanted to run. And so did she.

As she laced up her shoes, she thought of Daisy, of her blank stare, the pain crossing her eyes when Aubrey reminded her Josh was dead. Of her certainty that Chase was Josh. It was disconcerting, and made this whole situation that much weirder. She was missing something, something big.

She left the house with Winston, let him guide her. He went up the hill, toward 25th, legs stretching, and she knew he was headed toward the park. Tonight it didn't seem like such a horrible place to go. They raced up the hill, then settled in for a nice comfortable run. They circled Dragon Park, not stopping at the tree. She thought about Chase as she ran, and was back home in an hour.

Aubrey was hungry. That was something new. She wasn't used to these feelings: hunger, desire, contentment. She just knew she was about to have answers, and even if they hurt, even if they cut to the bone, there was a path to the light.

She fed Winston and was putting the finishing touches on a bowl of spaghetti when the doorbell rang. Winston scrambled to the door, nails clicking on the floor, and barked, three times, in quick succession.

She set the bowl on the counter and went to the door. Glanced out the peephole. Tyler.

Finally. She pulled the door open.

"I've been trying to reach you. Where have you been?"

When he didn't answer right away, she registered the truth. Tyler's skin had a grayish tinge to it, one Aubrey recognized. How quickly he had fallen. He'd used again and was trying to kick the heroin. He was in withdrawal.

"Hey, sis." He was shaking from head to toe.

"Oh, Tyler," she said. Her heart really did hurt for him. What he went through trying to get and stay clean she wouldn't wish on her worst enemy. It was hell. He got so very sick.

"Come in. What do you need?"

"It's that obvious?"

"You forget, we've done this before."

He tried for a smile, but only managed a grimace. He stepped into the house, and she shut the door behind him.

"Couch or bed?" she asked.

"Couch."

She got him settled in the living room. "What happened?"

"Got waylaid by a friend, looking for info on Derek Allen. I'm sorry."

"Why didn't you go to the clinic?"

"Did."

"So you have the methadone? Why haven't you taken it?"

"Did," he said again. "Isn't working. Not like it should."

He started to shiver. She covered him with an afghan, got him a glass of water and the tall plastic wastepaper basket lined with a trash bag. He was in for a rough night.

"Were you able to find anything—"

But Tyler was gone, passed out cold.

Aubrey supposed this was penance. She vacillated between love and hate for Tyler. The hate all stemmed from the fact that he knew her, knew what her life had been, what she'd been through, in ways Josh never had. She'd never told Josh what happened. She'd never spoken of it to anyone.

But Tyler knew. Tyler knew she'd been sullied. It was like everything that had happened to her was a result of her past. If she'd kept the door closed that night, she would have led a completely different life, with a completely different outcome. Most importantly, Josh might still be alive.

If only.

She got Tyler some water and retrieved her spaghetti. She ate in the kitchen, not wanting to sicken him with the smell if he woke up. The food was so good. She ate like she hadn't eaten in years, with gusto. She even had seconds. Then she cleaned the kitchen and tiptoed into the living room. Tyler was still asleep but restless, a fine sheen of sweat covering his face.

She took her laptop and went to her bedroom. Tyler would wake soon enough, needing food or water or the bucket emptied. She'd take advantage of the lull to send a note to Chase. Just a quick *Hey, how are you? I'm home. Call me.*

Meghan didn't want her to mention anything about Josh, not just yet. Aubrey felt like she was going to go mad, waiting. After five years, she finally had a spark of hope, and she didn't want to wait any longer. If she hadn't known all the parts of him, there was such possibility. She'd spent five years having to believe he was dead, for that was the only way he'd abandon her. But what if . . . ?

She made a promise to herself. She wouldn't hide from Chase. She'd tell him all of her story, all the blank spots she'd glossed over, and let the chips fall where they may.

Before she started to type, the phone rang. It was Chase. As if she'd summoned him from thin air.

With a smile, she answered. "Hey. How are you tonight?"

"Fine. All good. Did you have a nice run?"

"How'd you know I went for a run?"

"You're out of the hospital before dark, that's why."

"Wow. You already know me so well. What time is your flight tomorrow?"

"I'll be there in the afternoon. I have a car, don't worry about picking me up. Aubrey—" He broke off, and she heard something odd in his tone. "We need to talk."

Her heart started beating double time. "About what?"

"Just . . . things. I have something I want to say, but I want to do it in person. Okay?"

She fought to keep the tears from her voice. "If you're breaking up with me, you can do it now and save the plane fare."

"Whoa, no. That's not it."

"Then what is it?"

"Tomorrow, honey. I have to go now. Sweet dreams, okay?"

"Yeah, you, too." She hung up the phone and started to cry in earnest.

She couldn't lose him now. Not now. Not when everything was starting to come together.

She opened her email again, planning again to send him a note.

And saw a new mail, from an unknown address. With only two words in the subject line:

He's alive.

Her heart took off. She clicked on the mail. It took a moment to pull up. The image began to scroll onto the screen, pixel by pixel. Dark and grainy, like an art house black-and-white.

Except this wasn't an art house photo.

Aubrey's hand went to her mouth to fight the sudden nausea that threatened to overtake her.

Josh. Josh standing in a darkened corner, facing the camera. A woman's white-blond hair hovering at his waistline. His eyes closed, head thrown back in ecstasy.

She shut her eyes, willing the photo to disappear, for the shocking pain that lit her skin to fade. When she opened her eyes, the photo was still there, and a fine rage began to build, fiery hot, lighting her from within.

She didn't know who was playing with her mind, but she wasn't going to fall for it. Not again.

CHAPTER 36

Aubrey
Five Years Ago

Aubrey drove Arlo's car to the house. Arlo was silent, drumming his fingers on his knee, still smelling like tequila and stale vomit. She didn't care. She just wanted to get home.

The house was dark. April had turned into a blackberry winter; the windows were glazed with an edge of frost along the sill. Aubrey parked on the street, for some reason not wanting to be in her own driveway. She was overcome with dread. Something was so, so wrong.

Arlo tripped as he was getting out of the car, and went down hard on his knees.

"Whoops," he said. Normally they would be laughing; Arlo was still a little drunk and very ungainly, but now, all she could do was grit her teeth and go around the nose of the car to help him.

"What's this?" he said under his breath.

She could see him in the glow from the street-lights. He was on his butt, staring at his hand.

"I'm bleeding," he said.

"Come on. Josh has a first aid kit in every bathroom. I'll patch you up."

Eerie, the similarities: Josh had patched her up

just hours before. Her lip throbbed in turn with the memory, and she realized her neck was sore. Whiplash rearing its ugly head.

Arlo held out his nonbloody hand, and she hauled him to his feet.

They entered through the front door, and Aubrey smelled something she couldn't identify.

"Josh?" she called. Total silence. "Josh? Where are you?" Nothing. Not even the sound of nails scrabbling on the hardwood floors, a noise so natural, so normal, that not hearing it made her tense immediately.

"Winston? Wiiiinston. C'mere, boy!" The dog didn't respond to her, and she felt the hair rise on the back of her neck.

"What's that smell?" Arlo could scent it, too, apparently.

"Arlo. Stop where you are, okay?"

He listened without question, and she stepped into the living room and turned on the lamp.

It took a moment to process what she was seeing. Winston was lying by the fireplace, unmoving. There were smears of red along the hardwood floor.

Arlo was staring at the floor and his hand, in turns. He looked up and met her eye. "Aubrey, we need to call the police again. They'll have to listen to you now."

Aubrey whirled to him, eyes wide, then dashed from the room, flipping on lights as she went. "Josh? Josh? Oh, God, Arlo, there's blood everywhere."

She stopped in the door to the kitchen. Viscous fluid covered a large area, about four feet wide, in a strangely configured puddle that looked a bit like the outline of Italy.

"Holy fuck," Arlo said, joining her in the doorway. "Don't go in there, Aubrey. Don't disturb the evidence."

She wheeled on him, her voice a screech. "How can you be rational at a time like this?"

She tore back into the living room, to Winston. The dog was breathing, but out cold. Aubrey collapsed next to him, frantically petting his unmoving head. She heard Arlo on the phone, all traces of drunk gone from his voice. He sounded so old, so serious, so grown up.

"This is Arlo Tonturian. We called earlier to report Josh Hamilton missing. We're at the Hamilton home right now, and there's blood everywhere." His voice dropped to a whisper, cracking on the last note. He thought she couldn't hear, but she could. And the words cut a knife through her soul.

"I think he's been murdered."

CHAPTER 37

Chase

Once he hung up, he at least felt like he could sleep tonight. Even her voice made him calm. His earlier doubts were gone—he thought he might actually be in love.

This was not how he'd expected the story to go. He'd never felt like this, not as a grown man, at least. She was everything he'd ever wanted, even as messed up as he knew she was.

He would tell her the truth tomorrow and hope she'd forgive his subterfuge. And pray like hell Josh Hamilton really was dead as a doornail. Because he didn't want anything to come between him and Aubrey. Not ever again.

But he had to go carefully. He still had questions, questions he didn't want to ask Aubrey. He didn't want to ruin what he had with her.

He pulled the card out of his pocket.

Dialed the number. Got voicemail. Debated hanging up, then steeled himself. *You have to do this, Chase. You can't quit now.*

"Sergeant Parks, this is Chase Boden. We met at Aubrey Hamilton's house earlier in the week. I was hoping you'd have time for a quick chat. Please call me back."

He was surprised when the phone rang five

minutes later. The caller ID showed a 615 area code. Parks.

"Hello?"

"Mr. Boden? This is Sergeant Bob Parks. What can I do for you?"

CHAPTER 38

Josh
Six Years Ago

Josh Hamilton was drinking coffee in the Starbucks across the street from Vanderbilt's campus, as was his daily habit once his time at the hospital was finished. The coffee shop's clientele was mixed: young, shiny-haired coeds and jeans-clad, sunglasses-wearing country music stars; aging, exhausted doctors and beautiful young trophy wives. It always gave him something to look at.

He settled into his favorite seat by the window near 21st Avenue. It had been a hard day. He'd just finished his first set of rounds on the surgical floor, and he was so tired his hands were shaking, and so exhilarated it would take hours to come down from the high.

Medical school was challenging, hard on the brain and on the body, even with a little bump here and there—they all did amphetamines; it was like mainlining caffeine. He'd resisted when they were first offered around but soon gave in. You had to do something to stay awake forty-eight hours straight. He'd known school would be difficult, had even desired that a bit, but he'd had no idea how taxing it would be on the body, and the mind. And today, he'd been faced with a wholly new challenge.

He'd always known what he wanted: to be a family practitioner. An old-fashioned make-house-calls, get-involved-in-patients'-lives, deliver-three-generations-of-babies-out-in-the-woods doctor. He'd seen *Doc Hollywood* when he was a kid and the message stuck. The idea that people who had less than he did deserved to be taken care of in exactly the same fashion as people with millions was intoxicating. He knew it would take a special man to be that kind of doctor. And he was certain he was up to the challenge. Made of all the right stuff. Honestly, he'd dreamed about it for so long he already felt he was.

But rounds this morning, his first surgical tour—he'd been completely seduced. With the slash of a knife, people could be made whole again. It was a skill he could bring to bear on his practice. If he was trained in surgery, he could be the only doctor those people would ever need. He'd be able to fix everything they had wrong himself.

The surgical resident had encouraged him to think long and hard about coming on board. His scores were fabulous; he'd be welcome in what-ever residency program he chose. Chances were he'd be able to land a slot here at Vanderbilt, with the right words in the right ears.

But to specialize in surgery meant another five years of training, at a measly salary that wouldn't begin to pay off his student loans.

He couldn't afford that. They couldn't afford

that. He wanted to give Aubrey the moon and stars. She'd grown up with next to nothing, basically the clothes on her back and little else. He wanted to give her indulgences, luxuries—jewelry, cars, houses, art. Trips to exotic locales, richly woven clothes. He had to start earning, now, to meet his lofty goals for their life. He didn't want to do this because he thought she'd love him more, not in the least. She'd had so little beauty in her life; he wanted to give her back some sparkle.

His haunted young love had grown into an exquisite young woman, one he was proud to call his wife. They were a perfect match. She was strong and loving and smart and selfless.

And patient. Aubrey was one of the most patient people he'd ever met. He didn't know if that was a result of being brought up without parents, having to share all her belongings with practical strangers, or whether it was ingrained in her personality. He wished he'd known her parents, could judge how much of them she'd gotten. Nature, nurture, all that.

But they'd died when she was so young, and he wasn't the kind of kid who hung around parents at that time. Which changed. When Aubrey's parents died, something shifted inside him, and he became a grown-up. Ten, and as mature as a twenty-year-old. He needed to be strong for her. Even then, he had an affinity for the curly-headed girl. There was something so incredibly different about her.

Different, and beautiful, and—as she was exposed to new, not-so-nice things—a quiet strength. Though she flouted the rules when they weren't to her liking, she was a good girl. Deep down inside, she was pure.

Unlike him. He was just a man. Just a man with a dream, and a wife he'd put up on a very high pedestal.

He sipped his coffee and pondered his life. He'd committed to paying for school himself, through a series of student loans coupled with savings—he'd started saving for college the day Aubrey's parents died, knowing somehow, inside of him, that he'd need to do this himself. He scraped and scrimped and saved every dime of his allowance, not indulging in records or candy or video games like his friends, approaching his growing stash with a miser's eye. But that money had run out at the end of his undergraduate career, and the loans were piling up. More training meant even more time before he'd even start making enough to begin paying off the loans.

He could ask his father for help. Tom had some money stashed away—he'd told Josh that before he left for school. Pulled him aside, told him he loved him, that he was proud to be his father, and that he'd been saving for him just like Josh saved for himself. It was an emergency fund of sorts, all slated for him. If he didn't need it now, he'd inherit it when Tom died. Daisy didn't know about it. It wasn't for her—God knew if she found out about spare change lying around, it would be spent immediately. But it was Josh's whenever he felt he wanted or needed it.

Becoming a surgeon, fulfilling a dream, this would certainly qualify for raiding Tom's funds.

What was he thinking? He needed to save that money for an emergency. A real emergency. No, he would find a way to pay off the loans himself. He needed to find a source of income on the side, most likely from a part-time job. He barely slept as it was; medical school wasn't exactly a restful experience, and the uppers meant he'd go for days, then crash, hard.

He could probably go to work somewhere like the medical examiner's office, as a tech. He'd done his pathology rotation, hadn't minded it much. And he knew a guy who worked over there; he had an in. The money wasn't insanely good, but the hours weren't bad. He didn't see himself slinging hash or drinks, though bartending could help things add up very quickly.

Then again, he was the one who held lives in his hands every day. Perhaps it would be better for Aubrey to take on the extra work. Maybe she could do some tutoring on the side, just a little extra to pay for groceries and the like. Or work in that coffee shop near their house that she loved so much. He'd seen the owner around, a pretty elfin thing, dark hair in a pixie cut, drinking at Sam's after the store closed. He could always approach her, see if she'd be willing to take on his wife for some part-time work. Then they'd be comfortable enough while he dedicated himself to a surgical residency.

She would do it if he asked. Aubrey would do anything for him.

His coffee was empty. He needed a refill. He went to the counter and scored some more, then returned to his seat and cracked his shiny new surgical text.

Normally he was great at blocking out the conversations around him. But when two men sat next to him, he couldn't help but overhear them. They were whispering, which drew his ear in the first place. People talking at normal levels weren't trying to hide their conversations—in fact he sometimes suspected such people wanted to be overheard. These two were being furtive, and it piqued Josh's curiosity.

He shifted his body so he could be a few inches closer. They didn't seem to notice. One was black, gently accented, and the other was an older white gentleman, impeccably dressed, who seemed much more relaxed and merely listened, encouraging information as it was needed.

From what Josh could ascertain, the black man needed a doctor. A specialist. So he must be sick. The white guy just smiled and nodded and said, "We'll find someone for you. Someone good who you can trust. Don't worry. I promise it will be okay."

The black man obviously didn't feel he was being taken seriously. He grew more and more frustrated until he finally stood and set his coffee on the table, said, "Mark my words." And left.

Josh stifled an internal giggle—the "Mark my words" had sounded a bit like Arnold Schwarzenegger saying, "I'll be back."

He glanced at his watch: 7:30 p.m. He needed

to get home to Aubrey, to Winston, to dinner, to sleep. To get up and do it all again.

He began to gather his things. The white guy sitting next to him had crossed his legs and was staring into space. Josh debated with himself, then shrugged. Why not? What did he have to lose?

"Sir? Excuse me."

The man tore his gaze from the deep space universe he was studying and glanced at Josh with an annoyed sigh.

"Yes, I'll watch your things. Go, go," he said.

Josh laughed. "Oh, no, sir. I'm actually leaving. It's just that I couldn't help but overhear your conversation. Your friend is ill and needs a specialist? I'm a doctor here at Vanderbilt. Fourth-year medical student. I know most everyone on staff. If you tell me what's troubling your friend, I could give you a recommendation." He stuck out his hand. "I'm Josh Hamilton, by the way."

The man studied him with his right brow raised ever so slightly. As if making a decision, he finally smiled, politely, and said, "Well, isn't this just serendipity." He accepted Josh's hand in his. "Derek Allen. Your offer intrigues me. Would you like to grab dinner and discuss things? Perhaps my colleague could be talked into joining us, and he can hear your suggestions firsthand."

Josh glanced at his watch.

"I should really be getting home."

"Oh, surely you have a few minutes. At least let me buy you another cup of coffee. You may be just what the doctor ordered, pun intended."

Josh had a feeling about the man. Something told him to call Aubrey and tell her he was going to be late.

"All right, Mr. Allen, let's go get some dinner. I'll just let my wife know I'm going to be gone awhile."

CHAPTER 39

Aubrey
Today

The sun was high in the sky when Aubrey reached Dragon Park. Sweat ran between her breasts and down the small of her back, but she pushed on, passing the mosaic dragon, until she reached the oak. She stopped short about one hundred feet from the tree and looked around.

Would he be here, waiting? Would he know that she'd figured it out?

She didn't see anything out of the ordinary, just the usual accumulation of parents and kids, dogs and plaid blankets and Frisbees, spread out across the grass. Still, she approached cautiously.

Two feet away, she could tell something was different.

She shoved her hand into the darkness and instead of feeling the note she'd secreted inside, she felt nothing. Emptiness. Something compelled her to reach in farther, and this time, she did feel something. It was soft, and square, and attached to a hard piece of parchment. She eased it out gently.

The parchment was an envelope, good Crane stationery, the old-fashioned kind.

And the soft square was a blue velvet box.

She closed her eyes. Recorded every movement, every sound, every smell. Honeysuckle on the wind, jasmine, mud, sweat, blueberries, the crying of a child, the bark of a dog.

When she felt like she would be able to remember the moment forever, she opened the box.

In it was a large diamond. Loose. The pointed end was pushed into the velvet liner. She was afraid to take it out, but having seen some of the sparklers her friends sported, she knew this had to be in the three- or four-carat range.

Her heart beat mercilessly. She slid the box closed and opened the note.

It had two handwritten words, handwriting she more than recognized.

Josh's handwriting.

I'm sorry.

She looked at the stone again, and suddenly it wasn't perfect. A large crack began, running across the surface, and with a rending creak, the diamond split in half and inside was the photograph of Josh, wound around a stranger, and the photo began to move, bucking and thrusting in her hand, and his face came from the black-and-white and said, "I'm sorry, I had to, I didn't have a choice."

Let no man tear them asunder.

Oh, God. She knew what this meant. She knew . . .

Aubrey woke, sweating, crying. Betrayed. Five years of hell, five years of worry, and he was alive, out there. Letting her suffer. Letting them all suffer.

Aubrey didn't remember her dreams often. It was something she'd turned off when she was a child, effectively muting her brain when she woke in the mornings. She had enough nightmares that she needed something for self-preservation, something to protect her and keep her whole. So she'd trained herself to forget.

It worked 90 percent of the time. So long as her life was on an even keel, the bad dreams stayed at bay. But things were on anything but an even keel now, and Aubrey had been dreaming extensively for the past few days, and they were staying with her long after she turned back the sheets.

The morning after seeing the email, she woke exhausted, like she'd been running for hours. As she thought about it, she realized she had: that was a whopper of a dream.

Winston must have heard her crying in her sleep because he was wedged firmly against her side. When she woke and shifted, he moved with her, a low woof questioning if she was okay.

She wasn't.

When she'd cried herself out, she rose and washed her face. The clock said 6:40 a.m.

Tyler.

She went downstairs and realized she was alone. Sometime in the night he'd crawled away—whether to give up and score a hit or because he was actually feeling better, she didn't know. She hadn't even heard him. After she'd seen the email, she'd collapsed, taken a couple of Ativan, and just huddled in bed, weeping.

She felt empty.

She didn't know what to do.

Chase was coming today. How was she supposed to face him? How was she supposed to function, knowing that Josh might actually be out there somewhere? Or that someone was trying to make her think he was? He'd think she was crazy. He'd run so fast and so far she'd never see him again.

Maybe she was.

She made a cup of tea and sat at the kitchen table. Put her head in her hands. Ran her mind over the details of the past week.

The cab, the man's walk. The confusion on his face when she turned him. The happiness he radiated when she'd seen him in the coffee shop. The caressing touches at the bar. The overwhelming sex.

Chase showing her pictures from his life, growing up with his family, his dad and mom and sister, happy and content. She watched him mature through the years.

Asking her questions, expecting answers to things she'd stopped thinking about, her life, her feelings, her dreams.

Encouraging her to disagree with him.

Chase Boden wasn't her husband. He was his own person. He wanted her, damaged and broken as she was. And she wanted him.

But Josh . . .

Five long years later, she was on the edge of the truth. Could Josh actually still be alive?

God, she didn't know. She doubted everything. Herself, her world. Her sanity. How could this happen? How could this be? All of the bits and pieces of the past week crashed together, and she realized that he could be.

Maybe Meghan was right. Josh had been waiting to be declared dead and had come back for the insurance money. He'd been hiding in plain sight this whole time.

And if he was alive? Would she discard Chase?

She said, "No," aloud, making the dog jump, even while she thought about what would happen if Josh walked through the door at this very moment.

She was living in a fantasyland. Josh was dead. She knew he was dead. Whoever sent that picture was screwing with her. Trying to unhinge her mind.

Aubrey had a strong desire to stick a knife in the stranger from the hospital. She replayed his approach in the cafeteria, but this time, when he broke off the piece of chocolate, she gutted the bastard and left him gasping and bleeding on the cafeteria floor.

She was sick of being manipulated. Derek Allen was playing with her. He was dangerous.

It was time he learned she was as well.

CHAPTER 40

Daisy
Today

Aubrey had left, Tom was asleep, and Daisy wanted to weep. She wanted to gnash her teeth and wail and rend the scratchy, nasty sheet into ribbons. It wasn't right. Her son couldn't be dead. He couldn't. She would have felt that. She would have been able to tell.

Wouldn't she?

She wanted to go find him. They were keeping him from her. What had she ever done to deserve such hatred, such spite? She'd always been a dutiful wife, a good mother. And yet despite all of her giving, she was treated like pond scum by the very people who should love and appreciate her the most.

She should be treated with respect.

Instead, she was stuck lying in the bed, practically motionless, on a sheepskin that smelled of acrylic and must, forced to suffer these indignities.

She hurt. So very badly. Despite the fact she should be healing, despite her bones knitting and the swelling reducing, something was very wrong. She could tell. It was worse than what they told her, or they just didn't know. But she felt the pieces of her life dripping away, slinking into the void. She wasn't going to survive.

She had told Tom how she felt, and he scoffed.

"Of course you are, sweetie. You just hurt now. We can get more pain meds for you. But the doctors are very encouraged by your progress, and they think you'll be out of here next week. You're doing great. You're just fine."

He didn't take her seriously. He'd never taken her seriously. Always faithful Tom trying to placate her, trying to remake the world in his own image.

Fuck that. She wasn't going to sit back anymore.

She had sent Tom away and tried to explain to a nurse what she was feeling inside. Something open. A hole, a vastness in places that were supposed to be solid. The nurse told her it was just the morphine.

It wasn't the drugs, or her imagination. She actually got upset enough the nurse called the chief resident on shift and asked him to come in and take a look.

Pass the buck. In case there *was* something wrong.

Daisy waited for the doctor to appear. Hospitals weren't conducive to impatient people.

He finally arrived, all smiles and good cheer. He was handsome, a bit thin through the chin and jaw, but with lively hazel eyes. He pulled a chair up next to her and settled in like he had all the time in the world.

"So, Miss Daisy, tell me what's going on."

So she did. She told him all that had happened—her family insisting her son was dead, the hole inside her, the way she'd been treated, how much she hurt, and not just the physical part. He nodded and patted her hand. She felt so comfortable she even told him she'd been drinking too much, before the accident, but that was only because she was so very, very lonely.

The doctor—his name tag read *T. Lowe*—asked, "Have you ever talked to anyone about this before, Daisy?"

"No. I mean, yes, of course, but no one really listened."

"I think I'd like to have a friend of mine come by and talk to you. Her name is Ann Frazier. She's a great listener."

"Is she a shrink?"

"Well, in a way. But she's a specialist. She deals only with neurological injuries. With your severe head trauma, you are probably having some very strong emotive responses to things. That might be why you're feeling like something is so very wrong. It might help to have someone who's very trained in this exact situation in to have a chat. I promise, if you don't like her, you don't have to talk to her. Deal?"

He smiled, perfect teeth glistening, and she didn't feel like she could do anything but agree. She didn't want him to think she wasn't a good sport.

"All right. If you think it's best. But I don't

know that talking is going to fix what's happening inside me. I swear something is wrong. I can feel it."

"Your mind can be making that feeling strong, Daisy."

"This is in my chest. I swear, Doctor. Something's wrong in there."

He stood and patted her on the hand again. "Okay, Daisy. You've convinced me. I'll set you up for an echocardiogram first thing in the morning. But I'll also schedule you some time with Dr. Frazier. You'll like her. I went to medical school with her at Vandy, I've known her for years. She's a good egg."

"Did you know my son?" The words popped out of Daisy's mouth before she could stop them. She didn't want him to leave. He was kind and understanding, and she hadn't felt that level of kindness for a very long time.

"I'm not sure. Was he a doctor here? I don't get out much, as you can imagine."

"He was in his fourth year of medical school when he . . . His name is Josh Hamilton."

Saying his name aloud was like a dose of icy water. She tensed up as she said it, and Dr. Lowe did as well.

"Oh, my. Miss Daisy. I didn't realize. Yes, I knew your son. He and I did a surgical rotation together. He was a fine man, a fine doctor. I'm so sorry for your loss."

"He's not gone, Dr. Lowe. He's not dead. I just saw him. He's alive."

She started to cry, and Lowe comforted her the best way he knew how. He grabbed the nearest nurse and had her give Daisy something that made her feel like she was floating fifty feet up in the air. She liked the way that felt.

It seemed to take hours to come down to the bed again. She must have slept, because the sky was lightening outside and her mouth was incredibly dry.

Tom came, and the shrink. She was a nice woman, and talked to them both. She had some idea of what Daisy was feeling—she'd been in a bad car accident herself when she was a child, had a head injury. They didn't think she would make it.

It's why she wanted to be a doctor.

Frazier kicked Tom out of the room then, and she and Daisy had a long, soul-searching talk. A full fifteen minutes. That's how long it took for Daisy to realize they all just thought she was crazy. They were humoring her. The bastards.

Daisy shut down and refused to speak anymore. Frazier promised to come back, and Daisy told her not to bother. When the shrink had left and Tom came back, Daisy explained that she was never to come again.

Tom tried to argue with her, but she was adamant.

The nurse came and gave her another shot, and Tom went away. Daisy slept. When she woke, it was to an unaccustomed level of silence. She looked around, trying to understand why things were so still. Her eyes swept to the right, and she saw a man standing in the doorway to her room. He was partially in shadow. Was it that nice young doctor?

He moved, and Daisy felt her heartbeat skip. It made her breath come short, and she gasped. It wasn't Dr. Lowe. It was someone else. He frightened her.

"Who's there?"

The man came closer. Once his face was out of the shadows, she drank him in. Dirty blond hair, deep brown eyes, high cheekbones.

"Oh, my God," she whispered. Her chest hurt. The pain was immense, enormous. She didn't know if she could handle it. Her shoulders felt like someone was holding them down. She needed to ring the buzzer for the nurse. Something was wrong. Something was terribly wrong.

The man came closer to her bed and looked down on her. She couldn't get any air. She was starting to see spots.

Wrong. Wrong. Blackness. Dying. This wasn't how it was supposed to be.

The man leaned closer, right into her face, so she could see him clearly. As her heart ceased to beat, in that space between the end of the pumping and the connection to her brain that told her she was done, she heard the words. Whispered, as if on a breeze.

"Hello, Mom."

CHAPTER 41

Daisy came from blackness. She was crying. Inconsolable, hysterical. The nurse summoned Tom, who rolled in, bleary-eyed, and tried to make sense of Daisy's ramblings.

Which pissed her off. She was making perfect sense in her head, but no one could understand her.

Josh is alive. Josh is here. He came to visit. He stood over my bed and stroked the hair back off of my face. Why can't you understand me?

"Blum, gargh, ssssive."

"What's going on? Is she having a stroke?" Tom was shouting; he was so loud, so loud.

And that's when everything inside broke.

She felt it, a tearing in her chest. Like something pulled away from its proper spot. She said, "Oh!"

"Daisy, my God, Daisy. What's wrong?" She saw the panic in Tom's eyes. The nurse was struggling to pull him away.

"Daisy, are you in pain?"

But Daisy couldn't answer. The pain was too intense, too strong. Too . . . too . . .

The sirens were going off, clarion loud. A mechanical voice rang in her ears.

"Code Blue, Code Blue, room 566, Code Blue."

The pressure hurt. She was smashed, run flat, the air leaking out of her.

She couldn't see. It was fuzzy and dark.

Screaming. Her chest was on fire. No breath, couldn't get any air.

Hands, everywhere.

"Intubate."

"Charging to two hundred."

"Clear! Everyone clear!"

Her body leaped into the air and landed back, hard.

"We got her back, we got her back."

"Wait, wait, wait, wait, not yet, not yet. She's still in V-tach. We're going to have to shock her again."

"Get the epi."

"Shit, we're losing her. Come on, hurry, hurry."

The pain stopped.

Daisy drifted now, in and out. She felt so light, so free. She looked down on her body. There were eight people surrounding her, shocking and pumping and sticking needles into her veins, pumping air into her lungs. Frantically trying to save her life. She almost wanted to sneer, *See? I told you something was wrong.* But she didn't feel any of it. Just floating, like she'd done earlier, when the nice doctor had listened, actually listened to her. He was the first person in ages who had. He'd known Josh, known he was a good boy.

And now she could go to God, unburdened, free. She could go . . .

She couldn't go yet.

She forced herself back into her body, to feel the sticks and thumping and pain.

It was an agreement she had with herself. A deal. A deal she'd made with the devil. She couldn't go without telling the truth. To someone. To anyone. Whether they believed her or not.

"Son," she croaked.

"What's she saying?"

"She's asking for her son."

She couldn't shake her head. The damnable device was screwed into her skull so she couldn't. She tried again.

"Sonssssss."

"Sons? Are you saying you want to see your sons?"

She managed to get her eyes open, blinked twice, for yes. Tom was hovering nearby, his face coated in tears.

"She's only got the one. Had the one, I mean," he said.

Daisy blinked fast, hard. Tom edged closer. "Daisy, what are you saying?"

"Sons. I. Have. Two. Sons." She grunted out the words, hard and fast, with no doubt left as to what she was saying.

And then, her truth told, her conscience clear, she let herself slide away, into the black. It wouldn't matter now. It wouldn't ever matter again.

Dear Josh,

I am back on my feet.

I may have worried you in the past few months of letters, and for that, I am truly sorry. I wasn't really as serious about it as everyone thought. And last week was an accident, really. I slipped. I had too much to drink, and too many pills, and not enough to eat. I have gotten rather skinny; all the running has shaved off most of my body fat. No more curves. But if you come back, I promise I will put on weight.

I really thought I'd gotten past this. But I feel you everywhere, and see you everywhere. You lurk on the street corners, wait for me as I leave school, haunt my runs. And the tree, I see you in the tree. I know you're out there somewhere. I know it.

I just want to be with you. That's all I was trying to do.

Always,
Aubrey

CHAPTER 42

Aubrey
Today

Aubrey was attempting to pull herself together when her cell phone rang. She recognized Tom's number and answered, trying to keep the terrible knowledge she'd learned from her voice.

But Tom was crying, too. "Aubrey, you need to come. Daisy's in a coma. She had a massive cardiac arrest. I don't know if she's going to make it. We're back in the intensive care unit."

So Josh was alive, and Daisy was dying. That wasn't irony; it was cruelty. Some sick, cruel joke the universe was playing on her.

"Oh, Tom. I'm so sorry. I'm on my way."

She went down the stairs, saw Tyler was back and asleep, shivering and sweating on the couch. She wrote him a note, told him to hang in there, that she was pulling for him, and to call her with any news he'd learned.

Winston woofed at her quietly, almost a question, and she went to him, put her arms around him, and fought back tears.

"Oh, baby. I don't know what to do."

He nuzzled her and she let him, then stood and grabbed her keys.

She drove to the hospital in a trance.

How was she supposed to do this? What was she supposed to do? To think? To feel?

She was numb. This could have been some sort of joke. It really could. Right?

The hospital was so close she was there before she could wrap her mind around what was going on. The valet nodded in acknowledgment and took the car, and she went inside. The creepy corridors, the long hallways, the smell—it all was foreign again, strange, different. Her whole world was altered. The colors wound together in a blur, a kaleidoscope of images—Josh at the center.

God, she could hardly draw the details of his face into her mind. The dark hair, the blue eyes, yes, but the minute qualities, the little bits that she used to know better than the back of her hand, were gone.

His head thrown back in ecstasy as he got head from a strange woman.

The ICU was on the fifth floor. When she arrived, she was denied entry. She asked the nurse to let Tom know she was there, and she left to get him. They returned a few moments later, Tom looking haggard and drawn, his skin pale. He fell into Aubrey's arms, and she hugged him automatically. He smelled of fear.

"What happened?"

"They think that one of the broken rib slivers poked a hole in her heart and they missed it. She's been telling me all day something was wrong, and I just didn't listen. They thought she needed a shrink, that it was in her head—" He broke off, sobbing, and Aubrey led him to the ugly gray chairs and sat him down. There was a box of tissues strategically placed nearby. Aubrey handed one to Tom.

When he had calmed a bit, she asked, "So what's the next step?"

"They're trying to get her stabilized and they'll do surgery as soon as she can handle it. Pretty soon they're going to have to go in whether she's stable or not. They're saying it's fifty-fifty right now."

"I'll take those odds, Tom. Daisy is the most stubborn woman I know. She's fighting in there." The words sounded empty, flat. But they seemed to help Tom, because the tears began to slow, and he worked his way back to calm. She sat with him while he composed himself.

"The police came by to check on her. They're going to charge her with DUI and vehicular assault, they want to set a court date. You have to tell them it wasn't her fault, Aubrey. You have to let them know she didn't mean any harm. We can't let them charge her with assault."

Well, we can. But she patted his arm. "Let's cross that bridge when we get to it. You should probably talk to a lawyer before you do anything."

"You're right. Of course you're right. I will."

He went silent, pulling the tissue between his hands until it shredded.

"There's something else. When I got down here, she was going in and out of consciousness. She said the strangest thing before she went under all the way."

"What's that?"

"She said she had sons. Two sons."

"You must have just misheard her."

"No. She was very clear. And I've been thinking about it since she said it. You know she was married before me, right?"

"Sure. To Ed Hardsten. Josh's biological father." He tensed, and she smoothed her hand over his arm. "Josh always felt you were his father, Tom. Always. You gave him his name. You gave him your love. And he loved you, very much."

"Thank you, Aubrey. Though I guess it doesn't matter now. No, Daisy was married briefly before Ed Hardsten. To a soldier who died while he was on assignment. Very top secret stuff. She never talked about him; she only mentioned him once, before we got married. She didn't want to go into our wedding day with lies between us. But she wouldn't tell me much about him."

"Do you know his name?"

"No. It was years earlier, when she was just a kid. It pained her to speak of it, so I never pushed her."

And that was why Daisy had married Tom in the first place. Security and love, no questions asked.

Tom continued, "But what if she had a child with him and didn't tell me? Or had a miscarriage or something? She always held something of herself back from me. Could this be it?"

"Does she have any papers or anything from that time?"

"I'm sure she does. I don't go into her desk."

Of course you don't. "Do you want me to?"

He looked torn for a minute. Then the most decisive look she'd ever seen from him crossed his careworn face. "Yes. Yes, I do, Aubrey, if you're willing. I know Daisy hasn't been much of a mother-in-law to you. I understand if you'd rather stay out of this. But if there's something there, and she wakes up, maybe we can put her mind at ease. She was so upset, so disturbed. You should have seen her. It was horrible."

He started to cry again and Aubrey shushed him, patting him on the back like she would a small child.

Children, rather. The idea that Daisy had more than one child freaked her out. But for Tom, and for Josh, who might actually be out there somewhere, she'd go digging.

A nurse who had just hung up the phone came around the desk to them. "Mr. Hamilton? They're going to take her into surgery, sir. She's crashing again, they don't want to wait any longer."

"Go, Tom. I'll handle things out here."

"Thank you, Aubrey. I love you."

The words blew her away. Very few people had ever told her they loved her. Her parents, when they were alive. Josh. Meghan. And now Tom.

"I love you, too." And she meant it.

CHAPTER 43

It was cresting six and the sun was fighting its way into the sky, reluctant but inevitably persistent. Aubrey left the hospital and went directly to Meghan's house. She hadn't decided yet whether to tell her about the photo. For some reason, she felt like she needed to keep it to herself. But she'd make that call if it came up.

Sons. Daisy said she had two sons.

Meghan lived in an A-frame in Sylvan Park, and Aubrey knew she was a morning person. Sure enough, when she rolled up to her house, Meghan was outside on the front porch in a robe and slippers, drinking a cup of coffee and reading a book. She parked, and Meghan waved at her with a smile.

"What's up, buttercup? You're moving bright and early today. But you look like crap. Don't you sleep?"

"Rarely, it seems. I need your help," Aubrey said.

"With what? I'm still looking into Derek Allen. I asked Daniel to pull everything he could find on him. We're meeting later this morning to talk about it. You have another problem, sugar?"

"Daisy took a turn for the worse and is back in

surgery. She said some crazy stuff and Tom wants me to look into her files, see what I can find."

"Crazy stuff like what?"

Aubrey leaned against the column that held the roof up over the porch. She hadn't had breakfast, even tea, was running on fumes. "Like she has more than one son."

Meghan rocked back in her seat. "Seriously? Wow. That's . . . intriguing."

"I don't know. She could have just been corked out of her brain on morphine. Tom asked me to look into it. You game? You are the one who was married to the PI, after all. I don't really know what I'm doing."

"Hell yeah, I'm in. Let's do it!" She stood and started down the stairs.

"Um, Meghan? This isn't a clothing-optional field trip."

Meghan stopped and looked down. "Oh, yeah. Give me a sec."

She roared back inside and came out five minutes later, hair wet and glistening, combat boots unlaced, miniskirt only slightly askew.

They got in the Audi and buckled up. "I need to stop by the house and check on Tyler and Winston first. Will only take a second."

"Tyler's back?"

"Sweating it out on my couch."

"Bless his heart."

"You know it."

The drive was quick. Meghan offered to stay in the car, just to be safe.

"He doesn't bite, you know."

"He hates me."

"He doesn't hate you," Aubrey said. "You just represent all the worst ills of society to him."

"I don't get it. I'm a rebel. You'd think he'd love me."

They'd been through this before. Tyler felt like Meghan was a poseur, just faking being this romantic rebel to make her coffee shop cool to the college kids. Aubrey didn't think Tyler had any room to complain, considering. They'd argued about it more than once.

"Fine, stay here. I'll be quick."

Winston was thrilled to see her. Tyler was sitting at the kitchen table, eating a box of cereal. Without a bowl.

"Feeling better?" she asked, the suspicion in her voice clear. He usually didn't eat when he was coming down.

"Not really. But I thought I should try something. Your moms-in-law okay?"

She collapsed in the seat next to him, rubbed Winston's ears.

"No. She's in emergency surgery right now. I need to go by their house, get some things." She was hedging, and Tyler knew it. He sat back in the chair and eyed her.

"What kind of things?"

"Not money, Tyler. Records. Seems Daisy might have had more than one child, but no one knew about it until now. Is there any tea?"

"Do I look like your waiter?"

It was her turn to eye him. "You're obviously feeling better, smart-ass. Anything I need to know?"

He shook his head. "The pills started to work. I had to go back and get some more, didn't get back here till late. You were passed out in the bed."

"It was a long day. Meghan did a search online and found some news about Derek Allen. Did you ever see the guy you overheard talking about Josh?"

"Yeah, though I don't think he saw me. Dark, Mediterranean dark. Greek or Italian like. My height. Probably fifty-five, sixty. Silver hair."

"That sounds like the guy who was at the hospital. That's Derek Allen."

And then Aubrey remembered where she'd seen him before. The accident. She couldn't believe the penny hadn't dropped before now. It was the hair: he'd gone completely gray over the past five years.

"What is it? You look like you've seen a ghost."

"Uh, maybe I have. I just now realized Derek Allen is the man we rear-ended the day Josh went missing."

Tyler's eyes went to the table. "I don't know about you, Aubrey, but I don't believe in coincidences."

She touched his hand. "Neither do I."

"There's something I have to tell you."

She pulled back, shoved her hands in her pockets. Something in his voice . . .

"What is it?"

He hesitated, then the words poured out of him. "Josh. His death. It's my fault."

Aubrey took a deep breath and sat down. "What do you mean?"

"Dude who gave me info on Derek Allen? He was a guy I knew years ago, back when I ran with the G2 crew. We were looking for alternate revenue streams. I mentioned Josh worked at Vandy and had access to all kinds of great drugs. I didn't know he was going to tell anyone, especially not this Allen dude. I was just bragging. I got popped the next week, hadn't talked to him again until now. That's why I slipped, I had to use to make him trust me. At first, he thought I was a narc."

Aubrey shut her eyes. There it was. The key. The link. What she'd been missing all along. The how behind Josh's downfall.

A coldness filled her. How simple and cavalier he'd been with Josh's life. Tyler, her brother, her helper, had betrayed her savior.

Something in her felt like it was going to burst.

Pull it together. Don't do something you'll regret.

Tyler reached over and grabbed her hand. "Aubrey, I'm sorry. I'm really, really sorry. I'd do anything to go back and redo that conversation. I had no idea it was going to end up this way."

"You're the link. You're the reason he's dead," she said softly, and his face went ashen. Tears came to his eyes.

"Aubrey, forgive me, please. I didn't know what I was doing. I was so fucked up back then."

She nodded once, removed her hand from his. Stood up. "Thank you for telling me. I'm glad the methadone is working. I'm glad you're feeling better. I have to go, Meghan is waiting for me."

His face collapsed into a grimace. "I will never understand what you see in her."

Her voice was steady. "She was there for me when I had no one. I will never understand why you don't like her. She's never been anything but nice to you."

"Something about her I don't trust. You be careful around her. I'm going to go lie down. That is, if it's cool that I crash here for a while? I completely understand if you want me to leave, and never see me again. If I were you, I'd want me dead."

She did. God, she did.

She was fighting hard against the fear, the worry, the pain. The overwhelming desire to grab her kitchen knife and slice her foster brother's throat. But she didn't. It took all her effort, but she found the calm inside. At least she knew now how this had happened. Knowing made it easier.

And with everything that was going on, Tyler and his very loaded weapon couldn't hurt. Tyler had been her bodyguard before. It was his turn to watch her back again.

"Clean up after yourself, and let Winston out, would you?"

"When will you be back?"

"Soon."

He scrutinized her, his dark blue eyes running over her face, making her flush.

"Are you really okay, Aubrey? I know you're upset. You have every right to kick me out."

She patted him on the shoulder. "I'll be fine. If you find anything else out about Allen, let me know immediately. I'll be back in a bit."

He hesitated, then gave her a hauntingly familiar half smile. "Bring some food, yeah? You eat like a single white girl."

"Shocking, Tyler. I am a single white girl."

"Yeah, yeah, I know. Just bring home some meat or something. Lean Cuisines and cereal can't sustain a growing boy."

She pulled a twenty out of her wallet and handed it to him. "Order pizza or a sandwich."

Tyler eyed the money, and she immediately saw what he was weighing. "Thanks," he mumbled. She was interested in this new reluctance to take money from her; the humility of it was rather fascinating. Twice now he'd made conscious decisions about whether to put the money into his arm. Maybe he *was* changing. Or maybe he was acting out of guilt and regret. Well, he should.

Stop, Aubrey. Stop.

"Today?"

Meghan stood in the doorway, hand on a cocked hip.

"Sorry, Meghan. I'm coming."

Meghan and Tyler stared at each other. Aubrey felt the intensity of their glares; the room practically crackled with animosity. She debated saying something, trying to smooth things over between them, shrugged and patted Winston's head one last time.

"Come on," she said to Meghan, took her by the arm and dragged her back to the car. There was no reason to share what she now knew about Tyler's role in Josh's disappearance. It wouldn't change anything. It would hurt; Meghan wouldn't be able to see past the new information, and would want to blame Tyler for everything.

Once they'd gotten in, Aubrey asked, "Why do you hate him so much?"

"It's not hate. It's disappointment."

"What do you mean?"

Meghan shot her a glance. "He should have straightened himself out and helped you heal after Josh died. That's all."

"Oh. I never expected that from him, Meghan."

"You should have. He was the closest thing to family you had."

"I'm glad I have you. You're my family," Aubrey said, giving Meghan a squeeze on the arm. "And you are definitely a better cook than Tyler. I would have starved."

The sun returned to Meghan's smile and the flame to her eyes. "So, we're off to dear old Mummy's house. I bet you there are wire hangers all over the place."

And Aubrey thought, *You have no idea.*

CHAPTER 44

Aubrey had always felt nervous in Daisy's home. Even with Tom's sanction, it seemed wrong to be snooping in the woman's things. But this was important, and Aubrey reminded herself that it might all be a moot point anyway, especially if Daisy didn't make it.

She was almost glad for the distraction. After Tyler's revelation, she'd taken to checking her email every five minutes—she'd actually set up the mail account on her phone. She hadn't been using that function; she never used her phone to access the Internet anymore. It was something she'd tried to instill in her kids at school, too: if you need information from the Internet, do so at a computer, not your phone. She hated watching people walk around with their eyes glued to their palms, bumping into people because they were so absorbed in their own little worlds that they couldn't interact with reality anymore.

She had morphed into the worst kind of hypocrite. Like an ex-smoker who eschewed any contact with their old lifestyle. She used to use her phone all the time. Maybe she had texting PTSD. And really, who could blame her?

She checked it again, saw nothing new. No

surprise there. In the After, Aubrey didn't have a lot of contact with people. Very few emails, and those only from good friends and spammers. She'd closed her Facebook account, and had never been on friendly terms with Twitter. She had her habit: she checked her email once a day, usually preceding writing a note to Josh. She told herself she was fighting the rising tide of technology, but the truth was, she never felt safe online. She felt so . . . exposed.

"You expecting a call?" Meghan asked.

Aubrey lied smoothly. "Just hoping for an update from Tom."

Meghan had already broken into Daisy's desk—she wasn't going to waste any time. She turned around and eyed Aubrey. "What's the sudden interest in this woman, Aubrey? She's been nothing but a bitch to you for years. My God, she testified against you, did her level best to get you sent to jail for life. And here you are, acting like you actually care."

Meghan was right. In all honesty, Aubrey didn't know what had come over her since Daisy's accident. Manning the late-night shift, trying to communicate, to help. Yes, Daisy hated her, but Aubrey liked to think she was the bigger person. She just hadn't ever had an opportunity to show it. Or maybe it was Chase. Maybe opening her heart to someone had allowed her to forgive. Or, maybe, to find the final thing to sever all ties for good.

Die, bitch, just die.

Maybe not.

She arranged her face carefully. "Josh would want me to take care of his mother, Meghan. We're here to dig into *her* life, not psychoanalyze my motivations. Did you find anything?"

Meghan stood up, her brow furrowed. "No. Nothing of use. Everything here is current, just tax stuff and phone bills and bank statements. Filing cabinet?"

Aubrey glanced around. "In the closet."

The filing cabinet was locked. Meghan went back to the desk and started rifling through again, came up with the key. "Ta-da," she cried, holding it aloft. She unlocked the cabinet and started sifting through the files.

Aubrey had never spent any time in Daisy's office. She wasn't exactly sure why Daisy had an office in the first place. Daisy didn't do anything. She didn't work. She didn't have friends. Oh, she had the people she called friends, acquaintances from the club, people she tried to one-up. But actual girlfriends, people she confided in? Aubrey couldn't remember Josh ever saying anything that would lead her to believe that Daisy was anything but a bitter, shriveled-up woman, old before her time.

Her office reflected that life of isolation. No pictures, no homey touches. It was frank and utilitarian and clean. Too clean. It was the office of a woman desperate for control.

"Bingo," Meghan said. Aubrey heard clinking, looked over to see Meghan pulling out two bottles of vodka, one fresh, one half empty.

"Is Daisy a drinker?"

"I guess. I really haven't spent a lot of time with her since Josh . . ." *Say it, Aubrey. Say it. You don't want to mess up now.* ". . . died."

"Hmm. Check this out," Meghan said.

She handed Aubrey a file folder that had aging yellow cuttings from *The Tennessean*. Front and center was a photo of a young woman, no older than Aubrey was now, with a wide smile, frank eyes, and a microphone in her hands. The piece was called "New Voices," and the name under the photograph read *Daisy Dee*.

Aubrey read it quickly, shocked to find out her mother-in-law had been a lounge singer. A pretty good one, from the sound of it. She'd been honored along with a few other session musicians and singers as the best the city had to offer in the way of country music.

Good grief. She checked the date on the article heading. This was from before Josh's birth.

Daisy, a country singer.

Would wonders never cease?

The article mentioned that Daisy had gotten her start in the Nashville music scene after being widowed.

Aubrey showed Meghan the paper. "Check this out. Daisy was a singer."

"That's not all. God, there are medals in here. Bronze Star. Purple Heart. Tom wasn't in the military, was he?"

"Those must belong to her husband who died. Tom said he was in the service. She was married to him briefly before she married Josh's real dad."

"So she's had three husbands? Wow. Daisy really got around. What's the deal with Josh's biological dad?"

Aubrey sat in the desk chair, pushed off, and whirled around in a circle. "Bad news, that one. I met him once, when we were kids. He showed up and I thought he was a pedophile trying to steal us. But he'd just gotten out of jail. Josh was blown away. Daisy had told him his real dad died. He told me he had no earthly idea that his father was still alive, but I think he did know. I remember that day . . . Josh was wrecked. It really messed him up. He rebelled against Daisy completely then. Basically cut her out of his life, even though he was stuck living here. That's when he and Tom got close. And he and I got closer, too. Which made things with Daisy that much worse. I think she always blamed me for Josh finding out the truth."

Now Meghan was interested. "What was his dad in jail for?"

"He was convicted of identity theft. It wasn't as common back then as it is now. But there were all kinds of allegations against him, including an attempted murder. He was a classic crook. He got out early for good behavior before Daisy ever had a chance to tell Josh he was really alive." She went quiet for a moment. "I didn't like him. He was a handsome guy, all smiles, but something about him made the hair stand up on the back of my neck. He just seemed wrong, somehow."

"Where is he now?"

"Hardsten died a little while back. Before we got married. Got on the wrong side of a knife in a bar fight."

"Figures. Once a criminal . . ."

Always a criminal.

Like father, like son?

Another chill paraded down Aubrey's arms.

"Yeah. Anything more there?"

Meghan shook her head. "Nothing that screams 'I had a child no one knows about.' Though you have to admit, Aubrey, Daisy was certainly holding things back from people. Sounds to me like she's an expert at compartmentalization."

"So where do we look for a kid?"

"Adoption records."

The word *adoption* made Aubrey squirm. Somewhere deep inside, she'd always hoped someone would come forward to claim her, to give her a history, a family, a home. It never happened. As was required by the State of Tennessee, she'd gone to the monthly "adoption days" in Nashville, sat at a lunch table while eager couples walked past her without a second glance. She was cute, with her dark eyes and curly blond hair and long, coltish legs, but she had a fatal flaw: she wasn't a baby. The couples who came to these events were looking for someone little, someone still impressionable, who could be molded in their image; kids who didn't remember their real folks, who wouldn't cringe when they were asked to call their new strangers Mom and Dad.

Those Saturdays had been among the worst in her life. Every fourth Saturday of the month, they were prodded into the showers, dressed in the finest handoffs they had, and bused to the school, where they were lined up like show ponies. Or slaves. Eager children with one goal in life: to be loved.

She desperately wanted to be saved from the hell she was living in, and being adopted again would make everything okay.

It never happened, but soon enough, she was loved. By Josh.

Meghan caught that something was wrong. She was watching Aubrey with her little pixie head cocked to one side and her lips pursed, but let the moment go without inquiry. She smiled and patted Aubrey lightly on the shoulder.

"Come on, sugar. Let's hit the courthouse. See what we can dig up."

"Wait. I need to show you something."

Aubrey reached into her bag and pulled out a sheet of paper. She'd printed out the photo, was carrying it around like having it on her would make it disappear from the world.

She handed it to Meghan. "Someone emailed me this last night. The subject line was 'He's alive.'"

Meghan unfolded the paper. Aubrey could see the faint outline of Josh's body through the back. Even prepared for it, the pain sliced through her.

Meghan folded the paper, anger etched on her features. She was pale, and looked furious.

"Are you okay?"

Aubrey choked back a sob. "Of course I'm not okay. Someone's playing with me, trying to manipulate me. But I can't sit back and pretend nothing's happening." She grabbed the photo. "Clearly I didn't know him as well as I thought. What if he's been out there this whole time, living it up with some strange woman? I'm just his wife. Why let me know he's okay?"

"If this photo is even real. It could be something doctored up to make you doubt him."

"But who would do that? Who would want to torture me like this?"

Meghan gritted her teeth. "I don't know, but we'll find out."

PART THREE

Years of love have been forgot in the hatred of a minute.

—EDGAR ALLAN POE

CHAPTER 45

Josh
Six Years Ago

"So, Dr. Hamilton, what made you want to get into medicine?"

Josh was across the table from Derek Allen at Jimmy Kelly's Steakhouse, eating hot corn cakes and drinking an incredible glass of wine, waiting on the most expensive filet he had ever ordered. Allen didn't seemed fazed by the prices, ordering filets and lobsters and the $180 bottle of Nickel & Nickel cabernet sauvignon casually, as if he did it every day.

Josh was impressed. Someday soon, that would be him.

"I want to help people. I know that sounds cliché, but it's true."

"And what kind of doctor are you training to be?"

"Well, interesting you should ask that. Today was my first day of surgical rotation. I thought I wanted family practice, but now . . . there's something special about surgery. Though it means more schooling. More money. More everything."

Allen was looking at him with the same small smile on his face, almost like he'd known what Josh was going to say.

"And your wife? What will she think?"

Josh shrugged. "We'll figure it out. We always do."

Their meals arrived. Josh cut into the steak; it was perfectly done and smelled like heaven.

"It's hard to start your professional life in a financial hole. What if I could find a way to help you along?"

Josh stopped eating, fork poised over his plate. "What do you mean?"

"A little side job, to make ends meet."

"I was thinking of taking a position at the morgue."

"Oh, this would be much more fun. And much more lucrative."

Josh put his fork down. "What is it you do, exactly, Mr. Allen?"

Allen put his elbows on the table and steepled his fingers. His smile was crooked, and he leaned in so he wouldn't be overheard. "I'm a bit like you, actually. I make people feel good."

Josh walked out of his dinner with Derek Allen halfway through his very expensive filet, panic driving him back to his Audi.

What the man wanted was impossible, and there was no way in hell Josh was going to get involved.

Allen's "problem" was a simple one. He was a dealer, albeit a fancy one. He needed good, pure product for his upper-class clientele. Pills, especially. For while Nashville's elite wasn't going to be caught dead with a needle in the arm, a little bit of Oxy on the tongue was a whole different matter.

Allen needed a source who could get him pills. Simple as that.

Josh had balked immediately, started to rise, but Allen had grabbed his arm and said, "Sit. Down."

Josh sat, but didn't move to pick up his fork or wine again.

"Good. You need to think this through carefully. It isn't chance that led you to be here. Why do you think I was at that particular coffeehouse? I know you, Dr. Joshua Hamilton. I've been watching you. I know about your little upper issue. Adderall, is it? Tsk."

Josh froze. When he could form cognizant thought again, he leaned across the table. "Who told you that?"

Allen smiled. "I think you and I could do business together. I'm a good boss, I take care of my own. You'll get everything you need to finish your schooling and take care of your wife, and no one needs to know."

"I don't do drugs. And I don't run them, either."

"Bullshit. You started by taking wifey's pills, and when you couldn't do it anymore without her noticing, you struck a deal with the pharmacist at the hospital. An expensive habit you've got going on there, Doctor."

"You're crazy."

"Come, now. Look at your hands, they've been shaking since you sat down. Your pupils are pinpoint, you're sweating."

"It's hot in here."

"Hamilton, stop. I know all about it. All about you. Your friend in the pharmacy works for me."

Allen sat back, took a deep drink of his wine. Josh followed suit, trying desperately to calm himself. *Oh, God. Bob, you fucking idiot. You're working with an outsider? You told? Who else have you implicated?*

If the school found out, he'd be expelled, and he'd never get into another. *Oh, God. Oh God oh God oh God.*

Play it cool, Hamilton. He's fishing. Just play it cool.

"I don't know what you're talking about. And I have to go now. My wife will be waiting for me."

"Three thousand a week. All I need are a few pills here and there. Think about what I proposed, Josh. You're going to want to do this. I'll make it worth your while, and I'll protect you. And if you don't play ball, there will be consequences."

Josh nearly knocked over his chair trying to get away from the table.

In his car, he wanted to cry. This wasn't how it was supposed to go. He wanted to kill Bob, the fucking prick. He started to drive to the pharmacist's house, then pulled to the side of West End and had himself a breakdown.

God, Aubrey couldn't find out. If she knew he was *supplementing*, as he thought of it, she would freak the fuck out. She was so antidrug it was insane. That's why she'd had the leftover Adderall in the first place; she didn't like how they made her feel, so she'd tossed them under the sink. She hadn't noticed when they disappeared. He'd been refilling the prescription for a year, but when it ran out of refills, he needed a new source.

Bob was that source. He did it for most of the med students. Skimmed off the top of the bottles coming into the hospital.

And now, because Bob was a stupid motherfucker, Derek Allen wanted Josh to get involved as well.

Oh, God. He needed a drink. He needed a shitload of drinks.

He put the car in drive and headed toward Sam's.

CHAPTER 46

Aubrey
Three Years Ago

The lines on her wrist weren't natural.

It was an interesting revelation. Aubrey stared at the thin white flesh, now marred, confused for the briefest of moments before she remembered.

It was like this every day when she woke. The drugs they were giving her were too strong; they were numbing her brain, making her see flying things out of the corners of her eyes.

The bandages had come off yesterday. The cut was a thin line demarcating the flesh, the inside of her delicate wrist scored. Forevermore she would be able to identify her wrist's north from south, a permanent latitude etched into her skin.

They didn't understand.

She rolled onto her side. That was an improvement. The restraints had been overwhelming; she'd been panicked the whole time she was in them. The idiots thought she was fighting to get out; they were wrong. It was the idea that she *couldn't* that made her frantic. So they'd drug her, and she'd wake still tied and panic again. A vicious cycle, one that only stopped when one of the other patients, the one in the bed opposite hers, pointed out what the issue probably was.

They finally unhooked her, and she calmed immediately, taking huge, deep breaths, moving her fingers and arms and legs. She didn't try to get up, just moved all her parts, like a stunned fish finally put back into water.

They added claustrophobia to her growing list of "issues."

Bipolar. Depression. Suicidal ideations. Antisocial personality disorder. Narcissism. Delusions.

They sat with her in the afternoons with a wide, thick book called a DSM-IV and tried to explain all the things that were wrong with her.

They were the ones who were insane, but Aubrey had to concede one point: she did have a problem with panic. Being tied down, being forced to do what others wanted—she had a major issue with that. And depression, well, shit, who wouldn't be depressed if they were in her shoes? Her husband was dead. Missing. Dead. Whatever.

Let her out, let her get her own clothes on her back and sleep in her own bed, however grim that might be, and she'd be right as rain.

She hadn't exactly been trying to kill herself. She didn't think so, at least. She had been drunk. Rip-roaringly drunk. And she'd fallen, tripped over the dog into the kitchen. The beer bottle she was carrying broke into fifteen or so sharp green pieces, and since she couldn't stand up, she managed to get herself seated Indian-style on the kitchen floor and, weaving, began picking up the pretty green shards.

She was just drawing, the glass a permanent pencil. Pretty pictures, Christmas on her wrist. She told them that over and over, but they didn't believe her.

The glass was sharper than she expected, the flesh inside her wrist thinner. The blood that bloomed was so bright and red, contrasting with the dark green glass, a wreath tied in a bloody bow. It was fascinating, so she pushed a little harder to see if she could make the bow bigger.

She wasn't trying to kill herself.

Not that she hadn't tried that once before . . . but she was fourteen then. Fourteen and alone in the world and scared and dirty and not realizing what promise life held. Tyler had found her, saved her life. And things had gotten better after that. The kids at the group home had taken her seriously. She'd been mythologized. She was popular. Cool. She had taken a bottle of pills—not aspirin or Tylenol, like the poseurs did, but a bottle of codeine she found in her therapist's purse. Turned out someone had herself a little pill-popping problem.

And that same someone had realized her drugs were missing and returned to the group home in time to help Tyler get Aubrey to Vanderbilt's emergency room for a stomach pumping.

She shivered at the memory. The handcuffs, the tube full of charcoal being shoved down her throat, being forced—yes, that was her issue, any-thing or anyone making her do something against her will. Coming to just long enough to rush out of the bed, trying to make it to the toilet to vomit, the coal-black streams dripping from her mouth and nose, the ER staff screaming at her, grabbing her arms to force her back to the bed, tying her down.

That lovely little incident cured her of ever trying something like that again. No, if Aubrey wanted to kill herself, she'd do it right. She'd have Tyler do it for her, with a needle full to the brim of the highest-grade heroin they could afford.

She hadn't tried to kill herself with the bottle glass. This had been an accident. A legitimate accident. Just a mistake. A simple, stupid, drunken mistake.

A simple, stupid, drunken mistake that cost her six fucking weeks on the psych ward.

She didn't think they'd ever let her go. It was day after day after day of pointless bullshit, of crafts and group and personal sessions and life coaching and career development—for fuck's sake, people, she was a teacher, and a damn good one at that. She developed an aversion to being touched. She started smoking just for an excuse to see the sky. She'd never been a smoker before; it had a certain glamour to it. She pranced around outside during the breaks, puffing away, ignoring the ticklish cough that started after just a few puffs, just so freaking happy to feel the air and sun instead of the screaming buzz of the fluorescent bulbs and the pockmarked white cardboard ceilings.

The last time, when she was fourteen, Tyler had come to visit her, and reamed her ass out good for her stupidity. "It's never that bad, Aubrey. No matter what, it's never so bad that you want to end it all. Do you understand me?"

Sage advice from a boy who'd grown into a man with a drug habit so severe he had to live a life of crime to afford his fix. Poor thing.

When she thought about that, she sobered up. Aubrey truly felt sorry for Tyler. He couldn't come visit her now. He was with the last class up at Brushy Mountain doing a nickel for possession with intent.

A tisket, a tasket, a gray-and-yellow basket.

Fuck, she was still really high. The drugs they were giving her messed with the language center of her brain. She'd developed a sort of verbal dyslexia, and couldn't make the words come out in the proper order, even though she was thinking them clearly. Green. Green, not gray.

Where was she? Oh, that's right. She rolled over and looked at her wrist again. She needed to get a tattoo on that scar. She wondered if they could actually draw the line down the scar itself, or if they could anchor it, the white streak surrounded on either side with black, a bit of living chiaroscuro to make the right impact. Oooh, that would be pretty.

She just wanted to go home. Home to the emptiness that was her life. Home to the small, shabby house on West Linden she'd made sure wasn't homey in the least. Home to Winston, one of the only things from During she could stand to have around. It wasn't the dog's fault Josh was dead.

Josh was dead.

Aubrey had gone on quite the bender when the trial was over. It was interesting; she didn't have the claustrophobia in jail, where they were constantly telling her what to do. Maybe because they weren't kind. They weren't well-meaning. They didn't stare at her with sad eyes and ask how she was feeling about that.

"Rob hates you, Aubrey. He thinks your curly hair is a harbinger of death on the wings of flesh-coated Buick hoods. How does that make you feel?"

"It makes me feel like Rob is a psycho fucktard who needs to be shot, or better medicated. Can I go now?"

That outburst got her into isolation, the place she'd really wanted to be all along. No more of this pretending to be friends with the staff and listening to other patients' crap. She could smoke alone, shit alone, eat alone, sleep alone.

It was a comparative heaven.

They finally released her, on a blustery January day, with the threat of snow in the sky. She had never been so happy in her life. Even without Josh, even with her memories, this—being in her own home, away from the crawling eyes of constant organization and management and analysis—this was bliss.

And Rob really was a psycho fucktard. When they let him out, he shot up a Sprint store. They should have listened to her.

CHAPTER 47

Aubrey
Today

Meghan and Aubrey assiduously avoided speaking about the photo, kept their focus on the adoption records. But the courthouse yielded nothing. Neither did an online search. Aubrey was getting frustrated, but Meghan just smiled.

"Relax, sugar. This stuff can take forever. Especially if Daisy didn't want anyone to know about it. The odds of us finding information in the first place we look is slim to none, and Slim's out of town. I think we need to expand our search."

"To where?"

"Outlying counties. Let me make a couple of calls, see what we can dig up. I'm supposed to meet Daniel in fifteen minutes."

"Can I come?" Aubrey asked. She wanted to hear exactly what Meghan was finding out. She understood that she would need all the information she could glean in order to . . .

To do what, exactly, Aubrey? Clear his name? Allow Josh to come back?

And the money, Aubrey, don't forget the money.

It was Thursday. Chase was coming today, and the money that would change her life would be coming tomorrow.

She had a flash of Daisy lying incapacitated, and realized there would be no legal battle for the cash anytime soon. If Aubrey wanted the money, she could take it. Disappear forever. Five million dollars was a lot of money for a girl like her. *Think of the life you could lead.*

She shook off the voice. That voice had always created issues for her. Real and imagined.

Meghan shook her head. "I don't think you want to come. It's going to be technical, no fun at all. How about I meet you later?"

Aubrey bristled at Meghan's tone. "You don't want me there?"

Meghan raised her hands, palms first. "Hey, chill. I'll be honest with you. I don't know what he's going to say, and I didn't know if you wanted to put yourself through that night again."

"Sorry, Meghan. I'm just on edge is all."

"I understand."

"But I want to be there. I checked out of this so long ago. It wasn't right, and it wasn't fair to Josh. If I can help discover what happened to him, maybe I can start moving on."

Meghan pushed her hair out of her eyes. "Fine, you can come. Leave the car here, we can walk. We're meeting for coffee at the Hermitage Hotel."

"Nice. Hope he's picking up the check."

"Yeah, me, too."

"Let me call Tom, give him an update on what we've found."

Tom didn't answer, though Aubrey wasn't

surprised. The ICU was very strict about where phones could be turned on. She left him a message, and they set off in silence.

Aubrey hated thinking about the night Josh went missing, but it was more important than ever that she focus on every little detail. Like Tyler's revelation. Maybe there was even more that she'd missed. Anything could be the key.

The key to what, Aubrey? The voice again, that chatty little devil who loved to sit on her shoulder and throw spears at her. *Clearing your husband's besmirched name? Resurrecting him for the masses? Or are you doing all this for yourself?*

Yes, she wanted to go along. She was so close now. So close to finding out the truth.

It took five minutes to make the walk, mostly uphill, and Aubrey's legs felt the pleasant burn of exertion. She needed a run, something to clear her head, to help her focus. Running had become a crutch for her, but more than that, it was her sanity.

The doorman greeted them with a smile, and Aubrey realized how they were dressed: she in jeans and a T-shirt, Meghan like a punk rockabilly singer. All in all, they'd probably assume Meghan was the talent and simple, austere Aubrey the assistant. Which suited her just fine. She was used to Meghan drawing all the attention.

Meghan must have realized it, too, because she put a little extra swing in her hips and added a lascivious wink as they entered the lobby. Always on, that was Meghan for you.

The Oak Bar was downstairs, to the right of

the Capitol Grille, nestled in the corner of the hotel, and Meghan led the way. The place was legendary, dark and paneled and quiet, breathing out an air of mystery and charm. Just to be in the Oak Bar was a statement of belonging: to the city, to money, to class.

Aubrey had only been there once.

Josh had taken her for their first wedding anniversary. They'd sat in the corner, eating double-stack cheeseburgers and drinking peaty Scotch until they were legless. It was, as Aubrey recalled, an absolutely perfect evening.

Of course, all evenings with Josh were perfect.

That picture.

The idea of him enjoying someone else's attentions made her grit her teeth. She realized she was standing still, staring into the room as if she knew she didn't belong. Meghan was already taking a seat at a table on the far side of the bar, back in the alcove, where they couldn't be readily seen from the bar's entrance. Aubrey breathed a sigh a relief; for a moment she'd thought Meghan was going to sit at the table she and Josh had shared seven years ago. She couldn't have handled that. She could barely manage the memories she had.

Meghan was watching her curiously. Aubrey smiled and started toward the table, noticed Meghan's attention shift to somewhere behind her. She glanced over her shoulder and saw a man coming up fast. She stopped, thinking to turn and introduce herself, but he came flying by and made a beeline for Meghan.

Meghan stood and said, "Daniel Cutter? I'd like to introduce you to Aubrey Hamilton."

Cutter stopped short and turned. She could have sworn he looked shocked to see her, but he quickly composed himself and started back her way, hand outstretched.

"Mrs. Hamilton. It is such a pleasure to officially meet you. Let's sit down, and I'll tell you what I know, okay?"

Aubrey crossed her arms and sat. Meghan and Cutter ordered food, but she settled for tea; she didn't think she could handle anything more.

Once the waitress had disappeared, Meghan leaned forward. There was an edge to her voice that Aubrey didn't recognize. "So, Daniel. What have you found out?"

Aubrey put up her hand. "Can I ask a question before you start?"

Cutter was a stocky guy with a sure jaw and penetrating blue eyes. He turned them on Aubrey. "Of course."

"Was my husband involved in a drug ring?"

Cutter didn't move. "How did you come to that conclusion, Mrs. Hamilton?"

Aubrey shook her head. "I was told my husband might have been involved with some less than savory people, from a friend of mine who overheard a jailhouse rumor."

"Would you mind telling me what you were told?"

"Would you mind telling me if my husband was killed because of a man named Derek Allen?"

Boundaries established, he sat back in his chair. "Your husband was a very interesting man, Mrs. Hamilton."

Aubrey shook her head. "What does that have to do with Derek Allen?"

"Well, everything and nothing. You see, your husband vanished the same night Mr. Allen was found in an alley in downtown Nashville with a hole in his stomach."

Aubrey looked over at Meghan, whose mouth was open in a small O.

Aubrey was tired of playing games. "Mr. Cutter. Either tell me what the hell Derek Allen is doing and what his tie is to my husband, or I'm leaving."

He held up his hands. "Sorry. I needed to know if you were up to hearing all of this. Derek Allen was a drug dealer. And, as you already suspect, your husband worked for him."

Aubrey shook her head. "Impossible."

"It's very possible. It's true, as a matter of fact."

"And you knew this how?"

"Let's just say I had an interest in Allen's business and leave it at that." He tapped the side of his nose. Aubrey felt Meghan's body grow very still.

Cutter shrugged. "I'm clean now, Meghan. I've been in treatment. I'm working the program, like you always wanted."

Aubrey grabbed Meghan's hand under the table, tried to send her a silent *I don't care, it doesn't reflect badly on you.*

Meghan squeezed her hand back and unfroze.

"If Josh Hamilton was working for a drug dealer, why wouldn't this have come up years ago? During the investigation, or the trial?"

"Because Derek Allen is very good at keeping his silent partners silent."

"Did he kill my husband?" Aubrey asked.

"I don't know."

Aubrey shook her head. "I'm having a hard time believing your story. It's rather fantastical. Josh was a doctor."

"Where did he tell you he went all those nights?"

"He had a second job. At the morgue."

Cutter gave her an opaque look. "Which he was using as the delivery service."

Aubrey was trying to wrap her head around that tidbit when he suddenly leaned forward. "Have you considered that your husband might still be alive?"

He's alive.

Aubrey tried to keep the emotion from her face. She glanced at Meghan, sucked in her breath, and scooted back in her chair. "I think Derek Allen is trying to make me believe that he is."

She let her voice waver, tears threatening. "I'm sorry. Please, would you excuse me?"

She stood and practically ran to the ladies' room, bypassing the world-famous men's room, a black-and-green art deco masterpiece. Josh had taken her in there the night they'd come for their anniversary, made a big show of announcing a lady was present, all of it. She didn't think it was as beautiful as some did, preferred the quiet serenity of the women's modern nude space next door.

She slammed the door behind her and locked it. Son of a bitch.

She splashed water on her face. *Pull it together, Aubrey. You know he's dead. You know it. The insurance payout comes tomorrow. Derek Allen is just sniffing around, hoping for a cut.*

Using her, using Tyler.

That thought made her very, very angry. Aubrey didn't like herself when she was angry. She punched cops and stole from her mother-in-law and landed herself in psychiatric wards.

She stared at herself in the mirror, willing the hectic red spots on her cheeks to go away. She shut her eyes and ran her hands through her hair, her fingers catching on the corkscrew curls.

Breathe, Aubrey. Breathe.

Her cell phone trilled, shattering the silence, making her jump.

She cursed and dug it from her bag.

Chase.

Oh, shit. With all that had happened, she'd totally forgotten the time.

She swallowed and answered, trying to sound normal.

"Hey."

"Hey yourself, sweetheart. I miss you."

"You, too."

"Everything okay? You sound tense."

"Ha. Wow. You can hear it, huh?"

"Yes. What's the matter?"

What's the matter? Oh, wow. How to answer that? Let's see. People are starting to find out my husband was involved with a drug lord. I think I might be in danger. I don't think I should see you again. I want to see you so badly my skin itches.

She finally found her voice.

"Daisy. Daisy had a heart attack, or something like it. She's still in surgery, they found a hole in her heart. She's not doing well. I was there all night. I'm just really tired."

Her first lie to Chase. She should mark it on the calendar.

"Where are you now?"

"Um, at the Hermitage Hotel, of all places. Having tea with Meghan."

"Why aren't you at the hospital?"

"Meghan needed me. I'm just in the bathroom for a second. Listen, I should go."

She could hear the hurt in his voice. "Oh, sure. I understand. I just wanted to let you know I'm catching an earlier flight. My meeting was cancelled this afternoon. I got a car, you won't need to pick me up." He hesitated a moment. "That is, if it's still okay with you that I'm coming. Last night, well, I know it sounded ominous."

Aubrey bit her tongue. Tears burned in her eyes. She didn't know what to do. She had to make a decision, and do it quickly.

"It's fine. Great. So I'll see you at the house?"

Relief flooded his tone. "Definitely. Four thirty. I can't wait to see you."

"Me, too, Chase. Fly safe."

She hung up the phone and slumped down into one of the chairs in front of the makeup mirrors.

Pull yourself together, Aubrey.

It was no use. Her head began to spin, and her breath came short. The walls of the room began to close in around her. The waves of anxiety plowed through her. Her rational mind said, *Aubrey, you're having a panic attack. Breathe.* But her nervous system was already in overdrive.

It was all too much. She couldn't handle this. Tears came, and with them, short little breaths that finally got some oxygen to her brain. It took another minute to get her breath back, then another reassembling herself, using the mouthwash to erase the taste of bile that lingered in her throat. She had to get back out there, or they'd get suspicious.

You can do this, Aubrey. You're close. You always wanted to know what happened that night. And now, you're going to find out.

With a last look in the mirror, she squared her shoulders and headed back to the bar.

CHAPTER 48

Josh
Six Years Ago

Josh woke to the worst hangover he'd had in years. He rolled over, groaning. The light pierced his eyes and he flung a pillow over his face.

He didn't remember coming home, getting undressed. Clearly he'd been sick—there was a trash can by the bed.

It took a moment for the horror of the previous evening to catch up with him.

Derek fucking Allen.

He managed a shower, pulled on his jeans and a T-shirt, and went downstairs to find Aubrey sitting on the couch in the living room, drinking a cup of tea and looking extremely pissed off. Even Winston looked mad at him.

"Hi," he said.

Her head didn't move. "You're alive then?"

"Apparently. I'm a little hazy on what happened."

"Cab dropped you off at three. Poured you onto the doorstep. You could have called."

"I would have. Honey, I'm so sorry. I . . . lost myself last night. The pressure, school, everything, I just—"

Aubrey stood up. "Stow it, Josh. Don't dig the hole any deeper."

He couldn't help the tone in his voice. "What do you want me to do? What do you want me to say? I'm sorry, okay? I had a bad day and I tied one on."

Her eyes were sad, so sad. "You seem to be having more and more bad days lately, Josh. I have to go to work now. I already called you in sick. Try to get some sleep."

She left, and the dog skulked out of the living room behind her, through his doggie door into the spacious backyard.

He rubbed his forehead. Advil, water. *Stat.* Then he could go on feeling shitty about things.

His cell phone started to trill. He put his hand in his pocket. The number was unknown.

He ignored it. The phone rang again. Same unknown number.

Then a text came in.

Did you have fun last night, lover boy?

There was a photo attached to the text. He opened it, saw the picture, and his heart stopped. He didn't remember. He didn't remember at all. But there he was, clear as day, getting a blow job from a strange woman, in the same clothes he'd worn last night.

"Fuck!"

A second text came in.

> Meet me at Dragon Park - Blakemore
> entrance - 20 minutes, or the photo
> goes to your wife's phone.

It felt profane to meet Derek Allen at Dragon Park. The park was theirs, his and Aubrey's. He'd courted her there, made love to her in the soft grass, carved their initials into the lovers' tree. They'd played there as children, and as adults. How dare Derek Allen ruin it for him?

He jogged down the street to the park, repeating the same words over and over in time with his feet. *What have you done? What have you done? What have you done?*

Allen was sitting on the stone wall facing the dragon. Josh walked the last few steps, fists clenched. He wanted to kill this man, wanted to bash his head against the rocks. He had to keep his temper in check.

The park was quiet this morning, deserted. The skies were cloudy and dark. Rain was coming, forcing its way into town, keeping people inside. He stepped over a small pair of yellow rubber boots that had been left behind, wondering if the child who'd left them was barefoot now.

Allen didn't smile. "Have I made my point yet?"

"You have. What the fuck is this? You followed me?"

"Oh, not me. A private investigator. You've been under scrutiny for a while now."

Josh collapsed against the stone wall. "Why? Why me?"

Allen shrugged. "Because no one will ever believe you could do something illegal. You have the face of an angel. You're connected, and you already have a path in. You shouldn't break the law, Josh. Bad things happen."

"And if I don't agree?"

Allen did smile now, wide and amused. "What would Aubrey think if she knew you'd been with another woman?"

"I don't remember anything about last night."

"And you think that will make it okay for her? You'll lose her, and I don't think you want that to happen. I'm not asking for much. A few pills. And you get the money to move into a surgical residency and live the life you want. Simple. Easy." He snapped his fingers, then stood up.

"You'll show up here on Wednesday nights with the product. Eight p.m. You might want to up your jogging program so it will be a regular thing. Drop them in the old oak tree over there, it has a nice hole for them. And don't get caught."

"What about the money?"

"I've opened a bank account for you." He handed Josh a checkbook. "Don't spend it all in one place."

"How am I supposed to explain this money to Aubrey?"

"You'll figure it out. You've been lying to her for years. What's one more?"

"You're a son of a bitch."

Allen smiled cheerily. "I am at that. But one who's going to make you rich. So play nice, there's a good boy."

Josh bit back a retort. "And the picture? Is that the only one?"

Allen just laughed and walked away.

Josh collapsed to the ground. This wasn't happening. He was dreaming. He was going to wake up, snug and toasty next to Aubrey. They'd make love and have breakfast, take Winston for a walk. He would stop taking the uppers, clean himself up. Spend more time with Aubrey.

And in his heart, the lies began to form, and he knew this was the beginning of the end.

CHAPTER 49

Aubrey
Today

Aubrey felt like she'd interrupted something when she got back to the table. Meghan's eyes were sheened with tears, and Cutter was staring at his lap.

"I'm sorry about that. I don't know what came over me."

"It's no problem." Cutter gave her a brief smile. She sat back down, toyed with her straw.

"What can I expect from Derek Allen?"

Cutter shrugged. "It's been my experience that he's a dog with a bone. He's not going to walk away, not until he's satisfied Josh absolutely is dead."

"But why now? Why start all this now?"

"The money, obviously. And he's been in jail. He just got out. My guess is this is something he wants to handle himself. Otherwise, he would have told the police about Josh's involvement in his business long ago."

"You said he was shot the night my husband disappeared. Who shot him?"

Cutter didn't answer, just looked at her.

"You think Josh shot him?"

"I think that's a distinct possibility."

Jesus. Josh, what did you do?

She slid the card across the table. "One last thing. Any idea who is behind DC Investigations?"

Cutter picked up the card, then turned white. Meghan said, "Is that you? DC—Daniel Cutter?"

He nodded. "I can't believe he has that. It's an old card. I changed the name of the business years ago." He fished in his overstuffed wallet, pulled out a white rectangle, handed it over. "See?" The card was embossed with a large eye overlaid with a magnifying glass, with the name Sherlock's across the top.

"Sherlock's?"

"Gets business like you can't imagine."

"So why does Derek Allen have your old business card, Mr. Cutter?"

He was still pale, and Aubrey wondered briefly if he'd been the one to take the picture. It made sense. But it didn't matter. None of this mattered anymore.

"Like I said, I had a little problem back then. But I've cleaned myself up. I'm straight now."

Aubrey looked at her watch. She needed some time alone. She needed to think. She needed to batten down the hatches and make sure Derek Allen didn't ruin her life.

Damn you, Josh Hamilton, leaving me with this mess.

She stood up. "Meghan, do you think you can manage the rest of the day without me? I'd like some time to myself, if that's okay. And Chase just called, he's coming in early."

Meghan shot a look at Cutter, then said, "Sure, sugar. I'll go in search of the great mythological son of Daisy. Maybe Daniel here will help. You go home and get pretty for your boy."

Aubrey smiled, trying very hard to make sure it was a sunny, happy grin. "You're the best, Meghan. Thank you. And thank you, Mr. Cutter, for your insights. I appreciate your honesty."

"Watch out for this guy, Mrs. Hamilton. He's trouble."

She nodded and left, mounting the stairs to the grand hall, out onto the street. She didn't feel sunny. She felt overwhelmed. Too many decisions, too much happening. She ran down the street, back to the courthouse parking lot, drove home.

Tyler and Winston were perched on the front porch when she drove up—an eerie reminder of the previous weekend, when Daisy had pulled around the bend and seen Aubrey and Chase in the same spot.

The two were sitting in the sun, both sets of eyes closed. Tyler looked gray and unhappy but sober, and despite the spike of anger at his stupidity, she was glad to see him. She'd need his help to make all this work. Maybe a little deviousness would make him feel better. She wasn't worried about tracking down Daisy's other progeny, if there even was such a person. She needed to get all the pieces together from Josh's puzzle first.

She left the car parked in the driveway and got out. The dog came to her immediately, tail wagging, the whole back end of him moving in time as he snuggled up next to her. "Winston. There's my good boy."

"I'm not your good boy?" Tyler said.

She laughed lightly. "Not even close. But I'm glad you're here."

Tyler nodded in acknowledgment that what she really meant was *I'm happy you didn't take the pizza money and fall off the wagon again and get yourself fucked up three ways to Sunday and betray me.*

She sat next to him, took a stick from Tyler's hand, and tossed it into the yard for Winston. As the dog scampered away, she said, "I need to run something by you."

"Anything. Within reason, of course." He nudged her with his shoulder, and she smiled. God, they'd been through so much. He'd been a part of her life for nearly as long as Josh.

"I'm going to put a call in to my friend Arlo Tonturian. He's with the DA's office. He was a friend of Josh's."

"I remember. Why are you calling him?"

"I need to find out more about Derek Allen. He's involved in Josh's disappearance. I'm worried Allen's going to try and intimidate me, or hurt me."

Winston came back and gave Tyler the stick. He tossed it into the grass. "Allen is a seriously bad dude."

"Badder than you?"

He laughed. "Badder than me. Aubrey, this is a can of worms you do not want to open."

"I know you're trying to protect me, and I

appreciate it. But, Tyler, I'm starting to put this together, and if you know anything else, now would be the time."

He scratched his head, his words measured. "Can't you just take the money and get on with your life?"

"No." She showed him the photograph. "I received this last night. The subject line said, 'He's alive.'"

He glanced at the photo, his face tight. "But you know Hamilton is dead."

She shook her head, as if she could shake some sense into the situation. "I know it sounds insane. There was so much blood that night. So much. It was all over the place. He couldn't be alive. But there was no body. And the police certainly put me through hell."

"They thought you killed him, like everyone else. You had a window of opportunity. You were damn lucky the case fell apart during trial."

"Did you think I killed him?"

He met her eyes. "I know you, remember? I know what you're capable of. Murdering the man you love is beyond you."

Her hands curled into fists. "What if he'd done something terrible? What if I found out everything about him was a lie? Do you still think I'm not capable?"

His tone was wary. "What are you saying, Aubrey?"

She waved her hand, took a breath. "Meghan was married to a private investigator. His name is Daniel Cutter. He said Josh was working with Allen, running drugs. He thinks Josh shot Allen the night he disappeared. That Allen is now out for revenge, and could be coming after me."

"Whoa. Seriously?"

"That's why I want to call Arlo. I want to protect myself in case something is about to go down. Protect us. You're my family, Tyler. My brother. I may get mad at you sometimes, but I don't want anything bad happening to either of us."

She felt him puff a bit with pride at the title, but the tension continued.

"Still, the DA. It's dangerous territory. And you haven't exactly had good luck with the police in the past. Let me finish drying out. I'll keep you safe."

"Saving me again, Tyler?" She said it quietly. He didn't answer right away, just draped a heavy arm across her shoulders. Winston quit worrying his stick and joined them. She petted his silky ears.

"Do you remember that night at all?"

"Yes," she said softly. "Unfortunately, I remember all of it. Like it was yesterday."

"I damn near killed you. Just the idea of it, what you were going through, I wondered for a minute if I should just snap your little neck, make it look like he did it, then I'd have a self-defense claim, and you wouldn't have to live with it."

Jesus. Unpredictable had nothing on Tyler.

"I'm glad you didn't."

"Me, too. Though now, looking at all you've

had to deal with, I sometimes wonder if I did right by you."

She shook her head. "You did the best you could, Tyler, and I'll never forget that. But I'm not a little girl anymore. I'm capable of taking care of myself now. And I refuse to sit back and let Derek Allen take my life from me."

"You don't have to face the world alone, Aubrey."

They sat there together on the step, each remembering, not speaking, until her stomach started to growl.

"I'm going to call Arlo. It's the smart thing to do. And then I'll make you some lunch."

CHAPTER 50

Aubrey
Seventeen Years Ago

Aubrey was twelve when it happened.

Sandy had to work the late shift. Latesha and her latest beau were off somewhere. Julia was asleep in the upstairs bedroom, and Morgan was on a sleepover. Tyler was running on the streets with a bunch of his so-called friends. Aubrey was alone downstairs when the knock came on the door. She went to it, glanced out the peephole. Roger. Sandy's most recent acquisition.

Sandy wasn't all bad. She kept them fed and clothed, and Aubrey was grateful that she didn't try to force them out on their ears when she found out about Latesha and Tyler and the bedroom reindeer games that the three had been playing. It was rare for children in the system to stick in one foster home for the duration, but Aubrey had been with Sandy and her foster siblings for four years now, and that was practically a record. After Sandy found out about Tyler and Latesha, the woman who'd taken Aubrey to McDonald's and brought her to Sandy's came for a visit. She counseled Aubrey, asked all sorts of questions with dolls and such—anatomically correct dolls—but Aubrey assured her nothing untoward had happened.

Maybe Tyler had tried to feel her up once or twice, but that was normal, right?

The woman had pursed her lips and shook her head, then signed off on the house and went back to her own world. It was better that way. Things could have been so much worse. Sandy didn't abuse them, or yell and scream. She basically left them to their devices so long as they obeyed the rules. Sandy didn't necessarily love them, but she didn't hate them either.

But Tyler and Latesha had upset the gentle balance, and now they all had to pay the price. Scrutiny from the system messed with their freedom. Better to keep their mouths shut and let the heat die down.

Sandy seemed to like Roger, so they all tolerated him because a happy Sandy was better for all involved. Aubrey didn't care for Roger much—he had a lazy eye, and she never quite knew whether he was looking at her or not—so she avoided him whenever possible.

So when he came knocking, Aubrey followed the rules. She didn't open the door. She knew she wasn't supposed to. No one was allowed over when Sandy had to work at night.

She said through the crack, "Sorry, Roger, she's at work."

Roger gave her that lazy grin, the one Aubrey knew Sandy liked, a lot, and leaned against the door, pushing the wood against her.

"Come on, Aubrey. Lemme in. I'll just have a beer and wait. Sandy knows I'm here. I just talked to her. She's bringing home chicken after her shift. Someone covered for her, she's getting home early."

Aubrey cocked her head to the side and thought about that. Roger *was* Sandy's boyfriend. He was over here several nights a week anyway. The kids weren't allowed to have friends over, but no one said anything about Sandy's lovers.

She opened the door.

Roger came in and made a beeline for the fridge, where he helped himself to the beer Sandy had bought for him. "Make me some eggs, Aubrey," he commanded, and she did, knowing it was better to just acquiesce to Roger's demands. She'd watched Sandy and Roger together over the past few months, and he certainly got whatever he wanted.

She cleaned up after him and started to the living room to finish her homework. Roger followed, sat in the chair by the television. He put on a baseball game, drank a couple more beers. Aubrey had no problem working in the noise—she was accustomed to the cacophony that came about from having kids and people around at all hours.

At the seventh-inning stretch, Aubrey closed her notebook. "I'm going to bed. You should probably head out."

"I'm gonna wait for Sandy. Why don't you come here and give me a kiss good night?"

"Why don't you go jump, Roger?" She infused her voice with as much tone as she could, the sarcastic notes taken from Latesha and Sandy when they were annoyed. Roger just smiled at her. She started to walk by, but he put out his leg.

"Kiss me good night, Aubrey."

"No. Let me by."

He was fast. Before she could react, he'd leaped from the chair, grabbed her shoulders, and pinned her to the floor. He shoved his tongue in her mouth, and she nearly gagged on the taste of beer and eggs and man.

She pushed against him, but he was big, and heavy, and she couldn't get any purchase. She knew what was going to happen next. She tried to fight him. She tried to scream. But he just clamped one hand over her mouth and used the other to rip her shorts open. He put his hand between her legs, squeezing and kneading and pinching. That place was private, one she'd barely begun to acknowledge, and here he was, drunk and hot and moving on top of her like a wriggling bag of cement. She managed to get her mouth away and bit hard into his arm.

With a roar of pain, he smashed his forehead into her face. Her nose cracked; tears flooded her eyes. Blood began pouring down her face.

Roger slapped her, hard, then flipped her over, put an elbow into her back. "You little bitch. I'm bleeding. I'll make you pay for that."

He pulled her shorts down, knocked her legs apart with his knee, and she started to cry. Suddenly, his weight was gone. She got to her knees, then managed to get to her feet. The blood was everywhere.

Tyler was screaming at Roger. "I'll kill you, motherfucker! She's twelve. She's fucking twelve, and you come over here, try to use her like she's some party favor? What the fuck is wrong with you?"

"Fuck you, you little shit. She asked for it." Roger smacked Tyler, knocked his head sideways. Tyler exploded.

Roger was bigger, but Tyler was quick. He danced around Roger's body, fists flying. It didn't take long for Roger to go down. Tyler straddled his chest, pummeling his face. Over and over and over.

"Tyler!"

He glanced up at her, his face a mask of fury, tears streaming down his cheeks. The sight of her did something to him. He stopped hitting Roger. He stood, panting, covered in blood, his fists red and slick, and advanced on Aubrey. She cringed, but he pulled her into his arms and held her.

"I'm sorry, baby. I'm so sorry." He said it over and over and over again, into her hair, and they cried together like that, sitting on the floor next to Roger's unconscious body, until Sandy came home, and screamed and screamed and screamed.

The police came. The detectives had them separated. Aubrey didn't want Tyler to get in trouble, so she told them she had hit Roger herself. Again and again and again. They stopped the bleeding and gave her ice for her nose and asked her why she hit him. She didn't want to tell them. What happened was private, for her and Tyler alone. She didn't want people to know and look at her with pity—she got enough of that already from her teachers, from Josh.

Josh.

Oh, God, Josh.

How would she ever be able to face him again? Josh was good. Josh was hope.

And now Aubrey was dirt, just a scraping off a shoe.

She didn't deserve him. She was spoiled, tainted, like an apple left in the refrigerator too long, soft and mushy and rotten inside. She didn't deserve him, the golden boy, the one who always believed in her. Going to jail would be easier than facing him.

So she lied to the police.

"He was . . . bothering me, so I hit him. Tyler came home and saw me and tried to stop me. That's what happened. Just send me away."

And with that, she shut her mouth firmly against the world and let them do with her what they would.

They didn't believe her, of course. How could a small girl, barely five feet tall, with long legs and skinny arms, a colt, knock a full-grown man twice her size unconscious?

On the other side of the police station, Tyler was telling a different story. The truth, for once in his life. How he came home to find his foster sister being attacked by his foster mother's boyfriend. How they had words, how Roger punched Tyler in the mouth and told him to fuck off. How Tyler was forced to hit him in self-defense.

"What would you do?" Tyler asked the detective. "What would you do if you walked in on a man trying to hurt your twelve-year-old sister?"

Roger spent a month in the hospital, healing. He was arrested for attacking Aubrey, but Aubrey refused to testify, so he got away with probation. Tyler, on the other hand, pled down to aggravated assault. He and Aubrey were taken from Sandy's home—that was inevitable, of course—and while Tyler went in for his first stint behind bars, Aubrey's fate was much worse.

She was sent to therapy at the rape and abuse crisis center, and became the newest resident of an independent group home on Division Street. One for troubled teens. She was the youngest girl there, the smallest, the quietest.

And Monday morning, she would have to face Josh and explain why she'd moved.

She decided to lie. He mustn't ever know.

No one could ever know.

CHAPTER 51

Aubrey
Today

Aubrey went to her small office and looked up the number to the district attorney's office. Arlo had gone into criminal prosecution after Josh's disappearance, eschewing his previous path of contract law. She liked that about him, that he'd decided to try to make a difference.

And she really liked that he was always on her side. He never treated her like she was crazy, or breakable. Even when she was.

The secretary put her through, and she heard Arlo's deep voice answer, "Tonturian."

"Arlo? It's Aubrey."

"Aubs!" He sounded genuinely pleased to hear from her. "How are you? I was just thinking about you. Janie and Sulman were talking about a beach trip next month. You up for it?"

"Maybe. I need to talk to you, Arlo. It's important. Can you come to the house? Now?"

"Now? Can it wait until tonight? I've got a meeting in twenty minutes."

"Cancel it, Arlo. It's about Josh. And a man named Derek Allen."

She heard flipping papers, a muttered curse. "All right. Give me fifteen minutes. I'll be right there."

"Before you come, I need you to find out everything you can on Allen. He should be in the system."

He started typing; she heard a low whistle. "He is no good. Aubrey, what's this about?"

"Not on the phone, Arlo. Just pull everything and get here as soon as you can."

• • •

Arlo arrived twenty minutes later. His dark hair and beaked nose were so familiar, so comforting, Aubrey nearly threw herself in his arms.

"What the hell happened to the front of your house?"

"Daisy. She got hammered and drove into it. She's in bad shape at Midtown."

"I hadn't heard." The reproach was clear: *Because you don't ever get in touch anymore.*

"Listen, you better come in and sit down. I've made some lunch. You're going to want a full stomach. And Tyler's here."

Arlo tensed. "Is he straight?"

"Yeah. He's helping. So be cool, all right?"

Arlo followed her into the house. Tyler was sitting at the dining room table. They didn't shake hands, but Tyler nodded to Arlo.

She put a plate of grilled cheese sandwiches down, passed out glasses of tea.

Arlo put a stack of papers on the table, grabbed a sandwich, took a huge bite, scattering crumbs. Winston came and sat beneath his feet, lapping up the crumbly bits, happy to be of service. Arlo swallowed and asked, "So what's this all about, Aubrey?"

With a glance at Tyler, she filled him in: Derek Allen approaching her. Daniel Cutter claiming Josh was working for Allen, which made Arlo's face pale. And the email with the photo, which made the paleness turn to vibrant red.

"You're telling me this guy is claiming Josh was running drugs out of Vandy?"

Aubrey nodded. "Tyler? You want to tell him what you heard?"

"I was in holding downtown, there was a guy in there telling tales. We've figured out now it was Derek Allen. He said he'd run a pharmacy scam five years ago with a med student from Vandy. I don't believe in coincidences."

Aubrey said, "I think Allen knew who Tyler was. I think he let him overhear the conversation on purpose so he'd say something to me. And I do have a bunch of money coming to me tomorrow. He's probably gearing up to kill me and steal the money."

Arlo set his sandwich down, took a huge breath, ran his hand over his shadowy chin.

"Christ."

Aubrey nodded. "That about sums it up."

"Fucking Josh. If he weren't already dead, I'd kill him."

"What if he weren't dead?"

Arlo shook his head. "He's gone, Aubs. You know it, I know it."

"We never found a body, Arlo. If he was into something with these people, who knows what happened."

"The cops would have found something. They dug like mad."

Aubrey just shrugged. "Maybe they didn't dig in the right spot."

"This is insane. If that's the case, if Allen is coming for you . . . Aubrey, we'll need to get you somewhere safe."

"We can talk about that once you tell me what you found out."

Arlo opened the file in front of him. "Okay. Here's everything I could pull on short notice about Derek Allen. He made his bones in New York, on Long Island, with the Guiducci crime family. He had a reputation for being ruthless. They used him for the jobs the sane guys didn't want, and Allen took them all. It got to the point that they started to distrust him, to be scared of him, because he was off the rails, and they probably tried to take him out, but Allen was too smart for that. He floated around for a while, no one really knows where.

"Then he shows up down here, heading up a branch of the Dixie Mafia. They were doing a brisk business in hillbilly heroin, meth, all the nasty stuff, until he got sideways with one of his partners, who turned on him, tried to detach Allen from the business. He had no idea who he was dealing with. Allen cut him to pieces, left the parts at each of his crew's houses, as a message. He's a scary dude. And then he ended up gut-shot down on Lischey Avenue, opposite the body of another drug dealer, a Mexican working out of Memphis. The gun that shot him was found at the scene. It looked cut-and-dried, a deal gone bad—they shot each other. The Mexican died, Allen nearly did. But he pulled through, and because he'd violated his parole, having a gun on him, they sent him back to prison to finish out his sentence. The world was blessed with the removal of two more bad guys."

"You don't find it odd that all this just happened to go down the same night Josh disappeared?" Aubrey said.

Arlo took a large bite of his sandwich. Chewed and swallowed. She could tell he was thinking, processing. Finally, he said, "I can't believe this. How in the world would Josh even get matched up with a guy like Derek Allen?"

She slid two more grilled cheese sandwiches onto their plates, took the third for herself, and sat at the table across from Arlo. Raised her eyebrow at Tyler, who took a deep breath and said, "It was my fault."

Arlo tensed. "What did you say?"

"I mentioned what Josh did to a dude I knew. I think he told Allen, or told one of Allen's crew. Allen had lost his source and needed a new one, fast. Product is key for him. Josh was in a position to provide. And if someone took a picture of Josh behaving badly and threatened to show the school and Aubrey, I imagine he'd do most anything to keep that from happening."

"Blackmail," Aubrey said.

Arlo wiped his mouth. "Let me make sure I'm understanding you two. You're saying Josh was being blackmailed into running prescription drugs out of the Vanderbilt pharmacy?"

Aubrey said, "There's only one other scenario that plausible. Could Josh have been undercover, working with the police?"

Arlo shook his head. "Possible, but very doubtful. First off, it would be in the records. And Allen would have known. By all accounts, Allen had a nose for cops. Could always spot one a mile away. And his crew operated in secrecy. When Allen went to jail, they scattered. No one has any idea who was involved with him. The guy was a ghost. I really don't like this, Aubrey. We need to talk to Metro. They need to know what's happening. This is the first solid lead in five years, they're going to want to pursue it."

"No, no way. No cops. Please, Arlo. I can't run the risk of them deciding I knew about this all along and tossing me back in jail."

"I can protect you, Aubrey. I'm with the DA's office now. I promise they won't touch you."

She shook her head. "No cops. Not yet, anyway. You're an investigator, Arlo. Investigate."

"Aubrey, I'm an officer of the court. You've presented me with credible evidence of a conspiracy, blackmail, a possible murder, not to mention giving me some hope that we might, at long last, solve Josh's case. If he *was* involved with Derek Allen and his people, one of them might know where Josh's body is. I can't sit on this."

"A day. That's all I'm asking."

"Why do you think a day will help? What are you going to do?"

"Go through all of Josh's things, see if I can find a connection between him and this Allen character. I have the keys to Daisy's house. She has all his old boxes. I never really looked before. I didn't know exactly what to look for."

"Aubrey—"

"Arlo. Please. Let me try to put things right. You have so much to look into, it's not like you can get warrants and all that together today anyway. It's kept for five years. Another day won't matter."

Arlo glanced from her to Tyler, who nodded.

He threw up his hands. "Okay. One day. But I'm going to look into every detail here. And tomorrow morning, Aubrey, I'm going to pick you up, and we're going to talk to Metro homicide. You hear me?"

"That's a deal. Thank you, Arlo."

He polished off the last of his sandwich. "Don't make me regret this, Aubrey."

He gave her a hug, shook Tyler's hand, and left.

Aubrey let out a long breath, slumped in her chair. "God. This is unreal."

"You said it, sister. Arlo's a good guy. He'll keep his word."

"And Chase? What am I supposed to do about

him? He's going to be here any minute. Should I call and cancel?"

"No. I wanna meet him."

"I don't think that's such a good idea, Tyler."

Tyler stood up from the table. His simple presence was enough to remind her she had no real recourse; he'd get what he wanted regardless. But that didn't mean she had to let up without a fight.

"Really, Tyler. Come on. I don't want him to get rolled into this."

"That's why I need to meet him. I'll be able to size him up. I don't trust anyone right now, sis. There's too much at stake. This Chase guy appears just as all this is going down? You have to—"

Aubrey stepped right into Tyler's space, surprising him enough that he took a step backward.

"Leave Chase out of this, Tyler."

"You've got feelings for this man, Aubrey. I get that."

"I don't. I . . ."

That was a lie. She did. And Tyler knew it. He smiled at her, the leer unmistakable.

"Like I was saying, you like this man. I need to make sure he's not playing you for all you're worth. Literally. You come into a lot of money tomorrow. It's possible he's sniffing around, just like Allen. I want to protect you from getting hurt."

"Like you did with Josh," she mumbled.

"Well, maybe I didn't do such a good job with him at the end. But whose fault was that? I told you for years he wasn't the knight in shining armor you thought he was." She started to snap at him, but he held up a hand to silence her. "Josh was the one person you always kept the blinders on for. What about that chick you saw him with?"

A spike went through her heart. "She was just a classmate."

"A classmate you saw kissing his neck. Come on, Aubrey. You know something was up there. And now, this photo shows up. I keep telling you, something was going on with him."

"End of subject." Aubrey glanced at the clock. Chase would be here soon. She didn't see any sense in fighting Tyler on this. If Chase was going to be in her life, he'd have to meet Tyler sooner or later.

"Fine. You can meet Chase." She grinned at him. "But take a shower, will you? You stink."

Her cell phone rang. Meghan.

"Hey. Did you guys find anything?"

"We did. We found a birth certificate from the hospital. Daisy had a boy, down in Williamson County. The birth father's name was Michael Edwards. The kid would be thirty-three now. That's it, that's as far as we've gotten."

"Can you find Michael Edwards?"

"We're trying. The birth certificate doesn't have his social on it, and it's such a common name. We need more to go on. But we'll keep looking."

"Thank you, Meghan. Thank you so much."

"Sure thing. Everything okay there?"

"I talked to Arlo. He's pulling the threads. Everything is going to be okay."

She heard knocking at the front door.

"I have to go, Chase is here. I'll talk to you later?"

"Count on it," Meghan said, and hung up.

CHAPTER 52

Josh
Five Years Ago

The Tennessee Bureau of Investigation headquarters was up on a lonely hill overlooking the city. Their parking lot had one of the best views in Nashville. Skyscrapers shone in the sky, their glass reflecting the sun, enhanced by the Cumberland River meandering through downtown. From the Titans' stadium to the Batman Building to the courthouse and Shelby Street Bridge, the city's best face was revealed.

Josh Hamilton sat in the parking lot for a solid twenty minutes, trying to get up the courage to go inside, each one of those twenty minutes examining the gorgeous view before him, wondering if it would be the last time he could see the world as a free man.

It was a cool fall evening. The trees were just beginning to turn—the vista before him was sprinkled with crimson and pumpkin and fiery gold, a palette fit for an artist's brush. He loved this town. Loved his city. Loved his ties to the community—to Vanderbilt, to Aubrey. And here he was, about to toss away all that he held dear in the hopes that he could unfetter himself and spend the rest of his life in actual freedom.

It might not work. It was entirely possible that when he marched through those doors and announced that he had been helping provide OxyContin to Nashville's elite, he would be signing his own death warrant. Derek Allen was an unpredictable, mercurial man with a hair-trigger temper. Josh knew without protection he'd be dead. But he had to try. He had to do something. He couldn't live like this anymore.

The deal they'd struck had been working well for both of them. Allen got his pills; Josh got his money for school. He was good at what he did, and Derek Allen had come to rely on him as his main supplier. But now he wanted more, and Josh saw the path to his own personal hell—jail, divorce, public humiliation, because they would get caught, they absolutely would—unfolding before him. Even if it cost him everything, he had to put an end to this. Allen was insane and unpredictable, and damn if he was going to let the man ruin him anymore.

Allen deciding to get bigger, spread out, recruit more pharmacists to skim and doctors to write false prescriptions was one thing. But last week, the paper had done an exposé on drug abuse in the medical system, specifically targeting hospital pharmacies. In response, Vanderbilt announced that, in order to prevent these kinds of problems, they were about to change over their drug distribution to a robotic distribution method, which meant a complete audit of every pill in the system for the past three years. They would come up drastically short. There would be an investigation. Though they'd been very careful, Josh and Bob and Allen could get wrapped up in it, and then he'd be totally screwed.

Josh had to protect himself. He had to get his life back. He had to turn them in, rat them out, and maybe, just maybe, he could save himself. He was desperate.

And desperate men do stupid things.

He took in one last deep breath, then climbed from the car and started toward the doors.

Derek Allen stepped out of the vehicle next to him. Josh thought his heart might stop.

"Well, well, well. If it isn't my erstwhile doctor. Having second thoughts, are we?"

"Leave me alone, man. I'm just looking at the view."

"In the parking lot of the TBI? Bullshit. Get back in your car, now. There's work to be done."

Josh felt panic stream through him. "Not anymore. I'm out."

Allen laughed. "You're out, huh?"

"Yes. I don't want to work with you anymore. And if you don't let me go, I'm going in that building and telling them everything."

Allen took a step closer. Josh clenched his fists, ready for a fight.

"You get in your car and get back with the program, or your pretty little wife and I will have a nice, long chat. And the next time you'll see her, you'll be picking up the pieces of her body from the side of Interstate 40. Do I make myself clear?"

Allen wasn't kidding. Josh had seen firsthand what the man was capable of. He would hurt Aubrey. And he couldn't let that happen. He had to protect her. Had to protect his life with her. And that meant listening to Allen. Going along with his plan.

Josh had no choice. Not anymore.

CHAPTER 53

Aubrey
Today

Chase knocked on her door at 4:30 sharp. Aubrey had given up trying to tame her hair and instead let the curls riot over her shoulders. She wore a linen dress, flowy and clean-lined, and noticed just how far her collarbones jutted out. Too much running, not enough food. Sadness or happiness?

You're dillydallying, Aubrey. Answer the door.

It had only been four days since she'd seen him, but he seemed to have changed. He wasn't quite as tall as she remembered, his eyes not as dark.

But his smile lit her from the inside, and when he stepped inside the foyer and kissed her, it all came rushing back: the thudding of her heart, the strange sense of belonging, of comfort and safety and desire. Dear God, the desire.

She didn't want the kiss to end. But as with all wishes, that wasn't meant to be. Chase finally drew back and held her by the shoulders a foot away so he could look at her. He gave her a long, lazy smile that made her insides flip.

"You're stunning."

"You're sweet. How was your flight?"

"Well enough. It got me here, and that's all I

needed." He ran his hand down her arm, to the inside of her wrist, and used his forefinger to gently brush the soft skin there, tracing the scar. She was mesmerized, and had to force herself to pull away. What was it about him that was so alluring?

Josh, Aubrey. You need to think of Josh.

Truth be told, she didn't want to think about Josh. She was furious with him. Dead or alive, it didn't matter anymore. Her grief had solidified into a sharpness that shocked even her.

"Are you hungry?" She started toward the kitchen, and was relieved when she saw the flash of concern cross Chase's face. He felt it, too. He felt that zing, that connection, and didn't like to have it broken.

"I am, but not for food." Jesus, the way he pitched his voice, she felt it in her gut.

"That's nice to hear," Tyler said. He came into the kitchen from the living room, suspicion etched on his face. Chase immediately tensed, and Aubrey took a step forward and placed herself between the two.

"Chase, I'd like you to meet my foster brother, Tyler."

Chase's face broke into a smile, the tension immediately gone. "Hey. So you got to see this one grow up? That's fantastic."

Tyler just crossed his arms and did his best hard-ass impression.

"Okay. Not the chatty type. I get it. No worries. It's still nice to meet you."

Aubrey watched Tyler, waiting for him to

move, to acknowledge, anything. He just stood there. She finally walked over to him and pushed against his shoulder, knocking him off balance. She kept her tone light.

"This one is trouble, Chase. Stay away from him."

"Why are you messing with my sister?" Tyler growled.

"Tyler. Manners."

Chase smiled his wide grin. "That's okay, Aubrey. I respect his intention. Don't worry, Tyler. I've never met anyone like Aubrey, and I have no intention of doing anything to hurt her. She's been hurt enough as it is."

Tyler's eyes narrowed at that, and he cast a glance toward Aubrey. She just smiled at him. "It's all good, Tyler. We're going to have some food and chat. We don't need a chaperone. Why don't you go take a nap?"

"Do I look like I'm five? Fuck you."

Chase moved so quickly Aubrey gasped. He whipped around and got in Tyler's face. The two were eye-to-eye.

"Don't ever talk to her like that again," Chase cautioned.

Tyler took a step forward. "Or what? You're gonna beat me up?"

"Seriously. She deserves respect. You can talk to your woman that way, but not to mine."

Aubrey swallowed hard. Tyler didn't appreciate being challenged—she could see that immediately—but instead of lashing out or drawing his gun, he licked his lips, then smiled. Smiled his crazy beautiful-toothed grin and started to laugh.

Even Chase seemed taken aback, especially when Tyler punched him lightly on the shoulder.

"You're all right, man. I give you my blessing. If you're brave enough to get in my face, you're brave enough to take her on." He turned to Aubrey. "I'm going out. You be good."

"Be careful," she said, then surprised them both by grabbing him into a rough hug. They stood that way for a fraction of a second before he broke away. Without a word, he sauntered out of the kitchen, and Aubrey heard the front door close behind him. Just as quickly, it opened again. Tyler tossed a FedEx envelope inside the door, said, "You have a letter, Aubrey," and closed it behind him.

"Sorry about that," she said to Chase. "He's always been overprotective."

She picked up the envelope, saw the return address for the insurance company, and set it on the table. She knew what it contained. Notification of the pending bank transfer. Tomorrow was Friday. Aubrey was about to become a very wealthy woman.

Chase seemed oblivious to her reaction. "Glad we have his approval." He reached for her, kissed her deeply. Murmured in her ear, "Let's go upstairs."

Aubrey was tempted, so tempted, but she needed to talk to him, to tell him everything. He had to know what was happening, especially if the police were going to get involved.

She'd been so cool and collected before he showed up, but now, with him here, she was conflicted. All of her feelings were jumbled up inside, a massive ball of knotted yarn. For the first time since she was eight, she didn't know what she wanted.

"We need to talk first."

She led him to the living room. The plaster on the front wall was cracked from the accident— that was going to cost a mint to fix. But that didn't matter right now.

They sat, and she kept a small bit of distance between them. It seemed safer that way.

"What's wrong, Aubrey?"

She met his eyes. "It's about Josh."

"Ah." He sat back on the couch, crossed his legs. "I was worried about that."

"Worried about what?"

Chase's face was soft with kindness, gentleness. "Aubrey. You've gone through so much. His disappearance, being a suspect in his murder. Now his death declaration. I know you must be grieving. Is it too soon for us? Did Daisy's accident just bring it all back for you?"

That and the five million dollars about to be sitting in my bank account and Derek Allen and, and, and . . .

"I wish it were that simple, Chase. I met you, and I threw caution to the wind, and now everything has changed. There have been . . . developments this week. We may have an idea what happened to Josh. He was involved in something. Something bad."

"I know."

Aubrey sat up straighter on the couch. "Excuse me?"

Chase suddenly looked miserable. He took her hand, but she snatched it back. He sighed. "I need to say something before I tell you the whole story."

Aubrey's voice was tight. "What are you talking about?"

"You are the most incredible woman I've ever known. I . . . I came to Nashville looking for a story, and instead, I found you. That's why I want to tell you the truth. The whole truth. But some of what I say is going to upset you."

"A story?" Aubrey used the word like a curse. "What do you mean, a story?"

Chase took a deep breath. "I was doing a story on Josh for the paper. A missing-person exposé. That's why I was here last week. To flesh out the story. To hopefully meet you and interview you to find out more about him."

Aubrey whirled from the sofa. Winston jumped to her side with a woof. She touched his back to stop herself from lashing out at Chase, from scraping her nails down his face. "You *knew*? You knew Josh was my husband? You knew what happened? What I was put through?"

"Yes, but—"

"You've been using me this entire time." The fury finally lit, and she almost didn't recognize the hatred in her voice. "I'm just a part of the story, aren't I? God, how could I have been so stupid as to trust you?"

Chase was shaking his head vehemently. "It's not like that. Don't be crazy."

She must have flinched involuntarily because he reached for her hand immediately. She ripped it out of his grasp.

Calm, Aubrey. Calm yourself. Don't do anything you'll regret.

"Oh, babe, I'm sorry, I don't mean that you're crazy. Just that the idea of me using you . . . Okay. Please, hear me out. We can't move forward if I'm anything less than honest with you."

"We can't move forward at all. Get out."

He grabbed her arms; she yanked away and went to the window. He followed her. "I don't blame you for being pissed at me. I came across your story four months ago, and I got swept up in it. The idea of you and Josh, of what you must have gone through, of what might have happened to him. I pitched it to my editor, and he loved it."

His voice softened. "The more I learned, the more I wanted to see how the story ended. And it was horrible of me not to tell you exactly what I was doing when we met that first night. I stayed in town, talked to a few people. To the police, to the DA, the reporters who did the original work on the story. Everyone thinks you're guilty, but I know you're not. I know you had nothing to do with Josh's death.

"I lied, Aubrey, and I know it was wrong, and I am so, so sorry." He tried to pull her to him. She resisted, pushed against his chest.

"No!"

"Aubrey, please. I am not lying when I say I'm in love with you. Falling in love with you was the last thing I expected to happen. But I did. I love you. The story doesn't matter. I killed it. I told my editor there was nothing here, nothing new. I won't be doing the piece. I just want to be with you. Please, you have to forgive me."

She shook her head, forced the words out.

"I don't believe you. And you are not allowed to love me. You've lost that right." She was spinning out of control. She had nothing to lose anymore; her heart was a solid mass of stone. "And there's something else you need to know. Maybe it will help you finish your little saga. I think he's alive. I think Josh is alive. So fuck you, Chase Boden. Get the hell out of my house, and leave me to my fucked-up little life."

She started pushing him, backward, toward the door.

"Aubrey, please. I love you."

The fury bubbled over and she started to yell. "Get out, get out, get out!"

Chase stiffened, his face angry and tight. In that brief moment, he looked so much like Josh that she sucked in her breath and her mind started to whirl. Her heart felt like it stopped, then started again, taking off at a gallop.

Of course. She'd been an idiot not to see it before. It had all been staring her in the face this whole time.

Daisy said she had sons.

Brothers.

Josh and Chase.

Aubrey felt herself falling, heard Chase shouting. Then there was nothing.

CHAPTER 54

Daisy
Thirty-three Years Ago

Daisy was twenty, just shy of twenty-one, when she found out she was pregnant. Twenty, and already married for two years to a Navy SEAL who'd been stationed at too many posts to count. He was always being shipped away, off to foreign lands. He was a decent man, Chris, big and brusque and handsome, but gone so much. She was lonely. So very lonely.

They had a small house on the east side of Nashville that was easy to keep, and to stave off the boredom she experienced when he was gone, she was taking classes at Nashville State: English composition and Creative Writing 101. She'd started the community college classes at the beginning of the summer semester—something, anything, to keep busy. Chris had shipped off last month to some South American country; she wasn't allowed to know exactly where. He wasn't due back for a while.

She shouldn't have done it. But she was young and so lonely, married to a man who was never around. And Dr. Edwards, well, he was smart and sexy, and beauty and light and happiness and hippie—all in a little roll in the hay.

She knew better. It was a mistake, a terrible, huge mistake. She realized that before the sweat dried. Fun while it lasted, and all kinds of sexy since it was so forbidden. But wrong. She refused to see him again, dropped his class, and went on her way, trying to forget.

Six weeks later, there was no denying it. She was late, and sick, and sore, and scared. She went to the doctor at the Planned Parenthood in Williamson County, where no one knew her, and they confirmed the worst. She was pregnant.

How could she have been so stupid?

She was on the pill—every woman her age was on the pill. Chris wanted her to take it. He was afraid of orphaning a child. His work was terribly dangerous. But with Chris gone, she hadn't been particularly religious about taking them.

And now here she was.

She didn't know what to do. Or, rather, she did, but she was scared to death. The Planned Parenthood people were nice enough; they told her it would be quick and easy, especially since she was this early in her pregnancy. She went to the professor, waited outside his classroom, and told him she was six weeks gone. He was thrilled, and excited, and wanted her to keep the child.

She regretted telling him the instant the words came out of her mouth and his eyes lit up. He was from a bohemian world, where drugs and drink and casual sex were a daily thing, not missteps made by lonely young women.

Telling him was a disaster. She shouldn't have

told anyone, just gone and spread her legs and let the vacuum erase her folly. But she needed the money from him for the abortion—she couldn't take it from their family funds; Chris would notice a chunk of money missing like that.

Dr. Edwards—God, she didn't even know his first name—refused to give her money for an abortion. He wanted the child. He'd raise it on his own if she didn't want to be involved. He'd like for her to be. They had such a connection. Obviously they did—how else would they have made a baby with one brief, sweaty event?

The very idea panicked Daisy. Keeping the child wasn't an option. She was married, to a man who'd been gone ten weeks. Pretending the child was his would be impossible. She'd have to stage an early delivery and explain away why the child was full term. Chris wasn't an idiot. He'd put two and two together, and probably kill her. He was a good man, but even honorable men could be pushed beyond their limits when jealousy took the reins.

She didn't know what to do. She had no idea when Chris was coming back. And day by day, she grew bigger and bigger. She thought she was showing at just over three months. At four she finally started to feel better, not so sick, not so clouded. And by then, it was too late. She was past the time when they would legally abort the child.

Chris came home. She wore the baggiest clothes she could find, mostly his, telling him she'd missed him so much she'd taken to wearing his clothes. He teased her for getting fat while he was gone—she'd only put on a few pounds, but on her frame, it was obvious. But Chris hadn't ever been up close and personal with a pregnant woman. He had no idea. Though she caught him eyeing her stomach a few times, contemplatively scratching his chin, the excuses about the weight and his clothes were enough. Maybe he just didn't want to see. She often wondered about that after he was gone, whether he'd had some premonition that he would die and so, despite realizing his wife was pregnant by another man, kept his concerns to himself and gave her a final gift.

When he shipped out again, she was just over five months. She hadn't known how she was going to keep it a secret much longer, and was so relieved, so relieved, when he got his orders. Two weeks later the news came: Chris had been killed in the line of duty. They wouldn't give her any more details than that. Words were whispered that he had died in Nicaragua, but she could never get the Navy to admit anything.

At least he hadn't been publicly shamed. After the funeral, Daisy confined herself for the next several months, comically ballooning. When she needed to see the doctor, she followed her earlier pattern, driving twenty-five miles to Franklin and having the Planned Parenthood people help her. Friends and family assumed she was prostrate with grief. It was better that way.

Dr. Edwards (she found out his name was Michael, though she could never come to think of him that way) waited patiently for her call. He and his wife—yes, of course the jerk was married—were going to raise the child. His biological child. Daisy didn't know how a woman could agree to raise her husband's bastard child, and worried that the baby wouldn't be loved properly. But who was she to think those things? She loved her baby exactly enough not to kill him, and to give him away to a practical stranger.

When the time came, four in the morning on the fifth of March, when she felt like she was being sawed in half from the pain and her bed was drenched in amniotic waters, she didn't panic. She called Dr. Edwards. He and his wife, a beautiful dark-haired gypsy who seemed thrilled by the blessed event, picked her up in their Volkswagen Beetle. They drove her down to the hospital in Franklin—Daisy refused to have the baby any other place—and once the child was out, they left her there, in pain, throbbing and torn and empty.

She knew it was a boy. That's all she knew.

A son, who now belonged to someone else.

A husband, dead.

A lover, gone.

Daisy, widowed, childless, alone, and finally in a position to start over. She was free and clear to start her life, yet again.

She had always been a good singer. She could get work in the honky-tonks, singing backup or covers. And that's just what she did. She lost the baby weight as quickly as possible, sent out some demos and résumés, and landed a job two weeks later. She sang and flirted and had herself a ball, and tried so very hard not to think of the small bundle she'd given away.

Once, when she'd had a great deal to drink and was feeling especially lonely—because while she had a job, and friends, something inside her would never be right again—she tried to call the Edwards house. A recording gave her an immediate three-toned note, then said: "The number you have dialed has been disconnected or is no longer in service. Please check the number and dial again."

Gone. The man, the boy, the woman. All gone. The hole in her, the emptiness, the sneaking suspicion that she'd done the wrong thing, it all came parading back.

But she was too late. Remorse is a pointless emotion when you can't do anything to rectify the situation.

The next night, hungover, sad, lonely, she accepted the offer of a handsome man who wanted to buy her a drink. She needed the dog's hair anyway, and was running low on cash; tips weren't as plentiful when she wasn't on her game, and she wasn't on her game tonight.

The handsome man bought her a drink, then another, and another. Daisy was feeling better, more confident, surer, and he was a specimen, wide shoulders winnowing to a small waist, square jaw, straight teeth. Brown hair slicked back, jeans that filled out in all the right places. His name was Ed, Ed Hardsten, and several drinks later, when he offered to give her a ride, and he wasn't just talking about his car—wink, wink—she thought, what the hell. *What do I have to lose?*

Those were words that always came back to haunt Daisy.

The "ride" was an excellent one, and when Hardsten asked to see her again, she agreed. Languorously wrapped in his sheets, she hadn't felt like this much of a woman since . . . Well, she didn't like to think of that night, when Dr. Edwards took her up against the wall in the stairwell at the college.

She married Hardsten three months later. They bought a little house with a white picket fence and got to work starting a family. And she told herself how happy she was, day after day after day.

CHAPTER 55

Aubrey
Today

Aubrey came to on the couch, with a worried Chase inches from her face.

It was too much. It was all too much.

"Aubrey, are you okay? Please, listen to me. Please forgive me."

She held up her hand. "Stop. Just give me some space."

He handed her a glass of water. She drank it, mind still spinning, half with anger, half with relief. She set the glass down and pulled her legs up onto the couch, making herself into a small ball. She searched his face for any sign he knew what was going on. She saw only a man who had feelings for her, but he wasn't innocent anymore. She couldn't trust him. And her heart broke. It all crashed together again, and Aubrey shut her eyes.

Daisy.

Sons.

It all made such a sick, weird kind of sense now. There are no coincidences in life. Chase had been sent to her, a gift, a way out of her own grief. He'd been using her, and now she was being punished, yet again.

But she breathed out a sigh of relief. She

wasn't crazy. She wasn't seeing things. That's why he seemed so damn familiar.

"Chase, I need to ask you a serious question, and I need you to tell me the truth. Were you adopted?"

"What?" He whirled away, eyes blazing. "Jesus, Aubrey. You just drop this bomb that your dead husband might be alive, tell me I'm not allowed to love you, and then ask that? What the hell?"

She tamped down the anger, the betrayal, the urge to lash out. Got up and went to him. He didn't move, was breathing hard. She took his cheeks in her hands, looked deep into his eyes. Mad as she was, she was tempted to kiss him, but didn't. It was all over between them. She couldn't have him, and he couldn't have her. But she needed to know the whole truth, no matter where it took them.

"I know this sounds like it's coming out of left field. But you have to tell me. Were you adopted?"

He stood there, frozen, staring at her. Then he closed his eyes and sighed a great shuddering breath, took her hands from his face, and sat down hard on the couch.

"No one knows. How did you find out?"

"Educated guess. So you are?"

"Yeah. I found out two years ago, when my mom first got sick. She was diabetic, had been since she was a kid. The disease finally ravaged her kidneys, and she needed a transplant. Of course I was the first in line. But our blood types weren't a match. I asked what mine was, and the doctor gave me this look. I will never forget it, just this sideways glance, like, 'He doesn't know. Don't ruin his life.' It didn't take long to do the math—so I went to my stepdad and asked him about it.

"He wouldn't tell me who the woman was, but admitted my real father had a one-time-thing affair, and got the girl pregnant. She wasn't in a position to have a child, so she delivered me in secret and my parents took me home. They got divorced a few years later, and my mom remarried Robert Boden. My real dad left, and Robert Boden and my mother adopted me."

He eyed her. "Why are you asking me this, Aubrey?"

"Chase," she said softly, "I think you're Josh's brother."

Chase jumped to his feet and started stalking around the living room. Winston watched him, his head turning in circles.

"That's insane."

"It's not insane," Aubrey said. "It makes perfect sense. That's why you look so much like him even though you don't. Why you have the same mannerisms, the same set to your shoulders, the same walk. It's why Daisy finally admitted to all of us that she had sons—more than one. Because she recognized you, even though she didn't know for sure. Do you know your birth father's name?"

"Edwards. Michael Edwards."

"Chase, Meghan found a birth certificate with Daisy's name—your original birth certificate. Michael Edwards is listed as the father."

Chase's face was tight.

"I want to see Daisy. I want to ask her myself."

Aubrey sat back on the couch and watched Chase walk the room. "I don't know if that's going to happen, Chase. She may not make it. You may never have the whole truth. That's life, right?"

He flinched, and Aubrey was surprised to feel a pinch of pain in her chest. *You can't feel anything for him. You've been a pawn in his game all along, just like you were in Josh's.*

She steeled herself against him. She couldn't allow him to hurt her. He was just another man, like all the rest.

Wasn't he?

Watching him, in clear pain, she was torn between anger at him for betraying her and insatiable curiosity. Chase was Josh's brother. Somehow, she'd known it all along.

"Why did you lie to me? Why didn't you just tell me you were doing a story?"

"Because I am an ass, Aubrey. Because I thought the story was more important. Because I didn't count on . . . you."

"Me? Or what happens next?"

"What does happen next?"

"I don't know. You tell me. You need the ending to your story, don't you? That's why you've been sticking around, to see if Josh shows up for the money tomorrow. What are your plans after that?"

He stopped moving, his face pale. "That is not true."

Aubrey smiled sadly. "It's partially true."

He stopped pacing. "It's not. I am not playing games with you, Aubrey."

She chewed on her lip for a minute. She was such a terrible judge of character. Chase had lied to her, to them all. He'd used her to get at the story, and knowing that he was a part of all of this, even tangentially, was simply mind-blowing.

But by damn, he actually seemed to be telling her the truth now. If she couldn't recognize honesty when it bit her on the ass, she could recognize pain. And Chase was clearly hurting, badly. He stopped in front of her, dropped to his knees.

"Please," he said. "Please forgive me."

Aubrey shook her head quickly. "We don't have time for this. You have all your research, right? You need to see the story through. You need to find out the truth. Here it is. I think he's alive." She went to her bag and pulled out the photo.

He glanced at it, then handed it back. "I've seen it before."

"What? How?"

He laughed, short and hard and utterly humorless. "Sent anonymously to me. I was going to show it to you today when I confessed all my sins."

"It wasn't sent anonymously. I'm certain Derek Allen sent it. The man Josh was working with. He knows you're working on the story. He saw you at the hospital."

"What?"

She explained everything. Chase listened, then shook his head. "I can't believe it."

Despite her anger at him, she reached over and smoothed the hair back from his forehead. "But it's the only thing that makes sense, Chase."

Chase just shook his head. "Aubrey. I've been in this story for months now. I haven't seen anything that leads me to believe Josh is still out there."

She knew that. Of course she did. But what if he wasn't? There had to be a reason Derek Allen was terrorizing her.

"You said Cutter told you Josh was running drugs with Derek Allen?" Chase said. "Well, here's what I think was going on. I think Josh was being blackmailed. If there's one thing I learned about him during my investigation, it's that he would do most anything to make sure you weren't hurt. Blackmail fits."

Aubrey nodded. "That's what Arlo and Tyler think, too."

He reached for her hand, and she let him take it. "Aubrey. Let me help you. I'm here, telling you the truth. I refuse to betray you. Never again. I love you."

She flipped a hand, brushing the words from the air before they reached her. She couldn't hear this, not now.

Chase's lips tightened. "I see. I fucked up. And now you and I are finished, aren't we?"

She should say yes. She should. She knew that she couldn't have a future with Chase. Not after he'd lied to her, used her. And now that she knew he was Josh's brother? It wasn't right. It wasn't fair. Yet, she still didn't know what she wanted.

Despite herself, she leaned over and kissed him, lightly at first, then with a growing hunger. He responded in kind for a few moments, then broke away.

"I can't do this. I can't be with you if I don't know that you're mine. I know you don't want to hear it, Aubrey, but I'm not lying. I am in love with you. I felt it the moment we met, in the park. But I won't share you. With a memory of a man, yes. But not if he's out there. Not until we figure out what happened to him, once and for all."

Aubrey hated his words. Hated them and respected them and felt the weight of his resolve. Perhaps she was wrong. Perhaps he was an honorable man. Perhaps not. He'd lied to her. She couldn't ever trust him, not really. She wanted to kick and scream and smash his face in and, at the same time, wanted him to hold her and tell her it was all going to be okay. It hurt to think of not being with him. And she didn't know how to reconcile that with his betrayal.

Chase stood. "I'm going to go," he said. "I need to see Daisy. But I need to tell you something first."

"What's that?"

"The police are watching you and Tyler."

A small frisson of panic wormed into her

stomach. "Why?"

"You know why."

"The money. Those idiots still think he might come back."

Chase searched her eyes. "Be careful, Aubrey. No matter what happens now, I don't want you to get hurt."

She swallowed hard and nodded.

Chase touched her lightly on the shoulder, then glanced around the house like he knew it was the last time he'd see it. He took a breath and started to say something, then shook his head and left through the front door.

Aubrey closed the door behind him and collapsed against it.

She couldn't do this anymore. She would go mad. The only thing that would give her a chance to think was a run. She took Winston with her. She didn't feel safe by herself anymore.

CHAPTER 56

Josh
Five Years Ago

Josh's plan was simple: a straightforward exchange, a clean double cross. He was going to rob Derek Allen and take him down. And if Allen died in the process, all the better. Josh had finally admitted to himself there were only two ways this could go. Either Allen died, or Josh did.

Josh's next delivery was expected in a week. The order had been huge, so big that Bob in the pharmacy shook his head and said it was impossible. But he always said that, and always delivered. This time, in addition to the pills, Allen wanted prescription pads. Which really put Josh on the spot. Sneaking around the hospital stealing prescription pads was dangerous as hell. But he would do it, because the more ammunition he had, the better.

Allen was going into business with a new cartel, and this score was his buy-in. They were paying him a load of money, and he'd turn over all the goods in exchange for the cash. And Josh would take that money, and the score, right out from under his nose.

Josh knew it was stupid. He knew it was a massive gamble.

But the idea that he'd be free was intoxicating. Kill two birds with one stone—get Allen off his back and get out from under the blackmail. Start his life with Aubrey anew. Finish his schooling and go do some good for a change.

Josh kept to his schedule, his plan. When Allen called the meeting, he hung up the phone and told Aubrey he was pulling an extra shift at the morgue.

And Aubrey, sweet, loving, kind Aubrey, smiled and fixed him a sack lunch so he'd have some fuel besides coffee to sustain him overnight.

Josh drove the Audi to the river, looking vainly in the mirror for people following him. He didn't know if he could make yet another week like this, pretending, living a charade, not being honest with anyone, including himself.

Allen was waiting for him. Every time Josh walked into the warehouse, he was reminded of a scene from one of his favorite movies, *Ocean's Twelve*. And the fact that a heist film was one of his favorites wasn't lost on him. Maybe he had a bit of criminal in him after all. After his father's escapades, Josh was wondering if it was in his blood. Not this reluctant "can't believe I'm involved in this" feeling, but the idea that perhaps he was a mastermind in his own right, that he was just like the Night Fox.

No, that wasn't a good comparison. The Night Fox was a dupe. He fell for the long con and lost everything—his reputation most of all.

Though maybe it was a perfect comparison after all. Josh had allowed himself to be duped by Allen from the get-go.

The staging area, as Allen liked to call it, was a card table with a large paper map of Nashville spread on it. Allen held a pointer in his hand. He watched Josh walk to the table. Josh felt like sticking a finger in his collar and loosening it. His throat stuck, and sweat bloomed across his forehead.

He knows. He knows. He knows I'm going to screw him.

Son of a bitch.

He was fucked.

Allen gave a mock bow. "Nice of you to finally show up."

Josh crossed his arms over his chest and shrugged. Didn't offer any more. He'd learned the hard way: all Allen needed was a little ammunition. An excuse would do nothing but make the man attack.

Allen stared at him again, long and hard.

"We have an issue."

Josh just raised an eyebrow. Nonchalant. Uncaring. Inside his guts were twisting and his mind was screaming. He was going to die. He could just feel it.

"Here's the thing, Hamilton. The buyer wants to meet you, face-to-face. He wants assurances."

"No way. I'm not meeting with some dealer."

"Oh, yes, you are. You're going to assure him you can continue providing the product and prescriptions. I'm going to assure him I can continue bringing in the high-grade blow. And together, we'll shake his hand, and then you're going to take a wad of cash off him."

Josh felt the heat begin to rise. *Play it, Josh.* "You want *me* to rob him? No. Absolutely not."

Allen turned cold. Josh was reminded of a snake, coiled and waiting, impassive, safe only if left unprovoked. "*No* isn't part of the equation. You're going to do this. You're going to do it right. And we're going to walk away very, very rich men."

"I can't. I have no idea how to pull it off."

Allen cleared his throat. "Stop being such a pussy. I'll walk you through every step."

Josh glared at him. *Play along. Be yourself. Be the timid guy he knows and loves.*

"No way, no how. I can't do this. I'll screw it up. I'm a doctor, for God's sake, Derek. I'll blow it."

"No, you won't. You'll be fine. There's just one catch."

"Just one? What's that?"

"I don't know what night it's going to go down. My contact is flying in, but for security reasons he won't tell me when."

Josh ran his hands through his hair. "Derek. Don't make me do this."

"You're doing it, and that's final."

It was another two hours before Allen dismissed him, after drills upon drills of how they were going to make this work.

Finally, he set down the pointer. "Good. That

will work. Now, come here, kid. We need to have a chat."

Josh felt his heart jump into his throat again. Maybe he was wrong; maybe Allen did know. Fuck.

"Have a seat."

Josh took the chair. At this point, if he argued anymore, Allen was going to get suspicious. But he was caught by surprise.

"I'm really proud of you, kid. This is an important deal, the biggest one of my career. This dude is big-time, and I don't want his people thinking they can push me around. We're gonna show him we're strong, unstoppable."

"One question. Why?"

"Because I need them to understand I'm the right guy to do business with, and that we're going to be doing things my way, not theirs. We need to send the right message. We aren't going to be bought. They're going to work with us. For us. We're the ones with the product they want. And you're the one who can make it happen for me. You're my leverage. I just wanted to say thank you."

Josh was shocked, and his face certainly didn't hide that. Allen laughed. "I know. That sounds crazy to you. But you've added an element of class to this operation. You're smart, and I trust you. Do you see any issues with the plan?"

"Outside of me being the one who's supposed to rob this guy, and the fact that if I screw it up, his people will probably hunt us down and kill us both? No. It's solid."

"You're going to do fine. Don't worry about it. He won't see you coming. Just stick to the program and you'll sail right through." He hung an arm over Josh's chair, leaned in, the good cheer gone. "One last thing. You realize if I go down, we all go down, right?"

"Always."

"Good. I'm pretty sure this will happen sometime this weekend. So be ready. And no leaks."

"I can't this weekend."

"Yes, you can. And you will."

"No, seriously. My best friend is getting married, and I'm in charge of his bachelor party. I'm tied up the whole weekend. I'm the best man. I can't just not show up."

"I don't give a fuck." He smiled. "When I give you the signal, you're going to get yourself in place and get me that briefcase. Do you understand?"

"What's the signal?"

Allen stood, effectively dismissing Josh. "Trust me. You'll know."

CHAPTER 57

Chase

Aubrey shouldn't have forgiven him. Not that she'd said the words, exactly; there'd been no benediction, no blessing, just a sad stroke of his forehead and those limpid eyes, hurt flaring inside them, then compassion at his confusion.

How could he have been so stupid? How could he have allowed himself to be manipulated like this? He thought he was the one doing the game playing, yet it had all been a big joke on him, hadn't it? He'd lost Aubrey for good, and he was in over his head with this story.

He drove away from Aubrey's house, drove in circles for an hour, looping through Nashville, until he found himself at the hospital.

He wound his way around the crazy hallways. He finally found Daisy's room, but it was empty. A nurse at the central station told him she'd been taken back into surgery, and he could wait in the surgical floor lounge.

He hurried there, only to find Tom sitting defeated in a chair. He was asleep, chin in hand, a cooling cup of coffee to his right.

He should wake him, ask to help. Tell him Daisy was his mother, that he should be on watch with her. Sharing the duties.

He started forward, then stopped himself. What was he going to do? Wait? There were no answers here. She wouldn't know he was there. She wouldn't want to meet him like this.

Out then, into the Nashville evening again. To the drunken girls wandering Lower Broad and the anonymity of the tourist-packed streets, the vast sameness of it all.

He tried to lose himself. He walked the streets of Lower Broad for an hour, one thought purling through his mind.

He wanted Aubrey back. How was he going to get her back?

He drove his rental to the Sheraton, booked a room for the night. He took the elevator up to a space that was a replica of every hotel room he'd ever been in, took a shower, lay on the bed. How royally had he fucked up?

He should call her. Call and beg to come back over, to talk. To explain again, to find a way to make her understand. To find a way to keep her safe.

He didn't care about any of it, just knew that the thought of never seeing her again made him quiver in pain. He could fix this. He knew he could.

He started to dial her number, but hesitated. He shouldn't ask permission; he should just go over there, sweep her into his arms, use his body to explain. He had to do something to shake off this hideous feeling of dread that he was about to lose everything.

Because if he truly did lose Aubrey for good, he'd never forgive himself.

There was a knock at the hotel room door. He thought about ignoring it, but whoever it was, anything would be a welcome distraction from his current thoughts.

He set down the phone and flung open the door, only to be greeted by a familiar face.

"Hello, Chase."

CHAPTER 58

Aubrey
Five Years Ago

When Nashville Metro stood her in front of the white board for her mug shot, Aubrey cringed. She couldn't believe they'd arrested her. How could they think she'd murdered Josh?

The minute the cops figured out that she had a juvie record, they started pushing her, hard, and she lost it. On went the cuffs. It was unfair, and frightening, and she didn't know what to do. Thankfully, Arlo had hooked her up with a defense attorney who worked at the firm he'd interned at. The firm encouraged pro bono work, and so the lawyer was jovial, albeit a little reserved. His name was Hornby. Reginald Hornby. *Call me Reg.* He met with her on a Thursday, when it looked like the cops might actually try to press charges against her, nearly a week after Josh had disappeared. Asked all sorts of questions.

What was your relationship like?

Not was like, is like. It's very good. We love each other. We've loved each other for years, since we were kids.

And do you argue?

Like everyone, we have occasional spats. Nothing serious.

Money issues?

Of course. Josh is in medical school. It's expensive. But we have a budget, stick to it. Nothing unmanageable.

And you work a second job to help make ends meet?

Yes. Is that a bad thing?

No, no, just asking. Trying to get to know you and your relationship.

Aren't you going to ask if I did it?

Nope. I don't want to know.

What do you mean, you don't want to know?

First rule of criminal defense, Mrs. Hamilton. The less I know about exactly what and how you committed the crime, the better.

For the record, I didn't. This is all bullshit.

Of course it is, dear. Now. Was your husband seeing anyone else?

Are you kidding? Of course not. He wouldn't cheat on me. He wouldn't.

Don't get upset. I need to cover all the bases. Did he have any vices? Drugs? Alcohol? You know how these med students like their speed.

My husband would never do drugs. We have experience with that, in our family, and he knows what a bad road it is.

All right. He sounds like a pretty nice guy. Now, I need to hear everything about the night Josh disappeared. Start to finish.

And so she told him.

CHAPTER 59

Josh
Five Years Ago

Josh looked at his watch for the tenth time in ten minutes and tapped his fingers on the banister.

"Aubrey, come on already. We're going to be late."

"I'm coming, hon. Minor hair disaster."

"When is it not?" he murmured.

"I heard that."

A moment later, Aubrey appeared at the top of the stairs. Bedecked in a simple pink sheath, her curly dark blond hair piled on her head, a simple strand of pearls around her neck, she looked stunning, and highly annoyed.

"You're breathtaking," he said, and she shot him one of her most sardonic looks as she came down the stairs. She was wearing heels, and clung to the banister, which he found incredibly funny. He'd thought all women were born with an innate ability to totter around on those stupid stilettos, but his wife proved otherwise. Get her out of sneakers, clogs, or flip-flops and she had all the grace of an elephant on roller skates.

"Yeah. Forty minutes of straightening and the whole mess curled up again as soon as I turned the iron off. Why do I even bother?"

"Because if you didn't, you'd spend the evening wishing you had. It looks great, sweetie. You know I like it pulled up like that anyway. Grab your coat, we are so far behind."

"You shouldn't have played golf this morning then."

"You should have agreed to stay at the damn hotel last night, too, and I wouldn't have had to come home to shower."

"Touché." She grinned, and he smiled back. It felt good to smile. Good, normal.

Their bags were already packed in the car for the long weekend. Another wedding. They joked that they'd become like the characters in *Four Weddings and a Funeral*. But the spate of invitations that began rolling in three years earlier would finally end tomorrow, when the last of their tight group of friends pulled the trigger and joined the crowd of smug marrieds. And of course, there'd been no funeral, so maybe it wasn't the most apropos analogy.

Josh was the best man for this one, Kevin Sulman the lucky bridegroom. The wedding weekend had commenced Thursday with an around-the-world bar crawl—girls in one representative hemisphere devouring margaritas, the boys in another downing Guinness—and resumed on Friday morning with a more sedate golf round for the gents and a high tea for the ladies, followed by tonight's bachelor-bachelorette extravaganza.

Josh had tried to talk Kevin out of doing the bachelor party the night before the wedding. The last thing anyone wanted was to be hungover, standing in front of two hundred people in a stuffy church. But Kevin just shook his head and said, "Hell no, man. I ain't waking up in Thailand and scrambling to get home. All I want is a few beers, a couple of strippers, and Janie to fall all over herself worrying about me looking at titties all night. No sense giving her more to fret about than that."

Kevin always was the responsible one.

Aubrey turned in a circle, making sure she had everything, grabbed her bag, and met Josh's eyes. "Ready."

Josh set the alarm and held open the door to the garage. Only five minutes behind schedule now. That was dealable.

They settled themselves in the car, the Audi Quattro Josh got for a steal at an auction house. The engine was still throaty, and the car handled beautifully. They'd fixed it up, vacuumed and Armor All'd and waxed it until it gleamed. He pulled out of the garage carefully, then shut the door and headed out of the driveway.

"You know I'm dreading this," Aubrey said.

"Why? Men with tassels on their privates don't turn you on?"

"That's not what I meant."

He glanced over at her, then ran his hand up her thigh. She hadn't worn hose, and her legs were smooth. He pinched her knee at the spot he knew tickled and said, "Me neither. But it will all be fine. I promise."

"Josh, watch out!"

He turned his head forward, instinctively braking and throwing his arm in front of Aubrey well before he saw the black sedan that had stopped suddenly in front of them. He braced himself for the sickening crunch that followed: loosening his hold on the steering wheel, letting his muscles relax, taking his foot off the clutch. All this without batting an eyelash or thinking it through, just reacting. All those driving lessons from his father, all the near misses with his mother—both had swung their arm across to save him. And now he did it for his wife.

The car in front of them must have heard the squeal of the tires locking up because the driver hit the gas and lurched forward. That move saved them from serious injury. Instead of hitting the car from behind going forty miles an hour, the blow was cushioned so it seemed more like twenty. Still bad enough to crumple the fender and the hood and make the air bags pop free with a gigantic hiss. Still bad enough to knock the wind out of Josh. Still bad enough to hurt.

Once the shock of the collision passed, he knew he was okay. The pain across his chest was just the impact from the safety belt and the air bag. After a few tentative breaths he was able to bat the bag out of the way and reach for Aubrey. Surprise and fear and gratitude etched new lines on her face; her mouth was open in a round little O. Her hair had tumbled down from its clip, falling loose and curly around her shoulders, and her eyes were wide.

"Are you okay?"

She nodded. "I think so. Are you?"

"Yeah. I better check on the driver of the other car."

"Should I call the police?"

"Just hang tight for a second. Let me see how bad things are first."

She nodded again. Her face was blank now, the panoply of emotions that she'd first shown gone as reality set in.

Josh managed to get the door open without too much trouble. He didn't step from the car, but sort of fell out, just losing his balance for a moment. His knees hit the pavement, and he looked down at himself briefly, expecting to see blood or a severed limb. There was nothing. He was unscathed.

The driver of the black sedan had gotten out as well and was shouting at him. He was a middle-aged suit: perfectly combed hair, thin build, and obviously pissed off.

Derek Allen.

Fuck. The signal.

Josh put his hands up in the universal non-threatening "sorry, man" gesture, but Allen kept coming. Kept in character, putting on a little show for the crowd who'd gathered.

"What the hell were you doing? It was a stop-light. Are you a complete idiot?"

"Dude, I'm sorry. It was my fault. I looked away for half a second. Are you okay?"

That calmed the man down a bit.

"Please tell me you have insurance."

"Of course I have insurance. And I'm sure it will cover all the damage to your car."

Speaking of which . . . Josh walked to the front of the Audi, which had held its basic shape, even though the bumper and hood were mashed in. The sedan they'd hit was barely scratched, just a tiny dent where the Audi's fog lights had dug into the bumper. The sunlight sparkled in a deep scrape on the Audi's hood. Down to the metal. To the bone.

The fucker.

Josh looked at the sedan's minimal damage and shook his head. Aubrey had gotten out of the car now, and was looking forlornly at the front fender and hood.

"Oh, Josh. Our baby."

Allen's head whipped around. "You're pregnant?"

She shook her head. "No, not me. The car. It's our baby."

The flustered look dropped from his face, and he smiled. "Oh. I was . . . Never mind."

"We should probably call the police," Aubrey said.

Allen shook his head vehemently. "No, no, no need for all that. I'll just take your information. My car won't need much work. I can probably push that dent out. And if I have to pay to get it fixed, well, I trust you. You seem like a nice young couple."

A car horn sounded; traffic was starting to jam up.

"Why don't we push your car over onto the shoulder and get you out of the way?"

Out of the way. Josh realized his hands were shaking. What the fuck kind of message was this supposed to be, anyway?

Josh felt the sweat trickle down the small of his back, not entirely sure if it was from heat or frustration.

Allen continued his ministrations. "Why don't I call you a tow? I know a good one nearby, he'll treat you fairly."

Aubrey shook her head—she was never one to take help when she didn't absolutely have to have it. "We appreciate that, sir, but I've already called AAA."

Josh bit his tongue—actually, sliding a twenty at a random tow truck operator sounded much more appealing than waiting for God knew how long for the AAA folks to show, but Aubrey had already shaken Allen's hand and wagged her phone at him. Responsible Aubrey, always on top of things.

As much as it burned him to see Allen touching his wife, he had to admit, she was working her magic on him. He'd gone from furious to pussycat in a matter of moments, as soon as Aubrey stepped from the car. He was always amazed at her effect on people.

"Well then. I guess it's time for me to go. Sorry again for your troubles." He tipped an imaginary hat at Aubrey, then turned to Josh. He put his hand on Josh's shoulder and propelled him three feet away. Josh's dad had done that when he was growing up. It usually preceded a lesson, the hard way, the kind that ended in a belt. But Derek Allen just leaned his head in, smiled a vulpine smile, and said, "Just in case you were having second thoughts, I felt I needed to make a point. Don't even think about fucking this up for me. You see what I can do? One heartbeat, Hamilton, and it's over. Besides, I couldn't have you driving your own car to the meet, now could I? You have two hours. Do this right, or so help me God, I'll kill her."

He turned on his heel, got in the car, and drove off.

Josh watched him go, his heart beating triple time. He turned to Aubrey. She didn't seem to be paying attention to the interplay. She stood in front of the wrecked Audi, staring at the front end of the car. She had blood running down her chin, about to ruin her beautiful pink dress. That snapped him back to reality.

"Oh, shit, Aubrey, you're bleeding."

She wiped her lip with a grimace, then wrenched her gaze to his. "I think I bit my lip, that's all. I'm really fine, I promise." She glanced down at her chest, rubbed her shoulder. "I'm going to have a bruise, though."

He looked at her lips closely, the gash in her soft flesh. He couldn't do this to her.

He swallowed hard. "It needs stitches. Honey, I am so sorry." *Sorrier than you will ever know.*

"I know, babe. I know. I better call Kevin, tell him we're going to be late."

Aubrey got on the phone to tell the bride-groom his best man would be tardy for the ogling. Josh tried to keep his calm. This was not how he'd planned the weekend to go. Fun and romance and a little kink—they hadn't been able to stay in a hotel for a long time, and they were both look-ing forward to the illicit anonymity of the room. Aubrey was always looser at hotels. He wanted to touch her again, to hold her. To feel her heart beating next to his, like it had for so many years. If he fucked up tonight, he'd never be able to hold her again, and the thought made him want to cry.

Josh wiped the cold sweat that broke out on his forehead with his jacket sleeve. The idea of losing Aubrey made him physically ill. She was the most important part of his life. The only piece that actually mattered. And now, he wasn't going to have a choice. He was going to lose her one way or the other. He just didn't think it was going to be today.

A motorcycle cop in a helmet and shades swung by and put on his lights so people could be forewarned about the accident. He wasn't thrilled that the man Josh had hit had already left the scene, and gave Josh a ticket for failing to yield, or some other such nonsense. He didn't bother to look at it, just took the paper, folded it, and shoved it in his front pocket. He gave the cop the finger behind his back and went to sit on the guardrail with Aubrey, who was now gaily watching the proceedings like a queen awaiting coronation.

"You're going to mess up your dress, and you are in entirely too good a mood."

"I'm sitting on your jacket, so don't worry yourself. We're alive, and I'm glad for it. I should be suffering survivor's guilt, I guess. The poor car."

Josh glanced at the crumpled mess that was his pride and joy. "Poor car? Poor us. I don't know where we're going to get the money to buy another. The insurance company will never give us what it's worth."

"We'll figure it out. We always do, right?"

She took his hand and squeezed.

He stitched up her lip. The tow truck arrived in practically record time, just under an hour. After bidding their lonely, broken car adieu, they took a cab to the hotel and arrived there only an hour late. Aubrey insisted that Josh join the party as quickly as possible since he was, after all, the best man. She promised she'd take care of getting them checked in and calling the insurance company.

Thankful as always for the woman Aubrey was—capable, strong, resilient—he kissed her an extra long time, earning a look from a bellman, and scurried off toward the party.

And the moment her back was turned, he walked out the hotel's front door.

CHAPTER 60

Aubrey
Today

The run didn't help her confusion, but it helped her body. She felt more settled. More in control. She'd gone for two hours, two glorious, terrible hours. Her life—seven and seventeen and five, and now seven again, seven days of starting over, of finding peace—shattered into a million pieces.

The sun was gone, the night birds calling, mocking as she went up the steps. Another day over. She didn't know how she was going to find the strength to pick up the pieces and start over yet again tomorrow.

She fed Winston, worked up her courage, and called Meghan, who didn't answer. She left a cheery message so she wouldn't know anything was wrong and was just finishing a glass of juice when she heard knocking at the door.

Not just knocking, but the heavy slams that came from a fist turned sideways instead of politely rapping knuckles.

A cop.

Shit. Look normal.

She reacted irrationally, as she was wont to do when the police came calling. Who could blame her, really? She'd been on the losing end of their relationship for most of her life.

The banging continued.

God damn you, Arlo. You promised.

And . . . *Thank you for warning me, Chase.*

She opened it to the faces of two men she didn't recognize, both holding badges. The taller of the two said, "Aubrey Hamilton?"

"Yes? Can I help you?"

"Yes, ma'am. I'm Special Agent Tartt." He nodded to the smaller man, gray-haired and grim-looking. "This is Special Agent Hesley. We're with the Tennessee Bureau of Investigation. Ma'am, may we come in? It's concerning your husband, Josh Hamilton."

"What about him?"

If they noticed the sharpness in her tone, neither of them reacted.

"I think this is better suited for a sit-down, ma'am."

Jesus. What was happening?

She heard Tyler's voice in her head: *Play it, Aubrey. Play it hard.*

She sagged against the door a little. "Oh, my God. Did you find his body?" That would make sense. That was the right thing to ask. She didn't have to fake the tremulous voice; her whole body was shaking like a leaf.

"Ma'am, why don't you let us come on in, we can sit down and talk further."

She let them in, her mind spinning. All of the interaction she'd had with the TBI had been peripheral; she knew they were helping in the search for Josh, but she'd been at the mercy of Metro homicide instead. They were still cops, and because of that, she had no love for them, but they hadn't done anything to her, either.

She felt stronger now, more in control. She stood straight and looked the taller man in the eye. Saw concern, but nothing else. She led them into the living room. She was glad that she'd cleaned up after Tyler's big brother act and Chase's confession.

The three of them sat. She didn't bother to offer drinks, knowing they probably wouldn't accept anyway and wanting to get on with it.

"Mrs. Hamilton, are you familiar with a man named Chase Boden?"

There didn't seem to be any sense in lying. Too many people had seen her with him, at Sam's, the hospital, the coffee shop. Not to mention snoopy neighbors who might have seen them together on the porch, or walking Winston. And the cops, the day of Daisy's accident. It would all be very easily checked out.

"He's a friend of mine. From Chicago."

"Do you have any idea where Mr. Boden went this afternoon?"

"I'm sorry. I'm confused. What's going on? How does Mr. Boden relate to my husband?"

Tartt glanced at his partner, then sighed ever so gently and met Aubrey's eyes.

"Ma'am, this is going to come as quite a shock.

There was a sighting of your husband this afternoon."

"What? Where?"

"He was seen talking to Mr. Boden at the Sheraton downtown."

Her heart felt like it was going to burst from her chest. Had Chase known all along? Had he found Josh during his investigation?

"But . . . how can that be? Josh is dead."

Tartt said, "I understand this is sudden and confusing, Mrs. Hamilton. But your neighbor said she saw Mr. Boden here this afternoon. Was your husband here as well?"

She was thrust back five years, to the night the detectives had interviewed her. *As far as we can tell, Mrs. Hamilton, you were the last one to see your husband alive.*

Breathe, Aubrey. Breathe.

Tartt continued in his low, soothing voice. "Ma'am, can you tell us what happened this afternoon?"

The words blurted from her mouth before she had a chance to stop them. "Am I under arrest?"

Shit, Aubrey. Shut up.

The TBI agent leaned back in his seat and eyed her thoughtfully.

"Should you be?"

She waved her hand in front of her face. "Of course not. You'll understand that given my *history*, I may be inclined toward concern about false accusations."

Well said, girl. Give them some attitude. They

*didn't get that from you last time around. You don't
let them force you into saying anything you don't want
to say.*

"As it happens, Mrs. Hamilton, yes, I completely understand. And in this case, no, you are
not a suspect. Not at this time."

She inclined her head. The caveat was noted.

"Chase and I were seeing each other. We
broke up. Who claims they saw him with my husband?"

"I'm not free to release that information to
you right now, Mrs. Hamilton."

She tried to gather herself, tried to breathe.
Was it Arlo? Had he put someone on Chase, and
on Derek Allen, just to see what was happening?

They were watching her curiously. She pulled
herself together, cleared her throat. "I just don't
see how this could be possible."

"So your husband hasn't been in touch? No
contact?"

"Nothing since he kissed me good-bye at the
Opryland Hotel five years ago."

Tartt nodded. Clearly he was the spokesman
of the two.

"Well, ma'am, I'm not sure how to tell you
this, so I'm just going to come out and say it. Your
husband's fingerprints were found in Mr. Boden's
hotel room."

He sat back and watched her try to process the
information.

Josh. It wasn't anyone's imagination, not anymore. He *was* alive.

Joy and fear and something else, indefinable, began. *No time, Aubrey. You can't fall apart now.* She took a deep breath.

"That's impossible. Let me assure you, Agent. My husband is dead. He's been gone for five years. The state declared him dead last Friday. I believe you've made a mistake."

"You're sure your husband hasn't been in touch with you?"

"I'm sure. Where is Chase?"

"We were hoping you could tell us that."

"I have no idea where he is. And I'll say this one more time, so we're clear. This is the last I'm going to say it before I make a call and get my lawyer here. My husband is dead. And I think it's time for you to leave."

Tartt said, "Of course, Mrs. Hamilton. We understand. All of this has been quite overwhelming for you, I'm sure. We will see ourselves out. But I'm afraid we will have to talk to you again."

CHAPTER 61

She shut the door behind them and had to force her legs to keep her upright.

Josh was alive. He was alive, and he'd been talking to Chase.

Maybe she was hallucinating again. Falling into the paranoia trap she'd fallen into before. Had she just imagined those men coming to the door?

Just in case, she went to the medicine cabinet and took out the prescription bottle of Risperdal. She dumped two pills in her hand and washed them down with a Dixie cup of water. If she was seeing and hearing and imagining things again, the drugs would help.

Aubrey went back to the bedroom and opened up her laptop. She went to the email, searched through it, hoping against hope there was something, anything, that might give her a clue as to what was happening.

She saw nothing.

Josh's fingerprints in Chase's hotel room? Why would he go to Chase instead of coming to her?

And Chase . . . She forced his sexy half smile out of her mind. She couldn't afford to think

about him right now. If she allowed herself even
the smallest moment, she'd break into a thousand
pieces.

Think, Aubrey. Think.

She couldn't dare hope. She couldn't.

A shower. Wash off the grime of the run.
Think.

In less than three hours, her entire world had
been turned upside down. Her boyfriend was
using her for a story. A crazed drug runner was
after her money. Her husband was . . . alive?

It was too much to fathom.

*Call Chase. Call him, and find out what's happen-
ing.*

She was reaching for her cell when she heard
a phone ringing. It wasn't the landline or her cell.
Had one of the TBI agents left his phone behind?
She moved out of the bedroom downstairs toward
the living room, but the sound grew fainter.

The ringing stopped as she came back into
the bedroom, then, after a few moments, started
again.

She followed it to the source, realized it was
coming from her pillow.

Secreted inside the pillowcase was a small
black mobile phone.

Shaking, she answered it.

"Aubrey?" She recognized the voice. His voice.
Her Josh's voice.

Her legs buckled, and the bed stopped her from
hitting the floor.

The past five years of her life was lies. All of it.

Her voice broke. "Oh, my God, Josh. Where are you?"

"Aubrey, honey, listen to me very carefully. You need to get out of the house, right now. They aren't watching. I'm distracting them, but I don't have much time. In your closet, on the top shelf, behind the shoe boxes, there is a blue gym bag. Don't open it. Take it, and go to the train station. I'll meet you there. And Aubrey, this is the most important of all. If I'm not there, you get on the 9:02 p.m. to Grand Central in New York. You have to run, honey. Don't take anything but this phone and the bag. Don't tell anyone. Derek Allen is coming for you."

"But Winston—"

"I'll take care of him."

"Josh, I—"

His voice was like steel. "Go, Aubrey. Go, right now."

The phone went dead. She stared at it for a second, then forced her mouth closed and went to the closet. Exactly where he said it would be was a blue gym bag. She didn't know how long it had been in there. She didn't recognize it, hadn't seen it before, but it had clearly been in her closet for a while; there was a fine layer of dust on the top.

She threw on clothes, two layers of everything, just in case, pulled a baseball cap over her curls, then fed her arms through the handles of the bag and hoisted it onto her back like a backpack. It wasn't terribly heavy, but she could feel it was full.

Of what?

He'd warned her not to open it.

Why was she listening to Josh? He'd deserted her, put her through hell, and had just murdered the one spark of hope she'd had in years.

You love Josh, Aubrey. You always have. He is your everything.

It was simpler that way. The warm buzz of the pills made it all good. Smooth.

All in all, it took her less than two minutes to get out the door. She went out the back instead of the front, just in case, and took off at a run. She could smell something burning, saw thick black smoke rising from down the street. *I've distracted them.*

By lighting a fire. Smart.

It was 8:40 p.m. right now; she needed to set a fast pace to get down to the train station on time. She ducked through the neighbor's yard, and went out the back of the subdivision. There was a path that would cut straight across town to the station, probably a mile as the crow flew. During the school year it was quite active, with kids walking back and forth to school. Today, the students still gone for spring break, it was quiet. She jogged past the Montessori school, wondering what in the world she'd tell Linda about all of this.

As she ran away from her house, her life, her world, she smiled. Because in just a few minutes, she'd be with Josh again. And that was all that mattered.

Dear Josh,

The paper did a story on us today. An "it's almost the five-year anniversary" piece. Mostly about me, because, as I've told you before, your death created a bit of a stir in my life. The reporter had called and asked for a comment, but I said no. There was nothing to be said. So they created a world that wasn't entirely true, about how we used to have fights and how we used to make up. It was ridiculous, and I couldn't finish the article. Several parents took their kids out of school, something Linda shouldn't have to deal with, but there you have it. Even now, five years later, your disappearance is making waves.

I think back to the night you went missing, when Arlo and I looked everywhere for you, when we came back to the house and found your blood, how the police grilled me, and I want to give up. I want to believe like everyone else. No one but me has had any doubts about your death. I am the only one who ever thought you could still be alive.

But Josh, this is killing me. Slowly, yes, but every day without you is like the cut of a knife across my skin. What is it they say—death by a thousand cuts? That's what this feels like.

I am training for a marathon. Every step I take is in your memory, your honor. It's either that or join you.

Always,
Aubrey

CHAPTER 62

Aubrey
Today

It was 8:55 p.m. when she got to the train station. The parking lot was its usual chaos, and Aubrey quickly saw Josh's logic in sending her there. It would be harder to find them here than in the airport, with its long security lines making them sitting ducks for cameras and cops alike.

She should call Tyler. Tell him what she was doing. So he wouldn't worry. Wouldn't be looking. And Chase . . .

And then she saw Josh, and all thoughts of others disappeared.

He hadn't seen her, and he was pacing. God, she'd recognize his walk anywhere. It was something about the cock of his hips, the way they stayed somewhat still while his arms moved. He looked like a caged lion, a gunslinger, someone whose movements were never to excess. In addition to being varsity football, he was a swimmer, which was why his arms moved more than his hips. Years in the pool, off-season training, served to make his body and his gait very distinctive.

Just like Chase.

Chase doesn't exist anymore. There is only Josh.

He turned and saw her, and his face lit up in a smile. It wasn't Josh's face, not exactly, but it was his smile. She saw the years in that smile. She knew it was home. She was home.

The minute he saw her, his gait widened. His walk changed. She watched in fascination—he'd been doing it so she could spot him more easily, and now he went back to some sort of different stepping, so he'd disguised his most recognizable feature yet again.

She was impressed. It must have taken so much time to make all this work. His face, his voice, his walk.

But his face. His face was altered, somehow. Her Josh, but not her Josh. With the coloring, he looked oddly similar to Chase.

Chase, but not Chase.

Josh, but not Josh.

When she reached him, he handed her a ticket. "Follow me," he said, then walked away. There was no grand reunion, no kissing and hugging and crying. She waited a moment, then followed. He headed toward the northbound trains. A heartbeat later, he grabbed her hand and changed directions, down a staircase. She followed him, confused, but realized quickly that he was throwing whoever might be on their trail off yet again.

When they were at the bottom of the stairs, out of sight, only then did he reach for her, pull her into his arms, and hold her tight. It felt so

J.T. ELLISON

good, so right. She fit with him like she'd never fit with another.

This wasn't happening. This had to be a dream. The meds had kicked in fully, and she felt their warm buzz.

It was all real. It was happening. He was back.

"Josh—" she started, but he shushed her.

"There will be plenty of time to talk later. I need to get us out of here."

She understood. He needed to keep all of his senses about him to keep them safe.

She glanced around, taking in all the details. She'd read enough spy novels to know some of the tradecraft tricks, so she did her best to be subtle, glancing in the reflection of the parked train windows for people looking their way, looking for newspapers upside down in a signal or chalk marks on the station walls they passed.

She saw nothing.

He led her out the side entrance and up to Charlotte Avenue, where they caught a cab east toward the airport. Josh had the cabbie drop them off in the long-term parking lot. As the cab left, he took her hand again and they jogged to the short-term lot. After a moment, he veered off, back to the main parking lot. There was a black SUV in a slot. Josh pulled the keys from his pocket and gave them to her.

"You drive."

He climbed in the backseat.

"Where am I going?"

"The private airport, John C. Tune, off White Bridge Road."

She tried to talk as she drove, tried to ask questions. But Josh kept telling her there would be time for them to catch up later, and to pay attention to her driving.

Traffic was light. Twenty minutes later, they were on a small jet, buckled in, the plane in the air, and she finally saw his hands relax.

"Now can we talk?" she asked.

"Not just yet."

The excitement and drama was turning to annoyance. She wanted answers. She wanted a lot of things.

"Just tell me this. Why?"

He held her hand, tracing his fingers along hers. The familiarity was disconcerting. It felt so right, and so very wrong. Josh gestured to the pilot. "Please, baby. Not until we're safe. Alone."

He handed her a bottle of water, which she drank greedily. When she put it down, he pulled her close, into his arms. Stared into her eyes. Put his hand on the back of her neck. Her heart started to beat like crazy. She wanted this, so badly.

Slowly, he brought his lips down on hers.

Her eyes closed immediately, and she fell into the kiss. This was bliss. She didn't care, didn't care about any of it. Just being able to spend five more minutes with him was heaven.

Her heartbeat was off. Wrong. It was going faster and faster until she could barely breathe. She opened her eyes. Josh had stopped kissing her, was watching her thoughtfully. Her head began to swim; the walls of the plane started to close in on her. She had just enough time to register—*he's drugged me*—before the world went black.

CHAPTER 63

Aubrey woke to sunlight. It took her a full minute to get her eyes open. Her head ached and her mouth was bone-dry.

The events came rushing back. Chase. The TBI. The sprint to the train station. The plane.

Josh.

She swung her feet onto the floor. She was barefoot, and the floor was a whitewashed honey oak. She didn't recognize it. She did, however, recognize the voice.

"Good morning, sleepyhead."

He was sitting in a chair four feet from the bed. He shifted, set down a newspaper, and smiled.

"Where are we?" she managed.

"Someplace safe. Head hurt?"

She put a hand to her forehead. "It's splitting."

"Yes, I was afraid of that. Drink some water. It's by your right hand."

She turned her head carefully and saw the tall clear glass. Water became the most important thing to her. She gulped it down.

It didn't make her head hurt any less, but it did help her tongue, which was practically glued to the top of her mouth.

"What's happening? Am I dreaming?" she asked, setting the now empty glass down on the table.

He didn't leave the chair.

"Oh, Aubrey. It's a very long story. One which we will have plenty of time to discuss. But for now, I think it's best that you rest."

It was all hitting her now, the reality of her strange new world. "Not good enough, Josh. I want to know what's happening. I want to know where I am. And where the hell you've been for the past five years. You *bastard*! You left me all alone."

His voice sounded odd to her cottony ears. "I would never hurt you, Aubrey. Don't you trust me?"

Did she? She looked around the strange room, at her husband's strange face. This man, whom she'd promised to love, honor, and obey until death did they part? Death had parted them. Her obligation ended at death, right?

This man, who'd taken advantage of her. Who'd drugged her. Who'd whisked her away from her life. This man, who let her spend five years praying he was alive somewhere.

The love of her life. The destroyer of all she held dear.

He'd been as good as dead for five years.

And now she was supposed to trust him?

She sat up straighter, tucked her legs beneath her.

"No. I'm afraid I don't trust you a bit."

He laughed then. It was mirthless, and short.

"I can't say that I blame you."

"You have to tell me what's going on. Did you hurt Chase?"

Josh's new face froze. "Five years apart, and you're worried about *him*? God, Aubrey, I thought you'd be happy to see me. Happy to see that I'm alive. I just saved you from them. I saved your life. Allen was coming for you."

She heard the desperation in his tone. This wasn't going how he'd planned. And Josh was a planner, always had been. When things didn't go along their appropriate path, he always got upset. And she needed him clear and focused right now so she could figure out what the hell was happening.

Amazing how quickly they fell back into their old roles.

"Josh, I . . . Of course I'm happy to see you. I'm still in shock. Please, tell me, what's going on? Where are we? And what did you do to Chase?"

"Fuck Chase," he spat, and she recoiled. "I'm sorry. I didn't mean to be so hostile. It's just that . . . Aubrey, you don't know what it's been like. I've missed you so much."

"I've missed you, too. It's been hell for me. But I suppose you already know that."

His eyes closed, her words slicing across him like a knife. She didn't mean to cause him pain, but she couldn't seem to help herself. Five years, alone. He'd made his choice. A small wall began to build inside her, propping up her spine so she didn't simply collapse in a quivering heap. She had to hold it together. She had to know.

She could still see the hints of the man she'd loved in his new face. But he was a stranger to her now. A stranger who spoke like Josh and walked like Josh. *Josh, but not Josh.*

"You had plastic surgery?"

"I had to. What was I supposed to do? I was on the run."

She shook her head, looking into the stranger's eyes. "On the run. Five years without a single word. So why now, Josh? What's brought you back to me at last? Is it the money?"

"You never used to be bitter."

"Hey, fuck you, Josh. You clearly have no idea what I've been through, or else you wouldn't be so cavalier with your little quips. Of course I'm bitter. Do you blame me?"

He finally left the chair and dropped to his knees beside the bed. Clasped her hands in his. She let him, for the moment.

"Honey, you have no idea what being apart from you has been like for me. I've missed you every second of every day. It's been hell being apart from you."

"I think you better tell me what's been happening, Josh. From the beginning. Because I'm so confused I don't know what to think."

He nodded, the shadow lifting from his face.

"Aubrey, first . . . Can I kiss you? I promise I won't drug you again, that was for your safety. But, my darling, I've missed you so."

He turned his face to hers, and she couldn't stop herself. She wanted that kiss. She'd ached for it. And when it came, when his lips touched hers for the second time, she was surprised at how strange it felt. Familiar and strange, all at the same time. But not comforting. Not sexy. Not . . . anything.

It's just the stress, Aubrey. That's what's wrong. Just the stress.

She tried to relax, to accept what was happening. To experience the moment. Instead, her desire never rose. A chill went through her. She'd dreamed about this moment, begged for it, bargained and pleaded, just for one more chance to kiss Josh.

What the hell?

Josh noticed her lack of passion, too, ending the kiss at the very moment she started to pull away. She moved her head down, glanced toward the floor.

"It's been a long time, Josh."

"It has." He stood, waiting. When she didn't move into his arms again, he crossed them on his chest and smiled sadly.

"Where are we?" she asked again.

"Ocracoke Island. I've been living here for the past year. It's secure, as secure as I can make it, and it's the only place I know I can keep you safe. I can see them coming, you see. You have to take a ferry to get here. And I have friends here. They're close by."

He moved to the window, which he unshuttered and threw open. She joined him, looking out. A soft, warm breeze caressed her face. The sun was shining; it looked to be midafternoon. The beach came right up to the house, and the ocean spread before her, stretching endlessly out of sight.

"It's beautiful," she said.

"It should be. It cost me enough."

He laughed harshly, and she wondered if he was talking about money or something else. She turned away from the view.

"Tell me why, Josh. Please. I can't stand this. I need to know."

His look was another haunting visitation from the ghost of Josh past, right into her soul, the way he used to when they were children and she'd done something he disapproved of. When he was disappointed in her. "And you shall. Let's have some dinner. I think better on a full stomach."

He led her into the hall and down a flight of stairs into a modern, airy kitchen, with a white marble counter and whitewashed cabinets. The whole place had floor-to-ceiling windows that looked out over the sea, making the house feel like it was floating. She saw an infinity pool stretching away from the deck. It seemed to drop right off the edge of the world into the ocean. She had the sudden urge to fling herself into the sea. Death seemed easier than this new reality.

Josh grabbed her arm, almost as if he knew her thoughts, and sat her at the table. He poured her a glass of white wine and started putting together a meal. Fresh shrimp salad, fruit, cheese. Simple, light fare, fitting for the beach. Dizzyingly similar to meals they'd had on trips they'd taken just north of here, on Nags Head, with Kevin and Janie. When they were married. When they were a couple. When they told each other everything.

She ignored the glass of wine, poured water from the pitcher instead. Her stomach was churning, and she wanted her wits about her. She still had a headache from whatever he'd given her to knock her out. He'd drugged her, the bastard. Instead of trusting her and telling her the truth, he'd practically kidnapped her and taken her to his lair.

The dark abyss opened again. All this time, he'd been alive. All this time, he'd allowed her to think he was dead.

They didn't talk. There were no words to say after their disconnected kiss. She accepted a plate and nibbled at it, watching him. His long fingers, the broad shoulders, all that was the same. But his face was eerie: flatter, smoother, his eyes dark. His hair was bleached from the sun, or maybe carefully, skillfully highlighted. He looked more like Chase's brother than her husband.

She couldn't get a read on him, couldn't tell if he was happy or sad. His eyes used to have so much expression, and now they were empty. Soulless. Like him.

"Contacts?"

"Implants, actually. Safer, in the long run." He touched the parts of his face that were altered.

"Nose, chin, cheek, too. Just enough to get me past the facial-recognition systems so I can travel. Though I don't do too much of that anymore."

Implants. New bones in his face, silicone, fake. It was all a lie. He was a lie.

She put her fork down. "Why? Why in the world would you want to do this? For the money?"

He looked at her in horror. "Are you kidding?"

"What am I supposed to think?"

"God damn it, I was trying to protect you!"

And he stormed out of the room.

Aubrey let her head sink onto her hands. This new, strange Josh was unnerving. He was volatile. Unpredictable. The antithesis of the previous incarnation of her husband.

Unbidden, Chase's smile came to her. The feel of his body beneath her hands. The way he laughed. The differences between them were so stark to her now. She couldn't believe the variances had seemed so slight. Her mind had allowed the details of her husband to fade, to warp and grow dull. She realized the memory of Chase was more real to her at this moment than the physical version of Josh, somewhere nearby.

The old Aubrey would have curled up and cried, overwhelmed at the situation. She was different now. Stronger. Fierce. She wanted answers. She was ready for the truth, whatever that might be.

She took a few deep breaths, then went searching for Josh. She found him on the deck, sitting cross-legged in a spacious chair, his face turned to the sun. The waves lapped the beach below them, a gentle, constant roar.

She sat on the hard deck near him, drew her legs to her chest, wrapped her arms around them so she was as small as could be.

"Why don't you start at the beginning?"

CHAPTER 64

Josh
Five Years Ago

It all went south.

Of course it did.

There was a car waiting for Josh in the Opryland parking lot. He barely noted the drive downtown, arrived at his assigned spot in the parking lot Allen had chosen for their assignation, sweating bullets. He didn't want to do this, didn't want to be here, but if he could make it happen quickly and get back to the hotel before anyone missed him . . .

Yeah, right, Hamilton. Good luck with that.

Allen pulled up in his barely dented car. Another swept into the parking lot.

It was go time.

Derek Allen got out of the car, stuffing a weapon into the back of his pants. He saw Josh and smiled, signaled for him to come closer.

"Good, you're here. You have the gun?"

"Yes. You could have called. You didn't have to stage an intervention, wreck my car, and fuck with my life."

"Oh, kid. Just covering all my bases. Let me see the gun."

Josh handed it over. Allen took it and stashed it in his pocket. Josh noticed he was wearing gloves, kicked himself for not thinking of it. *Yeah, you're a bona fide criminal mastermind, Hamilton. Be sure you wipe the gun down after this.*

"Here," Allen said, handing him another gun. "This one's not loaded. Don't want you blowing your cock off or anything by accident."

"I wouldn't be so stupid."

"Kid, you're shaking. Take a breath and *get it together*. You know what to do. We practiced this. So man the fuck up."

They turned to face the second car. The parking lot was dead quiet, the moon casting shadows across the pavement. Josh shivered; he couldn't help it. He had a terrible feeling about this.

The other dealer stepped from his vehicle. He was dark and thick and surly. He had a large briefcase in his meaty hand.

The three stepped forward and met between the cars. Allen was the first to speak.

"Let's get this done, shall we? Javier, meet Josh. You wanted to put a face to the name. He's our link to the Oxy and prescription pads. Josh, this is Javier Cosmos, who's going to be helping us distribute deeper into the city."

Cosmos eyed Josh with distaste. He spit on the pavement. "He is just a child. How do we know we can trust him?"

Allen smiled widely. "You can't. Josh?"

That was his cue. The gun didn't shake in his hand. He was proud of that. He didn't want to look like the scared little boy he really was.

"I'll take the briefcase, Mr. Cosmos, with thanks."

Cosmos's face contorted, his black eyes narrowing. "Don't do this, Allen. We had a deal."

"We have a new deal now," Allen said. "I know how you people think. You'll kill me and absorb the kid into your organization so you don't have to give me a cut. That's not going to happen."

Josh advanced, and Cosmos shrugged and started to hand it over. The man looked pissed but calm and collected, like being robbed by a business partner was an everyday occurrence.

Josh got his hand on the handle of the briefcase, his eyes never leaving the dealer. He didn't see the move until it was too late. Cosmos was lighting quick. He shoved the briefcase into Josh's chest, knocking him backward onto his ass, and whipped out his gun. Fired.

But Allen anticipated the move and fired at the same time. The shots echoed through the Nashville night. A dog started to bark frantically, and the dealer collapsed on the pavement, leaking blood from a leg wound. He groaned and fumbled for his weapon.

Allen calmly said, "Shit. Missed." He fired again, and Cosmos stopped moving.

Josh ducked behind Cosmos's car. *Fuck. Fuck!* Allen had just killed the guy.

Crazy-ass motherfucker. And Josh was a witness. The only witness.

And he saw what was happening, clear as day. The gun Allen had used to kill Cosmos had Josh's prints all over it.

He realized he was holding the briefcase.

Allen chuckled, five feet to his right, moving closer. Hunting him in the dark.

"It's safe now, kid. Come out, come out, wherever you are."

Josh swallowed, pointed the gun at Allen, shut his eyes, and pulled the trigger. Nothing happened.

Son of a bitch. His weapon was unloaded.

Hamilton, you are a first-class idiot.

He looked around him for something, anything that could help. Cosmos lay dead on the other side of the car. His gun was by his side.

Josh scrambled under the car, twisting on the hard ground, lugging the briefcase with him. He came out the other side, right next to the body. His fingers found metal, and his heart stopped racing. He could fix this.

Josh took a deep breath, clutching the dealer's gun in his hand. He stood and pointed the new weapon at Allen. His voice was cool and steady. "Stop moving."

"Don't you even think about it, Hamilton. Give me the briefcase, and no one will get hurt."

He didn't waver, and Allen's face grew wary.

"I see what you were doing, Allen. This is a

setup for me, too. Get my prints on the gun, kill Cosmos, turn me in. You waltz away with the money and the pills, and I take the fall. Is that about what was supposed to happen?"

"Hey, now, kid. It's just the price of doing business. You've become a liability. I can see the struggle in you. You're ready to bolt, to turn yourself or me in, try to get your life back. I can't have that. The cartel wanted to cut me out, use you directly. I'm protecting you. And you belong to me now. You'll keep your mouth shut, or you know what happens. I destroy your pretty little wife. You get me?"

Something inside him broke. The months of agony, the betrayal, the pressure, it all exploded, and this time, he didn't close his eyes before pulling the trigger. The gun roared, and Allen dropped, shock on his face. His gun hand relaxed, and the weapon fell to the pavement with a clatter.

Oh, fuck. Oh fuck oh fuck oh fuck.

Sirens broke the distant air. The dog was still barking its fool head off.

Allen was dying, his eyes glazed in pain and shock.

Josh's mind cleared. He picked up Allen's gun and wiped it down, then put it back in his hand. He wiped the SIG down, replaced the gun by Cosmos's body. Stuck his head into Allen's car. The drugs were there. He grabbed everything he could, shoved the pills, coke, and Rx pads in his pockets.

The sirens were getting closer.

He looked at the scene. Prayed like hell the cops would pull up and think it was a drug deal gone bad and the two men had shot each other.

And he took off running, the briefcase heavy in his arms.

CHAPTER 65

It took him fifteen minutes to run to the house.

There was a path that cut through the neighborhood behind the houses. It wasn't safe for Aubrey to jog alone at night, but he was a man, and he was carrying a weapon. He'd risk it.

When he made it into his neighborhood, a thought hit him: Aubrey had the house keys.

Shit. An inconvenience, but a manageable one.

Aubrey had been upset with him when he wanted to stow a key outside. She didn't feel safe like that. People always left their keys outside. Over the doorsill, under the mat, under a rock. It was crazy, she said. Anyone with half a brain could find it.

So he'd gone a step further.

He hid the key in the garden of the house across the street.

He warned his neighbor, of course, just in case he ever saw Josh or Aubrey retrieving the key. But no one was home tonight or they were already asleep; the windows were dark. Josh crept to the rock and retrieved his house key. He didn't know what made him crawl under their porch and push the briefcase into the darkened space underneath the stairs.

Yes, he did. Bringing that into his house would

spoil his life even further. He just needed some time and space to figure out his next steps.

The little voice inside him had been screaming for the past fifteen minutes: *You have to get out of here.* He darted back across the street. It was so quiet. Their beautiful big house cast shadows over the street and allowed him to rush across and make it safely to the backyard without being seen.

He opened the door and scooted inside. Winston came running to meet him.

He petted him, buried his face in the dog's silky flank, then went to the kitchen and grabbed a hot dog from the refrigerator. Broke it into pieces, pushed the pill into one quarter. Fed the meat to the dog, bite by bite. The tranquilizer worked quickly; Winston was staggering before they left the kitchen. Josh got him settled near the fireplace.

He had to go. He had to go now.

He went into the kitchen, knocked over the chairs, made it look like there'd been a struggle. Lightning flashed outside, thunder on its heels, making him jump.

He took a scalpel from his emergency first aid kit in the bathroom, went back to the kitchen. He needed to make it look real.

He sliced the inside of his left arm deeply. He knew just where to cut; the blood began pouring from his arm. He sat on one of the chairs and let it flow.

When he started getting light-headed, he pulled off his belt and looped it around his shoulder, pulled it tight. Jesus, he had a new appreciation for stabbing victims. This hurt like hell. But the tourniquet worked. The blood stopped gushing from his arm.

Realized rain was pouring down. Good, that would wash him clean.

He managed to get to the bathroom, removed the emergency kit. Took a flashlight, and got out of there. He knew he didn't have much time. He took the bath towel and pressed it to the wound in his arm. Despite the tourniquet, it hadn't stopped bleeding entirely, and he was feeling sick and dizzy. He set to work. It took almost twenty excruciating minutes to sew up the knife wound.

Glanced in the kitchen—it certainly looked like he'd lost his life's blood in there.

Aubrey. I'm so sorry.

He bandaged himself up, took a last look at his life, grabbed a blue backpack from the hall closet, made his way across the street. Crawled under the porch. Emptied the contents of the briefcase into the backpack. Dug a hole one-handed and put the leather into the ground. Covered it back up with the dirt and set the old hose reel box, the one he knew they hadn't touched in years, back on top of the spot. No one would be able to see it. No one would suspect.

Pulled the backpack over his shoulder. The bleeding was under control. He hurt so badly it took his breath away. He dumped a pain pill in his hand and dry swallowed it. He needed to get away, now.

He just wasn't thinking. He was acting on instinct. Fight or flight. And flight was the only course of action he could see before him.

The path across to Dragon Park was even darker than before. He didn't know how he was going to get to Aubrey. They'd be watching. He was sure of it. The realization hit him and he had to stop and suck in his breath. There would be no recourse. They were going to hunt him down. He'd shot a man, for Christ's sake. If the police weren't already after him, Allen's crew would be soon, and the dealer's crew, too.

Tears pricked at his eyes. He blamed it on the Vicodin. He was well and truly fucked, and didn't know how to get himself out of it.

You did this to yourself, Hamilton. You deserve every bad thing that's going to happen from here on out.

He only had one option now. He had to disappear.

A moment later, his phone buzzed with a new text.

> Utterly bored. Come meet me for a
> drink? I'm in the Jack Daniel's Lounge.

Aubrey.

This time Josh did start to cry, hiccupping tears coupled with maniacal laughter that made his arm scream in pain with each inhalation. She couldn't know.

She could not know.

It was the only way to keep her safe.

He didn't allow the thought to form: *No, Josh. It's what's best for you.*

Using a burner phone, one of two he'd bought and stashed in the backpack, he Googled the Jack Daniel's Lounge at Opryland. Hit the Call button. The phone rang about fifteen times. A hurried voice answered. "Jack Daniel's."

"Hi there. I have a friend who's waiting for me. Pretty girl, curly blond hair. Bandage on her lip. Will you make her a gin and tonic, Tanqueray, with a thin slice of lime? I'd like to surprise her."

"Yeah, I see her. Sure thing, dude. Hope it works."

The man hung up.

Hope it works indeed.

Josh needed some time. Time to get away, to get on the road, to get the hell out of Dodge.

He broke down the burner phone. Took out the battery, buried it in the weeds. Took out the SIM card, crushed it under his heel against a rock, put it in his pocket. Repeated the process with his own phone, destroying it completely.

Started off, in the dark.

He knew exactly where he needed to go.

CHAPTER 66

Josh
Today

Josh watched his wife's reaction as he told her the story. She winced a few times but stayed silent and still, listening without interrupting.

She was quiet and reserved, holding back. This was not going the way he wanted. He'd expected a few flashes of anger, but he'd truly thought Aubrey would be so happy to see him that she'd rush into his arms and never want to let go again. She wasn't jumping in his arms. Instead, she was keeping her distance, on guard and afraid.

God, she looked just like she did when she was ten, and he was twelve, and he made her that valentine. She'd looked at it with the wariness of a cat about to bolt before its tail was pulled.

"Did you know about the investigation? The trial? They arrested me, Josh."

"Not at the time. I made it to Nags Head. Kevin and Janie's place. They went to Barbados on their honeymoon, I knew it would be deserted. And I knew where they left the key. I hid out there, and healed. The cut was worse than I intended. I got a fever. I nearly died."

That wasn't the whole truth. He had been aware, of everything. He'd been worried sick when she was arrested, but he knew she couldn't be found guilty. He'd been so careful. He just couldn't return to Nashville unless it was absolutely necessary. If she'd been found guilty, he would have turned himself in. But she hadn't. So he didn't. But he didn't think telling her that was going to make much of a difference. He hadn't played the hero. He wasn't sure why not.

"You shot Allen. You thought you killed him?"

"I had no choice."

"How much money did you get away with?"

"Almost two million dollars. I knew it would buy me some time."

"So how did you get to Nags Head?"

"Walked and hitched. Guy in an eighteen-wheeler picked me up outside of town. I was lucky he never came forward. Everything was predicated on luck. It could have fallen apart anytime."

"Right." She was quiet for a minute. "How'd you get the phone into my house? The police had me under surveillance."

"Loose surveillance. They followed Tyler when he left yesterday. I snuck in."

"Huh. Why didn't you just take the bag with you?"

"I heard your car. I panicked. I should have stayed, should have shown myself. I went out the window before the cops got back. I wanted you to leave with me then, but Chase . . ." He spit out his brother's name.

She laughed a little. "All this time, Josh. You

could have reached out. You could have told me. You could have trusted me. I'm the only one you could truly trust."

"I do trust you. That's why I'm telling you now, Aubrey. The whole night went wrong, from the very beginning. Nothing went according to plan. This is not what I wanted. This is not what I'd planned on."

"You seem to have made the best of it." Aubrey swept her arm out. "Living in style, plastic surgeries."

"I've been working on how to get us out of this mess, Aubrey."

"Oh. Okay." She stared out to sea for a few moments. When she looked at him again, her face was shadowed. "Why exactly did you come back, Josh?"

He reached for her hand. She didn't resist. "I came back for you, Aubrey. Now that I've been declared legally dead, we can start over. Fresh. You have the insurance settlement. We'll pull the money from the account the moment it hits, transfer it to mine. I know how to do it so no one will know—that's part of what I've been working on. With that money, and what I've got left, we have enough to last us the rest of our lives. You don't have to work, ever again. We can move to South America, live in paradise, swim, make love, read, dance. Have babies. Anything we want to do."

"So long as we don't ever come back."

"Well, travel isn't completely out of the question, though it's dangerous. We'd have to get you some work done, and—"

"Did you know about Chase being your brother?"

Her tone made him wince. "I didn't until Meghan found the birth certificate."

"You were watching her, too?"

"I've been watching all of you. I've seen it all." He couldn't contain the anger in his voice, the hurt. He'd promised himself he wouldn't, couldn't blame her. But he did; it poured out. "I know all about you and Chase. How you fucked him that night. You'd just met him, Aubrey. You didn't know him at all."

She looked at him sadly. "You're one to talk, Josh. I didn't know you at all, either."

His phone rang, interrupting their argument. Once. Then silence.

That meant only one thing. He did have friends on this island, friends who were keeping a close watch on the house today while he let his guard down and reconciled with his wife. A quick phone call was the warning sign that someone unwanted had managed to follow them.

Adrenaline shot through his system. He ran to the closet, grabbed the bag, rushed to Aubrey's side. He pressed a silver handgun into her hands. Her fingers closed around it like she held guns all the time, natural, comfortable.

"What the hell is this?"

"We have to go."

"What do you mean? Go where?"

"We have to leave. Now."

"Why don't you just answer your phone?"

"Aubrey. I don't have time to explain. If we don't leave now, we're dead."

A voice sounded behind them.

"It's too late for that."

CHAPTER 67

Aubrey
Today

Aubrey jerked at the familiar voice. She put her hand behind her, tucked the gun into her waistband.

Derek Allen advanced into the room. He had a wicked black gun in his right hand.

Josh immediately stood between Aubrey and Allen. He'd drawn so smoothly Aubrey hadn't even seen his arm move. He trained the weapon on Allen. The lethal twin eyes pointed at each other.

"Aubrey, I want you to go down the stairs and out onto the beach. There is a dock there, and a boat. Get in it, get down, and wait for me." Josh's voice was calm, collected, and dripping with menace. A stranger's voice.

Allen shook his head. "Don't you know I'd never come here alone? The boat's covered. You aren't going anywhere."

"Josh?"

Aubrey's voice was small, frightened. She hated how weak she sounded. Again, and again, someone was taking the choices away from her. Her whole fucking precious little life, other people had made the decisions for her. This time, it was her turn.

She could only hope Allen wouldn't shoot her on sight, just to get her out of the way. She stepped next to Josh, a show of solidarity.

"Both of you need to put the guns away. We will discuss this like civilized people."

Josh growled at her without taking his eyes off Allen. "Go in my bedroom and lock the door. Do it now, Aubrey."

"No. I'm sick of you telling me what to do. You two work it out. I'm no longer involved in this situation. I'm going home."

She stepped away, turning her back on them both, and went for the stairs.

The shot rang out before she made it four feet, the wood above her head splintering.

"Stop. Right. There." Allen wasn't fooling around. Aubrey whirled to face him.

"You bastard. You selfish, horrible bastard. How dare you shoot at me?"

"I didn't shoot *at* you, Aubrey, or else you'd be dead. I just wanted your attention."

"Well, you have my attention now." Aubrey stepped back to Josh's side.

"Where's the money?" Allen demanded. "Give me the money, and I'll consider killing you quickly."

Josh laughed, a hollow sound that gave Aubrey chills. "Not here. Do you think I'm an idiot? I'd never keep the cash on me."

"I don't believe you."

"It's true. Besides, it's all gone. Why do you think I risked coming back? I need the money from the insurance settlement to keep living."

"You're a liar, Joshua Hamilton."

Aubrey watched them, trying to figure how to get out of there. Allen's creepy voice, his blank, feral smile. It didn't take a genius to see the man was incredibly dangerous.

If Josh had been so careful, taken every precaution, managed to elude not only Allen but the authorities, too, for five years, how in the world had they been found so quickly?

Which led her to a moment of sanity. She'd disappeared. Wouldn't people be looking for her? Well, of course. People must be looking for her. She had no idea how long she'd actually been gone.

People like who, though?

Tyler? He'd rushed off to God knew where, clearing out to give her space to be with Chase. He wouldn't come around until after the weekend, she was sure.

Arlo? He'd come to pick her up, planning to take her to the police. Too late.

Daisy? Clinging to life in the hospital.

Tom? Worshipping at Daisy's shrine.

Linda wasn't expecting her back to work until next week.

Meghan would be worried, absolutely. Not right away, but if a day had passed, then yes, there was a chance she'd get concerned.

Her mind touched on Chase, and her heart constricted. Her breath came short, and she shut her eyes.

A wave of regret flowed through her. Her whole life had become the sum of its parts, and she was alone, surrounded by insanity, on a beach in North Carolina. But the police were supposedly watching. The TBI, too. If they were lucky, maybe they'd find her before she ended up dead on the beautiful white sand.

Josh shot her a look. *Distract him.*

It might be their only chance.

"How did you find us?" she asked.

Allen glanced at her briefly. "I put a tracker on you. In your running shoe. It was rather simple. You need to be more careful about locking your deadbolt."

Aubrey's first instinct was to take her shoes and throw them off the deck. She didn't, though. She only had the one pair. If they were going to get out of this alive, she might need them.

"How did you know he'd show up?"

"I didn't. But when I saw you in the hospital, I thought he just might. You are still a beautiful girl." He licked his lips, and she forced back a shudder.

Allen smiled, vulpine. "Enough of that. So, Hamilton, are you going to get me my money, or do I need to shoot you?"

"Hell no. I'm going to kill you, and then Aubrey and I are leaving."

He fired at Allen. Allen ducked and disappeared around the corner. Josh grabbed her arm and towed her toward the kitchen, firing over his shoulder as he went. "The deck," he whispered. "We can go off the deck, by the pool."

They ran for the deck, bent at the waist, hiding behind the kitchen island. The doors were open; they'd stormed into the kitchen after their fight and hadn't slid them shut.

Silence.

"Where is he?"

"I don't know," Josh answered. "You go first, I'll cover you. I won't let him hurt you, Aubrey."

Aubrey pulled up short. She smelled smoke. "What is that?"

"Shit," Josh declared. "He's going to try and burn us out. Come on, come on, come on, come on."

He pulled her out onto the deck, to the edge of the pool. There was a narrow circular staircase that led down to the beach. She started down the steps.

Shots rang out, splintering the water jug above her head. She froze on the stairs, clinging to the center pole. She couldn't see Allen, or anyone else; there were no clear lines of sight. Which meant he couldn't see her, either. It had been a lucky shot.

The smell of smoke was stronger now. Josh came down the stairs, gun swiveling left and right. The back of the house was on fire; she could feel the warmth of the flames.

"It's clear. Come on. Jump."

Instead of following the stairs down any farther, they dropped onto the sand. Josh went first; he turned to catch her fall.

As her feet touched the ground, a bullet caught Aubrey in the leg. She went down with a strangled cry, landed face-first in the sand, her heart doing triple time. The shot had come from nowhere. Josh scrambled across the ground, closer to her.

"Is it bad?"

Aubrey gave him a look of incredulity. The pain made her sick to her stomach. "He shot me."

Josh pulled off his shirt and held it to her leg. He had a knife in his pocket, which he used to rip open her jeans. Aubrey grunted in pain but bit her lip.

Josh was tending her leg frantically, repeating the words *I'm sorry* over and over and over.

The flames were getting closer now, embers sparking down their stairwell escape.

"We need to get out of here," Josh said. "The shot's not deep, it's just a graze. Can you put weight on it?" He grabbed Aubrey and helped her up. She set her foot in the sand. It hurt, but it wasn't unbearable. This was bad. She was going to slow them down.

They started to move, but Allen was suddenly on the stairs behind them, his weapon trained on them. He followed the steps to the beach.

"You little shit. How dare you try and run?"

Josh put himself between Allen and Aubrey. "It's over, Allen. I don't have your money. You've shot my wife. Leave now, and I won't kill you with my bare hands."

"You fucker, you shot me and left me for dead in that parking lot. You brought this on yourself, and on her. If you aren't going to repay me, then I might as well—"

The gun. Aubrey fingered the trigger of the gun in her waistband and took a deep breath. Despite her past, being around Tyler and his cronies, she'd never fired one before. She figured as long as she aimed for the middle of Allen's chest, that would work. It was their only chance. He and Josh were raising their arms, facing off, screaming at each other.

She whipped the gun out and pulled the trigger.

The recoil was shocking. She lost her balance and fell over backward, watched Allen turn her way, rage contorting his face. She'd missed.

Josh started to shoot. Aubrey's ears rang, and she ducked her head into her hands and squeezed her eyes shut.

Please, let it be over.

It wasn't. Allen grabbed Aubrey by the hair, wrenched her from the ground, and pulled her to her feet, putting her between him and Josh, the gun to her head. Josh stopped shooting immediately, raised his hands in surrender. His face twisted with fear, and finally, finally, she saw the man she used to know.

"Don't. Don't hurt her!"

Allen's vicious voice sounded in her ear. "Time

to end this, Hamilton. Say good-bye to your pretty little wife."

Allen didn't see she still had the gun.

Aubrey shot him in the side, smoothly this time, ready for the kick. He jerked, twisted, screamed in pain. He let go of her hair, and she fired again, catching him in the neck.

Allen fell to the sand, blood leaking out onto the sugar-fine grains, staining them crimson.

She wanted to pull the trigger again and again, but she held her finger still and watched him struggle, spitting and groaning, his words coming out in a mumbling curse. He was the reason her world had fallen apart, and she was the one who'd taken him out of it.

She smiled at him, imitating his rictus grin. His eyes widened. He slumped down into the sand. He struggled for a moment, then went still.

She stared at his chest, waiting to see it rise. It didn't, and something inside her, the old Aubrey, the terrible girl she used to be, tainted and spoiled and bad, cheered.

Then Josh was at her side, taking the gun gently from her hand.

"Let's go," he said calmly. "We need to get out of here."

Allen's warm blood was spreading through the sand. It reached her toes and she could only think, *I've just killed a man. Why don't I feel anything? I should feel something.*

Josh wrapped his arms around her shaking

body. "It's going to be okay, baby. I promise. It will all be okay. We're safe now."

"He's got someone else with him."

Josh shook his head. "He was lying. He's alone. There's no one here but us. And that's how it's going to be from now on. Us."

CHAPTER 68

Aubrey shouldn't have been surprised by the glossy speedboat anchored by the house's dock, but she was. Continually surprised. Her husband was a thief. A common criminal. A murderer. A liar. He had changed. There was nothing good about him anymore.

A quote floated to her mind.

Absolute power corrupts absolutely. Great men are almost always bad men.

God, wasn't that the truth.

Josh helped Aubrey into a life jacket. "Never gonna take a chance with you again," he said with a smile. "Okay?"

She nodded. She was anything but okay.

"Where are we going?"

He whispered in her ear, "Home, at least for a little bit. We need to get the insurance payout, and Winston. Then we can disappear. Don't worry. I'll protect you. I won't let anyone find out you killed Allen."

His assurances felt like threats.

"We killed Allen together."

"Yes, we did. Of course we did." He leaned down and kissed her, went to the wheel and started the engine. The boat roared to life with a throaty growl, and he maneuvered it out of its slip.

"It's all over," he said. "No one's chasing me anymore. We can live our lives, now."

"But your house . . ."

The house was fully engulfed in flames. Josh looked back at it once, and shrugged. "We'll build another one. Somewhere safe. Anywhere in the world. You get to choose."

Aubrey sat back against the seat, let her eyes close. They crashed through the waves, then hit the open sea, toward the mainland, where Josh let the motor roar. Spray hit her face.

"Why?" Aubrey finally asked. "Why did you lie to me? Why didn't you come back?"

Josh shook his head. "Oh, baby. I didn't have a choice."

It took a day to get back to Nashville. They docked the boat in Nags Head; Josh had a friend who had medical supplies, so they fixed up Aubrey's leg. Another friend of Josh's flew them back to Tennessee the next evening, the same man who'd piloted the plane down earlier.

Aubrey was amazed, and a little impressed— Josh had certainly cultivated a crop of people who could help him slip past the authorities when necessary. But the anger simmered, just below the surface, ready to strike. He'd had time to build himself a network of friends, but hadn't bothered to let her know he was alive.

They landed at a small, private airstrip in Manchester, Tennessee, an hour south of Nashville. A car was waiting for them. Josh drove them north toward the city, seemingly ignoring the fact that Aubrey wasn't partaking in his manic chatter. He had plans. Plans that would let them live happily ever after.

On the run. With all the lies hovering like ghosts between them.

"There it is," Josh said as Nashville's skyline appeared in front of them. It was just getting dark, and the lights of the city looked like circling fireflies. "Our town."

"I need to eat," she said, realizing she was getting dizzy. The pain in her leg was dull and throbbing.

Josh's expansive mood continued. "The world's your oyster. What are you interested in? Steak? Mexican? Italian? We could try Valentino's. Remember we always wanted to go there but couldn't afford it? We can afford it now, baby."

"That's . . . that's fine. Valentino's sounds good."

She didn't know how he could be so glib. Less than twenty-four hours earlier, she'd shot and killed a man. It didn't seem to have any effect on him. He was just so happy. So relieved. All the pressure was gone from his shoulders. His trial had ended. Hers was just beginning.

She gave herself a little shake. What was wrong with her? For five years, she'd begged, pleaded, bargained, prayed—anything that would bring him back to life. Her dreams had come true, and she just wanted some space. Some time to be alone. To think. To understand what she was feeling. Or not feeling.

To talk to Chase. To disappear.

Josh pulled up to the valet in front of the restaurant.

"We're not dressed," Aubrey murmured.

"It's Nashville. If the country stars can go to the five-star restaurants in jeans, so can we."

He swept out of the car and beat the valet to her door. He swung it open and reached for her hand. The maître d' gave them a look of derision when he heard they didn't have a reservation, but Josh slipped him some bills and he found them a table.

Josh ordered champagne for them, ostentatiously choosing a $420 bottle of Dom Pérignon. She fingered her menu, deciding. He ordered for them both, antipasto, frutti di mare, vitello Marsala. He spoke Italian now, apparently. He winked at her as the waiter conversed with him like he was native-born. When the waiter glided away, Aubrey gave Josh a tremulous smile.

"I need to use the ladies' room."

"Of course. I'm sorry, I should have asked."

He let her go.

She still couldn't breathe. She couldn't do this. This was not part of the bargain.

There was a phone at the unmanned hostess

stand, out of the table's line of sight. She dialed a number she'd memorized.

The phone rang twice. A deep voice answered. "Yes?"

She swallowed hard, fighting the tears that rose unbidden.

"Arlo? It's Aubrey."

CHAPTER 69

Fairy tales don't come true. Parents die and leave you alone in the world. Little girls get molested. Lovers die; husbands lie, and disappear, then try to pretend all is well.

Aubrey hadn't thought her heart could break anymore. She was wrong.

She hung up the phone and made her way back to the table. The champagne had arrived. The sommelier popped the cork expertly and poured. They clinked glasses. She took a deep drink, praying she didn't lose her nerve.

Arlo promised it wouldn't take them long.

And she needed to make a clean break.

Josh watched her for a long moment. "So. Where do you want to go, my darling? Anywhere in the world. What do you want? You say the word, and it's yours. I can finally give you the life you always wanted."

"No."

His face changed, a shadow crossing his unfamiliar eyes. "What do you mean, no?"

"I mean, no. As in, no way in hell. I don't want to live in South America. I don't want to have surgery, change how I look. I don't want to play this game." *Careful, girl. Careful.*

"What game? I'm serious, Aubrey."

"Serious about what, Josh? After all of this, did you actually think we were going to live happily ever after, safely ensconced in your new little world?"

He looked at her like he was seeing her for the first time. She could almost hear his thoughts: *Who is this woman? Did I create her? Or is this who she's always been?*

She'd been a criminal once, and here he was, asking her to go back to her old ways. But she'd changed, damn it. She'd changed for him. Hadn't she?

His voice was tight, his face hard. "I thought you'd want to be with me. With your *husband*. Do you know what I've gone through to keep you safe?"

"I don't care. Jesus God, Josh, do you have any idea what you put me through? Did you ever stop to think about what I've been dealing with all these years without you?"

He whispered, harsh and wild, "Why is it always about you? What about me? Playing dead isn't the easiest thing, you know. I gave up my life to keep you safe. And the surgeries, all the planning, sleeping with one eye open all the time . . . My God, Aubrey, I did this for *you*. For us. I've sacrificed the last five years to find us a safe place to live, a safe way to go on with our lives."

Aubrey shook her head, her curly hair standing on end from her hands restlessly pushing it out of her face. His face was hard. She didn't recognize him anymore, and it wasn't just the surgery.

"Please. You did this for *you*, Josh. Not me. Not us. There is no *us*. Not anymore."

She couldn't believe the tone coming out of her mouth, one she'd never used with him, one of derision and hate. Josh flinched like she'd hit him.

She crossed her arms and stared out at the sea of faces in the restaurant.

"This is over."

"What?" His voice was filled with dismay.

Aubrey spoke slowly, enunciating every word. "I'm going home. You can go on living this pathetic little life, but I don't want you anymore."

"Is it my face? I can have more surgery, go back to how I looked before."

She shook her head.

"You betrayed me, Josh. I can't do this. I can't pretend that all is well. I know this was hard on you—but Jesus, I've been grieving your *death* for five years. Five years. I've been through hell. I nearly died."

"I know."

She whipped her head toward him again.

"What do you mean, you know? You've been keeping tabs on me this whole time?"

"Yes. I risked a few trips back to see you. I couldn't stand to be apart. I've been watching over you, darling. And it was almost like you could feel me, my presence. When I was there, you'd look around like you knew I was watching. You even saw me a few times. I was trying to let you know I was okay, but you'd go straight to Meghan, who told you how crazy you were and dragged you to that stupid therapist. Fucking Meghan, messing with your head all this time. I should kill *her*."

Aubrey pulled in a breath. She couldn't believe the words she'd just heard. Had he just admitted . . .

"All those times I thought I saw you—"

"You did. That was me."

"Cruel," she whispered. Something inside her started to break, an unbearable rift forming. "How could you be so cruel?"

"I thought you'd understand. I thought you loved me."

"You used to be an honorable man, Josh. One who wanted to help people. One who wasn't seduced by the trappings of wealth and privilege. That's the man I loved. I don't even know who you are anymore."

Loved. She heard the past tense and realized it was true.

"I can't pretend this is all okay. You've been gone so long. I don't want to live a life on the run. I want to settle down. To have a family. Remember all the things we used to want? The dreams we had together?"

He was begging, pleading. "We'll have them now, Aubrey. It's over. I can finally give you the world."

"I don't want the world. I want to know that I can trust you. And I can't."

He set his glass on the table. "Of course you can. I'm the only one you really can trust."

She shook her head. "You always said that. I don't think it's true."

"I don't understand."

She looked at him, let all the walls down, let all the hurt and anger and fury and loss crowd into her eyes.

"You do understand."

"It's Chase. You want to be with him instead of me." His voice was tinged with frost.

She started to laugh. She didn't find his statement humorous, far from it.

"You have it all wrong, Josh. Yes, I have feelings for Chase, but that's not what this is about. You've betrayed me, in the worst possible way."

Pain in his eyes, sharp and intense. "Don't do this," Josh pleaded. "Don't do this to us. Not now. Not when I've made it all work."

She saw Arlo enter the room, with several plainclothes cops.

She stood. "Josh, *you* did this to us. Not me. I was just along for the ride."

He looked up at her. He had aged so much since he left. There was gray at his temples, lines on his face. Lines and gray they should have earned together, not apart.

"Aubrey, I still love you. Only you. You've been the love of my life since I was a boy. I don't know how to do this without you."

Without her. He'd done everything without her. Made life-altering decisions, turned into a criminal, disappeared.

"You managed for the last five years. Six, really, if you count all the lies you spun before you died."

He was starting to panic. Gone was the smooth man, replaced by the little boy she'd grown to love, the one who'd fallen prey to his fears.

"Aubrey, we're bound together. We always have been. We're meant to be together. You waited for me, for Christ's sake. How can you do this?"

"How can *I* do this?"

He was crying now. She couldn't handle that. It thrust forth the memory of the day he found out his father wasn't dead after all, but alive and well and fresh out of jail, and he'd just collapsed to the ground in the park, empty and broken, and cried. She couldn't do this. She just couldn't. The pressure was building, the words forming in her throat.

Don't. Don't. Don't say it.

People were starting to watch them now, forks poised above plates, glasses held in midair. She saw Arlo and his men out of the corner of her eye, waiting. This was how it had to be. Josh had to pay for his crimes. That was the right thing. And she had to pay for hers.

She nodded at Arlo, and he approached the table.

When Josh saw his best friend, he froze in place. His face turned white, his eyes wild.

"Oh, Aubrey," Josh whispered. "What have you done?"

What have I done? What have I done? He's right. I did this. It was all my fault.

Arlo stepped closer to the table. "Don't fight me, Josh. We'll get this worked out. But you're going to have to surrender yourself to Metro. It's time for you to come with me."

Josh looked frantically from Aubrey to Arlo. "This isn't happening. This can't be happening. You turned me in? Oh, my God, Aubrey. How could you?"

How could you, how could you, how could you?

She felt the tearing of her soul, the rage spilling into her bloodstream.

"How could *I*? You son of a bitch! You left me here all alone. You lied to me. You promised!"

The dam broke, and she launched at him, fists meeting his face, the fury of the past five years unleashing at last. Her voice was a wail, and her emotions, unchecked at last, allowed the words to come out. She couldn't stop them, couldn't stop herself; she was screaming them, over and over and over, sobs wrenching from her as she pounded her clenched hands against his chest.

She screamed until Arlo wrapped his arms around her and dragged her forcibly from the restaurant. Screamed until the men came to take her away, and shoved the needle into her arm with the sedative, and even then, as she faded into the darkness, she couldn't stop.

"We had a deal, Josh. We had a deal. We had a deal. We had a deal."

CHAPTER 70

Josh and Aubrey
Five Years Ago

Josh paced the living room. He had no choice; he couldn't do this himself. It would take time, and coordination, and he'd looked at every angle, every option, and there was nothing to be done for it. Aubrey would need to be involved.

Would she go for it? Or would she take a knife to his balls in the middle of the night? He really didn't know for sure.

He straightened at the sound of the garage door, the gorgeous specialty doors that looked like the front of a barn, stained a dark brown to match the front door and the stone face of the house. She'd taken the Audi to Whole Foods, would be laden down with bags of healthy food.

He needed a drink.

He went to the wet bar in the corner, poured a Scotch, drank it down. Liquid courage.

His wife's voice, sugar and light. "Hon, are you here?"

"In the living room," he called.

She came in with a smile on her face, holding a sheaf of paper. "Did you see this? Can you believe it? They screwed up the insurance, your mom's name isn't on it. They put me down as beneficiary. Daisy is going to shit herself when she realizes."

"Aubrey, honey. Come here. Sit down. We need to talk."

The smile fled. The gravity of his tone was no comfort; he couldn't help it. There was simply no good way to broach the subject, so he rushed in. He reached for her hand, caught it.

"The bank didn't make a mistake. I made you the beneficiary."

"What? Why?"

He took a deep, steadying breath. "You're going to be furious with me, but I need your help. I've made a terrible, terrible mistake."

He felt rather than saw her withdraw, her whole psyche pulling away from him. Then she carefully extricated her hand from his and drew her arms across her chest, to protect herself, to shield herself from him. The motion made him sick to his stomach. Her hair was wildly curly today—rain must be coming.

He choked back a sob. How was he going to do this? How was he going to forfeit the woman he loved, the life he'd fought for? Even something as simple as knowing the weather by the state of his wife's hair . . . He bit his lip, hard, pushing back his emotions. There was no other way.

He gestured toward the sofa, and after a

moment's pause, Aubrey sat, curling her feet under her.

He sat on the opposite end. "I need your help."

"What is this about, Josh? Are we in trouble?"

We. Thank God in heaven, she said *we.*

The story came out, from the start, each word bitter, each moment agony. She listened, pale, a hand to her throat. Toward the end, she'd compulsively scratched at her neck, and there were streaks of red lighting up the tender skin.

When he finished, he felt light, giddy. She hadn't slapped him or walked out, not even when he told her about the photos, about how he'd cheated on her.

She sat, still as stone, processing. He didn't push; he knew her well enough to know she needed time to adjust to her new reality.

That her husband was a criminal, a cheat, and a liar who needed her to help him disappear.

"I'm so sorry. I'm so sorry, Aubrey. I know how badly I've fucked up."

"You could kill yourself. Save us a lot of trouble." Her voice was so soft he almost didn't hear her.

"I've thought about it."

She looked up, eyes on fire. "Don't you dare. That's the coward's way out. We'll . . . We'll figure something out. Right now, I need you to leave. I need some space."

He didn't argue, didn't try to kiss her. He grabbed Winston's lead, snapped it on the dog, and took a walk.

• • •

Aubrey wanted to kill him on the spot. That's why she'd asked him to leave, so she wouldn't accidentally take a knife to his throat. Of all the stupid, idiotic things. Josh in a criminal enterprise was an absolute joke. Figured he'd managed to blow it.

She needed Tyler. Needed his brain. He'd know how to pull this off. But he was in jail, again. She'd have to figure this one out herself.

She had an idea. But she couldn't do any online research—that was too easy to trace. And she couldn't do a thing out of character. From this moment forward, she was onstage, and she had to give the best performance of her life, or they'd both go down in flames.

He'd asked for her help. She looked around their grandly appointed living room, still devoid of much furniture. After all he'd done for her, now he needed *her* help.

The tiniest bit of pride swelled in her chest. They could do this. They could find a way.

And to start with, no one would question her going to the library.

She wrote Josh a note and took the car. She was a regular fixture at the Vanderbilt library—she even had a book in the backseat that was due. Perfect.

She had an idea of where to look. She remembered one of her friends in the group home, if you could call her that, bragging about a book she'd read that would help someone disappear without a trace. Where would it be, what section? She couldn't do a search; she'd have to rely on her memory of the library's stacks and deduce where it could be under the guise of browsing.

She parked her car, walked in, swiped her card. She returned the book, smiled at the librarian behind the desk, casually pulling out a notebook and heading toward the children's section. They were used to her finding material for her kids. No one would bat an eye.

Walked down the aisle and made a right turn, back to the adult world.

She thought her best chances were in two areas in the library: travel and psychology. Travel didn't give her what she was looking for, other than a nice guide to various Caribbean islands, which she was tempted to check out just for fun, but she hit pay dirt in psychology. There were three slim volumes by different authors about personal security, and one specifically about how to disappear. Bingo.

She pulled it from the shelf and held it against her chest so no one could see it. She found an unlocked carrel, entered, closed the door behind her, took a deep breath, and started to read.

It was dark when Josh heard the garage door open again. He'd fed and groomed the dog, put away the groceries, cleaned the kitchen, and made tacos, just to kill the time. He'd been so relieved by her controlled reaction, but as the minutes ticked away, he started to wonder if Aubrey was even going to come back, or if she'd bring home the cops and just have him arrested and call it over.

She came in with a yellow notepad clutched to her chest, curly hair sticking out in all directions, face carefully blank. He didn't think he'd ever seen her look more beautiful.

"Light a fire. Read all of this. Then burn it. I'm going to take a shower, and then we'll talk."

He read the pages. Each sentence made him more afraid. He couldn't do this. He couldn't pull it off. It was too easy to trip up, to make a simple mistake that would cost them everything. *Don't Google yourself, don't Google the case, create disinformation*—every step would take years to plan out. Panic started to build in his chest. He had to turn himself in. That was the only choice.

Aubrey came down the stairs as he was feeding the pages into the fire. He turned, saw her floating his way, as ethereal and mysterious as the day he first saw her. He'd failed her. He'd failed himself.

He shoved the remaining pages haphazardly into the flames. "I can't do it."

"You can. And you will. Because I'm not ready to give up on you. I've forgiven your transgressions, Joshua Hamilton. Now you're going to pay me back."

It took them a week to make all the plans. In truth, it was simple, and elegant. He watched

Aubrey lay out precise lines, marveling at her ability to separate what he'd done from who he was, who he wanted to be for her.

He needed money, which meant he had to double-cross Allen, but that wasn't a problem. He hated the man for getting him into this mess; he was happy to fuck him over.

Finally, they had it all nailed down. He'd already taken out the insurance policy. Everything was signed, sealed, and delivered. All they had to do was get the date of the meeting, and he'd pull off the heist and be gone. Tennessee would declare him dead after a few years, earlier if his mother fought hard enough, which he figured she would, and then Aubrey would join him, and they could start life over again.

He didn't know how he was going to live without her that long.

Late one night soon after, lying in bed together, sated and warm, her leg thrown casually over his, the soft sheets kicked to the bottom of the bed, he started to worry again.

"They're going to think you did it."

Aubrey gave him a drowsy "Hmm?"

Josh sat up. "Wake up. We need to talk."

Aubrey dragged herself to an elbow, saw his face, and sat up the rest of the way. "What's wrong?"

"The police. When they investigate. They're going to think you were in on it."

She smiled languidly, dragged her hand up his thigh. "I am in on it."

"I'm serious. I won't do this if there's any chance you can be caught up in it. You have to swear to me you can make this work, and not get drowned in the process."

She grew serious. "All right. Worst-case scenario. They might think I was involved. They always look at the spouse first. I'm going to have to play this perfectly. That's my responsibility. You just have to stay alive and get out of town."

"No." He shook his head and got out of the bed, went to the window. Stared out at the moon-lit night. "No, I can't let it happen." He rushed back to the bed, dropped to his knees. Took her hands in his.

"Aubrey, I swear, if you're arrested, if it goes so far as a trial, I will come back and turn myself in. I swear it. And if I don't come back, you'll know I'm dead. Because that's the only thing that could keep me away from you. Only death can keep us apart."

"Josh—"

He kissed her, hard. "This is a deal breaker, Aubs. I'm willing to try this, running away, faking my death, the whole thing, but I won't let you go down for me. I swear it."

"You're not kidding, are you?"

He wrapped his arms around her, put his head on her chest, felt the strangeness of her body, sinewy and soft and his, her heart beating softly under his ear. He felt like he could hold her there forever, safe.

"I won't let anything happen to you, Aubrey. Ever. Deal?"

She kissed his forehead gently. "Deal. Now come back to bed. I'm cold."

EPILOGUE

They were on the patio, in the slope-backed chairs with extra cushions, the way she liked it now. The summer was intensely green, overwhelmed by the water. It had been a summer of rains and tornado warnings, of pain and withdrawal, of finding themselves. Establishing their relationship, one nonstop flight at a time.

Chase had brought the first printing of his article. It would run in the Sunday *Tribune*, a special report. It was good, solid investigative work—his editor was going to submit it to the Pulitzer committee. He couldn't think about that now. All he wanted was to let the joys and horrors of the past few months fade away.

He held the newspaper in his hands like it was a precious biblical tablet, cleared his throat, preparing to read the story out loud. She gave him a proud smile and nodded.

"It's called 'Love, Drugs, and Insanity: The story of a Nashville couple who deceived their whole world, and nearly got away with it.' A *Tribune* Special Report in Three Parts, by Chase Boden, with Shane Gert and Monica Page, *Tribune* Investigative Staff Reporters."

"I'm glad you got top billing."

He smiled. "Me, too. Okay, here goes . . ."

Nashville, TN: She seemed incapable of deceit. Innocent, damaged, dragged through life by her heels, Aubrey Marie Hamilton, a curly-headed twenty-nine-year-old Montessori teacher, was anything but what she looked like. She deceived everyone, including this reporter, over a five-year period after her husband, Joshua Hamilton, went missing. Acquitted of his murder, she'd resumed her life, waiting for the moment her husband was officially declared dead to capitalize on a $5 million life insurance policy and the money he stole from his partners in a pill-mill operation out of Vanderbilt University Medical Center. The story that ensued would make an excellent novel, but I've reported faithfully everything I've learned on this case.

When I began investigating the case of Joshua Hamilton, I never expected to become personally involved in the story. I went to Nashville to dig into what I thought was a fascinating missing-person story, and along the way found my biological mother, realized I was closely related to the missing

man, Joshua Hamilton, and, yes, I will
admit, nearly fell in love with Aubrey
Hamilton herself.

Chase stopped reading. "Too personal? Should
I skip that part?"

Daisy shook her head. "No, read it all to me. I
like it. You're a victim, just like the rest of us. She
sank her claws into you, too. I think it lends some
verisimilitude to the story. I'm glad people will
see what a spider she is."

Daisy adjusted her soft collar, the only tangible remnant of her terrible accident three months
earlier. She looked good, better than when he'd
seen her last. The scars on her forehead were
healing, though they still looked like she'd had
horns removed. She'd gained a little weight. Her
skin wasn't the pasty, sickly gray of a career alcoholic, but flushed prettily with the remnants of a
sunburn.

He'd flown down to show her the proofs of
the story, felt like he owed it to her since she was
as big a part of the story as everyone else.

When he finished, they were both quiet for a
time.

"Have you heard from her?" Daisy finally
asked.

Chase realized he'd drifted. He had a tendency
to do that now.

"I'm sorry. What?"

"From Aubrey. Has she been in touch?"

He nodded. "She's been writing me. Trying

to explain. She'd gone off her meds, she wasn't thinking clearly. All the excuses you'd expect." *That she loved me, and wanted forgiveness. Wanted to be with me, to twine around me in the night like she used to . . .* That she'd be out soon enough and they could be together. That Josh's betrayal was too deep. Letting her believe he was truly gone, breaking his promise that he would come back if she was put on trial, and if he didn't, it meant he was dead . . . no, she couldn't imagine ever seeing him again. That she understood Chase had lied to her, but when he'd come clean, told her the truth, she knew he really did love her. He was the only good thing in her life. The only truth.

Please, Chase. Please come see me.

He flicked a hand like it meant nothing to him. He didn't tell Daisy he'd cried like a baby when he received the first letter, and wrote Aubrey back a long, messy screed pledging his eternal love. In the cold light of day, when he'd crawled out of the bottle he'd fallen into after he discovered her lies, her treachery, he knew he'd made a magnificently bad mistake, but he couldn't seem to help the crazy feelings she dragged out of him. And truth be told, he didn't want to. She made him feel alive, for the first time in his life. That she was . . . unpredictable was simply part of the allure.

Poor Aubrey. The online photos of the Middle Tennessee Mental Health Institute made it look like a pleasant suburban doctor's office, its tall flagpole gaily snapping the American and Tennessee State flags, not a building that housed the criminally insane. He felt a stab of guilt, as he always did when he thought of her locked in there, stuck wearing white gowns and being shot up with Haldol—vitamin H, she called it—when she "misbehaved."

"I might write a book about it. True crime is a really popular genre."

Daisy smiled, picked up her glass. She held it like it was a cross to bear, her thirteenth station. Water. At least he thought it was water. She'd been sober since the accident. Started attending meetings in the rehab facility she'd been sent to when she managed to survive the heart surgery and started to mend. She even had her ninety-day chip. She'd been scared straight, or so she claimed.

"I think it would make an excellent story. I know you probably didn't have room in this piece, but if you write a book, make sure you mention that I hated to give you up."

He bristled. Always wanting to be portrayed in the best light. She'd been saying how much she regretted the decision to allow his father to take him, over and over, yet he wasn't sure he believed her. And now, Daisy wanted him to move to Nashville so they could be a family. No chance—when it came right down to it, he was afraid she might be as crazy as Aubrey.

"I had a letter from Josh, too," he ventured, and Daisy's eyes lit up.

"And how is my sweet boy?"

"Okay, I think. He seems . . . settled in."

"I can't believe they sent him to that place. After what that woman did to him, he should have been given an award, not sent to prison."

"Mmmm."

She was still in complete denial about Josh. Always had been, always would be. Aubrey was the villain. Josh was the innocent bystander. The innocent bystander who orchestrated a deal with the devil, talked his wife into covering for him, managed to disappear for five years, and very nearly pulled it all off.

The letter from Josh had been simple: *I'm sorry, about it all. I'd like to get to know you, see you again. Try to be brothers. Please come visit. My schedule's pretty open, ha-ha.*

Unlike Aubrey, held indefinitely in the psychiatric hospital, Hamilton was doing cold, hard time. Chase might go see him while he was here in town. Might. The only real contact they'd had was the night Hamilton had shown up at Chase's hotel, full of righteous fury, demanding to know why Chase was fucking his wife.

Ah, brotherly love.

To hell with Hamilton, it was Aubrey he wanted to see. But that would cloud his judgment. Let her do her time, come back down to earth, get her head screwed on. Then, maybe, they could talk again.

Jesus, Chase. You are as insane as the whole crew if you think that any contact with her is a good idea.

"Daisy—"

"*Mom*, please, Chase. I've told you time and

again. I am your mother. I would appreciate you calling me so."

He couldn't; he just couldn't. Mom was a sweet black-haired gypsy woman who'd taught him to read and chased away his nightmares and made him lemonade, whose grave he'd been neglecting lately. This woman wasn't Mom.

"I need to get on the road. I hate to run, but I have a flight back tonight, and I need to make a couple of stops before I go. I'll leave the paper with you."

She didn't fight but pouted a bit, waved him over for a kiss. He obliged. She smelled strange, a mixture of vinegar and honeysuckle, not pleasant but not entirely unpleasant.

"Come back soon. I miss you already." She wiped a tear from her eye.

Tom saw him to the door. "She loves seeing you, Chase. I'm glad you came by."

They shook hands, and once Chase climbed in his rental, he gave a sigh of relief. He was trying, really he was, but Daisy was a hard woman to love.

The sun was setting as he pulled out of the neighborhood. He couldn't help himself; he detoured by Dragon Park, and the shabby little house where it had all begun for them.

The echo of Aubrey was there, from the front door to the eaves, the small porch where they'd once sat, a moment in time full of sweetness and hope. The wall Daisy had plowed her Mercedes into had been repaired, but the stucco didn't quite match the rest of the house; it was off just a shade. Aubrey would hate that.

Leave, Chase. Get on the plane and go home. This is over. You can start a new life.

He thought about Winston, his trusting blue eyes, waiting for him to come back. He'd gotten a dog out of the deal, at least. And the image of the dog pissing on his parquet floors was enough to have him put the car in gear. He glanced at the house in the rearview mirror as he went. It was the past. The story was done. *Move on, Chase.*

Onto the highway, heading east, the lights of Nashville twinkling, beckoning.

That hair, tickling his thighs as she knelt before him.

Even now, even knowing the whole story, he was still drawn to her. She did that to men. Her gift, her curse, whatever.

Aubrey's hospital was near the airport. He cautioned himself against it. He simply couldn't get drawn in again. He couldn't.

But when he saw the exit, the wheel of the car took a right off Interstate 40, almost as if it knew something he didn't.

Two Years Later

Aubrey ran.

She was training for the marathon, barely three months away. It felt good to stretch and push herself. To feel the sun on her face, the wind in her hair. To be free. Finally, to be free.

The city was complex, bigger and louder and faster than she was used to, so she ran along the lake—Lake Shore Drive on her left on the way up, right on the way down. It was hot and quiet. She was doing the lake path's full eighteen and a half miles today. Plenty of time to think. To plan.

Her feet slapped the pavement in a familiar rhythm, as known to her as her own heartbeat. The sheer joy of her muscles moving, of being alive, filled her, and she smiled.

She had always been lucky. Nine lives. Like a cat.

She only hesitated for a moment before she dropped the letter in the mailbox near Hyde Park. She'd wanted to say good-bye to Josh in person, but that wasn't possible. So she'd written him a letter, told him what was happening with her life now.

She'd been putting it off, but no longer. It was time to start over, time for a clean slate. The future looked good, finally. Shiny and full of possibility.

Even at her leisurely pace, the run back went faster. She felt lighter.

She was dripping wet when she got back to their building. The air-conditioned lobby was frigid compared to the sultry outside air. She pulled the mailbox key out of her pocket, went to the boxes. She could have mailed the letter from here, but something made her take it away. She didn't want to sully her new life with it. She opened the box. Bill. Bill. Magazine.

Normal. It was all so very normal.

"Hey, Mrs. Boden. How'd the run go?"

She looked up to see their doorman coming from the back elevators.

"It was good, Billy. Thanks."

"Didn't take Winston with you?"

"Not today. I did the whole circuit."

He whistled. "I wish I could run like you."

Get a past, child. That will give you something to run from.

She smiled, friendly, appealing. Just a tiny bit of flirt in her tone. "Get a good pair of shoes. That helps. Talk to you later."

Billy grinned in return. "See ya, Mrs. Boden. By the way, this came for Mr. Boden." He handed her a package. Aubrey saw the return address and quieted her heart.

Almost as if he knew. How did he do that? Ships passing in the night.

She debated tossing it in the trash, but that wouldn't be fair. Chase deserved to have a brother, too.

The apartment was airy; picture windows overlooked the lake. Chase was at his desk, typing away. He was working on a novel. He looked up when she came in.

"Hey, babe. Good run?"

"Great. I'm going to shower. This came for you."

His face clouded for a second, but it disappeared so quickly she might have imagined it.

"Thanks. Want to go out tonight? There's a

new Italian place that opened in Hyde Park, and I know you need to get some calories."

"I'd love to. Let me get cleaned up and we can go early."

"By the way . . . ?"

She hated when he did that. Started a sentence, then stopped. She waited, towel to her neck, Winston rubbing along her thighs.

He gave her a lazy grin. "I love you." Then turned back to his laptop, fingers on the keys, the clatter of words pouring onto the page, taking him from her again.

She glanced out the windows, at the clouds starting to form, reflecting gray and white on the lake. The trees began to bend. A storm was coming. She'd gotten back just in time.

• • •

"Mail, Hamilton."

Josh accepted the plain cream envelope from the guard, smiled curtly at him, then returned to his bunk. As jails went, it wasn't so bad. It just killed him to be locked inside, locked down, unable to see the sun when he wanted. To be on someone else's schedule.

He recognized the handwriting, felt his heart kick into gear.

He didn't have to worry about opening it— that had been taken care of by the censors, as he liked to think of them. He liked to imagine he was in a Russian prison instead of medium security

in the middle of Bumfuck, Tennessee. Club Fed.
What a joke.

He pulled the single sheet of paper from the
envelope. As he read the words, he heard her
voice, sweet and soft in his ears. Just like when
he read all the others. She'd mailed him once
before, or had someone do it, a huge package of
letters. Some handwritten, some printed from the
computer's email. Five years of agony, just in case
he hadn't really understood what he'd put her
through.

His punishment.

This one, though, broke him in two.

Dear Josh,

I thought of you today.

*I was running and saw a rock in my path,
perfectly round and polished. It was eerie, so
much like right after you disappeared, when I
was walking on the beach and finally accepted
you were dead and that stone appeared. Now,
like then, I picked it up and put it in my pocket.
I will keep this stone, not brilliant or shiny,
but heavy and dense, as a remembrance. It will
have a place of honor on my mantel, and when
I see it, I will do my best to remember only the
good times we had.*

*I know you will hate this news, but I
wanted you to hear it from me. Chase and I
have married. It was the right decision, for
both of us, and we are happy.*

*We've been through so much, you and I.
From the time I was seven and you were nine
and you chose me to champion. I couldn't have
survived my childhood without you. You were
my savior, my knight in shining armor. The
love of my life. You will always hold a special
place in my heart.*

 *But my life, my future, is with Chase.
I hope you understand, and someday, you'll
forgive me. We could have been amazing, you
and I. Could have been one for the ages.*

 Take care of yourself.

         Always,
         Aubrey

He lay back on his bunk, on his side, facing the wall. Tucked the shabby pillow under his head and stared at the picture of his wife, sunny and curly-headed and blond, smiling at him from their wedding photo. The one little piece of her he still had. He traced the outline of her face with a finger and smiled.

"I won't be in here forever, Aubrey."

AUTHOR'S NOTE

Dear reader,

When No One Knows *first hit shelves back in 2016, it did so with a different epilogue from the ending you've just read. There were many editorial reasons for this, and I supported them all. But I've always felt something was missing. You see Aubrey mail a letter and run off into the sunset, but what did that letter contain? I'm all for an open ending, but over the years, this has always felt . . . too open. Too loose. It leaves too many unanswered questions.*

I wanted you to have the full experience, to see the story the way I conceived it. I am so happy that the original ending of this book has been added back into this mass market edition.

It's not often that an author gets a chance at a do-over. I am incredibly grateful to Gallery Books and my editor, Lauren McKenna, for indulging me in this dream.

I would love to hear your thoughts. Feel free to email me at jtellison@jtellison.com and let me know if you like the new, expanded ending.

All best,
J.T. Ellison

ACKNOWLEDGMENTS

When a book is five years in the making, there are a lot of people to thank.

Jeff Abbott—for teaching me about Scrivener

Blake Leyers—for the lunch that changed it all

Laura Benedict—for reading a thousand pages and then some

Jennifer Brooks—for editing the first go-round

Ariel Lawhon—for incessant cheerleading and Walden Ponds

Linda McFall—for believing in my dark side and encouraging me to let it shine through, plus a rocking good set of editorial letters

Rick Robinson—for the legalese

Valerie Gray—for a lovely afternoon's conversation and helping me see the holes

Marjorie Braman—for liking the concept enough to give me hope

The BMWs—Bodacious Music City Wordsmiths (JB, Del, Cecelia, Paige) for always telling me it was worth a try

Catherine Coulter—for the stellar advice

Harlan Coben—for giving me advice in my dreams and setting me on this path

Gillian Flynn—for the visceral beauty of *Sharp Objects*

Joan Huston—for edits and liking the new direction

Sherrie Saint—for the cop bits

Amy Kerr—for being the best right hand ever

Scott Miller—for helping conceptualize from the very beginning, and never giving up on this book

Abby Zidle—for loving it enough to bring me into the Gallery family

My parents—for listening (and listening, and listening) through all the iterations

Randy—for being a husband extraordinaire, and never letting me walk away from this one. I love you, darling, and don't worry, I'd never turn you in.

And last, but certainly not least,

You—for reading this far. Thanks for the support!